LOON LAKE LODGE

LOON LAKE LODGE

BY PHYLLIS ANN KARR
(MRS. CLIFTON ALFRED HOYT)

A Dialogue Novel after the Template of Thomas Love Peacock

WILDSIDE PRESS

Published by Wildside Press LLC.
www.wildsidebooks.com

"[W]hat is the use of a book," thought Alice, "without pictures or conversations?"

—Lewis Carroll,
Alice's Adventures in Wonderland, ch. 1

CHAPTER 1

Loon Lake was small enough to have belonged in toto to a wealthy lumber baron, Mr. Aloysius Woodbucks, who named it and decorated its shores with his mansion and its outbuildings. Also, covering most of his lake's neat little island, Mr. Woodbucks erected a fishing shack larger than too many a single-family residence. No sooner were these buildings complete, than the lumber baron clapped the entire property into a Perpetual Land Trust which, while allowing continual remodeling and replacement of the existing improvements, effectively banned any other development whatsoever.

After the original owner's death, his daughter Aloywisha made it her chief hobby for some years to run Loon Lake Lodge as an exclusive resort, occasionally proving her love of the Common Man by including a mere nameless millionaire among its guests. Her grandson Algernon "Gotcher" Lotsadoe proved his own ideals by turning the resort into a hippie commune. When the commune failed, the surrounding northwoods spent several years encroaching on the buildings, as was their right by the laws both of Nature and the Land Trust, until young Lotsadoe, now a stockbroker on the West Coast, sold the whole property to an entrepreneur who turned it into an elegant restaurant and museum which he advertised as the former hideaway of a famous Chicago gangster. This personage had indeed once passed through the northwoods, and according to one old-timer's speculation, might even have spent a night in Loon Lake Lodge while it was under the proprietorship of Aloywisha Woodbucks Lotsadoe; and the museum boasted several artifacts indisputably identifiable as belong to the famous gangster's actual era and city, so the promotion fell into the realm more of historical fiction than of out-and-out false advertising, and enabled the restaurant to survive a number of years in competition with another gangster's more authentic hide-out in the same general part of the world.

But perhaps our human taste for rubbing shoulders, at a safe remove, with the wicked and the notorious is not *quite* infinite, for eventually the true hideaway won out over the questionable. Or else the entrepreneur merely wearied of the northwoods and opted to seek richer pastures in

Las Vegas, where he was last sighted running an Arabian Nights casino, after selling Loon Lake and its buildings to a family named Eklektik.

CHAPTER 2

The Family Eklektik comprised two parents, Eliza and Elmer; two children, Freedom and Bugsy ("Ulysses Samson" on his birth certificate); and two pets, a green parakeet named Budgewiser and a mostly black Heinze 57 named Muttwump.

Eliza was a semi-retired feminist who had disowned her father's surname and called herself "Ms. Independence" for some years before marrying Elmer, a man who cared nothing about either feminism or male dominance, but only about model railroading, and who looked upon the Loon Lake property as ideal for his ever-growing collection of trains and layouts. Eliza had long found it more convenient to swim along with the current of convention in the matter of using her spouse's surname – besides which, "Eliza Eklektik" had such a melodious sound! She nevertheless enshrined her old ideals by dubbing her firstborn child "Freedom," and later regretting that the girl's personality failed to reflect these same ideals to any great extent, being fixated on needlepointing with an intensity reminiscent of her paternal parent's railroad enthusiasm. Bugsy's appellation derived from his love of both the insect world and any animated cartoons dating from before his birth, but these were only two of his many fascinations. Budgewiser officially belonged to Bugsy, having been a birthday present; Muttwump to the entire family, who – although well able to have afforded a pedigreed pureblood, had found him wandering, victim of the Throwaway Vacation Puppy Syndrome, and readily adopted him.

At the time this tale begins, Freedom was twenty-two, Bugsy twelve, and their parents aged appropriately. Muttwump was about four by the veterinarian's estimate, and Budgewiser old enough that the black lines had retreated from his nose band to leave his feathered brow broad and white.

Both Elmer and Eliza had inherited quite a lot of wealth in most of its various forms. Liquidating about half of it, they were able to pay cash down for the Loon Lake property and still have enough in bank accounts, investments, trusts, and securities to live at a munificently comfortable level – by the standards of the underpopulated northwoods – on the interest alone, without the various inconveniences of salaried employment.

At the same time, they were doubly blessed in that, having retained only one other piece of real estate – a cave in Colorado, which they looked upon as an escape in case of nuclear war or worldwide environmental catastrophe – they could luxuriate in the pretended need to practice what they fondly looked upon as household economy.

Freedom hoped, not only to produce collector dolls in needlepoint, but to sell these and her other designs to a publisher for royalties which she imagined in her inexperience might equal about what Hollywood paid for film rights to the current best-selling novels. Bugsy's plans for his adult career changed biweekly, and "How much money can a fellow make at it?" was frequently among his considerations. Not always, however. Of all the Eklektiks, young Ulysses was perhaps the most truly eclectic.

CHAPTER 3

Among their eccentricities, the Eklektiks clove stubbornly to the old-fashioned custom of gathering thrice daily around the table, wherever it happened to be found: breakfast nook, luncheon arbor, screened porch, fireplace barroom, kitchen, or that erstwhile guest room which they had converted into what Elmer liked to call the caboose. Their mealtime venue varied, not only with time of day, but also with weather, season, and general mood of the family or one of its members. Each of the abovementioned rooms had its own appropriately stocked china cabinet, complete with silverware chest; and if, in her heart of hearts, Eliza sometimes caught herself guiltily regretting that their country, era, personal ideals, and supposed need for household economy conspired to forbid them a staff of live-in servants for cooking and serving the food, at least such conveniences as rolling carts, microwave ovens, insulated covers, and ice buckets helped to get the viands from kitchen to table at an appropriate temperature.

Their cleaning-woman, Pearl Bonami, who came every day except Wednesday and Sunday, ran the dishwasher and usually got all the china and silverware back to the correct rooms. Of course, the family had to store some of its own leftovers—whatever failed to fit at once inside Muttwump—or risk spoilage; but Eliza comforted herself that this provided excellent character-building exercise for Freedom and Bugsy. And if occasionally one of them, absent-mindedly thinking of needlepoint or whatever, stored the lettuce salad in the freezer, or left the jar of mustard on the condiment shelf and put the pepper shaker in the refrigerator instead, this was a small enough price to pay for having children of good, egalitarian character.

As a resort, Loon Lake Lodge had had many guest rooms and a dozen light-housekeeping cottages. The Eklektiks had converted more than half of these into hobby rooms and workshops of various kinds, so that each member of the family had at least two or three. But I digress from the principal business of this chapter, which is to offer one small sample of the family's typical mealtime conversation or, as I believe it used to be quaintly styled, "table talk."

BUGSY

Honest! Brown and cream-colored zigzaggy stripes all across the carapace, and an underside just like the ivory tile in the northeast bathroom.

FREEDOM

I dreamed one time about cockroaches that lived in a bathroom so long they developed protective coloration.

BUGSY

Well, it sure to heck wasn't a dreamed-up cockroach! It was a real, honest to goodness long-bodied one—maybe a *lampyrida*—just about so big. *(He indicated the nail joint of his left thumb.)*

ELIZA

What a shame you lost your collecting jar.

> *Bugsy had found and eagerly collected his striped beetle on the island, but lost it on his return, when Muttwump overset the canoe by jumping out in sudden pursuit of a duck, which escaped.*

FREEDOM

They looked like clean ivory enamel, with shiny gold chevrons along the edges of their wings. For cockroaches, they were beautiful.

BUGSY

Yeah, well, too bad you couldn't bring a few back out of your dream with you. Hey! How about if I got that scuba-diving equipment? Mom?

ELIZA

Ulysses Samson Eklektik, not even in Loon Lake are you scuba-diving alone, and you are not going to badger any of us into learning the sport along with you, against our own inclinations.

> *If Eliza spoke a trifle wearily, it was because she had been over this and similar ground often before. In her own youth, she had believed with devout passion in the sacrosanctity of*

individual expression; but in parenthood she had learned there were limits which tended to fall in the murky borderland between individual expression and personal safety.

BUGSY

Aw, c'mon, Dad! Bet it'd look great in one of your layouts!

ELMER

Which one, son? Stripes or not, I don't see much chance to remodel an insect into a convincing tiger, say, or zebra, and even if I could, I very much doubt it'd be HO scale. In the science-fiction layout, now… hmm…maybe I could talk it over with Cliff Reed…

ELIZA

Darling, if you can find the space, time, and money for—what will it be?—your seventh layout—be my guest. But that collecting jar is probably broken by now, or lost beyond finding. And don't forget, we want to save plenty of guest bedrooms for our retreats.

The Eklektiks had not actually started holding these retreats as yet, but they talked about them whenever they felt that circumstances might someday force them to seek an additional source of income.
Today, hearing her mother once again raise the allusion, Freedom—hitherto rather lukewarm on the topic—was seized with sufficiently ecstatic inspiration to make her clap her hands.

FREEDOM

Mom! Dad! Let's hold one right away! Dad can have Uncle Cliff over to work on the layouts, and I'll invite Merlina, and we can get them together! Let's see, that means special invitations…

ELIZA

Not by special invitation only, dear one. We should certainly advertise as well. Let me see…

At this moment Budgewiser, who had the free flight of such portions of the lodge as boasted neither holes in the windowscreens nor doors opening directly on the outside, flew into the "caboose" dining room, landed on the table with a graceful plunk, cocked his head at the family, and announced, "Have you had a busy day?"

These comprised the only words the parakeet had ever learned to say and, this particular evening, they seemed less descriptive than prophetic.

CHAPTER 4

In fact, "Uncle" Clifford Reed stood in no blood relationship to any of the Eklektik clan. At the time they took up residence in Loon Lake Lodge, he had already been well established as a beloved if somewhat taken-for-granted local genius, a sort of middle-aged Gyro Gearloose whose habits, if mildly eccentric, were universally avuncular. Elmer had soon enlisted him for invaluable assistance, both electronic and artistic, in getting the various model trains of Loon Lake Lodge happily running through their respective layouts; and the children, then five years younger—so long had the family been playing with the idea of holding retreats—lost no time in adopting him as an honorary uncle.

Merlina, with whose name Freedom had so eagerly linked Mr. Reed's, was Mrs. Arthur Batique, a genial widow of rosy complexion and uncertain years—but presumably within Uncle Cliff's age range—who lived in the nearest town, Muskywater (pop. 814), where she ran the Yarn Barn, a boutique purveying both the supplies needed by local artists and artisans in many media, and a choice selection of the items they produced with said supplies. As plant life tended to provide hunter-gatherer tribes a more reliable source of groceries than the occasional major kill, so such transactions as Freedom's frequent purchases of colored yarns and plastic canvas filled Mrs. Batique's cash register far more surely than did the painting, handcrafted necklace, or needlepoint dollhouse she sold now and then on a commission of fifteen per cent, welcome though such occasional sales were to the artists involved. Merlina's business providing their meeting place, the two women had soon become friends despite a difference in their ages of perhaps as long as Freedom had been alive.

More often than not, Freedom's foraging expeditions to the Yarn Barn culminated in tea and conversation with the owner-proprietress in a cozy alcove added to the establishment a few years previously by popular request. If they chanced to be alone, their conversation customarily went on until that situation changed.

FREEDOM

Thank you again for pointing the "Snow Village" pattern book out to me, Merlina. If only I could have designed it first!

MERLINA

I keep telling you, Freedom, one set of designs like that hardly exhausts the market. Or even half a dozen. The more successful a trend is, the more demand it stirs up for similar patterns.

FREEDOM

You know, I think I almost have Dad convinced to build another layout, with everything in needlepoint. A "Santa Claus Land," maybe. I could design a Gingerbread Village...maybe I could even design special matching shapes to fit over the electric locomotive and train cars, and turn them into a real Santa Claus express. We could open it up for kiddy tours from Thanksgiving to New Year's. Uncle Cliff could do the landscape... You still haven't met him, Merlina, have you? Clifford Reed?

MERLINA

I rarely have time to meet anyone outside my Yarn Barn. And church circles, of course.

FREEDOM

If only you'd put in some model railroad supplies! Then we could get Uncle Cliff in here sometime, along with Dad.

MERLINA

I'm afraid, dear, that this area can hardly support more than one model railroad supplier, and I'm perfectly content to leave that business to Al Hopper up in Portfield.

FREEDOM

Yes, but that's an hour away, and... Well, okay, maybe you're right.

> Seeing by her friend's face that, whether or not Merlina was right in the absolute on this economic point, she was right about herself being the wrong entrepreneur to challenge Mr. Hopper's regional monopoly of the model railroad market, Freedom sipped her tea and nibbled away at a tray of Girl

Scout cookies until another gambit occurred to her relative to her pet social project.

FREEDOM

Oh, Merlina, what do you think about this? Not long ago, Uncle Cliff was telling us he'd read in one of his science magazines that they'd taken a poll. The question was, If medicine came up with a pill that, when you took it, would make you young again and give you an extra two thousand years of life, would you take it? And almost half the respondents said, "No"! Why would they say "no," can you think?

MERLINA

Why, yes, dear, I believe I can hazard a few guesses. For one thing, it would mean two thousand more years of fearing some painful disease.

FREEDOM

But this pill would cure every disease.

MERLINA

Accident, then.

FREEDOM

Oh, who really worries about an accident happening to them?

MERLINA

I do.

FREEDOM

People would just have to be a little more careful, that's all. Who knows—people might finally learn to drive safely! And then—

MERLINA

And then, there's the youth factor. Years ago I read in a novel somewhere that youth is a disease for which the only cure is time, and the older I grow, the more I agree.

FREEDOM

Oh, Merlina, you're not old! Not a bit of it. You're ageless.

MERLINA

Thank you… I think…but it's taken me years to get as far as I have, and I surely wouldn't want to have to start all over again! And maybe not get anywhere near this, not even in two thousand years, depending on how much the imbalances of youth are less a matter of inexperience than of hormones.

FREEDOM

All right, say they could adjust the pill and keep you whatever age you like for the whole two thousand years? Just think, you could stay just the age you are now—whatever it is—and never worry about the aches and pains of extreme old age!

MERLINA

That is a plus, certainly. And if they could take the extended age factor out of this pill, and let it simply enable you to live out your normal threescore and ten free of aches and pains, creaks and diseases, arthritis and carpal-tunnel, then I'd swallow it in a jiffy.

FREEDOM

But the extra centuries, Merlina! Think of all the things you could knit—

MERLINA

Freedom, a woman might get tired even of knitting. And think of the extra centuries of having to earn a living.

FREEDOM

Oh, they'll solve that.

MERLINA

I very much doubt it. More likely, someone will drop the bomb and whoever has taken that pill will be stuck with two millennia of the new Dark Ages.

FREEDOM

But it could never last two whole millennia. Wouldn't you love to watch civilization build itself back up again?

MERLINA

Not particularly, no. I fear the meantime would prove very uncomfortable.

FREEDOM

And help build it? You and all the other duomillenarians who had taken the pill?

MERLINA

Well, child… I'll meet you this far. If my Arthur were still alive, and wanted to swallow it, I'd take it with him. Since he's gone, I'd as soon not wait another two thousand years to be with him again in eternal bliss.

> *Freedom was too freethinking to feel quite confident about the existence of eternal bliss. But, too kind to say so, she remembered Mr. Reed's argument on the subject.*

FREEDOM

But since eternity is forever, what real difference can an extra two thousand years make?

MERLINA

Two thousand years' worth, from our viewpoint there. And who would want to go back to the end of a line that long, when the smorgasbord table is finally in sight?

CHAPTER 5

Freedom left the Yarn Barn that afternoon more than ever convinced of the desperation of Merlina's case. The older woman had in fact lost her beloved husband a mere two years earlier; but that had been almost a year before Freedom first set foot in the shop, having previously been spending the months of the academic year pursuing her college degree downstate, and those of the summer vacations swimming, fishing, and otherwise generally behaving less like a serious craftswoman than a passing visitor to her own family's resort-turned-residence. As a result of never having met the late Arthur Batique—and a little, perhaps, of her mother's ingrained attitude that most men were more or less inter-changeable—Freedom Eklektik felt, without pausing to examine the logic of her feeling, as if he had been deceased a very great while. Hence, she thought, it was high time Merlina laid widowhood aside and looked around for a second chance at romance. That Merlina showed no inclina-tion to do this struck Freedom as a warning sign of suicidal intent, an unconscious cry for help which must be answered as quickly as possible.

She returned home, therefore, with two bags of yarn, twenty sheets of plastic canvas, a new pair of scissors guaranteed to cut without leav-ing nubbins, a few spare needles, a guide to all the needlepoint stitches yet discovered, and so heavy a sense of matchmaking urgency that, even before putting any of her afternoon's purchases into play, she drew up a proposed advertisement for Loon Lake Lodge's inaugural "Rustic Re-treat," which she read at supper, to general approbation from the rest of the family—each of whom, however, had his or her addition or emenda-tion to suggest. The finished advertisement, as it soon appeared in both regional weeklies and on the notice boards of every library and town hall within a fifty-mile radius, a number of friendly craft, music, grocery, and gift stores, churches of the more liberal persuasions, and many restau-rants (though the family decided to avoid taverns, bars, and supper clubs for fear of attracting too boozy a crowd) read thus:

HAVE YOU HAD A BUSY DAY?

Refuel your inner self & reload your train of thought with a long weekend at Loon Lake Lodge Retreat House, where holistic ideas grow like blackberries, ready for picking.

There followed the dates of the inaugural retreat, Thursday evening through Sunday afternoon three weeks hence, along with mailing address and telephone number.

Since taking up residence at Loon Lake, Eliza had grown quite enamored of wild blackberries and all the delicious things that can be made therefrom. "Holistic" had been Bugsy's contribution: he thought the word had a catchy, New Age kind of sound and nobody else of the family liked to discourage him further, after overruling several earlier suggestions of his, pertaining to striped beetles, choice crayfish, and the appetite of the lake's bat population for its mosquito population. The genesis of several other words in the notice ought to be more or less evident. As for the dates, they were the absolute earliest to which Freedom could win the agreement of Pearl Bonami, on whom so much of the mundane labor must devolve.

Freedom enlisted Uncle Cliff's help in putting up the notices. For this and other bits of assistance she had enticed him to attend the retreat as a special, nonpaying guest (never mentioning how she hoped it might number his bachelor days). She took the preliminary step of nudging him to the Yarn Barn while directing her own steps to the library on the other side of the street.

Somewhat bemused—for he well knew that his young friend Freedom ("Freezie" to her intimates, though he had never quite stooped, adoptive uncle or not, to calling her that) knew the inside of the Yarn Barn as well as he himself knew that of the public library—Mr. Reed entered and looked tentatively around for whatever served as the shop's notice board.

The shop seemed innocent both of customers and persons to serve them when he stepped in, but after a moment Mrs. Batique made her appearance. They scarcely recognized each other: although living in an underpopulated area, they attended different churches and moved in different circles of interest as well as avocation; he, moreover, made his home in a small community twenty-odd miles distant, while she lived in a cottage behind her business. He guessed, by the fact that she had issued from the store's back regions and carried no handbag, that she must be either proprietress or employee; while she took him for a customer— likely on behalf of wife or daughter, although she did number a few intelligent and broadminded gentlemen among her regular customers. They began speaking simultaneously.

MR. REED

Good afternoon—

MRS. BATIQUE

Good afternoon—

Each stopped and nodded for the other to proceed. Mrs. Batique did so at once, since it was her business—as it was not his—to wait on the public.

MRS. BATIQUE

Can I help you, sir?

MR. REED

Er… Yes. Ms. Eklektik said…er…you could put this notice up somewhere?

After five years of friendship with the family and Eliza's formidable old feminist ideals, he would no more have distinguished mother from daughter by calling them "Mrs." and "Miss" Eklektik than he would have told the Pope—or anyone else, for that matter—a dirty joke.

Freedom being the only one of that surname whom she had met as yet, Mrs. Batique understood at once which Ms. Eklektik he meant. She smiled, accepted the handbill, and said oh, yes, she thought she could accommodate Ms. Eklektik.

He nodded his thanks and was gone from the establishment before she could finish reading the handbill or remark that, after all the business dear Freedom had given her in the last year, of course she would be going to the Loon Lake Lodge retreat herself.

* * * *

Meanwhile, across the street at the town's tiny public library, a woman of a certain age (fortysomething) brought an armload of books to the front desk and presented them along with her card. While waiting for them to be charged out, she read with some interest the advertisement the librarian had just good-naturedly slid below the glass as a favor to Freedom Eklektik.

Mrs. Penelope Wright was the author of half a dozen paperback novels. Aspiring to something more ambitious, in hardcover, she had depleted the establishment's easily-depletable stock of ancient histories, added a few old novels set in antique times, and felt in the mood to back up for a good start. "HAVE YOU HAD A BUSY DAY?" she read. Well, yes and no, she replied to herself, as honestly as she could, and proceeded selectively to scan key words of the Eklektik family's painstakingly phrased notice: **"Refuel your inner self... weekend at Loon Lake Lodge Retreat House... BRING A GOOD BOOK!"** *(Those last four words had been added by the librarian, Mr. Leif Pageturner, as his price for displaying the handbill so prominently.)*

MRS. WRIGHT

Loon Lake Lodge Retreat House?

MR. PAGETURNER

Yes. As I understand it, the Eklektiks are hoping to open the old lodge—their private home, now—to paying retreats.

Mrs. Wright had been on several retreats of the religious persuasion. But she had heard there was another variety, redolent of hot fudge and pillow-fighting, so she prudently inquired, "What kind of retreat?"

MR. PAGETURNER

I'm not sure, but from what I've seen of the Eklektiks, it should be worth checking out. And I'd love to get another look at the old lodge. Saw it just the once, and then just the part that was a restaurant at that time. And the little gangster museum. I was just a kid then.

MRS. WRIGHT

Are they... I mean...they're respectable, aren't they? —Well, of course they must be, if you're going yourself!

MR. PAGETURNER

Oh, they're a little eccentric, I think, but I've never heard anything bad about them. And aren't we all a little eccentric, one way or another?

MRS. WRIGHT

Must have been the "gangster museum" that got me a little worried.

MR. PAGETURNER

That was just a restaurant gimmick. Well before the present owners' time. Probably long gone.

CHAPTER 6

Reassured, Penelope Wright copied down the address and phone number of Loon Lake Lodge, went home with her books, and a day or two later dialed the number on her old-fashioned, large-receiver telephone.

The housekeeper-cook, being in the near vicinity of one of the lodge's almost equally old-fashioned—or "nostalgic," as the family called them—extension phones, answered.

PEARL BONAMI

Loon Lake Lodge.

PENELOPE

Hello? Loon Lake Lodge? Who am—I mean—*(checking her note, and finding the handbill must have included only surnames)*—is this Mrs. Eklektik?

Penelope was not bashful, precisely; but lifelong experience of being cut off in mid-exposition, coupled with excessive eagerness to get all her words out in order before the present train of thought was derailed, on occasion tied her tongue into somewhat Gordian knots. The housekeeper, however, on this occasion had no difficulty slicking through them to the meat of the inquiry, and replied she would fetch Miz Eklektik right away.

"Right away," in a dwelling the size of Loon Lake Lodge, could ramble into several long minutes. By a "long minute" the present author means to imply eighty-seven and a half seconds. In the present instance, these amounted to four long minutes...i.e., five and five-sixths minutes of the conventional length...toward the end of which time Muttwump ambled along and volunteered a loud bark at the telephone receiver, as was his custom whenever he found something out of place to his perception, and considered the humans ought to be alerted so

that they could come set it right. Both Freedom and Bugsy had passed through phases of leaving the telephone off its hook, a trait doubtless inherited from their father, who was still known to indulge it on rare occasion.

Now, Penelope Wright had in tender youth been bitten on the calf by a tiny dog who, going far to explain the word "pugnacious," had apparently taken exception to the long distance she was walking in her effort to place herself beyond the reach of his chain. As a result, she had suffered ever since from a deep dread of the canine race, so that Muttwump did little to reassure her as to the safety of Loon Lake Lodge as a retreat house.

Happily, before she decided to abandon the project and hang up, the mother of the family, alerted rather by Muttwump's bark than by the housekeeper (who was searching the wrong quarters of the lodge), arrived. "Good boy, Muttwump," she told the dog, rubbing him behind the ears; and Penelope, overhearing, thought, "Muttwump! What a nice, friendly, cozy name," and felt somewhat better concerning the presence of a dog on the premises; for, greatly though she feared them en masse, she was nevertheless capable of striking truces with individual friendly specimens of the species. Before returning the receiver perfunctorily to its cradle, Ms. Eklektik put it to her ear by way of precaution. Hearing no dial tone, but only silence, she essayed a greeting.

ELIZA

Hello?

PENELOPE

Oh, hello? Mrs.—Mrs. Eklektik?

ELIZA

Ms. Eklektik, please. Speaking.

PENELOPE

Oh, yes, I like 'Ms.,' too. Only some women, you know, get all upset and act as if they think you're insulting them when you use it.

ELIZA

The same sort of women who consider that of course one must know, by some mysterious osmosis, whether their marital status entitles them to 'Miss' or 'Mrs.,' and take it as an insult if one fails to guess which to use, from their naked names alone.

PENELOPE

I know. When 'Ms.' would solve the problem so nicely, for everyone! After all, males are all 'Mr.' nowadays, from the minute they're born.

ELIZA

Exactly.

PENELOPE

When in doubt, I always use 'Mrs.' It seems to me that single women are less likely to feel insulted if one doesn't guess right.

ELIZA

I question that. In my experience, single women are as likely to feel affronted by the suggestion that they lack independence.

PENELOPE

But as late as about a century and a half ago, 'Mrs.' didn't depend on being married. Mature women were called 'Mrs.' on the strength of their own accomplishments—actresses, authors, cooks and housekeepers—and nobody asked if they had husbands or not. Cooks and housekeepers could still be 'Mrs.' at the turn of the nineteenth into the twentieth century, though by then it seems to have been starting to cause some confusion. I'm…er…trying to revive the practice. That's why I…uh… call myself 'Mrs.,' even though I've never been married.

ELIZA

Yes, I see.

PENELOPE

When boys were 'Master' until they grew up, then 'Miss' for young girls might have been okay. But now that boys are 'Mister' as soon as they're born, why should marriage be the only way a woman is considered to have reached adulthood?

ELIZA

It shouldn't! And when women are called 'Mrs.' from the moment of birth, I'll go along with all my heart. Until then, married or not, I'd rather go by 'Ms.'

PENELOPE

Why not just address everybody as 'M.'? That could stand for anything—Miss, Mrs., Ms., Mr., Master—and even cover you when you've got a first name that could be either masculine or feminine, like Leslie.

ELIZA

Why not simply abandon titles altogether and treat everyone as equally worthy of respect, regardless of sex, age, accomplishments, or marital status.

PENELOPE

Good idea! Yes, I could certainly go along with that. Oh…er… maybe you're wondering why I called.

ELIZA

To tell you the truth, I have been trying to place your voice.

PENELOPE

You don't know me yet—

ELIZA

I know how you feel about Mr., Master, Mrs., Miss, and Ms.

Eliza uttered this interruption in so whimsical and friendly a tone that Penelope plucked up heart and pushed on.

PENELOPE

Well, I called about—you know—the retreat.

ELIZA

Ah! The retreat we're offering. Yes, we still have an opening.

As a matter of fact, they had several; but the Eklektiks were striving to be shrewd and worldly-wise. Ms. Wright, on the other hand, was striving not to let enthusiasm rope her into anything she might not like, and thus hardly knew whether to feel grateful that they still had one opening, or disappointed that the decision still remained for her to make.

PENELOPE

Well...er... What kind of a retreat is it? I mean, uh...

ELIZA

Relaxing and stimulating, both at once. A long weekend in a fine old resort overlooking a lovely northwoods lake, free from the work and pressures of everyday life, but filled with good meals and good conversation. We allow free discussion of both politics and religion, and will have on hand a first-rate arbitrator to keep it friendly. Among our other guests: a specialist in dream analysis; an authority in the textile arts; and L. Frank Craftlove, our local author.

PENELOPE

Well...er...ah...two local auth—writers, if I sign up. Penelope Wright? I've published a few...er...novels.

The name was not available to the elder Ms. Eklektik's immediate-recognition vocabulary, but the same diplomatic instinct that caused her to mask Uncle Clifford as the first-rate (honesty had just kept her from saying "professional") arbitrator, and Ms. Batique as an authority in the textile arts, now prompted her response.

ELIZA

Wonderful! I'll see if Leif can bring some of your books along—Leif Pageturner, our local librarian.

PENELOPE

Oh, yes! He'll... He's going to be there too, isn't he?

In this way, Ms. Wright found herself signed up for Loon Lake Lodge's First Annual Rustic Retreat, almost before she knew quite what had happened. Indeed, reviewing the state of her knowledge just after hanging up, she saw that her idea of precisely what kind of retreat this was to be still fell somewhat short of perfection. Nevertheless, if she considered anything better worth discussing than politics and religion (though she knew little of the first and less than she thought about the second), it was dreams. And if a first-class arbitrator would be on hand to head off the rancor which so often so marred debate of the first two as to render them taboo topics at many convivial gatherings, she felt the week-end should be worth a try. At worst, she consoled herself, she could always get back in her car and drive home again: it wasn't as if she would be marooned there among strangers…nor was Mr. Pageturner a stranger, she remembered with relief. In any case, she was too proud to phone back and cancel on second thoughts.

CHAPTER 7

Ms. Wright recognized Mr. Craftlove's byline, for his works were quite popular, though it was news to her that he resided in the same general area as herself. She promptly purchased one of his paperback bestsellers from the nearest bookstand, which happened to be in a small convenience store; but she cared so little for the work that she left off reading in the middle of page nineteen, and resolved, in courtesy, to pretend a total lack of acquaintance with his whole subgenre.

Craftlove was, in fact, a triad of authors, each moderately successful under his or her own name, who managed their collaboration over a distance. With two of the triad, a husband and wife who also published under a joint pseudonym and divided their time between Scotland and Florida, the present tale is unconcerned. The third had gentlemen's agreement rights to use the Craftlove name socially, and Ms. Eklektik—who indeed remained blissfully unaware that he had any other name, (his genre not being to her taste) of course seized on its popularity to help promote her own family's project, little dreaming that if anything could have caused Ms. Wright's second thoughts to outweigh her pledged word, it would have been *The Tentacle Pentacle from the Sewers*.

Had she only known it, her adverse reaction to this novel would have delighted its co-author completely, since he churned out this kind of profitable fiction as a scornful joke on people silly enough to pay money for it, and in private life devoted himself to the most extreme variety of right-wing Catholicism, under his own name penning erudite and scholarly volumes which contrasted the heavenly hierarchies with their infernal counterparts. These serious works circulated in manuscript among a carefully selected readership, but had yet to attract any commercial publisher, which rather increased their author's jaundiced view of the Reading Public.

Penelope Wright was Catholic too, but of an ultra-liberal outlook which rendered her as far from Mr. Craftlove in religion as if one had been a Southern Baptist and the other a South Seas Cannibal. (The present author knows too little about the tenets of these respective persuasions to intend any disrespect to either.)

* * * *

These, then, were the five guests who assembled at Loon Lake Lodge on the appointed Thursday evening: the author going professionally and sometimes socially by the name of L. (for Lycurgus) Frank (for "Frankly, my dear, I don't give a damn") Craftlove; the librarian Mr. Leif Pageturner; the fictioneer who preferred to go by the honorific of Mrs., Penelope Wright; the widowed shopkeeper Merlina Batique; and a friend of Mrs. Batique's, Dr. Mary Arrowsmith. A psychoanalyst who boasted one-sixteenth Native American blood in her ancestry, who had turned when approaching midlife to a broadly and ecumenically Wiccan form of religion (within whose circles she adopted the name "Moonglow) and who specialized both by medical and Wiccan training in the analysis of dreams, Dr. Arrowsmith had been recruited just too late for the Eklektiks to include her in their printed advertising—although they hoped, if things worked out, to include her in another retreat weekend as a paid rather than a paying attendee. Together with the eight Eklektiks—including Mrs. Bonami, Muttwump, Budgeweiser, and the informally adoped "Uncle" Clifford Reed—they made up an even thirteen, to Bugsy's great delight; and if any of his elders harbored superstitious misgivings, they kept them deeply secret, comforting themselves that the dog and the parakeet didn't really count.

A "long weekend," Eliza and Freedom had decided, should begin on Thursday afternoon.

To Freedom's great disappointment, her friend Merlina decided she would be unable to stay away from her shop on Friday. She lived near enough, however, to spend Thursday evening and plan on returning late the following afternoon. Freedom secretly regarded the Yarn Barn as so much wasted time that might otherwise have gone into growing a romance with Uncle Cliff; but she could hardly say so while the older woman remained unaware of any matchmaking scheme afoot.

Nor could Mr. Pageturner absent himself from the library on Friday, which tended to be what passed for its busy day, and he had independently adopted the same plan as Mrs. Batique. But that meant nothing to Freedom, although to the rest of her family it meant rebating a little of the price they would otherwise have asked him. This was something to Eliza's concern, since Merlina Batique's registration fee had been similarly truncated, leaving only three guests—Craftlove, Wright, and Dr. Arrowsmith—who were actually paying the full fee. Yet in her concern that the project would prove less a moneymaker than they could have hoped, Eliza was alone. For her husband, as long as his family were in reasonable health and his trains running in their ever-improving layouts, Elmer really worried about little else; Freedom cared too predominantly for her matchmaking scheme to bother her head with lesser details; Pearl Bonami cared about menus, place settings, bedding, and towels; Bugsy had not yet attained either an age or a state of want to render Higher Finance an immediately pressing personal concern; while Muttwump and Budgeweiser were forever in that happy state of unconcern with money achieved only by animals and presumably plants, inanimate nature, and bodhisattvas.

CHAPTER 8

The Thursday afternoon of the Retreat arrived, and with it such weather as made that part of the world a favorite among summer vacationers: clear and pleasantly warm, with just enough breeze from across the lake to waft away the mosquitoes and other small flying things. To be on the safe side, Elmer and his son lit citronella candles on iron stands around the pair of picnic tables, placed end to end for the occasion. All but invisible at the start of the supper, as daylight faded these candles in their blue glass globes gradually formed a ring of softly glowing bulbs around the tables. While giving enough light to eat by, it did not, even abetted by the radiance from Elmer's nearby barbecue stove, detract from the floor show of watching stars wink into the deepening blue sky, and the sadly rare fireflies, a.k.a. lightning bugs, rise from the weeds at the edge of the dark blue lake.

MRS. PENELOPE WRIGHT

There used to be so many more lightning bugs when I was a child, down in Indiana. I remember my cousin once told me there was a reward of a million dollars for the very rare pure green lightning bug, and we spent hours trying to find one and catch it, before I understood she was joking.

BUGSY

Rats! She was probably joking about the million-dollar reward, but I saw one of those green ones just last summer. Too bad I couldn't catch it.

FREEDOM

Oh, Bugsy, you just dreamed that.

BUGSY

Did not!

"UNCLE" CLIFF

Some of them really do look pretty green.

BUGSY

The one I saw last summer was green as a traffic light. Too bad it got away.

FREEDOM

Green, and it got away. That proves you dreamed it.

MR. LEIF PAGETURNER

No, it proves he saw it. Dreams are in black and white.

DR. MARY ARROWSMITH

I'm afraid that's a common fallacy. Most dreams are in color.

MRS. PENELOPE WRIGHT

I once had one in black and white. Of course, it was set in a London fog, so you'd expect it to be in black and white. Though I've always thought we should say, "in shades of gray," because that's what the phrase "in black and white" really means.

ELMER

I always thought of the Buster Keaton layout I'd like to do someday as in black and white, but you're right, Ms. Wright, it is in shades of gray. I wonder what a true black and white layout would look like…a checkerboard landscape, maybe, with white clouds reflected in a lake of…let's see…black slate? graphite? Just one red caboose, and the crossing lights for spots of colored relief…

FREEDOM (giggling)

What's black and white and red all over?

MR. LEIF PAGETURNER

A newspaper.

BUGSY

A blushing zebra.

MR. CRAFTLOVE

An Amerindian nun in the good, oldfashioned habit.

UNCLE CLIFF

Santa Claus in a sooty chimney.

MRS.MERLINA BATIQUE

Heartstrings variegated yarn Ombre…number eighteen, if memory serves.

MRS. PENELOPE WRIGHT

A chocolate sundae with ketchup on it.

FREEDOM (with a small shriek of laughter, which caused Muttwump to look up and thump his tail)

Wrong, all wrong! It's Dad's seventh layout, with the checkerboard landscape and red caboose! Hey, Dad—I bet I could needlepoint it for you.

Before the conversation could continue in this vein, Eliza, who considered that three more or less finished model-train layouts and three more in various stages of progress were quite enough for the time being and the space available, quickly wondered aloud what had happened to so much of the lightning-bug population.

UNCLE CLIFF

Pesticides, unfortunately.

MRS. PENELOPE WRIGHT

I'm afraid that's a large part of the answer, but I'd rather hoped geography had something to do with it. You know, more fireflies in the lower Midwest than up here in the north.

BUGSY

Yeah, partly the geography. There's a couple thousand species of Lampyridae, so what happens to the species in one area doesn't necessarily affect all the other species everywhere. But what does affect 'em all, and a bunch of other bugs too, is the cars. Ever notice how many bugs get squashed on windshields and radiator screens? When I grow up, I'm never going to break the speed limit.

FREEDOM

My kid brother is one of a kind—fortunately.

UNCLE CLIFF

Even at the speed limit, cars kill bugs. Maybe some kind of screen... gauze? supersonics? to turn them aside before they hit the glass or metal...

MRS. PENELOPE WRIGHT

But if the lightning bugs are still fairly thick down in the southern Midwest—Indiana and Ohio and Illinois and so on—I mean, there's more traffic on the roads down there than up here, so that theory wouldn't hold.

MR. CRAFTLOVE

Allow me to point out that all of our answers to the riddle were equally correct with Miss Eklektik's. And also equally wrong, since as the riddle is phrased, the answer should be something black, white, and red everywhere—"all over"—simultaneously, which is obviously impossible.

UNCLE CLIFF

Well, maybe in another dimension, an alternate reality. I think I read something like that in one of Tony Pierce's books...

MR. CRAFTLOVE (with a great sniff, because he considered the novels of Tony Pierce slightly inferior even to his own as fodder for the masses who bought and might actually read Such Stuff)

As for the problem of the fireflies, or "lightning bugs" if you prefer, you are all at best only partially in the right. The underlying problem, to which all these others are at most mere contributing causes, is the conspiracy to depress our nation's spirits by eliminating as many natural sources of beauty or pleasure as possible. In the case of fireflies, this is being accomplished by sterilizing the females of the species.

MRS. PENELOPE WRIGHT

Oh, please! Another conspiracy theory? If any group large enough to pull one of these great conspiracies off, could actually all work together long enough to accomplish anything—sweet Mortimer's mustache, they'd *deserve* to run the world!

UNCLE CLIFF

Exactly how are they sterilizing all the females?

MR. CRAFTLOVE

Not being a scientist myself, I must refer you to the published work of Drs. Owtrajeous and Philergaz, mostly in either the Father Janus Gazette or the Conspiracy Monthly.

DR. MARY ARROWSMITH

Oh, bosh! As if we really needed mock science to explain our problems.

MR. CRAFTLOVE (with a wry chuckle)

How easily you rise to the bait! And yet I have been in circles which would have swallowed such a theory and perhaps rushed out, in all serious enthusiasm, to seek in vain for the quite fictitious authorities I just cited. Your reactions seem, in comparison, quite healthy.

MR. LEIF PAGETURNER

The way I once had someone ask for articles cited in Amisov's gag article on the substance that dissolves *before* liquid is added.

UNCLE CLIFF

I can't remember much about my childhood, but I remember trying to check those references back when the magazine with that article came out… I guess I was about ten or eleven at the time.

ELIZA

I'm very glad you weren't serious, Mr. Craftlove, but if you were… Why the female fireflies only?

MR. CRAFTLOVE

The future of any species resides in a large population, even over-population, of its females. A single male is capable of impregnating any number of females—

BUGSY

Yeah, but that doesn't happen with every bug and every animal. They've got all kinds of different habits and so on, and some of 'em are strictly monogamous.

ELIZA

Bugsy, don't interrupt.

MRS. PENELOPE WRIGHT

Bugsy has a good point. What you're really talking about, Mr. Craftlove, is human beings.

MR. CRAFTLOVE

My argument cuts across species lines, Ms. Wright, but yes, it applies very forcefully to us. Is not the whole point and aim of human warfare, for instance, to ensure the fertilization of as many females as possible by the strongest and most virile males—that is, the victorious warriors?

DR. MARY ARROWSMITH

Your argument implies that as a general rule men exclude women from combat in order to preserve them. Unfortunately, the slaughter of civilian women by invading forces contradicts your theory.

MR. CRAFTLOVE

As does battle by long-distance weapons, from the bow and arrow to the guided missile. I speak of warfare at its pure fount and origin, Dr. Arrowsmith, before it grew muddied by generations who had forgotten its true *raison d'etre*.

ELIZA (who could no longer contain herself)

Rubbish, Mr. Craftlove! We got warfare out of the pure stupid machismo of the male sex, and women were excluded because at the beginning they were too smart to fight, and by the time they saw they were being victimized because of it, it was too late to stem the flood.

FREEDOM

Not all women. What about the Amazons? Joan of Arc? Molly Pitcher? Mu Lan? The modern Israeli army?

MR. CRAFTLOVE

Your last example is an ill-conceived experiment and a mistake, as the Israelis may eventually discover. That they ever attempted such a scheme at all can be explained only by the long-distance, push-button nature of too much modern warfare. For the rest, aberrations, exceptions, and daydreams of weak men and grandiose women, as fictive as such modern fantasies as, say, *Snowflake and Splinter.*

UNCLE CLIFF

Snowflake and Splinter? I enjoyed that one.

MR. CRAFTLOVE

You also enjoy Tony Pierce's novels, do you not? Which are, at least, blessedly free of heavy feminist ballast.

ELIZA

Even if they show women on an equal footing with men?

MR. CRAFTLOVE

Of course they do, since Pierce's aim is to attract the widest market possible. But perhaps Dr. Arrowsmith, as a practicing psychotherapist, would favor us with her professional opinion of the types to which the female warrior of modern fiction appeals?

DR. MARY ARROWSMITH

Really, I cannot draw any generalizations. Individual cases are unique, each drawing on its own special set of variables and modifying factors. It is entirely possible for a disturbed person to suck poison from *Heidi,* where someone in good mental health reads *Conquering Amazons of Gorre* unscathed.

FREEDOM

Anyway, what's wrong with a few daydreams about women turning the tables on men for a change?

MRS. PENELOPE WRIGHT

But in *Snowflake and Splinter*, women do the fighting because men are considered too valuable to risk their own lives and limbs. It's really a very male-dominated society.

MR. CRAFTLOVE

Your opinion, perhaps, Ms. Wright. I venture to say that most of the work's readership sees it as an example of female dominance.

MRS. PENELOPE WRIGHT

That isn't the book's problem. It's the problem of our society, that sees whoever does the actual fighting as automatically more powerful.

MR. CRAFTLOVE

Atypical as your opinion undoubtedly is, it credits the novel's author, a militant feminist—

Here Mr. Pageturner gave a cough which struck many who heard it as a warning note. Not being among these, Mr. Craftlove plowed ahead without interruption.

MR. CRAFTLOVE

—who, I understand, is planning a sequel in which her female warrior caste rises up and slaughters its masculine commanders—you credit her, I say, with more subtlety than she appears to possess.

MR. LEIF PAGETURNER (with another cough)

Mr. Craftlove, you're speaking to the author of *Snowflake and Splinter.*

MR. CRAFTLOVE (looking up and down the table)

I am? Here? Who?

MRS. PENELOPE WRIGHT

And you almost make me wish that I had written a book—a novel about…that is, I almost wish it really was the kind of novel you think—seem to think it is! I'd be very interested, Mr. Craftlove, where… I hope you'll tell me where you get your information about what I plan for the sequel. Who knows? The publishers might like your idea—whosever it is—better than the outline I actually sent them.

DR. MARY ARROWSMITH

Maybe from one of the same sources he cited in reference to that firefly conspiracy theory.

UNCLE CLIFF

Is there going to be a whole trilogy?

MR. CRAFTLOVE

As for where I got that information, I scan so many trade journals, and so quickly, that I can hardly say. If the idea interests you, by all means, utilize it.

MRS. PENELOPE WRIGHT

I'd hate to break anyone else's copyright, you see.

MR. CRAFTLOVE

Oh, a general idea alone can hardly be copyrighted, only what is done with it. Each one of us here present might write a fiction on the idea of a female warrior caste overthrowing its male commanders, and each treatment would be so different as to utterly baffle any lawyer attempting to draw up a case of infringement of copyright.

UNCLE CLIFF

I'd have some of the warriors discover that the men aren't really so bad. Maybe have one or two couples fall in love...

Penelope Wright, who had been on the point of expressing her opinion regarding the first nineteen pages of Pentacle Tentacle from the Sewers, *turned and looked at Mr. Reed instead, resolving to talk further with him some time when they could find themselves away from Mr. Craftlove.*

The single person at the table who took note of that glance was Freedom, who would have welcomed it had it been directed toward Uncle Cliff by her dear friend Merlina.

CHAPTER 9

Friday morning dawned to the sound of gentle rain, not unwelcome to the ecosystem of the area as a whole—which, as Uncle Cliff enjoyed pointing out, constituted a northern rainforest—but less than optimum for summer vacationers and for the retreat plans of the Eklektik family, who met at six a.m., summoned by Pearl Bonami, for a hurried conference on where to lay breakfast. Eliza judged the weather too depressing for the screened porch, and Bugsy, too warm for the fireplace barroom. Elmer wanted to reserve his "caboose" for closer friends. Freedom made a bid for feeding the throng in small groups (hoping to maneuver Merlina and Uncle Cliff together in a relatively intimate setting), but Miz Bonami—who saw Freedom's notion multiplying her workload—finally settled the matter in no uncertain terms by declaring that she would serve them all in the main dining room and nowhere else.

So the Eklektik women busied themselves moving the floral arrangements from porch to dining room and the Eklektik men set the long table, while Miz Bonami fried up pancakes and breakfast meats, Muttwump did his best to get in everyone's way, and Budgeweiser supervised it all from his cage. By seven thirty, the family Eklektik were seated two to a side at the far end of the table, with Miz Bonami to serve them, and all was ready for the first guests, who found their way to breakfast at seven thirty-five and three quarters.

To Freedom's delight, these first arrivals were her dear friend Merlina, who planned to return to her Yarn Barn for the day, and Uncle Cliff, a natural early riser and born gentleman, who opened the door for her, then seated himself to Bugsy's right. But—alas for Freedom's hopes!—at seven thirty-six and a half came Leif Pageturner to grab the chair beside Merlina, with whom he planned to carpool to Muskywater after breakfast in order to open the public library at ten; and half a minute later Penelope Wright, who tended to sleep late except when the excitement of new places, faces, and activities awoke her early, arrived to seat herself beside Uncle Cliff, so that the four guests sat in facing pairs and gender diagonals.

* * * *

MERLINA

What a lovely dream I had last night! Arthur, my late husband, was in a sort of crystal bubble, high in outer space. He had a comfortable kind of trapeze to sit on, and the moons and stars and nebulae and such around him were in softly glowing pastels on a background of such a deep blue it was almost black—like White Heart number forty-seven. I went floating up, the trapeze came swinging down, and I climbed aboard with him. So there we were together in the fine crystal bubble, floating up and up into deep space. He lay down with the trapeze for a pillow, and the rest of his long body stayed buoyed in place, as relaxed as in bed.

PENELOPE

Oh, that is lovely! Do you—that is, would you mind if I used it in a novel sometime?

MERLINA

Of course not. Please be my guest.

LEIF

I wonder what Dr. Arrowsmith would say about that dream?

BUGSY (in a recognizable if slightly unfair imitation of Dr. Arrowsmith)

Really, I can't generalize. Individual dreams are far too unique. I would need at least ten sessions with the dreamer, at about a million dollars a session, to begin to understand her particular mental processes.

FREEDOM (laughing)

Bugsy! Where on earth did you get "a million dollars a session"?

BUGSY (in wide-eyed mock innocence)

Well, aren't all these headshrinks expensive?

UNCLE CLIFF

Probably not quite that expensive, Bugsy.

PENELOPE

Anyway, either a thing is "unique" or it isn't. There can't—that is, grammatically, there's no such thing as "very unique," or "far too unique" or "especially unique" or so on. I know I'm trying to buck a whole stampede of steers here, but—

BUDGEWISER

Have you had a busy day?

All laughed, and Freedom seized her chance to redirect the conversation.

FREEDOM

Uncle Cliff, what do you think about Merlina's dream?

UNCLE CLIFF

It reminds me of science fiction. What a great way to travel around the universe, from star system to system!

MERLINA

As I like to imagine Arthur doing, enjoying all those beauties we can see only in photographs.

PENELOPE

And artists' renderings. I'd love to be able to paint the kind of deep-space phenomena and alien planetscapes I see at science fiction convention art shows.

UNCLE CLIFF

Science fiction conventions? What are they like?

PENELOPE

You mean you haven't ever been to one? I thought… That is, you seem to read so much of it.

UNCLE CLIFF

Yes, all my life. But I just read it, that's all.

MUTTWUMP

Arf!

Muttwump seemed, not to be commenting on Uncle Cliff Reed's last statement, but rather to be greeting Dr. Arrowsmith, who had just appeared in the doorway to the dining room. During the round of human "Good mornings," the psychiatrist seated herself beside the librarian, who poured her a cup of coffee while she waited for the pancakes even then on Miz Bonami's griddle. Mr. Pageturner returned at once to the subject of Mrs. Batique's dream, which that lady obligingly repeated with only enough differences in wording to reaffirm its authenticity.

MARY

Your whole tone of voice tells me that you loved your husband very much.

MERLINA

Yes, I did. We were very happy together.

MARY

Your love continues. Both yours and his.

LEIF

Speaking as a psychologist, Dr. Arrowsmith?

MARY

Speaking as a Wiccan, Mr. Pageturner. My psychiatric opinions stay in my office, and cost a great deal more.

BUGSY

Yeah, I thought so!

PENELOPE

"More" than what? Your Wiccan opinion didn't cost anything.

MARY (smiling)

I think it was the Mad Hatter who said, more than nothing is very easy. Sometimes our dreams provide windows into deeper realities than the merely psychological. Yours of last night, Mrs. Batique, sounds very much to me like one of these. I'd guess you may actually have glimpsed

Summerland—"Heaven" as many of us call it—and revisited your husband there in his happiness and continued love for you.

PENELOPE

Oh, how beautiful!

MERLINA

Yes…yes, that's certainly what it felt like.

FREEDOM

Yes, I'm sure he still loves you, Merlina. Too much to want to see you lonely. Maybe he was trying to tell you to look around for someone else to share your love.

MERLINA

I don't think I could ever find anyone else as good as Arthur.

MR. CRAFTLOVE (speaking from the open doorway, where he had somehow materialized without attracting the notice even of Muttwump)

But by all means, Mrs. Batique, don't let that stop you from looking around.

MUTTWUMP (waking up)

Arf!

> Mr. Craftlove entered the room and took his place in the one remaining chair, to Mrs. Wright's left, putting the two authors side by side and completing the complement of the weekend's scheduled guest list.

MR. CRAFTLOVE

Love in its physical aspect is, after all, the particular province of earthly life, and has no part in Heaven, which Dr. Arrowsmith so quaintly sees fit to refer to as "Summerland."

MARY

Now why, Mr. Craftlove, should the mere terminology bother you?

MR. CRAFTLOVE

Because, in this case, it carries its own misleading baggage as to the nature of that place where they neither marry nor are given in marriage, but are as the angels.

PENELOPE

I know that text, Mr. Craftlove, and in the first place, it doesn't deny the possibility that the angels may practice free love; and, in the second place, it says they don't marry there in Heaven—which I take to mean, no one is ever forced to marry anyone they don't want to—and leaves the chance open for happy marriages to continue right on from earth into the afterlife. Whatever it's called.

ELIZA

In that ancient society, of course, it was the women who were forced into unwanted marriages.

PENELOPE

Exactly! There's a verse somewhere in the Old Testament that says, "Some women make more desirable wives than others, but ANY man is a good husband."

MR. CRAFTLOVE

Ecclesiasticus, also known as the book of Sirach, and not to be confused with Ecclesiastes. Chapter 36, verse 20 or 21, if my memory serves. "Though any man may be accepted as a husband..." just so, in a society that allowed unmarried females no status whatsoever.

PENELOPE

But there's also a case where someone's unmarried daughters appealed to—Moses, I think—and got their father's inheritance.

MR. CRAFTLOVE

Numbers chapter 27, verses 1 to about 10. The daughters of one Zelophehad. I cannot remember that their marital status is actually specified; yet, since no husbands are in evidence, you could be correct in your assumption. They pled on behalf of their deceased father, arguing that his name ought not be withdrawn from his clan because he had left no sons; and their case did indeed bring forth a decision from the Lord specifying the laws of inheritance: sons first, then daughters, then brothers...

BUDGEWISER

Have you had a busy day?

UNCLE CLIFF

In a society where parents arranged the marriages, I imagine the boys were often as helpless as the girls.

MERLINA

But I surely do hope you're right, Dr. Arrowsmith, Mrs. Wright, about married couples in the next world.

LEIF

So do I. And as to whether we call it "Heaven" or "Summerland," I really don't see that it makes any difference.

MR. CRAFTLOVE

Only the difference, sir, between Truth and Error. In this case, between reading dreams as nightly fears and fantasies—psychological delusions—or as windows on eternal realities. Although, since both views amount to so much hogwash, you may after all have a legitimate point.

PENELOPE

But—look here—allow me to point out that we have absolutely no way of knowing, being sure about, what "eternal realities" actually are!

MR. CRAFTLOVE

We have the Holy Scriptures.

PENELOPE

Which tell us next to nothing about it. In fact, somewhere St. Paul— or the Pauline writer, I forget whether it's in one of his authentic epistles or one of questioned authorship—makes a point of being caught up to the seventh Heaven, of which no tongue can speak.

MR. CRAFTLOVE

The "third Heaven," actually. Two Corinthians, chapter 12, verse 2, and I subscribe to the view that all the Pauline Epistles, traditionally so called, are indeed from the pen of Saint Paul, with the possible though unproven exception of Hebrews. We have, moreover, considerably more about Hell, a.k.a. Gehenna, "where the worm dies not and the fire is not quenched." Eternally. Mark 9, 48, where Jesus Himself cites Isaiah 66, 24.

PENELOPE

But not necessarily forever! "Eternity" isn't the same as "forever"—it's another mystery that we can't understand here.

UNCLE CLIFF

Like the eleven dimensions needed to make String Theory work?

BUGSY (imitating Budgewiser)

Have you had a busy day?

> *All laughed, even Mr. Craftlove, who then at once turned his attention to his coffee and, finding it excellent, appeared prepared to view the world in a somewhat more benevolent light.*

PENELOPE

We were getting a little hot under the collar, weren't we?

MR. CRAFTLOVE

To coin a phrase. Well, I shall agree that we know next to nothing about Heaven or even Hell, if you will agree that the same mystery applies equally to "Summerland."

ELIZA

And since we don't know and can't know for sure, I think we should agree here and now to agree to disagree and not discuss religion at all until we can discuss it like gentlefolk, at least here in Loon Lake Lodge.

MR. CRAFTLOVE

Madam, though nothing this life offers can be better or more necessary to discuss than religion, pour me another cup of this superior coffee, and as long as I rest beneath your roof I bow to your will as our hostess. And if I have said anything to offend any heretic among us, let me most humbly apologize.

Here he looked, not at Mrs. Wright as Freedom might have hoped and expected, but across the table at Dr. Arrowsmith, who smiled in that quiet kind of way professional people sometimes show when regarding rank neophytes in some different and lesser course of study.

MARY

Accepted. What most interests me, Mr. Craftlove, is what dreams you must have, that you feel the need to reject them so definitively as mere "psychological delusions."

MR. CRAFTLOVE

Ah, Dr. Arrowsmith! I enjoy some remarkable nightmares. Nor, seeing that they furnish me with my most financially profitable fictions, do I wish to be cured of them at any price.

ELMER

Say, Cliff, what do you think about a Dante Railway layout, running all the way from the Inferno up to Paradise?

PENELOPE

Don't forget the Purgatorio! Everyone always ignores Dante's Purgatorio.

UNCLE CLIFF

We could use three levels. What kind of engine and cars?

LEIF

I think I know right where I can locate that poem about "The Hell-Bound Train."

FREEDOM

I could needlepoint little plastic covers, for you to change when the train goes from level to level.

MERLINA

Freedom, I'm afraid that some things simply aren't practical with yarn and needlepoint canvas. I could bring in a few color charts, though—just for ideas about a color scheme.

ELIZA (sighing)

Elmer, before you start work on yet another layout, no matter how exciting it is, I really think you ought to concentrate on all the ones you have going now, and whether or not there might be one you can bear to dismantle in order to make room for a new one.

ELMER

Fine idea! Maybe we can spend an hour or so showing our guests around the layouts we have, getting their opinion on it.

> *At this point, Pearl Bonami appeared in the doorway to the kitchen with a large serving platter and asked who was ready for hot pancakes.*

CHAPTER 10

Merlina ate just one more pancake, and Leif two, before leaving together in the latter's car for their last regular workday of the week. Expeditiously resetting Merlina's place, Pearl Bonami settled down to eat her own breakfast, while the rest of the gathering lingered over second, third, or even fourth cups of coffee to enjoy both their company and their leisure…Bugsy, who stoked his growing youth up for the day's activities on just one more pancake and cup of cocoa..

Elmer used this interval to describe in loving detail the half dozen various model trains and their layouts he was about to show off, with Uncle Cliff interspersing long technical explanations of the building and electrical wiring involved. His enthusiasm when expounding these neutral and more or less impersonal topics quite outweighed his native bashfulness, rendering him both voluble and, to any listener imperfectly acquainted with the subject matter, somewhat less than lucid; but a chill struck Freedom's heart as she watched Mrs. Wright gazing at Uncle Cliff in a lack of comprehension for the subject coupled with a growing appreciation for the speaker that did not bode well for the matchmaking project of which both Uncle Cliff and dear Merlina remained as yet the unaware subjects.

In the lodge itself Elmer had three of his layouts: the Lionel Safari Special in the old conservatory, the Bavarian Hamm and Swiss in the far corner of the sun porch, and the HO Transcontinental Line in the basement, on what had once been two regulation-size bowling lanes for the guests when Mrs. Aloywisha Woodbucks Lotsadoe kept Loon Lake Lodge, but which had suffered in the balmy days of her grandson's Hippie commune. Unlike the Safari Special and the Hamm and Swiss, which were largely deliberate flights of artistic fancy, the Transcontinental was as authentic a scale model as possible of cross-country America ca. 1880.

The Charley Iron Horse, the Lunar-Martian Express, and the Knights of the Rail Road Special were housed each in its own outlying guest cabin. Of these, only the last named boasted historical accuracy, being a recreation of the Great Depression following the Crash of 1929. The Charley Iron Horse postulated an alternate history in which a highly advanced American Indian civilization had first discovered Europe—rather than the other way around—and subsequently developed transportation by rails. The Lunar-Martian Express, which had barely been begun, as Uncle Cliff's special brainchild was frankly science-fictional, the tracks through simulated outer space intended to be rendered as invisible as possible by some artifice he was still in process of devising, but which would probably owe a great deal to black electrical tape.

In the first flush of his inspiration for a Hades to Paradise layout a la Dante, Elmer threw forth the proposal of creating it in the cabin on Loon Lake Island. Eliza, who suffered from a severe lack of desire to see more than six model train layouts on the property, who best liked the Knights of the Rail Road Special because it incorporated such of her own feminist principles as including women among the hobo population, and who could not bear that Uncle Cliff's pet Lunar-Martian project should be junked—no matter how far from completion—suggested that the Bavarian Hamm and Swiss already featured Alpine peaks, the tallest of which might well be recast as Mount Purgatory. Freedom, seeing hopes for her own pet idea fading, seconded her mother's idea for the Hamm and Swiss, but added the thought that a Santa Claus Special in the lake cabin might provide a wonderful tourist attraction, especially during those Decembers when the lake froze over soon enough to allow a frosty hike to the island, perhaps through a walkway of colorful Christmas lights. Uncle Cliff promptly began cogitating upon how the lights could be strung on tall poles affixed to the lake bottom, so as to form a path for all seasons: for swimmers in summer; rowboats and canoes in spring and autumn; and in winter, if the lake disobligingly remained open too long, planks might be laid down like a pier or a bridge—the light poles must of course be furnished with special projections.

At this point in the conversation, Eliza, who harbored secret doubts as to whether the terms of the Perpetual Land Trust would allow light poles in the lake, declared as hostess that she, for one, could drink no more coffee for a week, and thought it high time to visit the model train layouts in person.

Elmer always worried whether such tours should start with the layouts in the lodge proper, which were for all practical purposes complete or nearly so, or with those in the cabins, which, while far from finished, were fresher, newer, in some ways more ambitious, and in Elmer's view more innovative. Fortunately for him, today the others took the decision out of his mental hands. Fluffy white "fair-weather" clouds had begun mounding up like a whipped cream pie in the sky, and such pies showed a notable tendency in that part of the world to develop black bottoms on the spur of a moment; so the party reached a rapid consensus that they would rather see the Charley Iron Horse, Knights of the Rail Road

Special, and Lunar-Martian Express at once, while the outlying cabins could still be reached without the use of umbrellas.

Accordingly, they soon set out: the four Eklektiks and Uncle Cliff, Dr. Mary Arrowsmith, Mr. Craftlove, Mrs. Penelope Wright, and Muttwump. Pearl, who had seen more of all the layouts than really interested her, stayed behind to do up the breakfast dishes and start lunch; and Budgewiser had grown too old and wise a parakeet to manifest any great desire for quitting his cozy cage at that particular moment. Eliza, Mr. Craftlove, and Penelope Wright carried umbrellas along, just to be on the safe side.

CHAPTER 11

They set out eight humans and a dog, and after an hour and a half, returning to the Lodge proper, found themselves five humans, having somewhere lost Uncle Cliff, Mrs. Wright, Bugsy, and Muttwump.

No one but Freedom felt any particular alarm at this. That Bugsy and Muttwump should have gone off more or less together somewhere about their home property was a circumstance far too frequent to strike fear into the heart of even a doting mother, and Eliza had always aimed to instill her children with a certain independence of spirit. Nor was Uncle Cliff any stranger to the grounds of Loon Lake Lodge, knowing them by now as well as the family Eklektik. As for Mrs. Wright, Eliza ventured to suppose that she had stayed behind with Uncle Cliff to hear his fuller explanations of the Lunar-Martian Express.

It was this all too plausible theory that struck fear into Freedom's heart. Could not her own mother see what dangers lurked in another unattached female having Uncle Cliff apart to herself while Merlina was far away in Muskywater? Had Eliza forgotten that the aim was less to matchmake for Uncle Cliff—who was after all quite a comfortable old bachelor—than to fit poor, dear Merlina with a second partner to solace her declining days? Freedom could only hope that the four missing members of the party were all together, with Bugsy and Muttwump to chaperone Uncle Cliff.

In this hope Freedom was doomed to disappointment. Even as she hoped it, her kid brother was halfway to Loon Lake Island, with the family dog paddling happily alongside the rowboat. As for Uncle Cliff, he had discovered, while the rest were in process of quitting the cabin of the Lunar-Martian Express for that of the Charley Iron Horse, that in addition to writing adult fantasy, Mrs. Wright was likewise a reader of the related genre of hard science fiction, to which he himself was more particularly addicted. Both having read or seen certain of the stories, movies, and television shows wherefrom he had drawn some of his inspirations, they had lingered to discuss such matters as what fictional starship captain might make the best interstellar-train engineer, and which of the Martian moons—Deimos or Phobos—would provide the better site for a switchyard. While doing most of the actual vocalization on these topics, Mr. Reed always listened intently to whatever Mrs. Wright had to interject.

From there they quickly progressed to matters of a more general-interest nature, in which Mrs. Wright took a more equal part.

MR. REED

It's a doggone shame there's been so little follow-up on the Moon Landing and the Martian probes. We had so much hope, a few years ago!

MRS. WRIGHT

Haven't they just recently sent a deep-space probe out to Pluto and beyond?

MR. REED

Yes, they're still managing a little space exploration, in spite of the Republicrats. But we're not exactly where we should have been!

MRS. WRIGHT

I agree. Though I heard someone say at a convention somewhere that the Democritan Party was really more to blame.

MR. REED

Not as far as I can see. It's the Republicrats who think we're living in—

MRS. WRIGHT (*ironically*)

—the best of all possible worlds?—

MR. REED

—and any change for the better threatens to set us back.

MRS. WRIGHT

I'm an "Independent," but I find myself voting Democritan more and more. At least that party pays lip service to the idea that we need a lot of social changes for the better. In fact—I think the argument went—the Democritans try to direct all government funds into social programs, while the Republicrats, resisting all social change, are quite willing to see funds channeled into the space program.

MR. REED

That's false reasoning. Money doesn't fall into a black hole the minute anyone spends it. It stays in the economy, to get spent over and over again.

MRS. WRIGHT

Exactly! What difference does it make if more is spent a year on lipstick than education—or whatever—when millions of individual women are spending dabs of their private funds, while the state and local government are spending public funds—

MR. REED

—that came from taxes—

MRS. WRIGHT

Of course! So why shouldn't the same women who pay taxes spend a little of whatever money they have left on little luxuries like lipstick? In fact, some of them are teachers, drawing their salaries from the education funds, so it's actually the same money being spent in both cases.

MR. REED

My mother was a teacher. So was my father.

MRS. WRIGHT

Really? So were mine.

MR. REED

So our mothers were two of those teachers you just talked about, and we know how small a proportion of their paychecks went for lipstick.

MRS. WRIGHT

Actually, I don't. I never asked my mother, and I don't wear lipstick at all.

MR. REED

You don't?

MRS. WRIGHT

Or any other make-up. I found in high school that I'm allergic to it. I know they make it in hypoallergenic versions, but frankly I'm just as glad of the excuse not to bother with the stuff.

MR. REED

You don't need it.

MRS. WRIGHT

Neither do you.

Both laughed a little self-consciously. Then he resumed:

MR. REED

Except on stage.

MRS. WRIGHT

Are you in theater?

MR. REED

Amateur theatricals. My best part was Colonel Pickering in "My Fair Lady" *(adopting a British accent)* Don't you know?

MRS. WRIGHT

Good show! I'd love to have seen you in it.

At this point, seized with an access of Old World gallantry, Mr. Reed did something he had never before done—offstage— in his adult life. He took Mrs. Wright's right hand, raised it to his lips, and bestowed on it a respectful kiss.

With a slightly apologetic laugh, she pulled it away and explained that she didn't like having her hand kissed, any more than she liked being patted on the head. Both gestures might have been fine in their original context centuries ago, but they had a very patronizing effect when applied by modern American men to modern American women.

Seeing the somewhat abashed and embarrassed expression on his face, she compounded her explanation by adding that hand-kissing was akin to addressing a mature and accomplished woman as "Miss" simply because she lacked the appendage of a husband. Mrs. Wright was very careful to emphasize that this was why, though she herself remained unmarried, she preferred to be called "Mrs." Even though she sometimes had trouble persuading people to use it as soon as they knew she was in fact unmarried. That was why she frequently didn't mention the fact that she was unmarried, although she was. Unmarried.

Despite her care on this point, their conversational exchange somehow failed to regain the free and easy feeling that had graced it only moments before at the Lunar-Martian Express; so, leaving many things unsaid—such as how the Space Program might be set back on track, and why the Lipstick Argument might better be applied to cigarettes (which both agreed were equally obnoxious to the senses and hazardous to the health)—they set out at length to visit the rest of the layouts in the order Uncle Cliff knew Elmer to prefer, hoping that they might overtake the rest of the party before the rain fell.

CHAPTER 12

Bugsy, meanwhile, knowing the model train layouts almost as well as his father, had lost no time, but struck off alone with Muttwump almost as soon as the group as a whole had left the lodge building proper. Bugsy's idea was to visit the island cabin with a view to ascertaining whether it might indeed accommodate his sister's vision of a Christmas train (with or without needlepoint) or whether it might in fact be better suited to a scheme he had hatched even while listening to hers: a Bugland Special. In this diorama, larvae might at one station board chrysalis-shaped passenger cars, to emerge butterflies and moths at the farther terminus. There could be a honeycomb car, and a wasps'-nest car, et cetera. Anthills might dot the landscape, and possibly even an exotic termite spire or three… Spiders, who while not true insects fell almost equally into Bugsy's burning interest, could take the place of the marauding European Palefaces in the Charley Iron Horse layout. Bugsy felt confident that he could easily shift his sister's needlepoint enthusiasm from the North Pole to the Bugland Special, especially if he showed her certain choice color illustrations in his favorite books…if he wanted to. But did he really want to? He'd rather use real insects and arachnids, if and wherever he possibly could—a dream that assorted ill, in his young mind, with needlepoint. Only, if he could not convert Freezie to his own inspiration, they would surely have a fight about it. Then the final decision would fall to Mom and Dad, maybe with Uncle Cliff's input. And, unless Mom vetoed the whole Seventh Layout plan and commandeered the cabin for another purpose completely, it could end up as a Philharmonic Special shuttling musicians from one bubble dome to another across the landscape of Saturn according to old pulp space opera.

As for Muttwump, this morning he just wanted to be with Bugsy.

They repaired, therefore, to the rickety old dock, wherefrom Bugsy soon untied the rowboat and jumped in. He liked untying it first and subsequently aiming his small frame like a missile, to land—usually—in the middle seat as the boat drifted free of the piling. It was an aluminum boat, still fairly new since the family Eklektik had purchased it at the time of taking up occupancy and exercised the reasonable care of storing it every winter in the old green-painted boathouse.

Springing down an instant after the boy, Muttwump landed safe in the stern and looked on, panting eagerly, while Bugsy slid the oars up from beneath the seats, secured them in the oarlocks, and started to row.

Be it confessed that, although several lifejackets were stored in the boat itself and several more bedecked the dock, Bugsy set Muttwump the very bad example of ignoring them. He hated their orange bulk, and never wore one unless some adult eye rendered it absolutely unavoidable. He rowed well and swam better.

Arriving at the island, they heard several barks delivered by a second, unknown dog. This inspired Muttwump to plunge overboard and paddle to the narrow sandy shoreline without waiting for his boy to moor the boat to the island dock, which task, under the circumstances, Bugsy performed both quickly and carelessly before scrambling ashore to pursue his dog.

From the beach, two wooden flights of a dozen steps each, with rustic handrails and a square platform between them at the turn, led up to the "front yard," scarcely large enough for its wrought-iron chairs and table, in front of the guest cabin. The stairs, although dating only from the Lodge's time as a restaurant and museum, when they had been erected to replace a similar earlier structure, were already rickety with age, and the yard overgrown, as well as that adjective can be applied to a spot so tiny. The Eklektiks had talked recurrently of replacing the stairway yet again, perhaps with flagstone steps and an iron railing to match the lawn furniture (if such could be arranged under the terms of the Land Trust), and of clearing the front yard to accommodate a border of either roses or native wildflowers. No doubt this work must needs be done at last if the cabin were to be converted to a visitor-attracting model train layout; but it had not been done yet. The cabin boasted both a front and a back door, between which its two and a quarter cozy rooms snuggled bracketed like miniature volumes almost too small for their bookends.

Both these doors were kept duly locked but, as happens in certain dreams of a more or less disquieting nature, neither lock worked. While Muttwump in his efforts to pinpoint the unknown canine chased through the wild hazelnut bushes around the cabin, Bugsy burst in through the front door without even remembering the key hidden in an artificial rock near the step, and beheld a stranger lying fast asleep beneath the tattered blanket on the singularly lumpy old couch.

"Who the heck are you?" Bugsy shouted without reflecting on any possible danger to his underage self thus confronting a stranger and trespasser—who, at the sound of his voice, upreared himself somewhat groggily from his couch and echoed,

"Who are you?"

* * * *

**THE STRANGER (displaying an almost
immediate comprehension)**

Oh! Yeah, man, of course! You must be one of this property's present owners.

BUGSY

Yeah, but who are you?

THE STRANGER

One of it earlier owners, man.

Sitting up, the stranger displayed himself clad only in a pair of swimming trunks so psychedelic they probably ought to have been sold with a warning label, and went on,

THE STRANGER

Let me introduce myself a little more conventionally, friend. Algernon Lotsadoe, e.s.q.—"Gotcher" to my friends and well-wishers, who I hope will soon include you and your folks. I used to own this whole lake and all its buildings, back in the Age of Peace and Love.

BUGSY

Yeah, man? Well, we own 'em now.

At this moment, whines, barks, and scratching at the back door announced the strong desire of a canine presence for ingress to the human sanctuary. Saying, "Excuse me a minute, man," Gotcher Lotsadoe rose and in two steps reached the door, which he threw wide, admitting both Muttwump and the new dog, a brownish yellow mixed-breed of about the same size, who had obviously made friends with him outside.

GOTCHER

How are you, Pumpkin, old girl? And who's your new pal?

BUGSY

He's Muttwump. When was this "Age of Peace and Love," anyway?

GOTCHER

The era of the Flower Children—the Sixties.

BUGSY

Oh, yeah, I've heard of the Sixties. Yeah, I think my folks had even been born by then.

GOTCHER

To your generation, they must be what the Roaring Twenties were to mine. Yes, yes, how time flies, and all that jazz. Let me see… Hey, I guess I'm almost old enough to be your grandfather!

BUGSY

You can be my uncle, if you like.

Having one honorary uncle already, the boy saw no harm in adding another.

GOTCHER

"Uncle Gotcher!" Man, I like that! Making you my Nephew…?

BUGSY

Ulysses Samson Eklektik, e.s.q. "Bugsy," to my friends and uncles.

GOTCHER

Well, Bugsy my nephew-boy, sorry if I was trespassing, but the place still feels so much like home to me, I thought I'd just take a quiet little peek around, without disturbing anybody. Like, "for old times' sake." Used to run around here myself, back in the prehistoric when I was about your age, 'way back when my grandmother operated it as a guest lodge. I inherited it from her, y'know.

BUGSY

I guess that was before old What's-His-Name ran it as a restaurant and gangster museum, huh?

GOTCHER

Gangster museum? Oh, the shame! Oh, the disgrace! If I'd guessed, I guess I'd never have been quite so quick to sell it out like the money-grubbing stockbroker I was back in my corrupted, soldout to the Establishment period. Let that be a lesson to you, Nephew Bugsy. Well, looks like you folks have made the old place respectable again, anyway.

BUGSY

Thanks. My dad's into model railroading. In fact, that's why I came out here today, to check the cabin here for layout possibilities. I like bugs better, myself. All kinds of bugs. Even spiders, who aren't insect-type bugs, but they sort of get lumped in together.

GOTCHER

As creepy-crawlies.

BUGSY

Right! Good ol' creepy-crawlies. Great for freaking out big sisters with.

GOTCHER

And you know that because…

BUGSY

I got one. Well, not quite like the measles, I guess. She's ten years older, so it's sort of more like a live-in aunt. Not as pesky as Joe Coke's big sister, who's just two years older. Or Bud Wing's pest of a little sister.

GOTCHER

You should've heard the female persuasion of our old Flower Power Commune gripe about their brothers, big *and* little both. Like, neither gender's got a corner on complaining. Or reasons to complain, I guess.

BUGSY

Yeah, now I think about it, I've heard fellas complain about their brothers, too.

GOTCHER

And chicks about their sisters.

BUGSY

Don't let my mom catch you calling women "chicks."

GOTCHER

Feminist?

BUGSY

Like how.

GOTCHER

Yeah, all power to the Sisters, man, but thanks for the warning. What's your sister's name?

BUGSY

Freedom.

GOTCHER (nodding)

Yeah, if I'd heard her name sooner, I guess I'd've seen right off where your mom stands on things. Who else in the family?

BUGSY

Just Mom and Dad and Freedom and me and Muttwump there. *(Muttwump, secure beneath Gotcher's petting hand, wagged his tail happily.)* And Budgewiser—that's my parakeet.

GOTCHER

Well, Bugsy, remember this and be kind to Freedom: she was an only child for ten years while you were still twinkling in your father's eye. Good looking, is she?

BUGSY

Yeah, I guess. Looks a little like Laraine Day. You like old movies?

GOTCHER

Man, what you probably call "old movies," I grew up on when they were new.

BUGSY

I like 'em really old. Black and white, silent, the older the better. And cartoons. When you said "Oh, the shame" awhile back, you sounded just like Sylvester Pussycat.

GOTCHER

And you caught it! Stout lad.

> *At Gotcher's last two words, both dogs looked up eagerly, as if they thought the praise was aimed at them and anticipated a treat of the edible variety to accompany it. Gotcher laughed and patted what would have been his empty pockets had he been wearing trousers instead of swimming trunks. Bugsy likewise laughed, showed both canines his empty palms, and remarked how "wild" he found his new friend's swimwear. That he intended the modifier as a compliment was demonstrated by both his tone and the fact that he immediately afterward expressed a more or less burning desire to have an identical pair for his own lakely excursions.*

GOTCHER

You might be able to scare a pair up, Nephew, if you check out real carefully the oldest Goodwill places you can find. These are the real thing, Vintage Sixties.

BUGSY

Wow! I guess that makes 'em about as old as my mom and dad! Yours from back then?

GOTCHER

Assuming you mean the swim trunks, a relic of my sing-in-the-sunshine youth.

BUGSY

And you can still get into them!

GOTCHER

Slight correction. I can get into them *again*. How do you think they stayed in wearing condition this long? Stuck away in drawers and trunks during my misspent years as a corporate hireling of a stockbroker.

CHAPTER 13

Engrossed in their conversation, the new friends determined to repair to the mainland, where the son of the house might present his newfound ancestor all around. Recovering from the ancient dresser a pair of colorful inflated water wings, almost a match for and almost, indeed, contemporary with his swimming trunks, Gotcher accompanied Bugsy through the front door and down the steps to the dock, both dogs occasionally heeling but oftener bouncing along ahead.

They found the rowboat several times its own length from the dock, having seized its opportunity, after being tied with such careless haste, to pull free almost as soon as Bugsy's back was turned.

Filled with the plan of recovering it, Bugsy, Muttwump, and Pumpkin plunged in at once, while Gotcher lingered to reaffix his water wings to his person. By the time this delicate task was accomplished to his satisfaction, Bugsy and the dogs had achieved the rowboat and contrived to scramble aboard. Gotcher now jumped in (the beach here ending more or less at waterline in what is commonly designated a "drop-off"), and commenced paddling toward the boat even as Bugsy was wrestling the oars back into their oarlocks, with the well-meaning if cumbersome assistance of Muttwump and Pumpkin.

Gaining the boat before the boy could begin rowing, Gotcher attempted to scramble aboard in his turn, but, possessing no longer quite the agility of youth, upset and overturned it atop all four, with cries, splashes, and barks sufficiently vociferous to attract the attention of Mr. Reed and Mrs. Wright, who were even then proceeding from the cabin of the Charley Iron Horse to that of the Knights of the Rail Road Special.

Sprinting down to the lakeside, the longer-legged and swifter-footed Mr. Reed soon beheld the capsized rowboat, its oars floating away in either direction and looking, from his distance, like two toothpicks bobbing on the ripples. Even as he watched, Muttwump's black and white head broke the surface to the boat's hither side, followed almost immediately by that of a yellow-brown canine as yet unknown to Uncle Cliff—and, a heartbeat later, by his informally adoptive nephew Bugsy, whom he promptly queried, making a megaphone of his cupped hands, as to whether everything were all right.

"No!" the boy instantly called back. "Man overboard—I mean, underboard!" gesticulating backward as well as he could for splashing to keep himself afloat.

"Stay with the boat!" shouted Uncle Cliff, ripping off his shirt—fortunately, he was wearing one with snaps down the front, except for the topmost, a neckline button, which promptly popped off—preliminary to shedding his belt and trousers.

By now Mrs. Wright, albeit she would never have been chosen to race for any relay team, pantingly caught up with him. "Get help!" he directed her, kicking off both shoes, first the right and then the left. Stripped to V-necked undershirt, plaid boxer shorts, and navy blue socks, he hurtled himself into the lake and struck out for the boat, whilst she, still panting, turned and headed up toward the lodge...but paused when she noticed a large old bell suspended some few feet above the ground, by way of semi-functional lawn ornament.

She halted and, after a hasty investigation, found the clapper, with rope attached. The whole was slightly stuck, but yielded after a few adrenalin-laced tugs, and she achieved a dozen loud clangs before leaving the bell and running on toward the lodge.

She had not taken ten steps further before people came pelting outside, summoned by the clangs: Dr. Arrowsmith and Mr. Craftlove, Eliza, Freedom, and Elmer, and, from a different door (which appertained to the kitchen), Pearl Bonami, all demanding with a greater or lesser degree of simultaneity what was the matter. For answer, Mrs. Wright pointed lakewards and, subsequently recovering a modicum of breath, explicated that she couldn't be sure, but Bugsy and Mr. Reed and the dog—or dogs?—and maybe someone else were in the water with an overturned boat...but by the time she got all this out, everybody else was down at the shoreline, excepting only Eliza who, while naturally concerned for her youngest offspring, had already weathered too many alarms on his account not to have developed a realistic appreciation of his elasticity, and who therefore felt the greater immediate apprehension on behalf of her guest.

By the time these two women reached the others, who stood clustered on the narrow beach shouting more or less contradictory suggestions, Uncle Cliff and Bugsy, ignoring all their well-intentioned advice, had extricated Gotcher and his water wings from underneath the overturned boat and all three, accompanied by Muttwump and Pumpkin, were halfway back to shore; gaining which, to the accompaniment of further shouts of encouragement, the two dogs shook themselves vigorously—causing most of the onlookers to scatter away from the spray—whilst Uncle Cliff and Bugsy ran for the family's second watercraft, a canoe, and launched themselves in it, designing to right and recover the rowboat. Muttwump jumped in again after the canoe, while Pumpkin, after some perplexed hesitation, came at the snap of her own human's fingers and stood at his side.

Leaving Elmer and Mr. Craftlove to the all-important work of loudly vocal shoreline superintendance, the five women gathered around Gotcher and Pumpkin as the new and unknown quantity, Eliza's voice soon winning out as that of mistress of the house.

ELIZA

Who are you?

GOTCHER (examining his unfortunate water wings)

A thing of shreds and patches.

PENELOPE WRIGHT

Of ballads, songs, and snatches?

GOTCHER

But rather less than more, ma'am. Once I was a hippie, then I was a stockbroker, now I am a hippie again.

PUMPKIN

(a small, short whine)

MARY ARROWSMITH

Yes, so we all tend to come full circle in our lives. But I think our hostess wanted a few solid particulars as to your identity.

ELIZA

Thank you, Mary.

GOTCHER

Once, I was the heir of a real millionaire. In point of fact, the lady who first ran this as Loon Lake Lodge.

FREEDOM

Aloywisha Woodbucks Lotsadoe!

GOTCHER

My grandmother, in person.

ELIZA

Then you must be—let me see…

At this point, hearing several shouts of encouragement approbationarily directed at the action in the lake, Penelope Wright deserted the group around Gotcher to join the men on the shoreline. The stranger's obvious knowledge of Gilbert and Sullivan interested her, but hardly to the overweighing of Clifford Reed's heroism.

Uncle Cliff had contrived somehow, with or despite the assistance of the boy, dog, and male watchers on the shore, to get the rowboat right side up. (Mrs. Wright found she was just as happy not to have witnessed the actual operation.) He next hitched the rowboat's mooring line to the stern of the canoe and proceeded to row the latter slowly shoreward. As he neared the beach, first Elmer and then Penelope Wright stripped off their shoes and stockings—eschewing nylons, Mrs. Wright affected cotton anklets—and started wading in. Uttering a cry of "Geronimo!" Gotcher Lotsadoe raced down between and ahead of them, Pumpkin hard on his heels; upon witnessing which action Mr. Craftlove likewise waded in, socks, shoes, and all.

Eliza, Freedom, and Dr. Arrowsmith sensibly remained on dry land, replacing Elmer and Mr. Craftlove as shoreline superintendents, while Pearl Bonami even more sensibly returned to the lodge to finish her preparations for the luncheon to which, both watercraft once more safely moored, the entire party repaired with appetites comfortably whetted, lingering only to re-dress where necessary.

Mrs. Wright's fingers lingered tenderly for a heartbeat or two on Mr. Reed's shirt as she plucked it from the ground and handed it back to him…a gesture noticed only by Freedom, but upon whom it was very far from lost.

CHAPTER 14

Luncheon—the earlier-threatening clouds having drily folded their billows and passed away, possibly affrighted by the triad of umbrellas —was a picnic of bratwurst and hamburgers, which Uncle Cliff, Bugsy, and the newcomer Gotcher Lotsadoe—who eschewed the title "Mr."— presided over on the outdoor barbecue, leaving Mrs. Bonami and Freedom to bear the salads—potato, pea, tossed, and cherry gelatin—buns, assorted chips, and condiments to the table that Mrs. Bonami had already set with paper plates and their napkin-wrapped embellishments. The men naturally received all the initial compliments for the meal, to the annoyance of the hostess, who was not slow in pointing out all the feminine labor that had gone into everything except the meats.

Acknowledging her point at once, Uncle Cliff set forth ideas for rendering kitchens more cheerful and comfortable to work in. Observing the rapt attention Mrs. Wright paid his words, Freedom turned her head and drew the table's attention to the meal of another guest.

FREEDOM

What, Mr. Craftlove? Ketchup, mustard, and relish on your bun— and no hamburger?

MR. CRAFTLOVE

Today being Friday, Ms. Eklektik.

BUGSY

So what?

MR. CRAFTLOVE

I am, of course, fully aware of the alacrity with which most of my co-religionists abandoned the rule of meatless Fridays the moment it was relaxed. I, however, belong to the faithful minority who consider the old ways best in this, as in other matters.

ELIZA

Oh, my goodness! Pearl, don't we have some salmon patties in the freezer?

MR. CRAFTLOVE

No, please, Mrs. Eklektik. I am perfectly content. Pray put yourselves to no trouble on my account.

PENELOPE

As I recollect the old rules, they always allowed you to eat meat when your hosts served it. Courtesy and hospitality trumped mere Church discipline, every time. Also when you were traveling, when you didn't have anything else, and when you just plain forgot. For instance, if you ordered a hamburger and got halfway through before you remembered it was Friday, you were permitted to finish it rather than waste the food.

MR. CRAFTLOVE

Permission does not necessarily mean approbation, Mrs. Wright. As Jesus said, "Moses permitted it, for the hardness of your hearts, but it was not so from the beginning."

PENELOPE WRIGHT

Speaking of marriage laws, Mr. Craftlove, not of dietary customs.

UNCLE CLIFF

If it was a fast-order hamburger, someone might have been glad of the excuse to stop eating it.

MR. CRAFTLOVE

I am quite sure the same cannot be said of the hamburgers presently before us. Very well. For the sake of hospitality, I will accede this once to the relaxation of the old rules.

So saying, Mr. Craftlove, having both hamburger and bratwurst buns ready condimented on his plate, soon fitted the appropriate piece of meat into each, and commenced eating with relish.

PENELOPE

It's true, meat always tasted especially good on a Friday. We lost that, except during Lent.

MARY

Yes. You Catholics had the rest of the world trained to serve you fish every Friday. Then, as soon as you had re-trained us all to think it no longer mattered, you brought meatless Fridays back during Lent, and confused us hopelessly.

MR. CRAFTLOVE

The more so in that most of the secular world is unaware of Lent in any case.

UNCLE CLIFF

I'm not sure about that. There's Mardi Gras, and then there's Easter. Most people probably understand something about the time in between.

MR. CRAFTLOVE

Spoken like a true churchgoer! In our culture, Mr. Reed, most people are pagans to whom Mardi Gras means parades in New Orleans and Easter means chocolate eggs laid by a cute little bunny, with nothing in between but heart-shaped candy for St. Valentine's and green beer for St. Patrick's Day.

MARY

Mr. Craftlove, I'd appreciate it very much if you refrained from talking about "pagans" in that belittling, misinformed, and probably lower-cased way. Paganism, properly speaking, is as devoutly true a religion as Christianity, Judaism, Islam, Buddhism, or any other. And its most treasured law is one more form of the Golden Rule: "Provided it hurts no one, do what you will."

MR. CRAFTLOVE

With respect, Dr. Arrowsmith, I greatly suspect that most of your Pagans—with a capital "P," if you prefer—hear "do whatever you will" a great deal more clearly than they hear "provided it hurts no one."

MARY

Not having a note card ready at hand to challenge that rather indeterminate figure, "most of," I'll content myself with pointing out that every religion has its less than admirable adherents.

PENELOPE

I'd be very much interested to hear more about Paganism, Dr. Arrowsmith, but in the meantime, I can't help but wonder if Mr. Craftlove's "pagans with a lower-case 'p'"—maybe we should call them "seculars"—really do make up *that* overwhelming a majority of the population, considering how the "Born-Again" churches have been taking hold.

MR. CRAFTLOVE

Communion from a television screen! I put these "Born-Again" fundamentalists, Mrs. Wright, in the same category with our "lower-case" pagans. Given the choice, they would rather spend their Sunday afternoons with dragstrip races or football games—football, indeed, has arguably become the great secular religion of our age, as baseball was a few generations ago—but the quasi-religious pyrotechnics of a flashy televangelist will do to fill those idle hours when other sports are unavailable.

PENELOPE

I suspect you do them an injustice, Mr. Craftlove. Many if not most of them are surely sincere.

MR. CRAFTLOVE

In the throes of their emotional outbursts, no doubt. But how many of them remain sincerely devoted to washing in the Blood of the Lamb by the time of the opening kickoff?

PENELOPE

As many of them, I imagine, as of our own fellow churchgoers.

MR. CRAFTLOVE

Unfortunately, all too true. We have grown complacent in the venerable antiquity of our Church, secure as we rest in our knowledge of possessing Truth.

PENELOPE

Everyone believes their own religion is the Truth. If they don't, they look for another one.

MR. CRAFTLOVE

Most of them measuring "Truth" by their own convenience.

PENELOPE

I may disagree with the tenets of their creeds, Mr. Craftlove, but I will defend to the death their right to hold them!

MR. CRAFTLOVE

Spoken like a true Liberal, Mrs. Wright. That is, like an unconscious tool of the Devil.

UNCLE CLIFF

Hey!

PENELOPE

Rather, Mr. Craftlove, spoken like a true American, who believes in the principles of our nation's Founders.

MR. CRAFTLOVE

Indeed? And how much of our national scripture—I mean the Declaration of Independence, the Constitution, and so on—have you committed to memory, Mrs. Wright, or even read through?

MARY

But how many Christian fundamentalists have actually read their entire Bibles through from Genesis to Revelation, including the "begats" and the dimensions of Solomon's Temple?

ELMER

I've read the Declaration and Constitution through. And the Articles of Federation, and the Rights of Man, and the Federalist Papers, and chunks of Poor Richard's Almanack. Great bedtime reading. And the Gettysburg Address, too. I guess a person can soak in their main principles without memorizing them.

GOTCHER

By "bedtime reading," you mean boring.

PENELOPE

Maybe not. My own theory is that the best bedtime reading has to be interesting enough to take your mind off whatever might be keeping you awake, without being so gripping as to pump up your adrenalin. I'll have to give "our national scripture"—as Mr. Craftlove calls it—a try.

GOTCHER

Take it from me, they're only interesting if national concerns are what's keeping you awake.

ELMER

I find them real page-turners. Or would have been if they'd been written during the Age of the Railroad.

BUGSY

Yeah, Dad, we know—everything would've been better if it'd been written in the Age of the Railroad, even the Bible.

FREEDOM

Bugsy!

ELMER

Actually, the Gettysburg Address was, wasn't it? Wrote it on the back of an envelope while he was riding the train to Gettysburg, didn't Abe Lincoln?

MR. CRAFTLOVE (responding to Bugsy's last statement)

Ah, yes, the Protestant fallacy: idolization of the Bible alone, unbalanced by tradition.

UNCLE CLIFF (who, using the tip of the squeeze-bottle of mustard, was carefully inscribing his given name upon his bratwurst in its bun)

I think you're probably pretty well surrounded by Protestants here, Mr. Craftlove. Except for Mrs. Wright and Dr. Arrowsmith.

MR. CRAFTLOVE

But not, I trust, by Protestants of the shallow Bible-Belt variety! Rather, by members of churches for which there may well be greater hope. Still, in case I have inadvertently offended anyone here present, let me offer my sincere apologies and wishes for their happy and speedy conversion.

ELIZA

I really think we had better change the subject, at least for the time being.

PENELOPE

What are you doing, Mr. Reed?

UNCLE CLIFF

Oh, just putting my name on my bratwurst.

> *Mrs. Wright was strongly reminded of Jesus inscribing something or other in the dust with his fingertip during the squabble about the woman taken in adultery; but all she said was, "Oh, how charming!"*

The newest comer to the party was not, however, quite so ready to follow the lead of its hostess.

GOTCHER

Well, Mr.—Craftlove, is it?—there's actually three non-Protestants in our group here. I happen to be a firm atheist. Convert me, if you can.

MR. CRAFTLOVE

Not, perhaps, as difficult as if you were a convicted Born-Again. As a rule, it is easier to fill an empty vessel than to cleanse it first of impurities.

GOTCHER

From where I sit, all your religious superstitions look pretty much the same.

ELIZA

I think "superstitions" is rather strong.

BUGSY

Aw, come on, Mom! Isn't this the kind of good stuff our retreat was supposed to be all about?

ELIZA

Well, yes, but discussed like polite and civilized people, not like ranting savages.

PENELOPE

You're entirely right, Mrs. Eklektik.

MARY

Although one could question the stereotype of "ranting savages."

MR. CRAFTLOVE

Oh, by all means! The grossest heresy must be tolerated, if it is expressed in polite and gentle terms.

MARY

On the other hand, truth expressed in angry words takes on the sound of falsehood. The hotter the anger, the falser the statement rings.

MR. CRAFTLOVE

There is also such a thing as willfully mistaking holy anger—the passion of a strong conviction—for mere carnal rage.

PENELOPE

You know, I've always been rather confused about the difference between "holy anger" and "sinful anger." To me, they feel about the same.

MR. CRAFTLOVE

Might I suggest, with all due politesse, that someone of your liberal bias is incapable of feeling true holy anger, but only of confusing it with some species of mere carnal emotion?

GOTCHER

Hey, brother, I don't know which is least likely to convert me—your manners, your conviction, or your "holy anger."

MARY

As we NeoPagans pray, "Lord, save me from Thy True Believers!"

MR. CRAFTLOVE

As opposed to those who resort to conversion by force rather than by sound argument?

At about this moment, Uncle Cliff deliberately dropped a bite of bratwurst, which he had just prized off with his fork, to the ground near Muttwump's nose, who lost no time in snapping it up.

UNCLE CLIFF

Ooops. It just rolled right off my plate.

PENELOPE

Very scriptural: "Even the dogs may eat of the children's scraps that fall beneath the table."

GOTCHER

As Jesus himself got told off by that lady who was either a Syro-Phoenician or a Canaanite—one of the countless points on which your "infallible" Bible contradicts itself.

MR. CRAFTLOVE

The Gospels of Matthew and Mark agree on the principal points: that she was a Gentile, and that by pretending at first to refuse her, Our Lord taught His followers that all were to be admitted to the banquet.

GOTCHER (who, having demonstrated his attention to Mr. Craftlove's reply by carving off a bite of his burger, now dropped it on his own dog's nose)

Ooops! Dropped right beneath the table.

**FREEDOM (who had been watching the way in
which Mrs. Wright watched Uncle Cliff)**

Let me move that we table trying to convert Mr. Lotsadoe until dinnertime, when Merlina—Mrs. Batique—can join the effort. I'm sure she'll have a lot to contribute.

ELIZA

Dinner! Pearl, we'd better have the chicken tomorrow evening.

PENELOPE

Sometime during the Middle Ages, I forget exactly when and where, they considered poultry all right on a Friday. There was quite a controversy about it, I believe. Something to do with birds and fish having been created on the same day.

MR. CRAFTLOVE

And Science now places them on the same branch of the so-called evolutionary tree, thus echoing the first chapter of Genesis even while deriding it.

GOTCHER

Oh, yes, they like to make a big thing out of Morgan Robertson's *Futility,* too—that novel supposedly predicting the *Titanic* disaster. Sounds impressive and shivery as all get-out, when they just pick out the parallels. So I went and read the book for myself, an' lemme tell you all, there are a lot more mismatches than matches. Just like with science and the Bible.

FREEDOM

Please! Let's save all this for when Merlina is back.

BUGSY

And Mr. Pageturner, the good old librarian.

PEARL

There's some nice whole salmon in the freezer. We can have that tonight.

PENELOPE

You see, Mr. Craftlove? When we had to eat seafood on Friday, we didn't enjoy it—we thought it was a penance—and we never ate it except on days of abstinence. Now, we feel free to enjoy it any day of the week.

MR. CRAFTLOVE

Hmpf. Once, in the better and stricter days now gone, a rich Catholic family in their Cadillac, observed a family of poor fellow parishioners in their broken-down Ford drive into a McBurgers one Friday evening. Shaking their heads at this shopping-cart Catholicism, the rich family drove on to the area's finest restaurant, where they ordered lobster and king crab. I disapprove of the new-school priest who included this anecdote in his sermon at a Mass where I, as a traveler with limited choice that Sunday, found myself trapped. I recount it to condone the behavior of neither the poor family—if indeed they ordered burgers, which is far from proven, since even or especially in those days McBurgers doubtless offered meatless alternatives—nor that of the rich family, who ought to have invited their church acquaintances to join them at the fine restaurant. I mention the anecdote here and now merely to reassure you, Miss Wright, that it was indeed possible for a Catholic to enjoy seafood before the Second Vatican Council, so called, relaxed the wholesome discipline of happier times.

PENELOPE

What happened to "Mrs.," *Master* Craftlove? I really prefer "Mrs.," even if *(with a glance at Uncle Cliff)* I haven't ever been married.

UNCLE CLIFF

It seems to me that we put a lot of baggage on three or four poor little letters.

GOTCHER

I move we solve the honorifics problem in the neatest possible way and all just first-name each other.

BUGSY

Not me! I'd rather be Bugsy than Ulysses any day.

GOTCHER

And I'd rather be "Gotcher." By "first names," I meant including nicknames, wherever preferred. But you see my point—we've been cutting out the titles for years when talking to or about kids, and yet nobody deserves any less respect simply because they happen to be under the legal age.

MARY

Whatever "legal age" may mean. Eighteen, today, for serving in the military, but twenty-one for drinking, and so on with similar variations for driving, smoking, marrying…and we dare to wonder as a society why our young people seem confused even beyond what we might expect of raging hormones alone!

BUGSY

And we've gotta start paying grown-up prices for movies and restaurants and all that when we hit twelve—years before we get old enough for any of the good stuff. Tough being a kid, ain't it, Freezie?

FREEDOM

Speak for yourself, kid brother.

GOTCHER

We're all of us just kids, our whole lives long. We've just made a social contract that those of us who get big enough can bully the weaker ones around on grounds of age, race, gender, or whatever.

ELIZA

Have you ever been a parent, Mr. Lotsa—I mean, "Gotcher"?

GOTCHER

Sorry to say I've never had that happiness, Eliza. That's what qualifies me to explain exactly how other people should rear their offspring.

PENELOPE

By that reasoning, no one is better qualified to give marriage counseling than the unmarried people among us.

GOTCHER

Better still, your priests and nuns who are not only unmarried now, but have vowed as a career choice to remain so forever, which makes them feel eminently qualified to advise married people on all things relating to the wedded and child-raising state.

PENELOPE

How about this? Adulthood is the delusion of being all grown up.

BUGSY

Say whatever you like, there's still a difference between kids and grown-ups.

GOTCHER

Well, son, when you grow up enough to figure out what it is, let me in on the secret.

MR. CRAFTLOVE

Part of it, I should think, lies in learning that it is even less appropriate for a layman, who knows nothing whatever of a priest's education and labor, to criticize the clergy, than it is for a priest, who has for years heard his parishioners' deepest troubles and watched their children grow up, to pass along any wisdom he has thereby learned concerning marriage and parenting.

GOTCHER

Yeah, if you're going to pass a Canon Law that only priests with at least a quarter-century of parish experience can do it. What about sprouts fresh out of the seminary?

PENELOPE

People have to get experience somewhere. Isn't it a little like doctors? That is, if everyone insists on having only the most experienced surgeons—they'll all die out themselves in a generation, and where will the new ones have gotten their experience in the meantime? Who will they have operated on?

MR. CRAFTLOVE

Eliminate the death penalty as such and substitute the sentence that all murderers, rapists, and other such scum be subjected to the operations of beginning surgeons.

ELMER

Something wrong there, but I can't exactly put my finger on what it is.

FREEDOM

It's that we as a society make our criminals! We're responsible for them.

MR. CRAFTLOVE

Certainly we are responsible as a society for finding the best way to render them harmless to the rest of us. In no way are we responsible for their wrongdoing. To maintain otherwise is to deny the self-determination which permits the very concept of responsibility, whether individual or collective.

MARY

Would you hold the victims of mental and neurological diseases accountable for anything done by them in their dementias?

MR. CRAFTLOVE

I would hold that the insanity defense is greatly overused in our legal system.

MARY

An answer that betrays your lack of acquaintance with the field of health.

MR. CRAFTLOVE

Spoken like one seeking to undermine the whole basis of moral law by denying the very existence of sin and free will.

MARY

Yes, I do deny them, having seen more than enough cases to convince me that all "sin" so called, by which I understand destructive or otherwise antisocial behavior, results from purely physiological disease. In identifying and studying these various diseases, we have barely scratched the surface.

UNCLE CLIFF

All of them? *No* exceptions? It seems to me that both of you have good cases. Maybe most of what we call sin is the result of some disease or other, but don't we need a certain amount of responsibility even to study these sicknesses?

PENELOPE

Nobody may want to get sick, but sometimes what we do to ourselves—I mean, sometimes there's a voluntary cause. Like with smoking and lung cancer. Could it be a "sin" to do something you know is likely to cause a disease?

MARY

Possibly, when and if the connection is recognized. Which at our present state of knowledge is still the exception.

MR. CRAFTLOVE

I myself believe there is almost certainly a strong connection between television and Alzheimer's disease, not to mention the deplorable level of sex and violence in today's society. How many of our contemporaries are likely for that reason to give up their television sets?

GOTCHER

You mean the programming, man, or the flickering gamma rays or whatever our television sets are drenching us with?

UNCLE CLIFF

Yes.

BUGSY

There's nothing wrong with Bugs Bunny! I'm sick and tired of grown-ups thinking us kids can't tell the difference between cartoon violence and the real thing.

PENELOPE (in response to Mr. Craftlove's question)

About as many as give up playing their boom boxes full volume because of the evidence that that kind of loud noise causes deafness.

MARY

Or give up the cigarettes which are proven to cause cancer, both in the smoker and in those who must breathe the smoke at second hand.

UNCLE CLIFF

I had to give up bowling because of all the smokers. And there are still some restaurants where I have trouble playing a gig for the same reason. But it's been getting better. In fact a lot of people are giving up smoking, or at least trying to.

GOTCHER

Mainly because the "Stop Smoking" campaign has spawned a commercial industry large enough to rival the tobacco industry in terms of advertising products for sale.

PENELOPE

Maybe we need a commercial "turn down your radios" campaign.

PEARL

There oughta be laws. No smoking anywhere outside your own home, no playing music above a certain level...

ELIZA

Make the laws too stringent, and we could find ourselves with tobacco and boom boxes right where we were with alcohol back in the 1920s.

UNCLE CLIFF

How about some kind of filter that would let someone set the volume at full blast, but tone it down on its way out of the speakers?

MARY

But the point is, indulging in behaviors known to be harmful is in itself a compulsive disease, with roots that must be searched out and treated.

MR. CRAFTLOVE

Researching and treating them for the coddling of society in general being in itself one more compulsive disease, which also happens to be commercially profitable for the medical industry.

MARY

Mr. Craftlove—

> *Something in the tone of Dr. Arrowsmith's voice at this moment, even though it was directed at neither dog, made Muttwump bark and Pumpkin whine.*

GOTCHER

There, there, old girl!

ELIZA

The dogs remember our house rules better than we do: discuss anything, but please keep it polite!

GOTCHER

A loving dog's the noblest work of God. And vice versa.

PENELOPE

Which is pretty, but I don't know what it means.

GOTCHER

Ah, so somebody else in the world does still read the Bab Ballads.

ELMER

What about collective crimes?

ELIZA

Crimes of society, such as the suppression of women—

FREEDOM

And other minorities.

PENELOPE

Women are hardly a minority. The last time I looked, we amounted to slightly more than half the race.

ELIZA

Numerically, you're quite right. Unfortunately, too many of us tend to act like a downtrodden minority and proud of it.

MR. CRAFTLOVE

Which ones of you? The traditionalists or the libbers?

BUGSY (with a certain innocent relish)

Bet Dad meant the really bloody crimes against society. Like the Nazis!

ELMER

It's hard for anyone born and raised since World War II not to think of the Nazis in this connection.

MARY

Memes—germs of thought. Often benign and even beneficial, but in such cases as *Mein Kampf,* at least as deadly as any physical virus.

GOTCHER

Like a mob mentality that extends itself on and on through time?

PENELOPE

Or maybe—what do I want to say?—a disease that spreads through the people in power, and then everyone else goes along out of fear.

GOTCHER

Or because the octopus of bureaucracy masks the evil so deep, the mass of hirelings never tumble to what's really going on.

BUGSY

Hey, don't badmouth octopi!

GOTCHER

Sorry, Bugsy my man, you're right on. They're actually pretty gentle, reasonably harmless—most of 'em—and pretty damn intelligent. When you come right down to it, pretty much like most human beings. Even Republicrats, when it comes to their own interests.

Gotcher's last remark swerved the table talk into politics, which, while no more a forbidden topic for the weekend than any other, spawned a debate which went nowhere, led to no solutions either practical or practicable, and resulted in no other conclusions than which of the participants tended to the Democritan side and which to the Republicrat—a puzzle perhaps best left to the interested reader's own solution—while leaving both or all sides firmly convinced that they had won. In short, it differed from most political debates in remaining, thanks to the group's earlier hotnesses having put everybody on their guard, relatively polite.

CHAPTER 15

The time remaining between lunch and Happy Hour was allocated to leisure, spent either in small groups or in solitude, depending on the parties' tastes and preferred activities.

Bugsy went off with his new friend Gotcher and both dogs to circumambulate the property, revisiting sites where the boy listened with openmouthed circumspection to the man's accounts of how it was when he headed a hippie commune here, and they reversed roles when it came the man's turn to listen to what the boy knew of everything that had happened or been learned since. They also collected several beetles and one large *Chauliodes pectinicornis,* or fishfly, with strangely colored eyes.

Mr. Craftlove retired into his guest cabin to plot his campaign for the conversion of the atheist, while Mary Arrowsmith, allowing her Pagan side full reign, sought out the most suitable solitude wherein to commune with Nature. Eliza joined Pearl Bonami in planning supper. Elmer took advantage of Uncle Cliff's presence to work on their Charley Iron Horse layout.

After watching all these others safely ensconce themselves on their various projects and activities, Freedom went off in search of Mrs. Wright, whom she eventually located in the screened gazebo, scribbling away in a notepad propped on an old sofa pillow in her lap.

FREEDOM

Mrs. Wright...uh...Penelope...er... Good afternoon!

> *Smothering a sigh, Penelope Wright closed her notebook and capped her pen.*

PENELOPE

Freedom! How are you doing?

FREEDOM

Do you mind if I come in and join you?

PENELOPE

I'd say, "Be my guest," but actually I'm the guest in your gazebo. Aren't I?

> *Acting on this hint, Freedom entered the gazebo and seated herself on the small couch kitty-corner to the cushioned armchair in which Mrs. Wright sat ensconced.*

FREEDOM

What are you writing?

PENELOPE (who had learned, over the years that for most people this question was like, "How are you?"—an expression of friendly greeting, backed by no interest at all in the answer)

Oh—nothing, really.

FREEDOM

Oh.

> *They sat a few minutes in silence, listening to the sounds of summer, until Freedom got up the courage to broach the subject uppermost in her mind.*

FREEDOM

You...er...seem to be hitting it off with Uncle...Mr. Reed.

PENELOPE

Yes. He's a delightful gentleman. Everyone must like him.

FREEDOM

...What do you think of Merlina...Mrs. Batique?

PENELOPE

She seems like a dear soul.

She is! Oh, yes, she is! They'd make a lovely couple, wouldn't they?

PENELOPE

Who? Merlina and…er…Mr. Reed?

FREEDOM

Merlina's a widow, you know. She had a wonderful marriage and now she's so lonely, we're really afraid she's lost all her interest in life.

PENELOPE

Really? I hadn't gotten that impression.

FREEDOM

But Uncle Cliff was just made for her, don't you think?

PENELOPE

I…uh…think he would make any woman very happy.

FREEDOM

I knew you'd see it! In fact, that's why we made sure to have them both here this weekend—to get them together, you see.

PENELOPE

To make a match.

FREEDOM

I knew you'd see it. I knew you'd understand.

PENELOPE

But…isn't it really up to the two people involved? I mean, that is… they're both mature adults, aren't they?

FREEDOM

Yes, but that's just it! Don't you think middle-aged people need more of a shove than teenage kids? I mean, Uncle Cliff is so shy he's just turning into a confirmed old bachelor, and we all know he'd really love a wife. And Merlina—Mrs. Batique—needs someone just like him so very much. They'd be just perfect for each other!

PENELOPE

All they need is just that little shove?

FREEDOM

I knew you'd understand.

PENELOPE

Yes...I...think I understand.

FREEDOM

Then you *will* help us shove them a little, won't you? We *can* depend on you to help?

PENELOPE

I... Yes, if I can do anything to help, I... Yes, I will.

FREEDOM

Oh, I knew we could depend on you. Thank you so much, Mrs.... er...Penelope.

* * * *

After a few minutes devoted to more or less idle chitchat, Freedom left the gazebo, feeling well satisfied with her diplomatic effort. As soon as she was out of sight, Penelope Wright removed her glasses and wept into the cloth handkerchief she preferred to the era's omnipresent paper tissues. It was the fourth or fifth time in her life she had been called on to curb her own incipient interest in some member of the male persuasion because of another woman's (or, in one sad case, another man's) prior claim; and Clifford Reed had in short order won her incipient interest more dearly than any of the earlier parties.

Nevertheless, being a woman who believed in other women, she had given her word in good faith to the daughter of her hosts. She resolved, therefore, if she could not promote the match as actively and heartily as Freedom wished—which effort might go against her own deep convictions that people should be left free to make their own choices—at least she would take care to stand well back out of their way, and had best avoid finding herself alone again with Cliff...Mr. Reed.

This resolution made, she blew her nose, wiped her eyes, and took a few long sighs to calm her inward rage. Once, when seated in a comfortable coffee shop composing a poem, she had been approached by an eager stranger who took her pen and notebook as an open invitation to try to evangelize her into what seemed to be an especially Bibliolatrous brand of Fundamentalism, an experience which had put an effective end both to that particular poem and to all future attempts to write anything in a coffee shop or other semi-public place. Now, sensing that she must not allow something similar to stop all her compositional efforts in such an area as Loon Lake Lodge, she squared her shoulders, reopened her notebook, uncapped her pen, and returned as best she could to the verses she had been penning for that night.

CHAPTER 16

In due course, evening drew on, and with it Leif Pageturner and Merlina Batique, who, on returning from their daily labors in Muskywater, fell at once into the plan of going by first names. The party gathered in the old main lounge to partake of preprandial conversation and libations: white wine for Eliza, Freedom, Merlina, and Mr. Craftlove; red for Leif and Mary; whisky and soda for Elmer; Coke and rum for Gotcher and, after a moment of consideration, Penelope; and Coke without the rum (but with the lime juice) for Bugsy and Uncle Cliff. What, if anything, Pearl imbibed was between herself and the dinner cooking in the kitchen.

The reader may wonder how Gotcher Lotsadoe, from his appearance as, in some sense—former owner or not—an uninvited trespasser, had come to enjoy equal status with the other guests. The answer, of course, being that he owed it all to Mr. Craftlove's determination to convert him, which effort the said Mr. Craftlove, in his character as Advocate for the Truth, lost no more time undertaking, now that the librarian and the devout widow were on hand to help savor his conquest.

MR. CRAFTLOVE

Very well, Mr. Lotsadoe, if you dare deny the existence of God, how do you account for the order we see in the universe?

GOTCHER

Order? In *this* universe? Hey, man, when was the last time you poked your nose into scientific theory? The turn of the nineteenth century?

PENELOPE

I can never figure that phrase out. Does it mean when the 1800's became the 1900's, or when the 1700's became the 1800's?

LEIF

And what year, exactly, did either even happen—1800 or 1801; 1900 or 1901?

UNCLE CLIFF

Just a minute. I always get confused. The "nineteenth century" means the 1800s, right?

BUGSY

You got it, man.

MR. CRAFTLOVE (clearing his throat authoritatively)

Very well, then…Gotcher…if the universe is, as supposed by the so-called scientists you seem to favor, a place of mere chaos, how do you account for the fact that we sit here together, enjoying our libations and conversation, without all flying apart into our various component atoms?

GOTCHER

Are we sitting here, man? Ain't that the first question?

MERLINA

If not here, where are we sitting?

GOTCHER

Unless one of you can prove otherwise to me, nowhere.

PENELOPE

Wait—wait a minute? Is this that theory, "I alone exist, everything else is just a figment of my imagination"?

GOTCHER

Maybe. Unless any of you can prove otherwise.

MR. CRAFTLOVE

Ah-hah! By that outrageous theory, you yourself are God, and there-fore exist.

GOTCHER

Hold on there, man! Let's hear you prove I exist.

BUGSY

You were born, weren't you?

GOTCHER

Maybe, maybe not. Either way, *I* can't remember the event.

ELIZA

And I suppose you can't take your mother's word for it?

GOTCHER

Hearsay.

LEIF

Hardly hearsay! I'd call it first-hand testimony, since it affected her as well as yourself. Or are you going to call your own mother a liar?

GOTCHER

Not an intentional one, but she could have been tripping on mushrooms or something. And, if that accounts for it, she isn't my mother anyway, because I was never born.

ELMER

What about your birth certificate?

GOTCHER

Ever hear about a little thing called forgery, man?

UNCLE CLIFF

Who could've forged it, if nobody exists? And why?

GOTCHER

I never stated categorically that nobody exists, just asked you to prove it to me.

PENELOPE

Wait! Wait another minute here! If we can't even prove to you that you—or any of the rest of us—exist at all, we're never going to be able to prove God to your satisfaction!

GOTCHER

That's right. But, hey, people, all this was your idea in the first place, not mine.

FREEDOM

How could it have been our idea, if we're all figments of your imagination? If you're the only thing that exists, all our ideas have got to be yours, not ours. We're just reflecting them back to you.

GOTCHER

I repeat, I never identified myself as the Red King. For all I know, I'm as much a part of his dream as all the rest of you.

PENELOPE

Ah! But that makes the Red King—whoever he is—God, doesn't it?

GOTCHER

Well, if you want to think of God as a dreamer rather than a conscious creator, and if you can prove that the Red King himself exists, I suppose so. Okay, let's see you, as figments of a dream, prove the existence of the dreaming entity.

PENELOPE

And you really think you're smart enough to have dreamed up Lewis Carroll and W. S. Gilbert and all those other writers and thinkers and all, all by yourself?

GOTCHER

For the last time, I never said I was the dreamer! Maybe it's Lewis Carroll or W. S. Gilbert. I'm just asking somebody to prove it, one way or another.

PENELOPE

I sit corrected. But we still have to be *somebody's* thoughts, and what else would you call the thinker—dreamer—whatever—except God?

UNCLE CLIFF

Are we really all just electronic blips on a big computer screen?

BUGSY

Naw, not us, man, just our bank accounts.

All laughed at this, with the exception of Mr. Craftlove, who cleared his throat rather impatiently.

MR. CRAFTLOVE

This is preposterous! I propose here and now that we accept the hard evidence of our collective perception as solid reality, if we want to get anywhere at all.

GOTCHER

Fine with me, man, if we can agree on what our "collective perceptions" are, anyway.

ELIZA

If we couldn't have done that, you couldn't have asked for a Coke with rum and gotten back from us a drink you recognized as Coke with rum.

PENELOPE

That's a good point.

GOTCHER

It might be, if we could be sure that whatever you taste as Coke, rum, and a touch of lime are the same things I taste as Coke, rum, and a touch of lime.

LEIF

Oh, come *on!*

GOTCHER

All right, all right, for the sake of argument, we'll accept so-called tangible reality, insofar as we can all agree on it for social purposes, as our basis of hard fact. Provided you understand that this in no way obligates me to commit my personal convictions to whatever conclusion we may reach in our debate.

MERLINA

You wouldn't anyway.

PENELOPE

Nor should he. Philosophical conclusions are all right for killing time, but they're a shaky thing to base your whole life on.

GOTCHER

Ah-hah! Do I scent another old "Maverick" fan? "Work is all right for killing time, but it's a shaky way to make a living."

PENELOPE

"As my old Pappy used to say." Guilty as charged.

MR CRAFTLOVE

IF you please!

UNCLE CLIFF

Come on, everyone, let's try to be serious and keep to the subject for a few minutes at least.

PENELOPE

What an original idea! Uh… Don't you think so, Merlina?

MERLINA

Oh, I'm just along for the ride.

MR. CRAFTLOVE

Very well then, Mr. Lotsadoe, you choose to deny that the universe is orderly, or even—as I understand—that it exists at all. How, then, do you account for the fact that all of us perceive ourselves to be sitting here in this comfortable room, nursing our different beverages as we disagree vocally with one another's views?

GOTCHER

Hey, man, I don't account for it. I just enjoy it for whatever it might be worth. It's up to you to account for it, and up to me to wait with baited breath. Well?

MR. CRAFTLOVE (after a pause)

Let us apply Pascal's thinking here. If creation exists, and we believe that it does not, we stand to suffer—for example, by thrusting our hand into a fire. Whereas—

GOTCHER

Wait a minute, here—

UNCLE CLIFF

New rule! No interruptions. First let the speaker finish, then answer him. Or her.

> *Penelope Wright and several others applauded, at which Gotcher grinned, set his Coke with rum—or whatever it was— down on the nearest bookshelf—or whatever it might have been—and held both hands up in acquiescence. In the ensuing silence, broken only by a gentle snore from Elmer's corner, Mr. Craftlove again cleared his throat, and resumed.*

MR. CRAFTLOVE

If it exists, and we believe it does not, we stand to suffer. Whereas if it does not exist, and we believe it does, we will be all right.

GOTCHER

Okay, maybe…but "believing" and "acting" are different things. Hey, man, I'm not fool enough to go around toasting marshmallows on my fingertips over a blazing campfire! So I'm safe whether the marshmallows, the campfire, or my fingers exist or not.

UNCLE CLIFF

What about Occam's Razor?

PENELOPE

Yes, what about it? Oh—sorry!

UNCLE CLIFF

I'd finished.

GOTCHER

Well, Occam's old Razor isn't a bad tool, but that's all it is: a tool. Sometimes it works, and sometimes it doesn't.

FREEDOM

How can it ever work at all, if nothing exists for it to work on?

GOTCHER

Well, people, I understand we agreed to make things as we perceive 'em the playing board for this game, so I'm just going along.

MR. CRAFTLOVE

The trouble, my poor friend, is that in such a vital "game" as this, it is not enough simply to go along. God demands that we not only act as if we believed in Him, but that we believe in Him in truth, unless we wish to spend Eternity toasting marshmallows on our heads in the campfire of Hell.

PENELOPE

Now, wait just a doggone minute! What about the parable of the sheep and the goats at Judgment Day? *That* isn't a question of "Did you believe or not?" It's a question of "How did you act to one another, whatever you believed?"

MARY

"Show me your faith without works, and I from my works will show you my faith." To quote St. James from memory.

MR. CRAFTLOVE

Yes, I can see how the two of you, as a Neopagan and a shopping-cart Liberal respectively, would prefer those vague and easy-to-abuse citations to the harder home truths of the strict necessity of believing in Christ Jesus.

PENELOPE

Believing "in" Christ Jesus, or believing in the Abba—Father he taught? It seems to me that if we believe Jesus was God Incarnate, we can't use his personality as a mask to help us ignore what he taught—what he must have come to teach us! Like the sheep and the goats at Judgment Day.

BUGSY

Aren't we getting a little off the subject of whether God exists at all?

> *But before Mr. Craftlove or anyone else could respond to Bugsy's interesting question, Pearl Bonami appeared in the doorway to announce that supper was ready to eat in the main dining room—salmon for those who wanted it and stroganoff for those who didn't.*

CHAPTER 16

Pearl's earlier plan had been to cook salmon for all; but, finding a single whole fish in the freezer, she had doubted its power to feed a party of twelve. True, a repetition of the Loaves and Fishes Miracle might do something to help along the project of converting Gotcher Lotsadoe; but Pearl considered that Divine Providence as a general rule preferred helping those who helped themselves. Hence, the stroganoff.

To which almost everybody helped themselves, at least until after seeing that Mr. Craftlove had as much salmon as he wanted. Then, and only then, did Penelope Wright—who as another Catholic could have claimed equal rights with Mr. Craftlove to a fish she dearly loved—garnish her serving of stroganoff with a few bites of salmon. Elmer took a somewhat larger share, and Bugsy finished it off, thus providing his big sister the chance to send him a sharpish glance, which he ignored.

> *Hardly had all the diners filled their plates (with the single exception of Pearl, who was just settling into her seat, nearest the door to the kitchen), than Mr. Craftlove began his assault afresh.*

MR. CRAFTLOVE

Very well, Mr. Lotsadoe—Gotcher, if you prefer—what have you to say to the mass of anthropic coincidences, so called.

GOTCHER

Huh?

MR. CRAFTLOVE

Without which human life would be impossible. Whose hand but that of a Divine Creator could have fitted these together for our benefit?

PENELOPE

Oh, please! One of the saints—Aquinas himself, maybe, or one of the great medieval bishops—said there should be only light conversation during a meal, and save the heavy, serious talk for later—other times.

LEIF (raising his glass)

"Take a little wine for thy stomach's sake." St. Paul writing to Timothy. I imagine the sentiment could be much the same as that of whoever Penelope just cited.

PEARL

Please pass me the peas, someone.

Eliza did so.

MARY

I vote with Penny and Leif.

GOTCHER

Same here. In fact, I ain't even gonna hear one more word of proselytism until after dessert. Till then, you're just flappin' your jaws for the breeze.

PUMPKIN

Arf.

MUTTWUMP

Arf, arf.

BUDGEWISER

Have you had a busy day?

MR. CRAFTLOVE (briefly holding up both hands)

I surrender to popular opinion! For now, and in the devout hope that after dinner the popular opinion may turn to matters of ultimate importance.

BUGSY

Hear, hear! Meanwhile, anybody rent any good movies lately?

UNCLE CLIFF

No, but I'm just finishing a good novel. It's about a Catholic priest who goes into space, where she—

MR. CRAFTLOVE

One moment, if you please. I seemed to hear you apply the feminine pronoun to the antecedent "Catholic priest." Did I mishear, or you miss-speak, or are we talking of some other tradition than the *Roman* Catholic?

UNCLE CLIFF

No, I said "she." It's a science fiction novel, set in a future where the Catholic church is ordaining women priests.

MR. CRAFTLOVE

That will never happen. Therefore, the novel is unbelievable at its outset.

ELIZA

Just one moment! *Why* will it never happen?

MR. CRAFTLOVE

Because Jesus Christ our God and Savior ordained only men.

PENELOPE

Only male Jews, you mean! By that logic, we shouldn't ordain anyone to be our priests except Jewish men still practicing their birth religion!

ELIZA

And all from the Holy Land, too, don't forget! No Blacks, or Chinese, or American Indians, or Nordic Caucasians, or any other ethnicities.

LEIF

Wait a minute, Eliza. There are solid grounds for thinking that Galilee under the Roman Empire was almost as much a "Melting Pot" as New York city in the nineteenth century.

ELIZA

No American Indians, anyway.

MERLINA

And probably no Chinese.

PENELOPE

Well, maybe the novel is set in an alternate universe. Will you allow that, Mr. Craftlove?

MR. CRAFTLOVE

What is solid theology in one universe remains solid theology in all.

PENELOPE (about to mention two novels of which she has read only some of the reviews.)

Are you the L. Frank Craftlove who wrote *Clone's Palace* and *Frankenstein's Androgens?*

MR. CRAFTLOVE (sidestepping his co-authors, as per the conditions earlier described)

Potboilers for the masses should on no account be mistaken for solid fare.

PENELOPE

Then you admit you haven't always been strictly correct theologically in your own fiction, and if the masses are that ignorant—well—isn't it all the worse to mislead them?

MR. CRAFTLOVE

I beg this company's pardon for assuming it to be on a somewhat higher plane than that of the common masses.

FREEDOM

Don't pay any attention to him, Uncle Cliff! *We* know how smart you are. Don't we, Merlina?

MERLINA

I think anyone who reads science fiction must be quite intelligent. It's beyond me. I suppose I don't even make it up to the level of Mr. Craftlove's ignorant masses.

MR. CRAFTLOVE

Rather, ma'am, I should guess that you are too intelligent to read such tripe as my potboilers.

PENELOPE

Then please add me to that class, Mr. Craftlove. I swore you—that is, your novels—off after about chapter 3 of *Pentacle Tentacle*. But I'd love to hear more about the book you're reading…uh…Uncle Cliff.

BUGSY

Yeah!

GOTCHER

As one of Craftlove's ignorant masses, and proud of it, I say: man priest, woman priest, what's the difference? Come on, Uncle Cliff, tell us more!

UNCLE CLIFF

Well, the people in this story haven't discovered any warp drive or wormholes or anything like that, so time dilation applies to all space travel, and space travel is a life commitment. Once you go into space, you see, you can never come back to the world you left—*you'll* have aged just a few years, and the world will've aged centuries. So it's mainly colonists and merchants who go into space, and trade goods are fine cloth, handicrafts, artwork, and that kind of stuff, some specialty foods—almost no technology except a few toys, because technological things tend to be too advanced or, more likely, too outmoded for any planets the traders visit.

A lot of the starships are really flying monasteries and convents. That's why the Pope decided to ordain women—so a convent could go into space with women chaplains, instead of one or two male chaplains alone with all those nuns. And then what happens when the male chaplains die? The Pope could foresee them ordaining women beforehand to take their place, and decided better start with women priests. And even bishops, because apparently there are some…sacramental things… bishops can do that priests can't.

MR. CRAFTLOVE

Where this falls down is that inevitably all the nuns must die out, as well.

UNCLE CLIFF

Not necessarily, not if they can recruit new members at some of the planets they visit.

PENELOPE

Why would they visit any planets? If I follow this, going into space must be a sort of ultimate cloistered experience—discipline? So why break it by stopping at any planets at all?

UNCLE CLIFF

To recruit new members—spread the Gospel if necessary—and sell what they make. Of course, the starships are self-contained as far as it goes for basic necessities—hydroponic farms, even some livestock—

MUTTWUMP

Arf?

PUMPKIN

Arf, arf.

BUDGEWISER

Have you had a busy day?

UNCLE CLIFF

But people have to keep busy, so it's either stop whenever they find a populated planet, sell their excess brandy and artwork and crafts and so on, and get new supplies—or else take everything apart, recycle what they can and jettison the rest.

ELIZA

Commerce as good housekeeping.

UNCLE CLIFF

Anyway. The story is mainly about this one convent starship that leaves Earth carrying a bunch of colonists as paying passengers…

GOTCHER

Paying passengers, man? Paying with what, and why? Is the whole galaxy on a permanent standard currency?

UNCLE CLIFF

They paid ahead of time, and the sisters used the funds to outfit their convent ship before it left Earth. Once in space—planetary trade is pretty well barter system almost everywhere, because even if they find another planet that was originally colonized by people from Earth, inflation will probably have gone at a different rate, and, besides, what good would any one planet's currency be on the next planet? On shipboard, playing cards become the standard unit of currency.

ELMER

Playing cards?

UNCLE CLIFF

Yes. You see, when the original decks they brought from Earth start wearing out, the cards actually appreciate in value. Deflation, not inflation. Eventually a whole deck of matching cards is the mark of a—in our terms—a billionaire. One character has two unopened decks, still in their cellophane wrappers, which makes him so filthy rich—

GOTCHER

Brother, say no more!

MERLINA

But he can't spend his cards without breaking the deck and reducing its value.

LEIF

It's Mark Twain's story of the million-pound banknote. Unless there's something aboard he wants to spend a whole deck for?

ELIZA

But what good are cards if you can't play card games with them?

UNCLE CLIFF

The cards people actually play with are sort of pieced together by now, sometimes almost as many different backs as fronts in the deck.

GOTCHER

Maverick would love it, man.

PENELOPE

Or hate it like his worst nightmare!

UNCLE CLIFF

Some of the nuns take to making hand-printed cards, but they hesitate to release them into their passengers' economy.

MR. CRAFTLOVE (with a sniff)

Don't tell me these nuns play cards among themselves?

PENELOPE

Why not?

UNCLE CLIFF

Well, they don't gamble, not even for cookies, but they do play some card games during their recreational times. Like checkers, chess, backgammon, Yahtzee, and so on. Anyway, the playing-card economy does come into play in the first part of the novel, on the way out. There's a young couple among the passengers—Ellie Sonasound and Paul Fragonard—who love only each other and don't want to mix their genes with anybody else—especially not with some of the others the colony's scientific gene-mixing table has them scheduled for. All they want is just an old-fashioned Earth marriage, just the two of them.

MR. CRAFTLOVE

Quite exemplary. Laudable in its natural morality.

MARY

I question "natural" as it applies to the human race in general, but admit it in individual instances.

UNCLE CLIFF

Yes, and this one young nun—she turns out to be the main character, she's a young novice in part one, an ordained madre in part two, and the wise old matriarch in part three—Sister M. Celesta of the Holy Spirit—what does that 'M.' stand for, anyway? Most of the nuns have it in their names.

PENELOPE

'Mary.'

UNCLE CLIFF

Oh! Yes, that makes sense, doesn't it? Anyway, Sister M.—Mary—Celesta naturally agrees with Paul and Ellie, and sets out to help them. She has to find a madre willing to perform the ceremony. Most of the nuns feel very strict about not forcing their own ideas about morality on their paid passengers, even when a couple of the passengers themselves request it. There aren't any big technical troubles for the ship on the way out, no meteor collisions or major power failures or anything like that, but there's plenty of human friction. After all, once you're aboard a starship for a twenty-year trip, you literally can't get away from people you don't like. In fact, about half the colonists elected to spend the trip in suspended animation, either because they foresaw the personality problems, or were afraid of boredom, or wanted to save their best years for colonizing the planet, or some because the colony leaders asked them to as part of the Big Picture. There are still four empty suspended-animation pods when the ship takes off, and eighteen months into the trip seven people are asking to spend the rest of it in suspended animation, so they end up having to draw lots for the empty pods.

FREEDOM

But what about Paul and Ellie and Sister Mary Celesta?

UNCLE CLIFF

Oh, yes! Well, Sister Celesta lines up Madre Elisha—a lot of these nuns have male-sounding names.

MR. CRAFTLOVE

A not uncommon practice in the female religious life.

UNCLE CLIFF

And Madre Elisha agrees to do it if the colonists will build her a chapel when they reach their new home world, where she can live out the rest of her days as a celibate chaplain. Madre Elisha has decided she really doesn't like starship convent life, you see. Well, Paul Fragonard gets the billionaire, Anton Brubacher, to use one of his two never-opened decks to bribe old Dr. Lavallier, the woman scientist in charge of drawing up the gene-mixing pool, to give him Paul's place with all the other women, except Ellie, that Paul was down for. And then Ellie Sonasound persuades Dr. Lavallier, who used to be a Catholic herself before she gave it up in order to join the colony, to use the deck to fund Madre Elisha's chapel in return for giving her own daughter Ellie's chances with all the men, except Paul, that Ellie was down for. Dr. Lavallier is past childbearing herself, but the other colonists wanted her with them anyway for her expertise. Matching up her daughter with as many men as possible gives the best chance to keep the Lavallier genes in the population.

MR. CRAFTLOVE

You astound me. I should have thought they would have had both cloning and artificial insemination down to an art form.

UNCLE CLIFF

Hey, these colonists still have their own kind of moral standards. They still want to do things the old-fashioned way, what their leader Parke Tomlinson has convinced them was the original, Stone Age way of mixing and matching human genes. They'd even have been happy to let Paul and Ellie live together as husband and wife in every other respect, so long as they each took their turns mating with other people as per schedule.

MARY

Why, then, should the mere ceremony of a traditional marriage stop the other colonists from insisting on their schedule anyway?

UNCLE CLIFF

Because of the "forsaking all others" part of the traditional vow. Also, because Paul and Ellie hide out in the nuns' part of the ship until Anton Brubacher, Dr. Lavallier, and Madre Elisha can get Parke Tomlinson on their side and bring the rest of the colony around. And they write it in as a constitutional option that once their population reaches…I forget how many, five hundred?…other couples will be able to apply for traditional one-on-one marriages.

ELIZA

Doesn't Dr. Lavallier's daughter have her say in all this?

UNCLE CLIFF

She's one of the people in suspended animation until they reach the colony planet.

MR. CRAFTLOVE

Hmpf. Who authored all this?

UNCLE CLIFF

Perry Jernell and…let me see… Atra Menshous.

MR. CRAFTLOVE

Ah! Menshous and Jernell. *(So saying, Mr. Craftlove gave a dismissive sort of nod and devoted himself to the studious dissection of his dinner.)*

UNCLE CLIFF

Well, they spin a doggone exciting yarn. In the second part of the novel, when the nuns are returning to Earth, they run into mechanical problems, space debris, the works—and have to handle it all by themselves.

ELIZA

And do a better job of it, I hope, than if they still had a colony of squabbling passengers on their hands.

BUGSY

Yeah, what happens to the colonists? Do they get there safely, the planet where they were going?

UNCLE CLIFF

Yes, indeed they do. This part of the book keeps switching back and forth between the starship and the colony. I don't like that way of telling a story, because they always cut over on a cliff-hanger, and by the time you get back to that plot, you've almost forgotten what was going on, because the other plot is equally exciting. Why don't they pick quieter places to cut back and forth between chapters?

PENELOPE

I believe the editors insist on cliff-hangers, for fear the readers will lose interest otherwise.

UNCLE CLIFF

Well, I'm a reader, and I don't like it. It bothers me. Besides, the first and last parts aren't like that. Each of them follows just one plot, all the way through.

GOTCHER

Why didn't you read all the starship chapters through in order, and then go back and read all the colony chapters in order?

Uncle Cliff sat for a moment in silence, as if stunned by so revolutionary an idea, before slowly shaking his head.

UNCLE CLIFF

But that wouldn't be how the authors planned it.

PENELOPE

I often wonder how much of the text as printed is how the authors planned it, anyway. I really do think the editors ought to be named on the title page.

MR. CRAFTLOVE

They would then demand a percentage of the royalties in addition to their editorial salaries.

PENELOPE

Yes, but as things stand, the reading public has no idea but that what they're reading is exactly what the author intended, and any editor can commit any outrage whatever on the author's texts and get away scot-free, leaving the author to take full blame for anything! I'd gladly share my royalties with the editor, if it meant my not getting blamed automatically for every split infinitive, every "like" instead of "as," every unfortunate adverb, and—what's worst of all—all the meddling with plot and characters!

UNCLE CLIFF

Besides, I'd get confused, and might miss reading some chapters altogether. Anyway, part two ends when the starship gets back to where Earth should be, and it isn't there.

BUGSY

Wow!

FREEDOM

Why not?

UNCLE CLIFF

They never find out.

ELMER

Do they double check their charts and coordinates?

UNCLE CLIFF

They double check everything. And triple check it, and quadruple check it, and then run a complete scan of the solar system. Everything else is there, all right. But Earth is gone.

GOTCHER

I, for one, find that refreshingly logical.

MR. CRAFTLOVE

I do not. That mankind—

ELIZA

*Hu*mankind.

MR. CRAFTLOVE

If you will, though I should have thought that, in certain unflattering applications, you might have preferred the so-called 'sexist' terminology, which at least somewhat distances your gender's mistakes from ours. That *hu*mankind could wipe itself and even all other animate species from the surface of the earth, perhaps even from the upper levels of the oceans, possibly even from the greatest depths, conceivably even drain the waters, hopelessly pollute the atmosphere or actually cause it to dissipate away into space, leaving ours one more dead and blasted planet, one more Mars or Venus whirling its lonely way through space—still and nevertheless, this is a huge globe—huge at least in comparison with its crust—agglomerated of heavy, dense, and solid minerals, and I for one find it beyond the wildest reaches of imagination that our mightiest efforts could ever bomb this planet itself apart, nor shake it loose from Sol's gravitic attraction.

UNCLE CLIFF

Yes, the nuns talk all that through, themselves. They don't see how even the moon could smash Earth completely apart, and, besides, they can't find any debris. Besides, even if some kind of big enough rogue body had smashed the planet apart, it should've left another meteor belt in Earth's old orbit. They talk about all that, and even spend a whole year—by now a "year" is an archaic measure of time, since Earth's revolution was its whole basis, but they still find it convenient, and they're sentimentally attached to their oldstyle clocks and calendars—they spend a whole year searching the solar system. No sign of Earth.

BUGSY

Maybe it just moved away.

FREEDOM

Wherever to?

BUGSY

Another solar system. Maybe they figured out the sun was about to go nova.

UNCLE CLIFF

The sisters talk about that, too. Anyway, finally Madre Celesta—she's been ordained by now, and gets elected Mother Superior while they're searching the solar system—decides they'd better take the bad news back to the colony planet before they do anything else.

Meanwhile, back on the colony planet, all sorts of unique generational gaps have shown up. There are the colonists who spent the trip out in suspended animation. Now they're twenty years younger than the people they remember as their contemporaries, and also twenty years less mature, since the companions of their youth have been learning things and growing older all that time. The people who spent the trip awake see their one-time contemporaries romancing their children. And there's the further shock for the people who slept the trip away when they wake up and find people they remember as being their parents' age—in a couple of cases, their actual parents—now seeming more like their grandparents. One of the women who wake up finds that now her grandfather is the aged patriarch of the whole colony. Sort of like Rip Van Winkle in reverse.

MR. CRAFTLOVE

They must have been singularly dense not to have foreseen all this.

MARY

To foresee is not to experience. A person can know a thing very thoroughly in a theoretical and academic sense, and still be shocked by coming face to face with the reality.

GOTCHER

"I'll cut off arms and legs in theory all you like,
But not in practice."

PENELOPE

"Princess Ida," Act III, quoted not quite exactly, as I remember. But—well—this is why I distrust "thought experiments." Because so often things turn out so differently from the way I've thought them through ahead of time.

BUGSY

Yeah, but when the scientists who do the thought experiments are people like Leonardo and Hawking…

PEARL

They're still just human beings. Now, I know cooking. I've been at it all my life. And when I think a new recipe through in my mind, and see it all clearly as anything, and then it doesn't work out like I saw it, well, pardon me if I don't quite trust Leonardo, even if his brain was so much bigger than mine.

MERLINA

I used to have the same experience trying to invent new knitting and crocheting ideas.

PENELOPE

Maybe it's lucky for the great scientists that most "thought experiments" can't possibly be played out in practice.

FREEDOM

Isn't that why we call them "thought" experiments?

PENELOPE

And can never prove or disprove them, either.

GOTCHER

Maybe not with our present means.

PENELOPE

Anyway, Cli—er, Mr. Reed, what do the nuns do when they find Earth gone?

BUGSY

Yeah, what do they do, anyway?

UNCLE CLIFF

Once they're really sure, they turn around and head back to the colony planet to bring them the news.

ELMER

Pretty bad news.

BUDGEWISER

Have you had a busy day?

UNCLE CLIFF

I've just reached the part where they get back to the colony planet.

MR. CRAFTLOVE

I admire your persistence. I should have stopped reading at this mysterious vanishing of the Earth.

PENELOPE

I doubt you'd have gotten farther than the women priests.

MR. CRAFTLOVE

But what can we expect from the conjoined keyboards of Menshous and Jernell?

PENELOPE

Well, I, for one, would like to read it after you, Mr. Reed.

LEIF

Should be easy enough to arrange. One of our library books, isn't it, Cliff?

UNCLE CLIFF

Yes.

LEIF

Yes, I think I remember when you took it out. *(to the rest of the company)* One of our best patrons. He takes books out every month, half a dozen at a go, and always has them back right on time, read through all the way.

UNCLE CLIFF

Not all of them. There was one I gave up on once halfway through chapter one.

PENELOPE

One of Mr. Craftlove's potboilers, I hope?

UNCLE CLIFF

No, I don't think so…let's see… Something about some of the people had been snatched up into Heaven and some kind of evil dictator was trying to take over the world…

MARY

Oh, *that* series! One of the "Stuck Here" novels.

MR. CRAFTLOVE

While hardly recommending what LaStraw and Kennings have done with the idea, I cannot but envy their popular success. In fact, I had toyed with a similar inspiration but, alas! I "back-burnered" it, as they say, too long in favor of other projects, and unfortunately allowed lesser hands to beat my own apocalyptic vision into print. I confess, however, that mine would have been serious novels, more solidly theological and therefore in all probability less popular.

MARY

I would call the Bobbsey Twins more solidly theological than the "Stuck Here" series.

PEARL

Biblical, aren't they? The Stuck Here books, I mean.

GOTCHER

Yeah, man, in the same sense that *Peter Rabbit* is a gardening manual. They're based on what some 19th-century religious guru who read the New Testament like a crossword puzzle thought he found in there, and ever since then the drum-beaters have been using his "Rapturous" interpretation to whip up business for revivalist camp meetings.

PEARL

Well, they put 'em in the Inspirational Reading section down at Mc-Books, right along with the Prayer of Jaroch.

MR. CRAFTLOVE

Where my treatments would have fit far more comfortably.

PENELOPE

Yes, and McBooks shelves any historical fiction by a woman, no matter how serious or in what period—from *Kristin Undsetsdatter* to the Regency comedies of Georgina Hare—under the catch-all heading of "Gothic Romance."

LEIF

Classification is a perpetual problem. Nobody notices the nine hundred and ninety-nine books out of a thousand we catalog right, but everybody squawks about the one we get in the wrong section.

FREEDOM

Why not just recatalog it after the first complaint?

PENELOPE

Please let me apologize, Leif. I wasn't talking about libraries and hard-working library catalogers who make one or two isolated mistakes at the end of a long day. I was talking about sloppy and probably deliberate mis-shelving of whole classes of volumes at chain bookstores. I once found a copy of a famous Scifi writer's novelization of Mozart's "Magic Flute" shelved with the Westerns! Just one copy, with the—I think they call it the "stock card"—behind it, and sure enough, mass-printed right on the card, "Mary Winter Bradleigh, *Midnight's Daughter—Western*"!

MERLINA

Whatever sells the product best.

UNCLE CLIFF

But if people get stung too often, buying a book they think is the genre they read, and finding it a big disappointment, won't that turn them off reading? What's the good of selling a few more books right now and losing customers over the long haul?

MR. CRAFTLOVE

It is well known that the artists most in demand by prosperous publishers feature as many barely dressed females as possible because the decision of which books to fit on the convenience store stands is usually left to the truckers who deliver the boxes.

ELMER

Too much stuff being hauled these days by truck. They should go back to the freight trains. The best and most natural overland way to haul goods for any distance.

BUGSY

Yeah, Dad, and how many cars do we have lined up at every crossing on the Charlie Iron Horse layout?

ELIZA

Well—I, for one, would rather wait half an hour at a railroad crossing than be crushed inside my car by some trucker who thinks he or she is racing at the Indianapolis 500.

UNCLE CLIFF

Most truck drivers are good drivers. They have to be. Kind, polite, and always ready to help out.

MERLINA

Like most people. Most of us try to do our best, most of the time.

FREEDOM

It only takes one.

BUGSY

Hey, let's make a smash-up on that stretch of hill highway in the Charley Iron Horse—a semi and one of the little cars—like in that movie where the semi chases the hero in his car, and it's like the semi itself is doing it all on its own, you never see the truck driver at all.

GOTCHER

I could believe it.

MR. CRAFTLOVE

You could believe in a sentient truck more readily than you could believe in God?

GOTCHER

Hey, man, you're twisting language and context all out of whack. Besides, like the good folks just said, I've known some pretty darn nice truck drivers in my time, and heard tell of some pretty nasty smash-ups with trains, too.

> *Here Eliza suggested that gory accidents, whether involving trains, motor vehicles, or both, provided an even less suitable topic for mealtime table talk than did God, whereupon her husband moved happily back to the subject of model train layouts, where the conversation more or less remained, with occasional excursions into old moviedom, comfortably through dessert.*

CHAPTER 17

As Pearl enlisted Bugsy and Freedom to help clear the table of everything but the coffee carafe and cups, Mr. Craftlove returned at last to his pet project for the weekend.

MR. CRAFTLOVE

Very well, Mr. Lotsadoe—"Gotcher," if you prefer—to resume our consideration of weighty and serious matters—with the kind permission of…er, Leif and Penelope—think of the freezing point of water, the various effects of the moon on our earth, our optimal distance from the sun: these and all the various factors which, if a single one of them had differed by a hair's breadth, human or any other life would have been impossible.

PENELOPE

Not to change the subject—which is very interesting—but have you noticed how "hair's breadth" is becoming "hair's *breath*" these days?

MARY

"Breadth" is becoming an old-fashioned word, difficult to enunciate distinctly enough so that people who don't use it every day hear the "d."

UNCLE CLIFF

Someday they'll be wondering if us people of their olden times really thought of hairs as inhaling and exhaling.

MR. CRAFTLOVE

(clearing his throat)

To return to the subject which my fellow author has been good enough to style at least "interesting"—though less so than some minor verbal vicissitude concerning the letter "d"—I repeat, Gotcher, have you ever thoroughly pondered all these fortunate anthropic coincidences, as they have been called?

GOTCHER

I've pondered our place in the universe and what we're doing with it, if that's what you mean.

MR. CRAFTLOVE

That is perhaps sufficient for you to turn your present attention to this staggering mass of anthropic coincidence and ponder where we would be if even one small constant were otherwise than it is.

GOTCHER

Hey, man, the question is, do I really care all that much where I'd be or wouldn't be? Do you?

UNCLE CLIFF

Yes. I like being alive, and I've read something about "anthropic coincidences," but I think they were called something else.

MR. CRAFTLOVE

What various individual thinkers may call them matters less than the fact of their combined existence, enabling as it does our own.

BUGSY

Mom, can I be excused to go watch that movie about giant ants?

ELIZA

Yes, dear.

BUDGEWISER

Have you had a busy day?

> *Bugsy left for what he called the TV room, his sister the home theater, and Uncle Cliff the media room. Muttwump followed him and Pumpkin, after satisfying herself that no more treats were coming down to her from the table in the foreseeable future, followed Muttwump. Elmer poured himself another cup of coffee and started passing the carafe around the table. Meanwhile, at least some of the others tried to ponder anthropic coincidences.*

GOTCHER

Okay, so if we didn't have the moon to make the tides, we wouldn't be here. Kind of makes the moon God, doesn't it, man?

MR. CRAFTLOVE

You miss the point. It centers around no one single anthropic co-incidence, but upon all of them in combination. Whose hand put them together, like a puzzle, to enable our existence, if not that of God?

MERLINA

I like that.

PENELOPE

Well... I don't know. I'll have to think about it.

UNCLE CLIFF

Isn't it a more sophisticated way of saying the "Divine Clockmaker"?

MR. CRAFTLOVE

A clock is a thing of dry mechanism. What we are talking about here is a natural and organic inevitability.

PENELOPE

"I make things make themselves," as the Great Fairy says in that very under-rated book, *The Water-Babies*.

MR. CRAFTLOVE

We are speaking, neither of fairies nor of idols, but of God.

GOTCHER

No, man, we're speaking of coincidences. You called 'em by their right and proper name there. We're talking about a bunch of coincidences that came together and produced us to go around building fancy theories about them. And if they hadn't come together, we wouldn't be here to pester 'em, so maybe they regret doing it and are going to fly apart any minute now. So what?

MR. CRAFTLOVE

Even you have just personified them.

GOTCHER

I'm a human being. Us human beings personify everything. Show us three dots arranged like the points of a triangle, and we see two eyes and a mouth. Doesn't make all these coincidences God.

MR. CRAFTLOVE

Nor did I ever so imply. God's is the mind that was essential to choose and combine them into a universe capable of sustaining us.

MARY

Which argument are you going for, Mr. Craftlove? The "God so created things that eventually we would evolve to think it out" or "God told us in Holy Writ exactly how it was done"?

MR. CRAFTLOVE

You imply some sort of conflict.

MARY

Yes, I suppose I do. How can you possibly have it both ways?

MR. CRAFTLOVE

Easily enough, by seeing much of the Bible as allegory which we have so far interpreted only very imperfectly.

MERLINA

What about Adam and Eve?

MR. CRAFTLOVE

The first two beings, of whatever primate species according to our modern classifications, to achieve self-aware sentience.

PENELOPE

Just a minute. We simply cannot know how far other species may or may not be "self-aware" and/or sentient.

MR. CRAFTLOVE

I believe the best scientific minds concur upon the distinction in kind between our sentience and the mere appearance of thought in all other animate species.

PENELOPE

Depending on how you define "best scientific minds." And in that, religion follows science. Find me some text in the Bible that definitely states we have souls and animals don't, and I'll find you several that imply the opposite! I think science came up with this dichotomy between humans and other animals so it could feel free to perform any nasty experiments it wanted on animals, and religion went along because we're naturally so insecure in our own identity that we have to bolster our collective human ego. But when I put my finger down in front of a spider, and it stops, hesitates, and then turns around and scurries the other way—that certainly looks like recognition of danger and desire for individual self-preservation at work—so much so that we are simply unqualified to judge whether it is or isn't, and all our scientific efforts to argue it away as something else, could just as easily serve some other species to judge *us* as non-sentient and unthinking.

UNCLE CLIFF

For that matter, none of us human beings really has any proof that any of the rest of us human beings are thinking and feeling and so on. Evidence—in the shape of our words and testimony—but no actual proof.

MR. CRAFTLOVE

Ms. Wright... Penelope... I understood you to call yourself a practicing Catholic?

PENELOPE

Should that make me any less able to think for myself?

MR. CRAFTLOVE

Not as long as your cogitations lead you along correct paths. But when they lead you into dangerous places, you had better stop and unfold the one true roadmap, that of the Holy Church in which you pretend membership.

PENELOPE

I'm sorry, I don't see how making sure your reason must take you somewhere somebody else has already decided is the only proper conclusion, counts as thinking for yourself!

BUDGEWISER

Have you had a busy day?

UNCLE CLIFF *(laughing)*

Who says they don't know what they're saying?

ELIZA

Budgewiser's right. We had better hit the "Pause" button right now.

MR. CRAFTLOVE

It was my understanding that serious discussions of what ultimately matters were to form our principal occupation this weekend. I can bring myself to go along with banning them at mealtime, for the sake of necessary recreation, but if we are to banish them at any and all other times…

ELIZA

Not "at any and all other times," only when the arguments sink to personal name-calling.

PENELOPE

I'm sorry, was I…?

GOTCHER

Yeah, I guess we'uns were skirting pretty close to a regular bloodbath there. Our chatelaine is right. We'd better lay off the heavy topics a little while longer.

UNCLE CLIFF

Let's go help Bugsy watch that movie about giant ants.

> *All did so, with the exception of Pearl Bonami, who, after covering Budgewiser in his cage for the night, proceeded to clear away the remains of supper and load the dishwasher before turning in for a well-earned rest. In order to cover all meals, she was spending her nights at the lodge for the duration of the weekend.*

CHAPTER 18

After the giant ants had been defeated by some cinescientific formula which more than one of the grown-ups called almost as much into question as Bugsy called the anatomy of the ants, the group turned off all home media units while the librarian read the epic of "The Hell-Bound Train," which we do not reproduce here, for fear of treading on any copyright of that prolific author Mr. Unknown; the interested reader can find it where Leif Pageturner had, in Hazel Felleman's perenially reprinted *Best Loved Poems of the American People,* section III, and doubtless in other places as well.

Leif having completed his reading of an epic which Mr. Craftlove approbated as "exemplary," Bugsy as "a rattling good story," Gotcher as in the same class as Dante's *Inferno* but without the style, and Elmer as an interesting basis for a new model train layout, Penelope Wright, who had been somewhat acquainted with Unknown's poem, though not to the extent of memorizing more than the initial couplet, read the companion piece she had that afternoon composed.

THE HEAVENBOUND TRAIN

I lay myself down between ten and eleven,
And dreamed that I rode on a train bound for Heaven.
The passengers hailed from all rankings and places,
All ages, both genders, all creeds, and all races.

Also canines and felines and equines and birds—
All friends of St. Francis, love truer than words.
In silence, or singing, or soft conversation
Car after car trailed forth from the station.

We began to descend through a vast, windy tunnel
Which enfolded the train like a vortex or funnel.
The conductor came by calling out clear and well,
"Everyone, shut your windows! We're passing through Hell."

Were those shrieks of the damned, or the train's turning
　　brakes?
Were those lost souls, or mere window-dressing and fakes?
Being bless-ed and loving, we prayed in our ark
That Dante's Inferno was just a theme park.

Down, down plunged our train through the Pit's frozen fire,
Till it finally emerged at the base of a spire:
A crystalline mountain where zephyrs blew cool
Through green pines that bordered a placid blue pool

The conductor soon made his appearance again:
"We're reached Purgatory, where women and men
Are patched up and healed of every ill
That pestered and plagued 'em in Earth's stamping-mill."

Where Dante had filled Purgatory with pain,
We saw beds and warm bathtubs to soothe every strain
Of the "fever called living." For thought-forms grow worn,
And new symbols must out of old ones be born.

Our train reached the mountaintop summit at length,
And leapt off the track with its last ounce of strength—
Divine fingers caught it, Divine accents spoke…
What they said, I can't tell, for just then I awoke.

UNCLE CLIFF

That could make an even better layout.

BUGSY

Yeah, but I like the smoke and brimstone of the Hell-Bound Express.

ELMER

A little harder to do safely.

UNCLE CLIFF

Making it more challenging. Even so, I like the "Heaven-Bound" idea better.

MR. CRAFTLOVE

Well, the rhyme and meter may squeak by—barely—in a crude, greeting-card way. But the moral of this new version is deplorable.

Who would choose virtue, if the ultimate reward of everyone were to be Heaven, regardless of behavior?

PENELOPE

Pretty much the same people who choose virtue now. The trouble with hellfire-and-brimstone warnings is that the only people who take them to heart are the ones who are already trying to do their best. The people who might really profit by the warnings never pay any attention to them at all.

MR. CRAFTLOVE

Some few do, and mend their ways. Then there is more rejoicing over the one that had gone astray than over the ninety-nine—

PENELOPE

Who have meanwhile either been needlessly terrified out of their skulls or else reinforced in their smug, holier-than-thou righteousness.

MR. CRAFTLOVE

Would you rather a man committed murder, smug in the belief that he would go to Heaven despite his sins, or be converted in time by wholesome fear of Hell, and his prospective victim spared?

PENELOPE

As Charlie Brown once said in "Peanuts," I hate it when there are two sides to an argument.

UNCLE CLIFF

But how often does one of these fear-of-Hellfire conversions actually happen in time to save somebody from getting murdered? Seems to me they're more likely to come along with remorse for the deed.

MR. CRAFTLOVE

In good time to save whomever might have been the murderer's subsequent victim or victims.

Mary Arrowsmith might have here inserted a professional opinion, but Freedom, anxious about Uncle Cliff's having seemed to jump to the wrong woman's defense, was already trying to draw Merlina into the conversation by asking her how she felt about all this.

MERLINA

Why, dear, I think it would be very good to put the fear of God into bad people without upsetting good ones, if our ministers could only figure out how to do it.

GOTCHER

If common sense can't do it, ma'am, don't expect your ministers to.

MR. CRAFTLOVE

Indeed? And what, exactly, is it... Gotcher...that you define as "common sense?"

GOTCHER

The best and most comfortable way of getting along with the rest of this world, man! Which is the only one we know we've got.

UNCLE CLIFF

I agree with you about this world being the only one we *know* we've got, but I don't think that means we can rule out the possibility of there being any others.

GOTCHER

Yeah, "up there in the sky," but it ain't any heavenly pie, man, it's other physical worlds orbiting other material stars.

PENELOPE

One doesn't rule out the other.

MERLINA

All I know is, what I have left of this world would be unbearable if I couldn't look forward to meeting my Arthur again in the next. Don't try to take that hope away from me, Gotcher.

GOTCHER

No, ma'am, I won't. After all, who's to say our essences don't go on after death? Maybe to Jupiter or some other sphere that can't support physical life as we know it here. All I'm saying is, you don't need any God as a prerequisite.

BUGSY

Hey, Gotcher, aren't you the same guy who was arguing before dinner that we can't be sure about anything, not even this world around us?

GOTCHER

Consistency is the hobgoblin of little minds.

MR. CRAFTLOVE

Mr. Gotcher, if you are going to hide behind a misquote of Emerson in order to change your ground whenever it feels slippery, it will prove difficult indeed to save your soul. *Our* ground is sure, unchanging, and consistent.

PENELOPE

Oh, really?

MR. CRAFTLOVE

I refer you to the Gospel of Matthew, chapter 9, verse 18: "Upon this rock," said our Savior, "I will build my Church."

PENELOPE

But is the rock Gibraltar or Vesuvius?

UNCLE CLIFF

Yes.

GOTCHER

Why don't you just give up on me, man, and save your fellow believers?

Budgewiser had been left snug in his dining-room cage for the night, but the two dogs had settled with their humans in the media room, where they lay dozing in their canine wisdom throughout the movie and most of the ensuing debate. About now, however, both of them rose as if on signal and shook themselves vigorously, after which Muttwump trotted to the nearest doggy door while Pumpkin, a visitor on unfamiliar ground, thrust her nose peremptorily between Gotcher's hand and his knee. All laughed—even, to his credit—Mr. Craftlove—and elected to suspend further discussion in favor of bedtime.

CHAPTER 19

Very shortly thereafter, all were tucked away in their separate bedrooms, with the exceptions of Bugsy and Gotcher, who had decided to watch a late-night festival of horror films whose extreme age, and little else, rendered them worth serious study.

Elmer, who rarely had trouble sleeping, was soon sawing his nightly logs. Merlina of the Yarn Barn, Leif the librarian, and Dr. Mary Arrowsmith were not far behind him, had they known it, which they did not, for two principal reasons: the difficulty of pinpointing the instant when oneself passes through hypnagogic imagery into slumber, and the impossibility of recognizing the same in anyone else, especially anyone who lies abed in another room entirely, with closed doors between.

Eliza lay wakeful rather longer, deep in mental review of the day's events, and whether or not their first retreat was unfolding with reasonable success; she would have liked to talk this over with her husband but, unwilling to interrupt his peaceful snores, eventually she resorted to repeating over and over in her head every Mother Goose rhyme she could remember, falling asleep just as Jack B. Nimble successfully negotiated his jump over the moon.

Enabled as we are to watch them, so to speak, from above, as if the roof above their bedrooms were clear glass, we may see Mr. Craftlove kneeling late before a small traveling shrine of crucifix and holy pictures, which customarily occupies about twenty percent of his suitcase. A crystal rosary, its beads filled with Lourdes water, weaves its way between his fingers, and his lips are moving with a slight whispering sound. Respecting his privacy, we pass along and find Uncle Cliff still awake, though our only indication of this is his breathing, which lacks the involuntary peace of slumber; he lies quietly, however, with both eyes lightly closed and a curious smile on his pleasant lips…and now, at length, his breathing steadies into what in another person might develop into a very soft, very gentle snore.

Returning our glance to Mr. Craftlove's chamber, we now find him snug beneath his blanket, caught fast in the slumber of the godly man, while a battery-powered vigil candle casts its electric flicker before his portable triptych.

Of those who lie abed, only two now remain awake. Freedom Eklektik taps her teeth fretfully, no doubt refining with all her might her matchmaking plans for Uncle Cliff and her friend Merlina; also, we fear, regretting the unforeseen complication in the presence of Penelope Wright, who for all she knows might be scheming how best to spoil Merlina's chances.

Mrs. Wright is in fact tossing and turning determinedly in her bed, from time to time wiping away a tear. At last she sits up, turns her night-stand lamp back on, gathers notebook and pen into her hands, and spends perhaps half an hour scribbling. After which, she rises for a journey down the hall to the closest bathroom, where she swallows, with the aid of a mouthful of water, one of those pills marketed for the relief of motion sickness but frequently applied to the problem of insomnia. Returning to her guest room, she passes another interval in courting slumber before, getting up again, she wends her way back to the media room and joins Bugsy and Gotcher at their mini-festival of old horror movies, where at length, snuggled in an old armchair in a far corner of the room, she drifts asleep to the dulcet strains of Godzilla demolishing the city that could scarcely have time to rebuild between his visits.

When the last commercial is over, the last illegible credit line run, and the television set turned quietly off, Bugsy and Gotcher notice and bear Mrs. Wright safely to her bed, Bugsy leading the way and Gotcher, strong after years of various jobs involving manual labor, carrying with-out awakening the woman of letters. Bugsy then leads Gotcher to his own newly appointed guest room, Pumpkin shadowing her human, after which the son of the house himself retires, Muttwump settling at the foot of his bed. And now the entire house is at rest save for one hungry mosquito, still buzzing hopefully around the nightlight in the west wing bathroom.

That poor, lorn mosquito might feel happier in the bedroom of the son of the house. In lieu of football, basketball, or race-car motifs, Bugsy's bedspread is bedecked with designs of insects. Eliza had looked long for such a spread, with more or less matching wallpaper, and rejoiced when she found it.

CHAPTER 20

Despite her broken night, Penelope Wright arrived early at the breakfast site, which that day was in the luncheon arbor. She was in fact the third to arrive there, after Pearl Bonami the cook (who was at the moment invisible by dint of being in the kitchen) and Cliff Reed the honorary uncle of the family. Seeing him already seated alone at the far end of the table, Penelope hesitated at the door, torn between half-guilty delight and the wish that Freedom had not, in foresightful irony, taped and tucked pointer arrows guiding the way, without which arrows the authoress must infallibly have foundered in confusion until a great many more of the guests were safely castling the sign maker's choice for Merlina Batique.

Even while Penelope hung back, however, Clifford caught sight of her at the door and, rising, hailed her with a pantomimed tip of his imaginary hat. So espied, she saw no choice but to enter and let Freedom's matchmaking plan fend for itself.

UNCLE CLIFF

Penelope!

PENELOPE

Uh…er…Mr. Reed.

UNCLE CLIFF *(abashed)*

I'm sorry…weren't we…uh…on a first-name basis yesterday?

PENELOPE

You're right, oh, of course you're right. I'm sorry… Clifford…forgive me, I must've still had sleep cobwebs in my brain.

Meanwhile, in two steps he had reached the table's other side, where he swung out the chair directly facing his own place, then gestured toward the buffet on the table behind him,

with its array of covered steam trays left over from Loon Lake
Lodge's days as a lakeside resort.

UNCLE CLIFF

There are pancakes, scrambled eggs, bacon, sausage, toast and jelly, oatmeal, fruit compote, muffins…coffee, tea, hot chocolate, two kinds of juice, and milk. Can I…uh…help you to anything?

PENELOPE

Thanks… Clifford… I can help myself…uh… Don't let your pancakes get cold.

UNCLE CLIFF

I need more cocoa anyway.

PENELOPE

Well…in that case…as long as you're at that end…coffee for me.

CLIFFORD

Leaded or unleaded?

PENELOPE

Oh, leaded, please! I don't like the taste of decaf… Besides, I need the caffeine to get started.

> *He replenished his cup with cocoa and filled hers with coffee, while she garnished her plate with a muffin, dab of butter, and spoonful of jelly from a three-bowl serving unit that in other applications held a selection of salad dressings. The Eklektiks had not reached that pitch of restaurant perfection that furnishes grape jelly and orange marmalade in individually sealed plastic mini-containers.*

CLIFFORD

Cream? Sugar?

PENELOPE

I can drink it any way… Sometimes I'm not sure until I take my first sip. *(At this point, she noticed that the coffee condiments were on the buffet rather than the dining table.)* Well…this morning…just cream, please, a…dollop or two.

He creamed her coffee and they settled down at their places, facing each other.

CLIFFORD

I never learned to drink coffee, not even when I was in the Navy. But I like the aroma.

PENELOPE

That was quite an accomplishment—avoiding coffee in the Navy! How did you stay awake?

CLIFFORD

There was one time I didn't. I fell right back to sleep after being called, and *dreamed* I stood my whole watch, in every detail. It was so vivid, at first I didn't believe my mates when they described how they had covered for me.

PENELOPE

That's hard to believe. Dreams are a hobby of mine, and they're hardly ever so realistic you can't tell the difference after you wake up. At least, mine aren't.

CLIFFORD

This one was.

PENELOPE

Are you sure your friends weren't kidding you when they said you'd slept through your watch?

CLIFFORD

No—I mean, no, they weren't. At first I thought maybe they were, but there were too many other little clues. I figured it out later. I really did dream a whole watch, completely realistically—only some of the details in my dream—realistic and plausible as they were—didn't match what I found out had actually happened.

PENELOPE

Wow! Well, I did go to a dream workshop one time, where we had a kind of guided meditation session… I don't think I actually went to sleep, but one of the fellows did, and when he woke up, he really looked astonished. He reported that in that half hour or forty-five minutes or so, he had dreamed the session ended, and the workshop ended, and he went home and lived his life for twenty or thirty years, completely realistically, and that was why he was so surprised to wake up and find himself still at the workshop.

CLIFFORD

Kind of upstages my experience, doesn't it? I only dreamed a single watch, apparently minute per minute, real-time.

PENELOPE

I'm sorry, I didn't intend to upstage you. After all, we only had his word for what he'd dreamed. I'm just going by how sincere he sounded, and how surprised he really did look. My own dreams have never been that realistic.

CLIFFORD

How do you know?

PENELOPE

Well, you know…now you mention it, there are some memories, I can't feel quite sure whether they ever really happened or whether I just dreamed them. Oh, but then again, I still remember a few dreams I had when I was only three or four, and they were really…dreamlike.

CLIFFORD

How do you mean, "dreamlike"?

PENELOPE

Well, not with that kind of distorted landscape and oddly proportioned characters you sometimes see in artwork that's supposed to represent dreams. Maybe some people dream like that. I don't. One dream

I had… I must've been about three…we were in a sort of sun porch that I'm not sure our house at the time really had, and we were playing with a live crab made out of cheese. Another time back then, I dreamed it was night and I was standing in the living room watching a sparkler through the screen door. The sparkler traced several designs, and finally it traced a burglar's face, in profile. This scared me, and I ran into the kitchen to warn Daddy and Mommy, and little curls of smoke started coming up through the floor linoleum.

CLIFFORD

That's remarkable. I can't even remember things that actually happened to me when I was that young. Maybe that's what makes you a writer.

PENELOPE

Along with plenty of coffee. Don't know how much I'd get written without my morning cup of coffee.

CLIFFORD

Have you already written this morning?

PENELOPE

Well, no. I always bring my notebook along on these weekend getaways, with every good intention of writing Saturday, at least, before breakfast, but…I never do.

CLIFFORD

Do you go on many of these weekend getaways?

PENELOPE

Two or three a year. Science fiction and fantasy conventions, usually. Very different from this retreat. I've been on a few retreats before in my life, but they were very different from this one. They were religious—Catholic—mainly spiritual exercises and everybody was supposed to practice the rule of silence in between, but more than half of the attendees talked anyway, as soon as the retreat directors were out of hearing.

CLIFFORD

Mr. Craftlove would have chewed them out for that—unless he was too busy practicing the rule of silence himself. And why is he still "Mr.

Craftlove," now all the rest of us are going by our first names? As I remember them, the church retreats I went on sometimes, back in my teens, were pretty much like this one, only without the home theater. So you've been to "science fiction" conventions? I don't think I'd ever even heard about them before this weekend.

PENELOPE

But you read science fiction.

CLIFFORD

All the time. I think a lot of people read science fiction without ever going to conventions. Wouldn't conventions be for the writers only?

PENELOPE

Oh, no! They're places where the writers and the readers can all get together and mingle as fans—plural of "fans": "fen."

CLIFFORD

What are they like?

PENELOPE

Well, there are panels on various topics, serious or humorous—occasionally, more people are on the panel than in the audience; an art show for amateur and professional artists, with most of the works for sale by bids; a dealers' room where you can shop for books and jewelry and anything that fits the theme even vaguely; usually a banquet and a costume contest; games; movies; room parties…

CLIFFORD

Sounds like too much for one weekend.

PENELOPE

You're right. It's like a candy shop or fan emporium—you have to pick and choose. Some people just spend most of their time lounging around talking to their friends. Some camp out in the film room for the whole weekend. I've heard stories about one fan who lives in his car, just driving around from city to city for conventions. Maybe he specializes in a different activity at every con.

CLIFFORD

There are that many conventions?

PENELOPE

I think so. In fact, quite a few weekends of the year, this guy would have to pick and choose between several cities. Mind you, I've never actually seen him myself.

CLIFFORD

How do you know?

PENELOPE *(laughs)*

Of course, I can't be sure. Like the person who said, "I've never seen a ghost," and somebody else asked right back, "How do you know?"

CHAPTER 21

At this moment, Pearl Bonami appeared in the doorway to the kitchen.

PEARL

Have you all—both—got everything you want?

CLIFFORD

More than we can eat and drink, Pearl, thanks.

PENELOPE

Delicious! Wonderful coffee!

PEARL

Hmf. I expected more people before now. Where is everybody?

> *Gotcher, yawning hugely and with Pumpkin at his heels, lounged into the other doorway just in time to hear her last words.*

GOTCHER

Yeah, man, well, here's one more, anyway. And if I can make it at this ungadly hour, after a night of Godzilla and Frankenstein, why can't everybody else?

PENELOPE

Morning, Gotcher. It's interesting: you don't believe in God, but you believe in "ungodly."

GOTCHER

Hey, woman, I said "ung*a*dly," with an '"a," not "ungodly" with the "o."

CLIFFORD

Same difference.

GOTCHER

You know, man, that expression always bugs me. Not only is it a contradiction in terms—"same difference"—but they always put "difference" in the singular, and how can any one thing be the "same." The same as what else? Like, it takes at least two of anything to be "the same," doesn't it?

> *While the other two pondered these points in the privacy of their individual brainpans, the aging hippie shrugged himself over to the buffet table, where he plenished a bowl with eggs, oatmeal, breakfast meats, and a little fruit compote, and set it down at Uncle Cliff's right hand. Immediately returning to the buffet, he poured a cup of cocoa, heaped a large plate with portions of everything, brought them also to his chosen place at the main table and, transferring the heaped bowl to the floor for Pumpkin, settled down and began to break his fast.*

UNCLE CLIFF

Okay, same differences.

GOTCHER

Still a contradiction in terms, man.

PENELOPE

You've got—you raise—some very good points, man. It's an idiom, and idioms can be stupid. But think about any word long enough, and it can seem silly and pointless. All language is more or less arbitrary, and if everyone always tried to avoid using any word or expression that might bug anybody else, verbal communication would pretty well grind to a halt. As for "ungadly" versus "ungodly," I've always understood that "gad" is a—what d'you call it?—substitute word people use when they want to swear in polite company, like—oh—"Jeez" or "Jeepers Creepers" instead of Jesus Christ. So your "ungadly" really *is* "ungodly."

GOTCHER

Man, ma'am, it's too early in the a.m. to go this heavy. Let's see… At this impossible hour. That better?

UNCLE CLIFF

Except that it clearly isn't an impossible hour of the morning to be up and doing, because the three of us are up and eating, and Pearl was up and cooking a long time ago.

PENELOPE

And no hour of the twenty-four can be "impossible," or the clock would either stop, or else skip over it completely. So "impossible" in this sense is as much a contradiction as "same difference."

GOTCHER

So, if you can use "same difference," why can't I use "impossible hour" when I mean too damn early?

UNCLE CLIFF

I'd rather you said "too doggone early." Maybe it's only a polite substitution and we all know what it stands for, but it's still easier on the ears. My ears, anyway.

MR. CRAFTLOVE (appearing in the doorway in good time to overhear the last exchange)

Amen! The denser our population grows, the more important our manners become.

BUGSY (coincidentally coming up behind Mr. Craftlove)

Speaking of manners, you shouldn't let your dog eat before you do.

GOTCHER

Hey, man, if you remember, last night I held back and fed her the same time you fed Muttwump. Who I don't see around just now to eat with her, so she's eating with us. You can use whatever book of etiquette you like, but I regard dogs as people of the canine persuasion, and treat

Pumpkin accordin'. Don't I, old girl? *(As he spoke, he fondled Pumpkin's ears. She looked up at him and thumped her tail three times against the floor.)*

MR. CRAFTLOVE

This is one argument I refuse to enter.

So saying, he proceeded to the buffet table, followed by Bugsy.

MR. CRAFTLOVE

I will, however, venture to ask where the dog of the house may in fact be this morning. As well as our host and hostess.

BUGSY

Mom read somewhere that in an affair like this, the guests oughtta have some informal time to themselves, outta earshot of the retreat directors. So she made Dad and Freedom eat with her in the breakfast nook—little tiny place, just about big enough for the three of 'em and me, if I wanted, along with Muttwump and Budgewiser. They think I'm sleeping late. I'm still just a kid, so I can get away with it.

MR. CRAFTLOVE

I cannot deny that the bird, at least, has so far laid some claim to the title of retreat director.

PENELOPE

Have you had a busy day?

All laughed, chuckled, or at least smiled. Mr. Craftlove and Bugsy soon took their places at the dining table, the boy beside Gotcher and Pumpkin, the author of the male persuasion beside the one of the female.

PENELOPE

But did I actually hear you, Mr. Craftlove, admit that we have a problem with overpopulation?

MR. CRAFTLOVE

We should not have had one, had enough of us throughout the centuries practiced celibacy outside of marriage and fidelity within, waiting to wed until sufficiently mature or remaining permanently in priestly or professed religious life, whichever God intended for us, individual by individual or couple by couple.

GOTCHER

Better prove to me God exists, man, before you start telling me you know all about his diagram for our existence.

UNCLE CLIFF

But if people waited until they were sufficiently mature before they got married, there wouldn't be very many weddings.

PENELOPE

None—or almost none, like that "rare, most extravagant pair" in the poem—Dorothy Parker's, I think—"who waited till they could afford it," and ended up almost too old to totter down the aisle.

GOTCHER

And if, on top of that, everybody waited until they were married, nobody would ever get born at all!

MR. CRAFTLOVE

Which would certainly have nipped the overpopulation problem in the bud.

> At this point, Penelope remembered Bugsy's age and cast at him a slightly old-maidish glance, which he happened to notice.

BUGSY

Don't worry about me. We've got cable TV.

MR. CRAFTLOVE

Nor does one even need cable nowadays in order to see questionable programming, ripe as the networks have become.

BUGSY

Yeah, I sure hope they clean it up by the time I've got kids to raise!

All laughed.

PENELOPE

But why worry about cleaning up the programs before we've cleaned up the television commercials?

MERLINA (just entering)

Oh, but some of them are so funny.

GOTCHER

Ah! Top o' the morning to you!—Merlina, isn't it?

MERLINA

Thank you, and a very good morning to all of you…let me see… Catcher—

GOTCHER

It's "Gotcher," ma'am, but you were almost close enough for the cigar.

MERLINA (nodding around the table at each in turn)

Gotcher. Cliff. Penny. Mr. Craftlove. And Bugsy.

BUGSY

Don't forget Pumpkin.

> *Pumpkin looked up with a hopeful little whine and a few thumps of her tail. Meanwhile, Mary Arrowsmith and Leif Pageturner arrived behind Merlina, and all three repaired in close proximity to the breakfast table.*

MERLINA

May we give Pumpkin a little, too?

GOTCHER

Well… No, because there are too many of us. If everyone gave her just a little at every meal, she'd get fat.

BUGSY (sneaking Pumpkin a slice of bacon)

I can get away with it 'cause I'm just a kid.

UNCLE CLIFF

See here, m'boy, if you know what's good for you, you'd better stop swinging your age around.

BUGSY

Or what?

UNCLE CLIFF

Or I'll build an age machine, tuck you inside, and turn you fifty or thereabouts in a wink.

BUGSY

Wow! Sorta like a personal time machine?

PENELOPE

What a charming idea? Could I—Would you mind if I used it in a story?

MR. CRAFTLOVE

I believe that something of the sort has already been done, in *Portrait of Jennie*.

BUGSY

Oh, yeah, with Jennifer Jones and Joseph Cotten.

MR. CRAFTLOVE

Based, of course, upon the novella by Robert Nathan. Now, if the device were to be applied to horror fiction…say, a type of horrendous iron maiden, its spikes of time rather than iron, with which the mad scientist threatens captives in his dungeon laboratory…

UNCLE CLIFF

I won't stop you, if you want to use it that way. I'd rather see it in a romantic story, or science fiction. To get around the time dilation factor in space travel, for instance. But will there by any copyright trouble if you both use it?

PENELOPE

As I think Mr. Craftlove himself pointed out last night, naked ideas can't be copyrighted, only how writers develop them into finished products. Maybe fifty different writers could start with the same idea and produce fifty stories so wildly different you'd hardly know they'd all dived off the same board?

PEARL (having brought in fresh pancakes in time to hear this latest exchange)

Just like cooking. I say, give fifty different good cooks identical kitchens, ingredients, and recipe, and you'll get fifty dishes that all taste a little different. That's why I never leave any ingredient out whenever I give a recipe to a friend. What's the point?

PENELOPE

Good for you, Pearl! Recipes are to share, not to hoard up out of sight. As you say, nobody else will ever be able to cook it quite the same as you do, anyway, so why not give them the fairest chance you can?

MR. CRAFTLOVE

In fear, perhaps, lest one of them should actually outdo you and produce a better dish with the same recipe.

PEARL

Let 'em try. (*Immediately after delivering this ultimatum, she returned to the mystic sanctuary-workshop of her kitchen.*)

BUGSY

Hey, Mr. Craftlove, since all the rest of us are using first names and nicknames for each other, how about you?

Now, "L. Frank Craftlove" being a pseudonym, the individual in question might have opted for any masculine given name beginning with "L.," such as Lawrence, Lucas, or Ly-sander. Instead of which, in some freak of youthful inspiration he had long ago decided that should the question ever arise, he would answer,

MR. CRAFTLOVE

Lycurgus.

BUGSY

Licorice.

MR. CRAFTLOVE

Lycurgus. After the legendary lawgiver of Sparta.

Having decided that they had given their guests quite long enough for unsupervised chit-chat, when important questions concerning the day's schedule cried out to be settled, Free-dom had left her parents and reached the luncheon (today, the breakfast) arbor in time to hear the last exchange. Little as her general principles approved of agreeing with her kid brother on anything, she now could not forbear exclaiming,

FREEDOM

Oh, I like "Licorice"!

BUGSY

Well, thank you, Freezie.

MR. CRAFTLOVE

Yes, youth as a rule prefers levity to sober thoughtfulness… "Freez-ie."

FREEDOM (aside to Bugsy)

Little brother, I'm going to get you for that.

PENELOPE

And us oldsters have been complaining ever since—oh, ancient Egyptian days, at least, probably since the Old Stone Age—about how young people are going to the dogs.

MR. CRAFTLOVE

No doubt the first such complaint was lodged by Adam and Eve when their son Cain slew his brother Abel. And they were quite right.

UNCLE CLIFF

Funny, how long we've been going to the dogs without getting there, and how much we've been getting done along the way.

MR. CRAFTLOVE

My good Mr.... Clifford, have you taken a hard look lately at the world around you? Consider the abysmal state of society indicated by the dreary fact that my own novels are bestsellers.

PENELOPE

People don't necessarily read every book they buy. All the books I've bought—thinking I can read them any time—some of them have been sitting on my shelves for decades, waiting. Whenever I *really* want to get a book read, I find the best way is to check it out of the library, so I have to read it quick and get it back.

LEIF

Thank you. It's good to know that we actually are providing a service.

GOTCHER (giving Pumpkin a tidbit)

What's wrong with going to the dogs, anyway, man? Ask me, might be the best thing we ever did. If more human beings were born with half the virtues that come natural to dogs, the world would be a lot better place! Wouldn't it, old girl? (Scratching Pumpkin behind her ears.) Even at that, there are enough good-hearted people in the world to keep old hippies like me alive from day to day, so I guess we can't complain too much.

PENELOPE

No, *we* can't. What about all the people who *don't* survive? Can some of them complain?

MR. CRAFTLOVE

God in His infinite wisdom has predestined everything that happens for the best.

PENELOPE

Oh, please! God might be able to bring good out of our worst faults and rotten luck, but that isn't the same as making bad things happen as part of the recipe!

MR. CRAFTLOVE

As the Easter Liturgy puts it of the fall of Adam, "O happy fault, O necessary sin of Adam, which gained for us so great a Redeemer!"

PENELOPE

Adam and Eve were still expelled from Eden, Abel was still dead, and Cain was still punished for killing him. Just as at the "happy ending" of the book of Job, all Job's original children, servants, and animals are still dead, and his wife has to go through all that childbearing all over again, as if new children could ever really "replace" the earlier ones.

> *Dr. Mary Arrowsmith arrived in time to hear something of this last exchange.*

MARY

Wallowing in guilt is a way of reaffirming our ego. The concept of sin is a device to reassure ourselves that we are in control of our thoughts and actions, whether or not that is actually the case.

MR. CRAFTLOVE

As my esteemed fellow author lately observed, "Oh, please!" Lycurgus knew better.

BUGSY (in a whoo-whoo voice)

"Who knows what evil lurks in the hearts of men?"

FREEDOM

"The weed of crime bears bitter fruit."

At this point Eliza entered the room, closely followed by Elmer and Muttwump.

ELIZA

That's enough, children. Don't monopolize our guests' conversation with old family catchphrases.

UNCLE CLIFF

It's okay this time, Eliza. I guess we all know it's the Shadow who knows what evil lurks in the hearts of people.

MR. CRAFTLOVE

As did Lycurgus, which was why he laid down his exemplary laws.

MARY

Not all of which we would call "exemplary" today. For example, taking boys from their homes and putting them in military camps at the age of six.

BUGSY

Yuck!

ELIZA

Oh, dear!

MR. CRAFTLOVE

As opposed to our practice of sending boys and girls alike into public schools amounting to little more than war zones?

BUGSY

Aw, it isn't quite that bad. Anyway, we get to come home at night, and we still get most of the summer off.

MR. CRAFTLOVE

He also instituted the custom of eating together in common mess halls, which is of course what we sit here doing now.

PEARL (coming in, briefly, to check the steam tables)

Here, now! Don't you go calling my meals messes!

MR. CRAFTLOVE

With apologies, Mrs.—Pearl—I meant "mess hall" in the older sense, as in the Biblical "mess of pottage" for which Esau traded his birthright. If that dish resembled your preparations, Esau could justly have been considered a shrewd businessman.

PEARL (on her way back to the kitchen)

Okay, thanks, apology accepted.

LEIF

Lycurgus is also supposed to have forbidden house-builders any other tools than axe and saw, though that could be legend.

UNCLE CLIFF

What an interesting challenge! Maybe I could try it…

MARY

I dislike the use of such words as "legend" and "myth" to imply that this or that is "merely" fictitious, when myths and legends have in fact great and tangible power in the formation of our thoughts and our societies.

PENELOPE

As a fictioneer, I could object to your use of the word "fictitious" for exactly the same reason.

MR. CRAFTLOVE

I offer no such objection. Indeed, the kind of fiction I write justifies to perfection Dr. Mary's use of the word "fictitious."

MARY

I was just going to allow Penny's objection and look for another word.

PENNY

How can you have such a low opinion of your own work, Mr. Craftlove, and still be so sticky about nicknames?

GOTCHER

Good point.

MR. CRAFTLOVE

You have cornered me. I admit it. Very well, I will entertain suggestions—but not, I beg you, "Licorice"!

FREEDOM

Awww.

BUGSY

Why not? It's something to "lick" and something to "like."

GOTCHER

Hey, man, how about "Likely"? Can we call you that?

MR. CRAFTLOVE

I should prefer "Lycurgus," in full.

LEIF

Even though the original Lycurgus died what we'd call a suicide? Of course, his Pagan contemporaries considered it a hero's death. First, he bound his fellow Spartans to follow his laws until his return. Then he went to see the oracle at Delphi, satisfied himself that his laws were good, and starved himself to death so that he never could return and Sparta would be bound by oath to keep his laws forever.

UNCLE CLIFF

Why didn't he just go on touring the world for the rest of his life?

BUGSY

Yeah! Death by wanderlust.

GOTCHER

Which may yet prove to be my own fate. And not too bad, I guess, taken all in all.

ELIZA

The fellow Spartans who didn't like his laws—and I imagine there were quite a few of them, once they had time to think it over—could have sent a delegation to force him to come home and debate it all a little more thoroughly.

UNCLE CLIFF

It might not have been so easy to find him. The world was probably pretty big, even back then.

MARY

He might have feared that his own resolve would waver, and force him home in spite of himself. Our society has exchanged the ancients' strong identification with home for the modern mobility that allows us to move hundreds of miles and resettle in new places for the sake of work, retirement, or even whim. We have forgotten that in olden days exile could be seen as a sentence actually worse than death.

ELIZA

That feeling was a male privilege. In those same olden days, women were required to accept exile from their birth homes and resettlement with their husbands' families as a matter of course. A condition still with us today. In our own country we may not notice it so much because of the general mobility you mentioned, but whenever the question comes up, wives are still expected to drop their own jobs and other involvements in order to go wherever their husbands' lives take them.

ELMER

Seems to me you had a pretty loud voice in choosing Loon Lake Lodge as the property to buy, Eliza.

ELIZA

Oh, Elmer, I wasn't talking about us, I was talking about society in general.

MARY

Yes, we do tend to talk about "society in general," always or usually regarding our own personal selves as the exceptions.

BUGSY

"The exceptions that prove the rule."

GOTCHER

Never noticing how silly that "exceptions prove the rule" principle really is, man.

PENNY

However you slice it, Lycurgus still committed suicide, didn't he? So how can you admire him so much, Mr....Lycurgus, with your strict moral code?

LYCURGUS FRANK CRAFTLOVE

The ancients did not consider suicide a mortal sin, madam. Rather, as our librarian friend has so kindly pointed out, under certain circumstances they regarded it as the crowning act of heroism.

UNCLE CLIFF

But it was still suicide.

LYCURGUS

True; and, as such, we who are fortunate enough to live under the Christian dispensation know and recognize it as violating the Natural Law. But three conditions are required for mortal sin: the act must be sufficiently grave, the sinner must fully understand its gravity, and he—or she—must nevertheless freely and wholeheartedly consent to it. Suicide is, of course, sufficiently grave, with a deadly finality. But although the classical ancients recognized its finality, certain failures in their vaunted logic prevented them from perceiving its full moral implications, while the same circumstances they saw as rendering it heroic simultaneously constrained the full freedom of their will.

PENNY

So they went to Heaven.

LYCURGUS

They went, as Dante perceived, into the same species of afterlife they themselves expected—for the most part a dreary gray existence, free of actual pain but equally free of pleasure or happiness.

PENNY

If they expected that, didn't it make their suicides all the more heroic? What else are most martyrdoms but suicide by executioner?

BUGSY

The old attitude's still good for captured spies, like, too—when they bite down on the cyanide capsule in their back tooth so they won't be tortured into giving away secrets. And for people about to get captured and tortured to death by savages, like in that old movie, "Five Came Back."

GOTCHER

Quite an afterlife your God has laid out for us, man! Checkered all over into neat little plots of every kind of future existence any culture ever invented for itself: Greeks and Romans here, with a little Elysium Fields in the center; Egyptians here; Muslims with their houris over there; Dante's Inferno off in that direction…

ELMER

What a layout!

ELIZA

Our whole acreage wouldn't give you enough room for it, dear.

FREEDOM

Not even if we built platforms all over the lake. And where'd we sleep?

BUGSY

Dibs on Heaven for my bedroom!

PUMPKIN

Arf! Arf! Arf!

MUTTWUMP

(arriving, in search of his family)

Arf!

LEIF (laughing)

Now, where is little Budgewiser, to make the pet complement complete?

PENNY

And grace us with his unfailing wisdom?

ELIZA

Still in his cage in the breakfast nook, I'm afraid.

MERLINA

Never mind, we'll see him at lunch.

FREEDOM

Well, no, actually. That is, today we're having picnic lunches in small groups.

LYCURGUS

Oh?

ELIZA

Yes. We'll choose a topic, discuss it in small groups, and at dinner we can share whatever conclusions our small groups reached over the picnic baskets.

GOTCHER

Sounds okay, ma'am. How do we divvy ourselves up?

BUGSY

Bet you can trust Freedom on that one. She's probably got a list all ready to go.

FREEDOM

(producing a paper from her pocket)

As a matter of fact, I do. Here's what I thought: Merlina and Uncle Cliff, Mr. Craftlove—I mean…did we ever decide what to call you?

LYCURGUS

I would accept, as both quick and noncontroversial, the mid-name of Frank.

FREEDOM

Oh, great!… Frank and Penny, Leif and Mary, Gotcher and Bugsy, Mom and Dad, Pearl and me.

> *Penelope Wright darted an angry glance at Freedom and an apprehensive one at Frank Craftlove; but it was Uncle Cliff who spoke first, tapping his fingers a little, for his genius had this peculiarity: that he could never memorize the multiplication table, but had always to work such figures out anew.*

UNCLE CLIFF

That's…one, two, three, four, five, six groups. Too many. We might as well all ponder our own thoughts on the question, each one alone, over lunch. I suggest groups of four…that will make it three foursomes.

FREEDOM

Oh, no! Don't you see—

PENNY

Or four threesomes. Oh, at least, let it be threesomes!

FREEDOM

Even worse! "Two's company, three's a crowd."

UNCLE CLIFF

That applies for…other kinds of situations, not philosophical small talk. How about Elmer and Eliza join Leif and Mary, Bugsy and Gotcher with Freedom and Pearl, and…Penny and Frank with Merlina and me.

FREEDOM

Oh, if we've got to make it foursomes, at least let *me* make the fourth with Merlina and you and—

PENNY

Me. And Mr....Frank could join Bugsy and Gotcher.

GOTCHER

Hey, man!

ELFRANK

I should have preferred that either our own tastes and preferences had first been consulted—

FREEDOM

But I did my best to choose compatible—

ELFRANK

Or that a strict lottery system had been employed from the outset.

PEARL

That's okay. I'll pack three baskets, all different, and you can lottery for them.

ELFRANK

But if I am to be banished as often as this, let me at least land at last with the librarian.

LEIF

Fine by me. Us librarians never mind fraternizing with our primary suppliers.

MARY

Group dynamics is not my principal field of expertise, but the way our parties seem to be shaping up so far, let me suggest that Eliza might make a good fourth for Leif, Frank, and myself, leaving Elmer, Pearl, Bugsy, and Gotcher to comprise the third of our foursomes.

ELFRANK

You have misused the word "comprise." The foursome will comprise father, son, cook, and venerable hippie. They will not comprise it.

LEIF

Let's compromise and agree not to quibble about terms, as long as everybody understands what they mean in context. After all, language should be to communicate, not to fight wars about.

GOTCHER

Fine by this venerable ol' hippie.

BUGSY

Which one—our grouping or Leif's compromise?

GOTCHER

Both, man, both.

UNCLE CLIFF

In other words, yes.

GOTCHER

And let me hopefully guess our group gets Pumpkin and Muttwump, too—

PUMPKIN

Arf. Arf. Arf.

MUTTWUMP

Arf.

GOTCHER

Who contribute more of real value than any of the rest of us, man!

PEARL

I'd like to see them pack the lunch baskets.

GOTCHER

Meal preparation excepted, ma'am. Of course.

CHAPTER 22

After breakfast, the party broke up to pass time in ones and twos while awaiting the picnic hour: Bugsy and Gotcher, predictably, sought the lake, followed by both dogs; Pearl carried Budgewiser's cage to the kitchen, where his scolding chatter provided background and counterpoint to her labors; Frank Craftlove betook himself off alone somewhere to commune with the Infinite; Uncle Cliff took refuge with Elmer at the Lunar-Martian Express layout; Eliza lounged with Merlina over one last cup of coffee in the luncheon arbor; the librarian and the psychiatrist found a pleasant bower where they could talk of many things while glancing down from time to time at the two boys—one young and one superannuated—and their dogs; and Freedom at length ran Penny Wright to earth in the library, where the latter had hoped to elude the former and, at her appearance, regretted being alone.

FREEDOM

How could you? You know what we're trying to do, and yesterday you even promised to help.

PENNY

I said I'd try to stay out of the way. But it was—it was Uncle Cliff himself who insisted on—that is, asked—for foursomes.

FREEDOM

When you jumped right in to land yourself in the same group with him and Merlina and me! I was going to name Mr. Craftlove—I mean, Frank—two women and two men. Balance. Now Uncle Cliff will be alone with three women. One of them you.

PENNY

Before you blame me, stop and think. Your original plan had me paired up with Mr.—with Elfrank Craftlove!

FREEDOM

But that would have been so perfect! So right—

PENNY

Oh, *please!*

FREEDOM

You and he have everything in common. Don't you see that? You're both writers, you're both Catholic—

PENNY

We're farther apart as Catholics than if—than if he was an inquisitor and I was a Muslim! The Catholic Church isn't a monolith, it just pretends to be—which is one of its biggest weaknesses.

FREEDOM

And you're both opinionated!

> *At this accusation, Penny Wright drew a deep breath, as if she had been slapped, before replying in a chastened voice,*

PENNY

Am I? Really? I'm...sorry, if that's the way I come across to you. Well... How about this, then? We can monopolize each other and leave her almost as clear a field with...Uncle Cliff...as you had it planned originally.

FREEDOM

That's what I was going to do about Mr....Elfrank. Well, maybe it'll work out.

PENNY

Although...you know...something in me revolts, rather, at this business of leaving "her" a clear field with "him." Shouldn't it be as much the man's choice as the woman's?

FREEDOM

In fact, it might even work out better this way. Maybe Uncle Cliff won't be quite so bashful if he doesn't feel like he's quite alone with her.

* * * *

Penny wondered whether Freedom had even heard her opinion about the man's right to have his own choice in the matchmaking affair. But in her relief at pacifying and seeing the last for a few hours of the younger woman, she said nothing to prolong the painful interview.

Eleven a.m. arrived, and the groups assembled at the picnic table, where Elmer had helped Pearl carry and arrange the three large baskets she had packed with gustatory delectables. Since she alone knew the exact contents of each hamper, she declared that the other two groups should make their selection, leaving the last for Elmer, herself, and the two "boys" with their dogs, both of which last-named seemed interested in all three large baskets equally, sparing only the dregs of their attention for the extra, smaller basket carrying doggy treats.

Which of the two choosing groups—that comprising the hostess, psychiatrist, librarian, and bestselling author, or that made up of the young matchmaker, her two subjects, and the one she regarded as a potential spoiler—should make first selection was settled by Elmer's tossing a stray quarter he found in his pocket. When the eagle on its reverse side gave the decision to Freedom's party, further hesitation ensued as they debated which of the four should make the actual choice. Merlina stood aside at once, opining that any basket of the three would suit her fine. Freedom nominated Uncle Cliff to choose, he being both the one man in the group and the person who would bear the basket to their luncheon site; but, there being so little difference in the faces the baskets presented to the world, he stood pondering until Penny seized the middle basket and put it into his hand, ignoring the frown that creased Freedom's brow at her impulsive action.

Mary Arrowsmith made short work of second choice, simply taking the basket nearest her left hand and presenting it to Leif Pageturner, as the nearer of her group's males, to carry. The baskets being thus distributed, the groups struck out, each to find a site where their conversation might remain unheard by the others.

Freedom commenced subtly guiding her group toward the gazebo where the previous day she had cornered Penny Wright, hoping that it might provide a constant reminder of that author's promise. Uncle Cliff, however unwittingly, spoiled Freedom's design by pausing at one of his own favorite spots along the way, beneath a cluster of shady oaks, and asking if this wouldn't be a fine place to spread the blue and white checked picnic tablecloth Penny was carrying over one arm. Unable to protest without too obviously tipping her hand, Freedom acquiesced; and soon the foursome were enjoying ham sandwiches, potato salad, corn chips, homemade watermelon pickles, fresh peaches, golden cupcakes, and a choice of iced tea or lemonade.

Penny mixed the two beverages half and half in her tumbler, explaining that the British had used to call such blended potations "twists," and that one or two centuries ago they had included even a compound of coffee and tea, though nowadays the only twist remaining in popular usage was the "shandy" composed of lemonade and beer.

Merlina was inspired to top her own tea with lemonade, remarking how often people added both lemon and sugar to their tea anyway. Freedom commented a little stiffly that she preferred her tea straight, and Uncle Cliff, who never used caffeinated drinks of any complexion (except cola, cocoa, and hot chocolate), pronounced the subject of twists very interesting and quietly continued to swallow his lemonade straight. This subject disposed of, Freedom reminded them of the scheduled activity: to discuss God in their small groups, with the ultimate view of curing Gotcher's atheism.

PENNY

Maybe first we should decide what atheism is, exactly—diagnose what we want to cure him of.

MERLINA

Why, isn't atheism just…atheism? Godlessness?

UNCLE CLIFF

Not believing that there is a God, anyway.

PENNY

But not believing there is what kind of God? "Theism" is—anyway, can be used for—a certain attitude—interpretation—whatever you call it—about God that had developed by early modern times.

UNCLE CLIFF

The Divine Clockmaker?

PENNY

Well, I'm not sure it includes the Divine Clockmaker—I just read about it a few weeks ago—but it does seem to include our standard image of the white-bearded old man sitting on a cloud throwing smiles and/or thunderbolts at the world. Maybe also that all-seeing eye on top of the pyramid on our dollar bill.

FREEDOM

I thought that was a Masonic symbol.

UNCLE CLIFF

Well, Freemasons believe in God, too.

PENNY

Anyway, if "theism" means the theory of God as the stern old white-beard on a cloud, "atheism" can simply mean not believing in that particular image of God.

MERLINA

What's wrong with that particular image of God? I've always rather liked it. Found it comforting to think of a kind Father always watching over me from Heaven.

UNCLE CLIFF

Not quite so comforting for the ones He's throwing His thunderbolts at!

PENNY

When Jesus let Himself be crucified between two thieves, wasn't He identifying Himself with the lowest of the low—the very ones Yahweh throws His thunderbolts at?

FREEDOM

But it wasn't God Who thunderbolted those thieves, it was the Romans.

UNCLE CLIFF

God works through us. On us through each other.

MERLINA

And through other natural means. I think it was God's thunderbolt that struck down my Arthur, but I also believe it was thrown in perfect love, maybe to save us from something worse.

PENNY

I wish I could feel as sure about that as you do. I rather think that God doesn't directly plan everything bad that happens to us—weeps when we suffer, and suffers with us.

FREEDOM

Sooner or later, we all die.

PENNY

Yes, and go right into Judgment Day. That is—I was taught there's an individual judgment for each of us at death, and then there'll be a general Judgment Day at the End of the World, but I don't believe that any longer. I mean, God lives in eternity, right? And all historical time is visible in an instant from eternity. So I think that at death each of us pops right into the big general Judgment Day, apocalypse and all, and goes on from there. After all, people suffer just as much from fiery accidents if they happen on our roads here and now as if they happened at Armegeddon, so I think Armegeddon is going on around us all the time, interweaving right through historical time.

UNCLE CLIFF

I like your theory. It would mean we don't really need a scientific End of the World in historical times, so astrophysics is safe to go on theorizing about whether the universe will expand forever or collapse in a Gnab Gib—

FREEDOM

"Gnab Gib"?

PENNY

Oh! "Big Bang" in reverse!

UNCLE CLIFF

It would also help explain this business of seeing your whole life flash before you in an instant, just as you flash from time into eternity.

FREEDOM

What do you think about all that, Merlina?

MERLINA

Oh, I just trust God to know what He's doing.

PENNY

Yes—we don't any of us have much choice about that, when it comes right down to it—but we aren't going to convert our friend Gotcher that way!

MERLINA

But I didn't come here to convert anyone. I came to get away for a weekend.

FREEDOM

That's right. This whole "convert Gotcher" project only got thrown at us when he suddenly showed up yesterday, and I think it was Mr. Craftlove—Elfrank—who started it, wasn't it? Merlina came to rest and relax and...meet some new people.

UNCLE CLIFF

(with a chuckle)
Well, we're doing that with a vengeance!

PENNY

How can we think of converting him to believe in our notion of God when we can't even agree about whatever "our" notion of God might be, let alone figure out what Gotcher's non-notion of God is—or maybe I should say his notion of non-God? His non-notion of non-God?

UNCLE CLIFF

Well, I seem to remember that we tried asking him that, and he wriggled very neatly out of giving any solid answer at all. Or can there even *be* a solid answer to the question? Can we say it's even a solid question?

Meanwhile, the group comprising psychiatrist, librarian, horror novelist, and hostess had settled in the gazebo Freedom would have liked to claim, where their conversation, over cold fried chicken, biscuits, pea salad, potato chips, mixed pickles, fresh oranges, peach pie, and a choice of iced tea or lemonade, had reached the following point:

MARY

His very denial of God can be seen as evidence of his concern with the idea. People who don't care about a subject rarely bother to deny it; they simply ignore it—have little or nothing to say about it one way or any other.

LEIF

Do you mean that he's in the stage of denial, maybe over something traumatic that happened in his life?

MARY

Possibly. Kubler-Ross's five stages apply to other aspects of life besides death.

ELFRANK

He is well advanced into middle age. If not old enough by now to be responsible for his ideas, when?

MARY

"Adulthood" is largely an illusion. As a society, we agree on it because we want to feel responsible. It's a game we play to hide our lifelong weakness and immaturity from one another and from our own selves as well.

ELIZA

He really hasn't told us very much at all about his life. But he doesn't act like he recently lost somebody very dear or important to him.

MARY

The loss could have come many years ago, and scabbed over, until his denial of the power we commonly call "God" became an ingrained habit.

ELFRANK

Or he could simply have gone with the flow when atheism was fashionable, and continued clinging to it as to a tattered old security blanket.

LEIF

Where's the security in thinking God doesn't exist and there's no life for us beyond the grave?

ELFRANK

A great deal of security and even comfort in that notion, for one who is conscious of having lived such a life as any just God must condemn him eternally to Hell for doing.

ELIZA

Oh, I can't believe Gotcher has lived that evil a life!

LEIF

Nor I. I'm not denying the existence of Hell, Frank, and I'm not even saying there's nobody there at all, but anybody who is there has got to be a thoroughly unrepentent mass murderer, at the very least.

ELIZA

Or rapist. Possibly even somebody who would commit murder gratuitously, if she or he could.

LEIF

Anyway, not some poor Catholic who ate a hamburger one Friday a couple of years before Vatican II.

ELFRANK

Your assurance is touchingly innocent of insight into the finely tuned Catholic conscience.

MARY

But how nearly is even the finest conscience, Catholic or otherwise, attuned to the perception of God?

ELFRANK

Very closely indeed, if we apply ourselves to God's own directives as provided us in Holy Writ.

LEIF

Pardon me there, but other religions have their own holy scriptures, to which they are attached as devoutly as we are to our Bible.

ELFRANK

Other religions labor in error.

ELIZA

What about us, then? There are probably as many different interpretations of the Bible as there are Christian churches and Jewish synagogues, and most of them seem to be incompatible with all the others.

ELFRANK

The fault of having abandoned solid tradition and properly trained clerical guidance in this as in other matters.

LEIF

Pardon me again, but that's a load of manure—

ELFRANK

Which is very useful stuff for fertilizing fields. As I have read in some translation of the seventeenth or eighteenth century, when society was more earthily aware of her dependence upon agriculture, "The blood of the martyrs is the manure of the Church."

LEIF

Be that as it may, if you're right, then why are your own church fathers always quarreling among themselves about what this tradition actually is, and how that passage of Scripture ought to be interpreted?

MARY

I have met a few individuals who claim the experience of a personal revelation from God guaranteeing them of the divine authenticity of Scripture. Lacking such personal revelation—the reliability of which always remains open to question in any case—the rest of us have only the word of our fellow fallible mortals that any set of Scriptures, including the Holy Bible, really is the direct "Word of God." In other words, our assurance is hearsay.

LEIF

And these scriptures tend to date from the era when literacy was still a fairly new invention and writing seen as something magical, mystical, or marvelous in itself.

ELFRANK

While as for us moderns, our sensitivities lie confused and buried beneath a muck of more printed words than any person can read in a lifetime, let alone ponder.

LEIF

I moil in that muck for my daily bread and butter, and you've certainly contributed your fair share to it, Frank.

ELFRANK

I, too, moil in it for my livelihood; nor is it my fault, any more than it was Edgar Poe's, if the gullible book-buying public prefers such tripe to solid study. Happy the failed authors, whose lack of commercial success drives them to pursuits of greater spiritual profit, if only to their own personal salvation! But I ask no reader to copy out or study any potboiler of my casting off. If you would begin to know the Holy Bible, copy it out word for word.

LEIF

What, "begats" and all?

ELFRANK

Certainly, "begats" and all. With particular attention to the comparative dimensions of Solomon's Temple and his personal residence.

ELIZA

But if the Bible is God's direct instruction so pure and simple, why didn't She make its meaning a little easier to grasp?

ELFRANK

Possibly because *He* wanted us to expend some time and energy thinking about it.

MARY

How often we use "possibly" and "perhaps" to signal our deep opinion that such-and-such is the only true and absolute explanation!

ELFRANK

I trust that you will not accuse me of pontificating if I offer it as my opinion that "perhaps" we are ill equipped to convert any unbeliever to a creed so mismatched as our own—collectively speaking. His has at least the advantage of unity.

LEIF

Does it? As nearly as I can make out, Gotcher's atheism seems to have as many viewpoints in itself as our God-orientation has in the lot of us.

ELFRANK

His shifting viewpoints might be compared with the crew of an ocean vessel, while Gotcher himself is the prow, cleaving cleanly through the roiling waves of our various doctrinal disputes and disagreements.

ELIZA

Which really shouldn't be that much of a problem, should they? if we're only trying to convert him to a generic belief in God rather than to any one particular denomination?

ELFRANK

"Conversion" connotes bringing the converted to a conviction of the Truth, not to an artistic appreciation of some prismatic whirligig of partial reflections.

MARY

If you mean by that that you hope to convert all of us here this weekend to your own particular view of Catholicism, I can only say—and not very sincerely—"Good luck!'

LEIF

Maybe the rest of us should just sit back and watch Frank and Gotcher skirmish all by themselves, prow to prow.

ELFRANK

Perhaps that would be preferable to thrusting your various oars in at so many cross purposes.

> *As for the third of our groups, that comprising the present paterfamilias of Loon Lake Lodge, his son, the hard-working preparer of all three lunch baskets, the former master of the property, and the two dogs (the parakeet having been left for the afternoon safely in one of his several cages inside the main house), they sat around the island's rather ramshackle old picnic table, refreshing themselves with pastrami and cheese on rye, Waldorf salad, shoestring potatoes, pickled peppers, bananas, chocolate cake, and a choice of iced tea or lemonade; and comfortably tabled the whole plan to convert anyone to anything, in favor of appreciative comments on the favorable weather, the watery antics of the dogs, the deliciousness of the meal, and whatever other pleasant mundanities sprang to mind.*

ELMER

Y'know, we might be able to do it...a Santa Claus Express on the island here...

BUGSY

I like my idea better—the Bugsylvania Express.

ELMER

Maybe even start it on the shore and run the track across a bridge, make the cabin itself over into Santa's workshop at the North Pole... we'd have to make it a pretty good bridge, wide enough for folks to walk along beside the tracks...

BUGSY

Yeah, but Santa's only good for December. Bugs are good for the whole year round. I know where I can get some really great specimens of genuine *Egyptian Scarabaeoidea,* and *Anastrus neaeris*—not just the jewelry they make out of their wings, but the whole blue butterflies, mounted.

GOTCHER

Yeah, those are beautiful, man, but too bad you couldn't have live specimens instead of dead ones.

PEARL

Butterflies are pretty, but most bugs give most people heebie-jeebies. The best thing about winters up here is that we get a break from the bugs, most of them.

BUGSY

Aw, we don't have nearly so many bugs up here as they've got in Hawaii and South America and Africa and places like that. We don't even have as many in summer as they've got in some of those places in their wintertime. That's what'd make the Bugsylvania Express so great—people could see what we're missing up here. Like *Blaberus giganteus* this long! *(Holding his palms several inches apart.)*

PEARL

Ugh!

BUGSY

You mean "Yuck," or Ick"?

PEARL

I mean Santa Claus and Christmas are good pretty well the whole year around, too. There are lots of all-year-round Christmas shops. Except maybe the two weeks right after New Year's.

GOTCHER

Don't forget those weeks fall right in the Orthodox Christmas season, Pearl. Often used to think, before I washed my hands of all that kind of stuff, that maybe I'd just convert to an Orthodox system and do all my Yule shopping during the after-Christmas sales.

PEARL

The after-Christmas sales seem to come pretty well all through the month of December, nowadays.

ELMER

Might be too much work to lay track across the ice every winter, but maybe a footpath across the ice beside the bridge for wintertime visitors, give them a better angle for watching the train chug by…

BUGSY

Maybe Santa's workshop could have an insect museum?

GOTCHER

Do they still sell ant farms, man? I wonder if they could have a heated room for live butterflies at the North Pole? What'd you call it? Let's see…"aviary" is for the birds…

BUGSY

How about an "entomiary"? Yeah, man, wouldn't that be great? Not just butterflies, either…

PEARL

Don't you even celebrate Christmas, Gotcher?

GOTCHER

Not as "Christ's Mass," Pearl. Funny, how the Protestant culture hung onto that old terminology. But, yeah, most years I get kind of a bang out of the lights and goodies and like that. Could be a pretty cool fiesta, if the merchandisers would only go a little bit easier on it. But then, complaining about how much they commercialize Christmas is maybe the oldest, most cherished Yuletide custom of all—the old Pagans were already complaining along those lines back when Christmas was Saturnalia. And Santa Claus ain't too bad an idol, as idols go.

PEARL

Are you saying people treat Santa Claus like God?

GOTCHER

"He sees you when you're sleeping,/He knows when you're awake./ He knows if you've been bad or good…" Who does that sound like? At least ol' Santa gives the good children good stuff, which is more than you can say for some of our gods.

ELMER

In some places, bad children used to get lumps of coal in their stockings.

GOTCHER

Well, man, in some climates, when heating costs got high, people must've encouraged their kids to be bad, and get all the free fuel they could.

BUGSY

Would the Santa Claus Express be a pufferbelly? We could paint little Christmas ribbons and bows on the lumps in the tender.

PEARL

Watch the dogs.

* * * *

The dogs, emerging more or less *in tandem* from the waters of the lake, had just chased each other—or, rather, since no one could say which was chasing which—charged together up the island's bank to its picnic table, where both stopped at once, Muttwump on Bugsy's side of the table and Pumpkin on Gotcher's, where they set in simultaneously, as if by some doggish pre-arrangement, to shake themselves so that the shining droplets flew, less as the "gentle dew from Heaven" than as some tempest flying up out of the chthonic regions into the bright sunlight, to poise there a glittering nanosecond, each drop its own prismful cloudlet, before descending tablewards with a pattering accompaniment to the jingle-jangle of the several metallic identification, license, and innoculation tags on Muttwump's collar.

With a sharp exclamation, Pearl tried to fling napkins over the food so as to umbrella it against the cloudless localized cloudburst. Gotcher attempted to follow her example, as also did Bugsy, the last-named chiefly for the sport of the exercise, seeing that it was already too late to save the food from what was after all, at worst, a sprinkling of freshwater lake asperged from the backs of healthy dogs. More perilous to the picnic than this sprinkling was the way in which the chocolate cake somehow, in the process of being hastily draped, contrived to get its plate jostled an inch or two nearer the edge of the table, which, as already remarked, was no longer the most solidly balanced member of its treen species.

A second later, a chipmunk poked its nose into sight. Now, while these cheeky little striped rodents politely pretend now and then to be afraid of us humans, they may well fear dogs out of more than mere etiquette, for after two seconds of poised tableau, when the chipmunk suddenly darted beneath the table, both canines gave instant chase, juddering the table's leg so that the cake thudded to the ground—and well might the picnickers have rejoiced that there were no further casualties… except that they had already more or less eaten their fill of everything preparatory to dessert.

ALL

Whoops! *(or noises to that effect, not quite in unison)*

PEARL

Oh, *drat!*

BUGSY

Aw, it isn't too much spoiled. *(Salvaging as much of the remains as he could scoop up with both hands, and depositing it on the nearest paper plate, which happened to be his own, never minding that this still hosted small puddles of pickled-pepper juice, as well as crumbs of sandwich, traces of Waldorf salad, and one lorn shoestring potato.)*

ELMER

Better get the rest of it, before the dogs do.

GOTCHER

Aw, man, let 'em have it. This is their picnic, too.

ELMER

It's chocolate.

GOTCHER

So what, man?

BUGSY (continuing to scoop up as much as he could, his father and Pearl helping him, beneath the very noses of the dogs who, having been deprived of the chipmunk, by its own efforts, now turned their attention to the victim which of itself must remain immobile)

Dogs shouldn't eat chocolate.

GOTCHER

Who says?

ELMER

Muttwump's vet, for one.

GOTCHER

Man, Pumpkin ain't never seen a veterinarian in her life—far as I know—and just look at her for health!

PEARL

You mean she hasn't been spayed?

GOTCHER (shrugging)

Not by my directive.

BUGSY

Whoops!

GOTCHER

No more'n I begrudge her a bite or two of chocolate now an' then. Huh, old girl? *(The other three having pretty well recovered most of the cake, except for a few crumbs, which Muttwump continued to chase determinedly with his tongue, Gotcher held a loose handful of cake and icing down to Pumpkin, who licked it up, tail wagging, faster than the other dog could crowd in beside her.)*

PEARL

Well, let's hope she ain't in heat.

ELMER

What about rabies shots?

GOTCHER

Yeah, that worries me a little, sometimes. Y'see, folks, Pumpkin here just latched onto me one day—followed me home, so to speak, such as "home" was—and we've hung out together ever since.

ELMER

We can get you in Monday to our vet and get her a shot.

BUGSY

And a collar for the tag that shows she's had it.

GOTCHER

A collar? What about it, girl, you want a collar around your neck?

PUMPKIN

(looking for more crumbs between Gotcher's fingers)
Woof!

BUGSY

Make it a fashion statement. Get my sister to needlepoint her one.

PEARL

Bugsy, are you eating that dirty cake?

BUGSY

Not gonna lose out on this good stuff just because of a little good, clean dirt.

PEARL

And dog slobber!

GOTCHER

Hey, dogs eat stuff after we've got a little of our slobber on it, and it doesn't seem to hurt them any.

BUGSY

Ouch!…Pebble. Must've got stuck in the icing.

PEARL

There! You see? Serves you right.

ELMER

Hope you didn't break a tooth there, son.

BUGSY (feeling)

Yeah, that's a permanent one. Naw, don't think it's broken.

GOTCHER

Just goes to show how carefully people must've had to chew their cake, times when it had those little fortune-telling trinkets baked into it. Like at weddings, New Year's, times like that, you know, back in the old days.

BUGSY

Yeah? Sounds like fun. Maybe we could try it next New Year's?

PEARL

Don't hold your breath.

GOTCHER

Of course, I guess they had pretty bad teeth anyway, back then. More toothaches than headaches, more pulling teeth than filling 'em. We worry about coffee and tea and tobacco stains ruining our smiles, where our ancestors must've thought a smile was pretty good whenever all the teeth were there, no matter how badly stained.

> *At this point, had Mr. Craftlove been with on the island with them, he would undoubtedly have offered some comment comparing stains on teeth and stains on souls; but the reader may have observed how very far this group allowed their conversation to stray from the project of Converting the Atheist.*
>
> *The author may also remark that, catch-as-catch-can though Gotcher's approach to pet care was, Pumpkin may nevertheless have known what she was doing in roaming along with him rather than striking off again on her own, as it is obvious she could easily have done.*

CHAPTER 23

During that afternoon interval between lunch and dinner which—like life itself—seems so deceptively long until all at once it is over—the psychiatrist and the librarian somehow contrived to find themselves alone together in the little library of Loon Lake Lodge.

DR. ARROWSMITH

I'd think you'd have enough of looking at books in your nine-to-five job, Mr. Pageturner.

MR. PAGETURNER

"Leif," please.

MARY ARROWSMITH

Oh, must we be informal even here, away from the others?

LEIF PAGETURNER

Why not?… Mary, if I may. "Mary" has such a melodious, rounded sound—"Arrowsmith" such a sharp, pointy one.

MARY

Perhaps I prefer coming across as to the point…Leif.

LEIF

In certain times and places, I don't blame you. I hope we aren't in one of those times-and-places now…Mary.

MARY (laughing)

No, I guess we aren't.

LEIF

As to your question, I find it just a little bit frustrating, on my nine-to-five—actually, eight-thirty to four most days, ten-thirty to six every other Saturday, with Wednesdays and Sundays off—to handle all those books: charging them out; charging them back in; cleaning their covers; mending them when they need it; ordering new ones; cataloguing and processing them when they arrive—that is, library-stamping them, casing their dust jackets in plastic covers, adding the magnetic strips to their spines, and so on to get them ready for the patrons; choosing which ones to keep and process when donations come in—usually by the boxful—and which ones to put in our ongoing book sale right away; shelving them; reading the shelves to keep our permanent collection in order; designing bulletin board displays, putting the said displays up and taking them down; doing story hours for the kids…and never getting to read any of all these books! It's nice sometimes to relax in someone else's library and actually read a few lines.

MARY

Maybe I'd better leave you in peace until dinnertime?

LEIF

It's even nicer to sit and chat with somebody *sympathique*. That's why I usually go out to lunch, instead of snatching that hour to sit with a book. Have you published many books, Mary?

MARY

Only papers in various professional journals.

LEIF

Are there universities somewhere that teach fledgling newsletters and magazines how to grow up into "professional" journals?

MARY

Not exactly. But some, I believe, start out in life as departmental bulletins at prestigious universities and by dint of being sold over and over again to better heeled publishers, eventually grow up into finely printed monthlies or even quarterlies distributed to the whole field. Meanwhile, of course, the university department has started another bulletin to keep itself posted on its own doings.

LEIF

I wonder if anyone has done a biological study on the life cycles of periodical publications.

MARY

It wouldn't surprise me. I might even want to read such a study, if it ever came to my attention.

LEIF

I was hoping, of course, that you might have published a book or two for more or less popular consumption.

MARY

And have a few autographed copies somewhere about my person?

LEIF

Gutenberg forbid! No, I had in mind some title or titles we might acquire, through regular channels, for our collection.

MARY

No, nothing like that, I'm afraid. "Gutenberg forbid"?

LEIF

If there is a saint or a god of publishing, it almost has to be the inventor of the printing press.

MARY

Haven't I heard somewhere that some other party actually beat him to it?

LEIF

Possibly—as someone else actually invented the telephone first, and the light bulb, and the sewing machine, and Coca-Cola, and of course Shakespeare's Plays—which everybody seems to have written *except* Shakespeare—and America, which everybody seems to have discovered *except* Columbus. What of it? It's the reputation that counts, and the popular belief that shapes subsequent history, rather than the sober truth. Didn't you say something like that yourself last night? And so I say, according to popular theology, Johannes Gutenberg remains the god of the printing press and therefore, by extension, of the publishing world.

MARY

"God," or "patron saint?"

LEIF

Much of a muchness, in this application. What else are today's patron saints, but the lesser gods of the ancient pantheons?

MARY

I believe that the Catholic Church created a minor scandal, a few decades ago, by going through its calendar of saints and banning all the ones who couldn't be proved absolutely historical.

LEIF

Not exactly "banning," as I understand it: merely relegating the legendary ones to the limbo of purely private devotion. As far as I know, the Catholic Church carried out no raids for St. Christopher medals and suchlike, simply disqualified good old Chris from having schools and parishes named for him. Since the legendary saints are the ones who are most obviously old Pagan gods in disguise, the concession to private devotion is more remarkable than the expunging from the official list. Still, I hold that assigning demonstrably historical persons to the roles of patron saints puts them in the same position as the minor deities of old. In a way, their unquestioned historical reality even cements their position in the heavenly pantheon.

MARY

What do you think about angels?

LEIF

They fit right into the pattern. It looks very much as if entities of some kind exist somewhere just beyond our usual corporeal perceptions. Other cultures have called them gods and goddesses, spirits of the Ancestors, elves and fairies, and so on. We call them angels and saints, ghosts and demons, aliens from outer space, possibly even Bigfoot and Yeti. What do you think?

MARY

I'd add another set of candidates: thought forms of our own creation, which can grow into obsessions, occasionally beneficent but more often destructive.

LEIF

Yes, obsessions certainly take on a hard solidity of their own.

MARY

The danger intensifies when a number of people share an obsession, as the world witnessed in Nazi Germany.

LEIF

Some thinkers say that all humanity is really one big organism.

MARY

Why limit it to humanity? I would say, all the world, with everything in it. Even all the universe.

LEIF

Inanimate as well as animate?

MARY

Certainly. Speaking more from my personal religion than from my profession, I ask, What evidence do we really have that stones and stars and all such things lack their own individual types of life and even awareness?

LEIF

The word "profession" can mean religion. As in "This is what I profess to believe."

MARY

If we are falling into word play, the difference between "organism" and "orgasm" is a single syllable, between "immortal" and "immoral" a single letter.

LEIF

Which is entirely appropriate, seeing how often the ancient immortals were quite immoral, by the moral standards of mere mortals.

> *The two conversationalists shared a heartier laugh than the rather shopworn joke warranted.*

LEIF

Well, you know, I don't give either of us two much hope of converting our friend Gotcher, but…

MARY

We might stand some chance of converting each other.

LEIF

Not so much converting, as effecting a few minor modifications. We don't exactly seem to be poles apart on these matters, only a few degrees of latitude—if even that.

MARY

Further exploration might prove intensely rewarding.

> *At about this same time or a little earlier, Freedom located Mrs. Wright in the latter's bedroom, much to the latter's annoyance and, of course, without the knowledge of Freedom's mother, who had not thought it necessary to spell out to her daughter that the privacy of retreatants in their own rooms was to be strictly respected except perhaps at mealtime.*

MRS. WRIGHT (answering the knock at her door, and trying to hide her displeasure on seeing who it was)

Freedom! Is anything wrong?

FREEDOM

Everything! And it's all your fault! You should know.

MRS. WRIGHT

Oh, really? Well, I have done my best—

FREEDOM

Your best to spoil—to, to sabotage a really good woman's last chance for happiness!

MRS. WRIGHT

If she has any interest in him, why doesn't she do a little bit for herself? Ms. Eklektik, I may not have that much real experience in these matters, but neither do—I don't think you've got any more experience than I have—

FREEDOM

Don't play the "I'm older than you" card!

MRS. WRIGHT

Let me finish! You can't go around maneuvering people into what—whatever *you* think is best for them and expecting them to be "happy." That's playing God, and—whatever God is—we aren't God! At least, no individual one of us is—

FREEDOM

But if we only worked together—

MRS. WRIGHT

To force him—*and* her—into a marriage that maybe neither of them really wants? You think that would make them happy?

FREEDOM

Of course Merlina really wants it! And needs it, whether she knows it or not. If you'd had the talks with her that I've had—

MRS. WRIGHT

Maybe you should have a talk with Dr. Arrowsmith about things like that. As for me—

FREEDOM

Please just stay out of their way.

MRS. WRIGHT

No. Please, *you* stay out of their way and let things take their natural course.

FREEDOM

Mrs. Wright! If you'd only think about this for a minute—

> *But here Mrs. Wright shut her door between them. "A minute!" was echoing through her head. "I have been thinking about this—for much more than 'a minute'! If you only knew, Miss Misnamed 'Freedom'—how long I have been thinking about this! But, of course, whenever people say 'If you'd only think about this,' what they really mean is: 'Change your mind and see it my way.' And that, Ms. So-Called Freedom, is exactly what you should kindly allow him, and your poor friend Merlina—yes, and me, too—to do for ourselves!"*
>
> *By all of which may perhaps be glimpsed, in microcosm, the difficulties faced daily in international diplomacy.*

CHAPTER 24

As for Freedom, she stood half a dozen heartbeats with her fist poised to hammer against Mrs. Wright's door, then finally turned away, her breast heaving and shuddering. How did this cold, unfeeling old witch *dare?* Well, Freedom would never read any of *her* silly books!

All the same, the young woman guessed that her own mother might not entirely appreciate her daughter's various interviews and frustrations with one of the paying guests, no matter how praiseworthy Freedom's motive. It was in no small measure for this reason that the daughter refrained from seeking her mother out in the kitchen, where she knew Eliza had planned to spend much of the afternoon helping Pearl prepare dinner. (And where, incidentally, they might well press any stray household member into service with them.)

Accordingly, Freedom wandered. Peeping into the library, she overheard a little of the conversation between Leif Pageturner and Dr. Mary Arrowsmith, as quoted (in part) above; and, G-rated though it was, the daughter of the house turned away satisfied that this woman, at least, posed absolutely no threat to poor Merlina's fading chances with Uncle Cliff…for which reason Freedom was more than happy to leave the pair alone together.

Next her restless feet carried her away from the main lodge to the cabin her father and Uncle Cliff were converting into the solar system of the Lunar-Martian Express, where she found both of them, together with Bugsy, Gotcher, and the two dogs, deep in technical abstrusiosities about how to rig this or that special effect in the layout, in which they had by now progressed to include the entire cabin, for they discussed, among other things, how to construct a dome-shaped false ceiling whereon to project stars with the aid of a miniature planetarium.

Seeing little chance to detach Uncle Cliff from a discussion of which he was the very hub, and even less chance of interjecting needlework embellishments—which in any case seemed to have lost their old power to distract and absorb her thoughts now that she was suffering an attack of What Really Matters, Freedom drifted away with scarcely a word, and continued her abstracted meanderings until she reached the gazebo where yesterday she had achieved—as she then supposed—an understanding with the treacherous Mrs. Wright, and today found Merlina sitting with, of all people, Mr. Craftlove!

Here was danger from a totally unexpected direction, and to head it off, Freedom bravely joined them at once.

FREEDOM

Good afternoon!

MERLINA

Oh, good afternoon, Freedom!

MR. CRAFTLOVE

Miss Eklektik. Or "Ms.," if you prefer. Or should I take the liberty of your first name, even here and now, out of your estimable mother's hearing?

FREEDOM

With only the three of us, I think we can tell who we're talking to without calling one another anything at all.

MERLINA (half to herself, musingly)

The wood where things have no names.

MR. CRAFTLOVE

You allude, I think, to *Through the Looking-Glass and What Alice Found There,* a book written for love and hence more conversational than engrossing.

MERLINA

A lovely, quiet, friendly book.

MR. CRAFTLOVE

Such a book as I might turn my own hand to, had I the time to squander.

MERLINA

Why "squander"?

MR. CRAFTLOVE

The world already has the two *Alice* books, an achievement which Carroll himself was never able to duplicate. As for me, I have better uses for my time when not engaged in pandering to the masses for my daily bread.

FREEDOM

Couldn't you find some way to make a living that you might like better?

MR. CRAFTLOVE

None, perhaps, for which I would prove to have a better knack, if I may trust my agent, publishers, and royalty checks. It is a more or less tragic thing to have inescapable talent for an occupation little to the possessor's own taste and conscience.

MERLINA

Yes, I see how that could embitter someone. But why not write things more in keeping with your conscience?

MR. CRAFTLOVE

I have little creativity left over after my potboiler labors, therefore prefer to expend my leisure hours with fruits culled by greater laborers than I in the vineyard of things spiritual.

MERLINA

Well, why not write about angels and saints instead of monsters and murderers?

FREEDOM

Yes, why not?

MR. CRAFTLOVE

Because the book-buying public would rather expend their money on tales of monsters and murderers, God knows why. We must assume it has to do with the sin of Adam.

FREEDOM

Oh, *that* again! I wish people wouldn't always drag Adam and Eve into it. Haven't we got enough sins of our own to worry about?

MR. CRAFTLOVE

The sin of Adam *is* the sin of all humanity.

MERLINA

I've always thought the sin of Cain was a great deal worse than the sin of Adam. After all, what did Adam and Eve really do that was so terrible? Like any little children in loving homes, they wanted to be like their Daddy. And when they saw they'd been naughty, they tried to cover it up, like any scared little children. But Cain actually murdered his brother. Which he might not have done if they'd all still been living in the Garden.

FREEDOM

Oh, I don't know about that. There are times I'd like to murder Bugsy.

MERLINA

You wouldn't really, dear. That's just a figure of speech.

MR. CRAFTLOVE

Nor, admirable example as this Loon Lake Lodge property is of the best work of our Creator's Hands, is it the Garden of Eden. But I will grant your argument this much: that such a sin as that of Cain makes much better—that is, more saleable—copy than such a sin as that of Adam. Now, if Abel's ghost would only obligingly return, hair stringing down in bloody loops and eyes ablaze with accusation, to confront his murderer in the best style of Classical and Elizabethan revenge tragedy, there would be something I could work with for my bread and butter.

MERLINA

Wouldn't that rather spoil Abel's character as the good and mild brother?

MR. CRAFTLOVE

Um… Not necessarily. Abel is interpreted as the earliest Christ figure, and has not Jesus been shown, as early as the Apocalypse of John—alias "The Book of Revelation"—in the guise of Divine Avenger, blazing with righteous wrath? Moreover, it would not necessarily be Abel as he had actually been in life, but Abel as his brother's guilty conscience paints him… Hmmm.

MERLINA

Oh, dear! I'm afraid we've given him an idea.

MR. CRAFTLOVE

For which I thank you, ladies. A potboiler with, perhaps, some shred of moral and theological substance…

MERLINA

But why would Abel's ghost have to be accusing? Why not forgiving?

FREEDOM

Because ghosts are always scary.

MR. CRAFTLOVE

The ghost of murdered Abel might indeed be forgiving, with a mercy perceived by his murderer as accusation. "For by so doing, thou wilt heap coals of fire upon his head."

MERLINA (in answer more to Freedom than to Mr. Craftlove)

But why should the stories always show them as scary? In life, most people try to be as good as they can, most of the time. Why should we think that death automatically changes us all into monsters?

MR. CRAFTLOVE

The brief answer to your question is identical to that about angels and saints versus monsters and murderers: fearsome ghosts "sell," whereas kindly ones do not.

FREEDOM

What about Casper the Friendly Ghost? Bugsy loves him, insufferably.

MR. CRAFTLOVE

A mere cartoon creation, remarkable precisely in being set apart from the predicated general rule. If ghosts in general were to be regarded as friendly, Casper would dissolve into insignificance. But to answer the original question more fully, we should draw a distinctive line between "ghosts" and "revenants." The former term, considered from a religious point of view, provides a synonym pure and simple for "souls" or "spirits"—something each and every human being is presumed to have, in order to enjoy Heaven or suffer Hell. The latter term, "revenants," denotes such spirits as return to manifest themselves on Earth, in order to complete—or attempt to complete—some unfinished business which continues to disturb their afterlife. Such unfinished business must be somehow troubling, and frequently involves revenge or at least balance for the violence of their mortal deaths. Hence, revenants must almost by definition be troubled souls, and therefore frightening. The common question, "Do you believe in ghosts?" ought properly to be worded, "Do you believe in *revenants?*" Otherwise, an answer in the negative would logically mark the respondent, not as someone free from superstition, but as a blatant atheist.

FREEDOM

Gotcher would probably say they're the same thing. I mean someone who's free from superstition, and an atheist.

MR. CRAFTLOVE

Mr. Gotcher Lotsadoe's freedom from adult responsibility is not our present problem.

MERLINA

It is if we're trying to convert him.

FREEDOM

Does "adult responsibility" mean the same thing as "churchgoing"?

MR. CRAFTLOVE

More: it also entails searching out and selecting the right church and, once safely there, subscribing wholeheartedly to her tenets.

MERLINA

How many churches have you sampled yourself?

MR. CRAFTLOVE

Having by the grace of God been born into the right one, I have never needed to "sample" any other.

FREEDOM

In other words, you've just taken your own church's word for it—just like everyone else who believes the church they happened to be born into is the best and only true one.

MERLINA

When we say, "There but for the grace of God go I," aren't we really saying "God loves me—or us—best," which is like saying, "We're better than everybody else"? I find that attitude rather at odds with the ecumenical spirit.

MR. CRAFTLOVE

The "ecumenical spirit," so called, bland though it is, resembles cayenne pepper in this much: that it must be used sparingly and in appropriate dishes only, if it is not to spoil the entire meal.

MERLINA

Be that as it may, what about your calendar of saints? Aren't they "revenants," the way they pop into people's lives as angelic visions?

MR. CRAFTLOVE

Do not, I beg you, adhere to the common error of confusing the saints with the angels, as if a saintly man upon death became an angel—

FREEDOM

A saintly man or woman.

MR. CRAFTLOVE

In order to avoid being sidetracked into an argument concerning grammatical niceties, I stand corrected. As if a saintly human being upon death became an angel. The angelic orders represent an entirely different creation from humanity. Angels are not graduated humans, nor are human beings fallen angels. Humans can no more become angels, than dogs and cats can become human beings.

FREEDOM

A lot of people believe that dogs and cats *can* become human beings, and the other way round. Reincarnation.

MR. CRAFTLOVE

A lot of people are wrong. In this, as in so many other matters.

MERLINA (whimsically)

And you're the man to set them right?

MR. CRAFTLOVE

Not I, but the Church whose time-tested pronouncements I have the privilege and duty to convey.

FREEDOM

What about Galileo? Your Church was wrong about Galileo, wasn't it? About which revolved around the other, the sun or the earth?

MR. CRAFTLOVE

At the time of Galileo, society was still in process of mapping out which areas of human study belong properly to the realm of spiritual importance and which, such as what we today popularly call "science," fall into the area of pastime and avocation. The Galileo affair was a social problem, not a religious one. Moreover, while Galileo chanced to be correct regarding the sun, let me point out that the outer planets, in revolving around Sol, do in some sense revolve around Terra as well.

MERLINA (laughing)

I would still like to know why your saints don't count as "revenants"— "heavenly" revenants, since the modifier "angelic" sets you off so much.

MR. CRAFTLOVE

Your new and accurate adjective says it for me. The saints need not quit Heaven, even temporarily, in order to intercede on our behalf and cause blessings, like the mystical roses of St. Theresa of Lisieux, to shower down upon us. While the revenants vulgarly called "ghosts" are mere superstition.

MERLINA

(with a perfunctory glance at her watch)
My goodness, look at the time! If I want to change for dinner, I'd better get going.

FREEDOM

I'll come with you.

> *Making their polite adieux to Mr. Craftlove, who seemed if anything thankful for the opportunity to recollect himself in private while gazing on the tranquil waters of Loon Lake, the women rose and started back to the lodge. As soon as she judged they were safely out of his hearing, Freedom asked her friend, "Merlina, you don't…feel attracted to him, do you?"*

MERLINA

Who? Frank Craftlove? Oh, my goodness gracious, Freedom, what ever put that idea into your head?

FREEDOM

You were sitting there alone with him, talking.

MERLINA

We happened to come up to the little gazebo at the same time, from entirely different directions, and when we caught sight of one another, I suppose it didn't occur to either of us that there was any reason to make a sudden change of plans. After all, we're both of age, and we aren't living in Victorian times. In fact, I'm considerably more than "of age." Without knowing for sure, I'd guess I've got at least a good ten years on Elfrank Craftlove.

FREEDOM (breathing a sigh of relief)

That's good.

MERLINA

Yes, I enjoy being the age I am.

FREEDOM

Oh, Merlina, you aren't old!

MERLINA

Nor yet young, and quite comfortable as I am.

FREEDOM

But still young enough that you *might* want to get married again?

MERLINA

No, not really. Well, I suppose, if another man as good as Art should happen to come along my way. But men like Arthur are few and far between, and any lesser specimen simply couldn't measure up—it wouldn't be fair to him.

FREEDOM

I'm sorry I never met him. But I can think of at least one very, very good—and unattached—man we've got right here with us this weekend.

MERLINA

Yes, I have lunch with Leif sometimes at The Coffee Cup, and he does seem to be a man who should make some woman a very good husband. But he's far too young for me!

FREEDOM

Oh, I didn't mean the librarian! That is...yes, I'm sure he's very good too, but I meant...Uncle Cliff.

MERLINA

Oh, but, Freedom, haven't you noticed? He seems to have an eye for Penny Wright.

FREEDOM

I think you must be imagining things, Merlina!

MERLINA

Do you? Well, well, let's just wait and see.

FREEDOM

If he is, I'm afraid he'll be disappointed, and maybe need someone good to pick up the pieces. Because it looks to me as though Mrs. Wright must be attracted to Mr. Craftlove.

At this, the older woman laughed.

FREEDOM

Well? But don't you think they'd make a perfect match, Merlina?

MERLINA (laughing again)

Oh, Freedom, dear Freedom, it wouldn't last long enough for a honeymoon! When angry sparks start flying as soon as two people meet, that's no sign of romantic attraction in real life, only in cheap romances!

FREEDOM

But they're both writers, and they're both Catholic.

MERLINA

I'd call that a large part of the problem. Don't matchmake, Freedom. Just leave them alone, and you may be surprised how good your Uncle Cliff's chances are with Penny Wright.

FREEDOM

But she isn't nearly good enough for him.

MERLINA

Suppose you let him decide that for himself, child.

Freedom fell silent, letting her friend ramble on about the beauty of the afternoon, the moss and acorns and pine needles, the birdsongs and mushrooms, squirrels and chipmunks, the glances of sunlight catching briefly in the rippling surface of Loon Lake, the people pouring with shouts and waving arms out of the Lodge...

CHAPTER 25

It transpired that after shutting her door in Freedom's face and stewing in her own room until she judged the coast was surely clear, Penelope Wright had sought relief from the turmoil of her thoughts by wandering through the Lodge until she reached the room where Budgewiser was perched in his cage, contentedly if rather scrappily chewing away at his cuttlebone. Knowing, as did all the guests, that the family frequently gave their budgie the flight of the house—as, indeed, her own family had used to do decades before with their own pet parakeet—Ko-Ko, long in bird heaven—the author felt safe, after making a careful check of all the screened windows, in opening the door of Budgewiser's cage and coaxing him onto her outstretched finger.

When he proved coaxable, she guardedly brought her finger, with its birdy burden, forth again from the cage and stood a few moments gently stroking Budgewiser's little white forehead with the forefinger tip of her free hand, before he dodged, gave himself a generous shaking, spread his wings, and began happily flying up and down the room in all its three visible dimensions and perhaps, for all we simple mortals can really say, its eight (or however many) invisible-to-us dimensions as well.

Budgewiser flew, and Penny Wright watched, and suddenly Pearl Bonami entered the room—all unaware—and quick as a bat the pet bird winged his way out the open door.

"What?!" exclaimed the cook, feeling the small rush of air above her head.

"Budgewiser! Budgewiser!" cried Penny Wright.

The two women gave chase down the hallways and through several rooms of Loon Lake Lodge, until the bird espied another opening door, where Bugsy was just coming in to run down a book his father and Uncle Clif wished to consult *a propos* of their plans for the Lunar-Martian Express layout, and flew over the boy's head as featly as he had earlier over the woman's, this time to gain the great out-of-doors.

Budgewiser flew. Bugsy, threatened with being bowled over in the doorway by two hollering women, discarded all memory of the book, turned, and was first in the race after the budgie. Merlina and Freedom, made aware as earlier described of the commotion, lost little time joining the chase. Elmer, Uncle Clif, and Gotcher, hearing the hullabaloo, rushed forth from the cabin of the Lunar-Martian Express to swallow the scene before them at a gulp and meld into it, bringing the total number of pursuers up to eight or—in consideration of Bugsy's immature bulk, seven and a half or, perhaps more exactly, seven and five-eights, along with the two dogs, all shouting and waving their arms (or tails) after one small bird, who, however, possessed of the gift of self-powered flight, easily held the upper hand or—should we say?—wing.

Eliza, wondering what might be keeping Pearl, came looking for her in time to notice something out of the ordinary going on outside, make her own egress by a nearer door, and run after the others. Mary Arrowsmith and Leif Pageturner heard the noise, distantly, but did not as yet leave the library, reasoning that if it were some emergency of both a general and a serious nature, such as the end of civilization as we know it due to a meteor strike, the outbreak of nuclear war, or the Armageddon of the Fundamentalists, they would learn their doom in due course without the need of rushing forward to meet it.

This leaves only L. Frank Craftlove to be accounted for. He, still seated encircled by the posts of the gazebo, attempting, with eyes closed and head leaning back on the high rattan chair, to commune with the Infinite…finding his meditations imposed upon by the tumult and turmoil without, rose and existed the edifice…to feel something small and fluttery settle on the crown of his head.

Still calm from his latest excursion into the realms of Ultimate Reality, he raised his right hand, closed it gently around whatever was nestling in his dark hair, and brought down the parakeet or—more properly speaking—the budgerigar who, cocking its striped head, looked up at him with shiny black eye and inquired if he had had a busy day.

"You got 'm?" cried the son of the household, first to reach the gazebo. "Hey, it's okay!" he shouted to the others as they came rushing up. "Frank's got 'm! Is he okay?"—turning anxiously to the author, who responded rather bemusedly,

"As nearly as I can determine on immediate inspection. Here…" he offered, extending his hand as if to turn the bird over to the boy.

"No," panted Eliza, "you'd better keep hold of him—Frank—if you'd be so good… Bring him back to the Lodge yourself."

No sooner said than begun; and, in its due and natural interval of time, completed: Budgewiser safely restored to his cage in the erstwhile taproom, where the bulk of the company spread itself out and settled down for a preprandial Happy Hour, Elmer serving as bartender, while his wife returned with Pearl Bonami to the kitchen, and his son went in search of the two missing guests (who were still together in the library).

ELMER

A wooden nickel for your thoughts.

MERLINA

Whose thoughts?

ELMER

Anyone's. The first one who speaks up.

UNCLE CLIFF

Wouldn't that be you, Elmer?

FREEDOM

Dad's thought was to ask the question.

PENNY

If a "Wooden Nickel" is a house drink, I'll try one. Uh… What's in it?

FREEDOM (mischievously)

Brandy, bourbon, gin, rum, Scotch, and a dash of vermouth.

PENNY

Oh, no, really?

UNCLE CLIFF

She's making it up. I think. I've never tasted anything stronger than an after-dinner cordial.

FREEDOM

Uncle Cliff is strictly a root beer or lemonade float man. Like you, Merlina.

MERLINA

You don't mean ice cream in lemonade?

UNCLE CLIFF

Yes, indeedy, I do mean ice cream in lemonade. One of my family's favorites from 'way back when. But not before supper.

PENNY

Well, I'll just have whatever Uncle Cliff has, thanks.

MERLINA

So will I.

ELMER

Three root beers, coming right up.

GOTCHER

I'll have the same, with a shot of rum.

FREEDOM

Oh, ick! Just let me have a glass of Chablis, Dad.

GOTCHER

We drink rum in Coke. Why not in root beer?

UNCLE CLIFF

Why spoil the taste of Coke or root beer or any other soft drink?

ELFRANK

The man makes an excellent point. Therefore, I will request a simple Scotch and—not liking to spoil our area's superior drinking water—bottled plain soda.

ELMER

(holding up the bottle for him to see)
Hope our Scotch meets your approval.

ELFRANK

(glancing at it)
Fine, fine. I am not so very difficult to please.

MUTTWUMP

Arf.

Looking, they saw that, Gotcher idly fondling the head of his own Pumpkin, the family dog was apparently desirous of similar attention.

FREEDOM

Muttwump! Go find Bugsy.

Muttwump looked at her for a moment, shrugged his ears, and trotted off along the hallway Bugsy had earlier taken. Pumpkin, with a glance back at Gotcher, followed Muttwump. Budgewiser seized this opportunity to query the room at large as to whether it had had a busy day.

MERLINA (laughing)

Well, if we haven't, it certainly isn't through any fault of yours, little bird.

FREEDOM

Yes! Thank you so much for catching him, Mr.—Frank.

ELFRANK

Thanks are hardly due me. I rather think that your small bird, finding the great outdoors a trifle wider than its miniature brain could encompass, simply sought the nearest island of human sanity that was not pursuing it after the fashion of a hurricane.

FREEDOM

You mean he'd have come back if we hadn't chased him? I don't think so.

ELMER

Can't say, either way. Budgewiser's never been outside before.

PENNY

I'm sorry—it's all my fault. I never should've taken him out of his cage. I only thought—I used to have one myself...

UNCLE CLIFF

You only thought, just because the people who live here give their bird the flight of the house—how revolutionary! Of course, Budgewiser would never have flown outside if it had been one of the family who opened his cage. Perish the thought!

ELMER

In fact, I'm surprised this was the first time.

PENNY

Thank—Thank you.

ELMER

Freedom. Can you come help carry people their drinks?

UNCLE CLIFF

I'll help, too.

Promptly snatching up a pair of root beers, he presented one to Penny Wright and settled down to consume the other as close as he could settle to her armchair. Noting all this with secret dissatisfaction, Freedom bore Gotcher and Merlina their beverages, enduring a wink with which the latter meant to remind her of their very recent conference regarding certain matters of the heart—and, in stoicism, returned to the bar for her own glass of wine, leaving her father to fend for Frank Craftlove.

This Elmer did, to an accompaniment of small talk, and was just pouring a beer for himself when Bugsy returned with the last pair of guests, Muttwump and Pumpkin half helping herd them in, half getting underfoot.

The librarian opted for a beer like Elmer's, the psychoanalyst for white wine like Freedom's, Bugsy poured himself a cola, and so the room settled down again in a minimum of time; when Craftlove recommenced the conversation.

ELFRANK

So tell me, Mr. Librarian, how long do you estimate it will be before both you and I are out of the work to which we have accustomed ourselves?

LEIF

I don't follow you, Frank.

ELFRANK

I mean, of course, that the Internet is about to free society from the tyranny of long writings. Even now, greater and greater numbers of people abandon that leisurely, old-fashioned correspondence waged via the Post Office, in favor of brief and snappy e-mails. Bit by bit, I foresee these e-mails taking entirely the form of whimsical photographs and cartoons. Eventually all of these, rather than merely some, will achieve nonverbal humor, stirring laughter with no need of captions. By now literacy will be needed only for filling in personal address books—if, indeed, these addresses have not already taken the form of codes and ideograms.

UNCLE CLIFF

How are you going to build codes without numbers and letters? You can't use nothing but ideograms.

ELFRANK

The Egyptians and the Chinese did.

PENNY

Which formed their written language. They didn't read them out as ideograms—they read them as words.

UNCLE CLIFF

I never tried it, so I'm not sure, but I think it'd be the dickens to do math with ideograms.

ELFRANK

Very true, and therefore numerals may survive, although the prevalence of calculators throws even this into some doubt. For the rest, a system will evolve of international ideograms, the use of which will result in a truly worldwide sign language, erasing communication barriers at least on the Internet. Though more traditional tongues remain in local use for oral communications, literacy in the old-fashioned sense will dissolve away.

LEIF

Fahrenheit 451.

ELFRANK

In some analogous sense, although without the need of firemen kindling bonfires of books and other print media. We social insects will have accomplished it freely, with no other tyrants than science and commercialism.

UNCLE CLIFF

I don't think you can blame science for any dystopia you've dreamed up yourself.

ELFRANK

Blame? Dystopia? Friend, for mankind at large—

FREEDOM (speaking for her mother)

*Hu*mankind.

ELFRANK

Yes, by all means, *hu*mankind, if you are so eager that women share the...responsibility, and drawbacks, if any. For *hu*mankind at large, it will be less dystopia than eutopia. Translated into ideogrammatic form, no longer will Bible and Koran serve as shibboleths setting the world's religions one against another. Though I fear we will have time to translate comparatively few of our so-called literary classics into ideograms before the last generation capable of such efforts has died out.

GOTCHER

That's going to be a pretty thin generation, man. Consisting of people old enough to know the alphabet, young enough to learn your ideogrammatic idiom, and literary enough to appreciate 'em both. Not many, man. Not many at all.

UNCLE CLIFF

What about plays—stage literature? What happens to Shakespeare when you put him into ideograms? How are the actors ever going to get the words right? Won't it all become just paraphrasing?

ELFRANK

And if it does? Have you so little faith in the power of Shakespeare's plots, characters, and situations, as to suppose his works rely completely on his exact choice of archaic words?

UNCLE CLIFF

Archaic? Maybe not so much as you think. I read somewhere that Shakespeare invented an incredible number of the words we still use every day.

LEIF

And you must admit that the word-choice adds an important dimension, not only in Shakespeare's, but in all great literary works and even in all good translations.

ELFRANK

Even so, small doubt that some ideogrammatic translations will prove better than others. But as for the greatest works for the stage, they will, I imagine, remain virtually word-perfect in the repertoire for generations, perhaps even centuries, passed along by rote from actor to actor.

LEIF

To be put back into hard copy once writing is re-invented.

GOTCHER

Or maybe uncoded again. Hey, man, he never said anyone would burn books on purpose. Just that we'd all stop using 'em.

PENNY

They might be able to pass along musicals and operas singer to singer, but what about the musicians?

ELFRANK

Oh, we will allow musical notation, like mathematical, to remain in use. Possibly even the directions—"andante" and so on—which few besides musicians understand anyway.

UNCLE CLIFF

"Andante and so on" are perfectly good words. They just aren't English words. First you said all this is going to be worldwide, and now you're implying only us English-speakers are going to become illiterate?

LEIF

That's right, Cliff. He has left a hole there.

PENNY

Some musical annotations are in English. I once met one in a composition by an American composer—a concert-band arrangement of some film music, I think—"vicious, angular."

UNCLE CLIFF (curious)

How do you play music viciously and angularly?

PENNY

I never could quite figure it out.

ELFRANK

No doubt some genius of the ideogrammatic idiom could do so. Very well, let music have all its annotations in ideogram.

PENNY

But, see here! If people can memorize Shakespeare, they can just as easily memorize the Bible and the Qur'an!

MARY

True; and once people have such a good bone to quarrel over as a set of religious shibboleths, they're not likely to give it up without a good fight.

UNCLE CLIFF

What about scientific papers?

ELFRANK

As many as the general public is capable of understanding anyway, will no doubt enjoy translation into ideograms, which will render them, at least, no less comprehensible than they are in printed forms of traditional languages. A further advantage being that one ideogrammatic translation will work for all.

LEIF

But the original scientist will have to have written it in his or her own language to begin with.

UNCLE CLIFF

Yes! Or there'd be nothing to translate from. Maybe the scientists could write their own in ideograms to begin with, but I doubt that any system of ideograms could capture all the nuances that good scientists need to record and share their work. It's hard enough to do in written vocabularies!

PENNY

And if your ideograms ever got that complex, it wouldn't be long before they'd split up into hundreds of local dialects, and we'd be right back where we started.

ELFRANK

Very good. Let the scientists, mathematicians and musicians retain traditional literacy, as one more secret of their Mysteries, while the rest of the world—

LEIF

The translators will have to be literate, too.

ELFRANK

Not necessarily, when computer programs can be written to perform the task with far greater accuracy, consistency, and technical precision than any human is capable of.

PENNY

"Consistency"—like always using the same word—ideogram in this case—to translate the same word? I once saw someone boast about how accurate some translation of the Bible was because it did that—but doesn't that ignore all the nuances of usages changing over time, and different meanings for the same word? Like the foreign student trying to paraphrase a Shakespeare sonnet, whose Dutch—I think it was—and English dictionary gave nothing but the Dutch equivalent for "a playground" for the English word "fair."

ELFRANK

Reserving the right to question the accuracy of "a playground" even for "fair" as an English noun, I beg to point out that such absurdities would be far less likely to happen with either computer translations or ideograms.

UNCLE CLIFF

If scientists, mathematicians, musicians, and translators can still be literate, why not actors?

MARY

And, no doubt, priests.

MERLINA (laughing)

My, oh, my! You're all taking him so *seriously!* Don't you see he's just pulling everybody's leg?

ELFRANK

Am I?

GOTCHER

Yeah, man, you really oughta be writing science fiction.

ELFRANK

I believe there are those critics—though, for myself, I never read them—who consider supernatural horror a subgenre of science fiction.

LEIF

A world without books is a pretty horrific scenario, however you get there.

BUGSY

I think we're gonna get there by crowding the books out with videos. We'll all still be able to read, we'll just spend our time watching movies and stuff instead.

LEIF

The boy makes a good point. We've already committed more shelves to videos than I enjoy counting.

MARY

The public library shelves, or your own?

UNCLE CLIFF

Careful—he might say "Yes." Going by my brother's and my sister's video libraries, and what I see in the public library, where you have to go through the video shelves to get to the Incredible Shrinking Bookshelves.

PENNY

Why, don't you have a home video library yourself?

UNCLE CLIFF

No, not with all the good old 78 r.p.m. records we stocked up on years ago and now we don't have anything left to play them on. The video format still in use just now has been around so many years, they're overdue to change it, and then everyone's video libraries will be obsolete. The books will still be readable.

BUGSY

Until they're all in ideograms.

LEIF

They still manufacture phonographs that play all the old speeds— thirty-three and a third, forty-five, and seventy-eight. Even sixteen and two-thirds, I think, if you search the right catalogues.

PENNY

It isn't the same. The new phonographs can play old 78's but... they...pick up every pop, every scratch—make them sound terrible.

UNCLE CLIFF

I keep hoping I'll find a really old turntable in an antique store sometime, one I can buy cheap, get back into working condition, and wire up to my modern speakers.

FREEDOM

Merlina, don't you have an old phonograph in your garage?

MERLINA

Oh, no, that one isn't nearly old enough, Freedom! Why it can play 45's and 33's! If it still works at all, of course, after all these years of damp and disuse.

PENNY

I know just what you mean. My folks and I still have boxes unpacked from two moves ago! High time to do some—uh—home archeology.

MARY

Not a bad term for sorting through one's own old clutter.

PENNY

And—have you ever noticed?—the older anything is, the harder it is to throw away, even stuff you really should've thrown out without thinking twice, at the time.

UNCLE CLIFF

All the little stuff antique stores will delight in after a century or so.

MARY

And archeological digs, after a millennium or so. Even—maybe especially—things whose context the very owners have completely forgotten in their own lifetimes. And I'm speaking, you understand, of mental as well as physical clutter.

LEIF

We wonder why we have so much trouble reconstructing our ancestors' past, when we can hardly reconstruct our own.

PENNY

I remember, when I was just a kid, saying "We should drop the Bomb on the Russians before they drop it on us." I must have picked that up from grown-ups around me, but I'm sure I was absolutely sincere at the time. Now, I can't even begin to reconstruct that mindset. But I know I felt it, once.

UNCLE CLIFF

That was the Cold War. Speaking for myself, I can't remember very much at all about my childhood. It happens I was in the Navy circling Cuba during the Missile Crisis, sailing around and around, knowing we could find ourselves in World War Three at any minute. But I hadn't joined the Navy for that or anything like it, I joined up to get an education in electronics.

LEIF

Would the bombs we had back then even work any longer?

GOTCHER

The Big Brass would tell you "No," and explain all the reasons we've got to go on "improving" and testing new super-weapons for decades after we already had enough firepower to blow the world up several times over.

ELFRANK

A misapprehension of sloppy thinking, the result of alarmist propaganda. It would take a great deal more than our puny bombs to shatter this globe as Dark Vater's Doom Star shatters Princess Elala's home planet.

ELMER

Might not exactly blow the whole world apart, but what difference would it make to us if we were all killed and dead?

ELFRANK

Some remnant would always survive—if nowhere else, in shelters dug far beneath the surface of the planet.

GOTCHER

Whoo, boy! "Some remnant would always survive"—more science fiction.

UNCLE CLIFF

Hey, don't knock science fiction. It has a way of coming true.

GOTCHER

Sorry. More myths and fables and fairy-tale fantasy, then.

MARY

Don't knock myths and fables, either. They contain some of the most powerful symbols and archetypes our race has ever discovered.

PENNY

And fairy tales—fantasy as a genre—predates science fiction by millennia. I hate this business some authors have of writing a really fine fantasy and then arguing themselves silly to try and prove it's "really" science fiction. That's classifying the genres by: "If it's good, it's SF—if it's bad, it's fantasy." Making fantasy second-rate by definition.

FREEDOM

You're the science-fiction reader, Uncle Cliff. Which do you prefer, science fiction or fantasy?

UNCLE CLIFF

Yes. That is, I probably read more technical SF, the nuts and bolts stuff, but I cut my teeth on *The Lord of the Rings*, I call the Covenant Chronicles really good, and I wouldn't try to classify either of those as hard SF. Or any of Anthony Pierce's Zanth and other fantasy novels, though he does do some series that are solidly SF, too.

ELFRANK (with a faint snort)

To quote a capsule review: "The first novel of Anthony Pierce's only new trilogy this month."

PENNY

As a big fish says somewhere in *Pinocchio,* "Mine is a personal opinion, and ought to be respected as such." I've only read—read only—one

Anthony Pierce novel so far, but it made me laugh so much that I fully intend to read more.

UNCLE CLIFF

You can borrow some of mine. I have six or eight.

ELFRANK

The finest tip of an iceberg which dwarfs the one that sank the *Titanic*.

ELMER

Talking about old records, like we were a minute ago. Once they've got a good format, why keep changing it? LPs played just fine, what's this business of shoving them out for, what d'you call 'em?—CD's? Not like it is with model trains. HO stays HO, and you can always find it. Maybe they add a new line here and there, but they don't scrap all the old formats because they've got something newer.

UNCLE CLIFF

Maybe not, but sometimes we really have to search for the older stuff, and end up getting N.O.S. out of dusty boxes from the back room.

PENNY

"N.O.S."?

UNCLE CLIFF

"New Old Stock." Old, but never used.

PENNY

Superannuated virgins? *(to herself: Like me.)*

GOTCHER

Y'wanta know why they keep changing these formats on us? Same reason they keep right on developing and testing new bombs! Oh, yeah, they *say* the new stuff works a lot better—smoother, more dependable, and all that jazz—but it's really to keep the Big Business Juggernaut running roughshod over the ecosystem, man. Kicking hobnail boots right in Mother Nature's face. Making jobs so we can all live like mass-produced millionaires right up to the blazing—or whimpering—end.

PENNY

Isn't it—in large part—that is, I tend to put a lot of the blame on any economic theory that says only material goods have any "productive" value, and human services are more or less unproductive drudgery. It might have been different in Adam Smith's day—with a numerically huge servant class—but today we've got sales outlets crammed with cheap, unsold junk that factory workers got paid more money for turning out than "service" people like teachers and nurses earn for really valuable work.

LEIF

I'd have to take a harder look at comparative pay scales, but I'm reasonably sure Adam Smith—the eighteenth century giant, not his modern namesake—didn't originate the idea of goods being valuable productions and services mere unproductive busy work. I'm sure that idea goes back to the years before they were calling the general subject "Economics," and that by reading back farther you might find that the venerable Adam Smith actually modified the older idea somewhat to the service people's advantage.

PENNY

Thank you. Maybe I'll tackle *The Wealth of Nations* again.

GOTCHER

Hey, man, maybe we *oughta* bomb ourselves right off the face of the home planet. Give poor old Mother Nature a chance to start everything up from scratch.

BUGSY

Like in that old cartoon. Anyhow, I'm sure glad they developed videos.

PENNY

I think I know what cartoon you're talking about. The humans bomb themselves into extinction, and then the animals find the Bible in the wreckage of a church, and an owl reads it and says, "Looks as if they had a pretty good set of rules. Trouble was, they didn't follow them." So the animals recreate civilization the way it should have been, and it ends up with them coming into church for Christmas Eve service, very Dickensian, all in old-fashioned costume, smiling and wishing one another,

"Merry Christmas." It made a deep impression on me when I saw it as a kid, but now I can't help wondering how a nuclear holocaust could kill all the humans and leave the other animals unharmed.

ELFRANK

One might suggest that God spared all those creatures guiltless of making and using the Bomb. And may even have given souls to the animals, in lieu of the human forfeiture.

FREEDOM

Animals don't need to be given souls all of a sudden. They have souls anyway, just as much as we do.

ELFRANK

That remains debatable. I do not, however, say that I myself suggest this solution, only that someone else might.

GOTCHER (shaking his head)

You ain't making the case any better for God, man! The fact is, we aren't all of us humans guilty of the Bomb. A heck of a lot of us have been protesting it for all we're worth, and ought to survive right along with the animals, if there were any of this famous "divine justice" in your God.

BUGSY

Yeah, the one you saw with the Bomb, that was a new version of a famous cartoon they made after World War One. I've seen 'em both, back to back.

MERLINA

Yes, I can see that with only the weapons we had before the atom bomb, it might have been possible to imagine us killing ourselves off and still leaving animal survivors.

LEIF

Possible, but highly unlikely, considering how many of us there were even at the time of the First World War.

ELFRANK

I trust you are not about to introduce that dreary and long disproved Malthusian argument of impending overpopulation into the discussion.

PENNY

Malthus has *not* been disproved! If anything, the twentieth century has proven Malthus' point beyond his own wildest—

ELFRANK

What? Would you call yourself a Catholic and advocate birth control?

UNCLE CLIFF

Let her finish, if you please.

PENNY

That is…uh… Thank you, Cliff. The thing is, Malthus argued only that the population *could* increase at a geometrical rate, if it were unchecked, and then spent most of his book examining the checks that kept it from increasing so rapidly. One of them, by the way, was a high standard of living, that keeps it down naturally—

ELFRANK

If by "naturally" you mean techniques available to the selfish rich.

UNCLE CLIFF

Shh!

PENNY

Not necessarily. They can just as well use techniques approved by the Church. The point is, if we want to avoid overpopulation, we should work to better living conditions for everybody. And if you're about to push abortion into it—Malthus demonstrates how the availability of infanticide in a society actually tends to *increase* the population, because people feel free to have babies, and then find they can't bear to expose them, after all—so the number of babies engendered and not killed outweighs the number that would have been conceived in the first place, if infanticide hadn't been available. I suspect he'd make the same argument about abortion on demand, so, if you want to keep the population climbing, you should welcome legalized abortion!

ELFRANK

Now, see—

PENNY

In fact, in spite of our two World Wars, the twentieth century has seen a population growth that Malthus himself never predicted, only thought possible without the natural checks to population. Of course, war itself is only a short-term check, and, in the long run, another spur to population increase. When I was a kid, the world's population was about two billion, and some author whom you would have loved, Mr. Craftlove, said it was increasing by only one percent a year, and called that "reassuring." Well, I worked it out, and at one percent a year, compounded yearly, I saw we were going to hit six billion by the turn of the twentieth century.

BUGSY

Like that game with the checkerboard? Put one cent on the first square, double it on the next square, keep on doubling, and by the last square—

GOTCHER

You could just about pay off the National Debt.

PENNY

Well, I…guess…I'm done.

GOTCHER

Yeah, but I'm not. I'd like to go back to this business about us wiping ourselves out and leaving the animals to take over. It's something like the story of Noah's Ark, right there in your Bible, man. Let's just say for a minute that all those other folks except old Noah and his family really were guilty enough to deserve what happened to them—

ELFRANK

Not such a great stretch of the imagination, if they resembled society today.

GOTCHER

All right, man, say they were. My point is, God saved his so-called "righteous remnant" that time—if you believe it—didn't he? Along with at least some of all the innocent animals. Now, suppose the whole Noah family had gotten themselves washed overboard during the storm, and left the animals to start society up again all by themselves?

UNCLE CLIFF

At a single breeding pair for each species, the gene pool would have been much too small to prove viable.

GOTCHER

Gene pool wasn't that much better for the Noah family, man! Like I say, the whole story's bullshit.

MARY

As so-called historical fact, of course it is. Its power lies in its archetypal meaning. The Deluge appears long before the Bible in human history. The pre-Biblical account which actually constitutes a very short section of the Gilgamesh Saga is no doubt itself a late occurrence of a deep-seated common fear that reoccurs whenever any of us either experiences an actual flood situation or suffers a nightmare about rapidly rising water.

PENNY

I've had that one over and over, all my life. Different details, but always the tide—or whatever—coming up too fast.

ELFRANK

It might be to your eternal profit to interpret the water as fire.

ELMER

Here, now. It's one thing to talk about religion, but no more of that!

GOTCHER

Yeah, man, if there do turn out to be any Pearly Gates, I'd rather take my chances alongside her than you.

ELFRANK

If we are to have no commentary regarding eternal destinations, that last opinion should be banned as well as mine.

PENNY

Frank's right. Fair is fair.

GOTCHER

Like the Chinese say, once a word is spoken, a whole team of horses can't pull it back. I can only apologize for what I say, man, but for what I think—my thoughts are my own.

MERLINA

As are everyone's.

MARY

The Gospel of Thomas quotes Jesus as saying that if you bring forth what is within you, what you bring forth will save you.

MERLINA

But if bringing forth whatever you have within you hurts somebody else?

FREEDOM

How far does anyone have the right to save themselves by destroying someone else?

ELFRANK

While eschewing the so-called "Gospel of Thomas" as apocryphal writing of a probably heretical nature, which had much better have remained lost, I would propose that if, by "destroying someone else," you mean bringing the second party to a proper sense of the error of his—or her—ways, the first party has every right, if not actual duty.

GOTCHER

One party's destruction is another party's salvation. Whatever all that may mean.

LEIF

No writing "had better remain lost." If nothing else, the Dead Sea Scrolls and Nag Hammadi Library and such newly discovered ancient texts give us more windows on the mindsets of the time of Jesus and his earliest followers.

ELFRANK

What remains heresy now, was equally heresy then.

PENNY

Not necessarily. Up until—I think about the middle of the nineteenth century—it was perfectly okay for a Catholic in good standing to question Mary's Immaculate Conception. Every time the Church says all Catholics absolutely have to believe something or other, the Church makes it that much harder for thinking people to stay Catholic. And why? What difference does it make to living a good Catholic, Christian life according to the Beatitudes and Jesus' parable of the Final Judgment, whether you believe that Mary was immaculately conceived, or not? Besides, every time they try to stamp out any heresy and erase it from believers' minds completely, it just surfaces again a few centuries later in the minds of people who think it's their own brand new insight.

> *Gotcher applauded. After a few seconds, Uncle Cliff joined in, then some of the others. Penny Wright flushed and hung her head, as if more taken aback by her own tirade, than pleased with it.*

ELFRANK

One might suggest that the gravest of all errors—this time I shall not go so far as to label it "heresy"—is supposing that orthopraxy does not hinge upon orthodoxy.

BUGSY

Ortho-what?

GOTCHER

Let's see: orthodoxy is "right thinking," so orthopraxy's gotta be "right doing." Give me orthopraxy any old time, and I kind of think Jesus would have said the same.

ELFRANK

How can an atheist appeal to the authority of the Son of God and Second Person of the Trinity?

GOTCHER

Hey, man, I don't have to believe Jesus was any of that to believe that what he was, was a pretty fair guru and practical moral philosopher.

MERLINA

Saint James says,"Show me thy faith apart from works, and I by my works will show thee my faith." Doesn't that apply to orthodoxy and—what's the other word, again?

LEIF

Orthopraxy.

PENNY

What a good word. I love it! Orth-o-prax-y.

> *At this point, Eliza reappeared, in her role of hostess, to summon the company to the crowning meal of the day.*

CHAPTER 26

They found a fine pork roast in possession of the table, wafting forth a tempting aroma as it held dominion over serving bowls of whipped potatoes, gravy, green beans almondine, a fine chopped cranberry-orange relish, steaming rolls, assorted pickles, and that stick-to-the-ribs satisfaction which still goes by the title of "dressing" or "stuffing," even when it is no longer stuffed into whatever roasted meat or fowl may or may not (as in the present case) boast a natural cavity to contain it.

As had been their wont all weekend, in deference to the advertised subject of their retreat as well as the expressed opinion of Frank Craftlove, all bowed their heads for a moment while Uncle Cliff produced a brief and ecumenical ad-lib blessing, Craftlove crossing himself with enough ostentation to justify Penny Wright (in her own mind) not doing so, whilst Bugsy surreptitiously, Gotcher and the dogs openly if in polite silence, ogled and sniffed the food. The preliminaries thus executed, Elmer carved the roast—a task he performed quite capably, in defiance of all the assorted jokes concerning modern men's and even women's incompetence in this area—whilst around him the passing of side dishes happily commenced.

Little conversation happened beyond the essential pleasantries of distribution, until all were served and munching. After the lapse of enough time to have tasted everything, Merlina complimented the cook heartily on a delicious supper.

ELFRANK

I should have called so sumptious a repast "dinner," when served at this hour of the day.

UNCLE CLIFF

We've always called it "dinner" at midday and "supper" in the evening, in my family.

PENNY

And in mine, it's always been "lunch" at noon and "dinner" in the evening. Except on Sundays, when "dinner"—the big meal—could come anytime between about two o'clock and four or five o'clock, and if we got hungry in the evening, we snacked.

LEIF

Interesting. As nearly as I've been able to figure out, medieval and early modern custom put "dinner"—the principal and most elaborate meal—rather shortly after midday, followed by a light evening supper and maybe a bedtime snack actually munched in bed, at least by the classes who had servants to bring it to them there. By about the middle of the nineteenth century, "dinner" was moving down later and later in the day, its noontime place being taken by "nuncheon," "luncheon," or "lunch," a word that originally could mean a snack at any hour of the day. As the dinner hour settled at eight or even nine p.m. for the upper classes, a light formal meal called "tea" appeared in the late afternoon—toast, cake, maybe some boiled eggs, things like that. In the lower classes, this became an early evening "high tea" very much like our Midwest American country "suppers."

PENNY

Once an English friend explained to me their mysteries of caffeine consumption, and why I couldn't get a cup of tea after lunch. First thing in the morning, it's tea—in bed, if you have anyone to bring you a cup. At breakfast—I'm not sure, but I *think* that was the one time you could drink either. At "elevenses" in the morning—what we'd call "coffee break"—it's always tea. After luncheon, always coffee. Midafternoon, including the intermission or "interval" at a theater matinee, always tea. After dinner and during theater "intervals" in the evening, always coffee.

BUGSY

Huh! I thought the English always drank just tea. All the time.

UNCLE CLIFF

Sounds like they drink more coffee than we do.

PENNY

And very good coffee, too.

UNCLE CLIFF

I'll have to take your word for it. I like the smell of fresh coffee, but just the smell. I don't drink it.

FREEDOM

Uncle Cliff got all the way through his hitch in the Navy without drinking a single cup of coffee.

GOTCHER

How did you stay awake?

UNCLE CLIFF (repeating—as all of us tend so often to repeat—this time for the benefit of the group, what he had already shared with Penelope alone)

Well, one time I didn't. One time they called me for my watch. I answered, but fell asleep again right away, and dreamed I got up and went through my whole routine, duties and all, down to getting back in bed. I must have dreamed it all in what I think they call "real time," while my buddies covered for me by taking my duties. Afterwards, when I woke up for my next watch, I could hardly believe it.

PENNY (like Cliff, repeating herself for the collective benefit)

One time—years ago—I went to a dream workshop—a workshop on dreams...where one fella woke up out of a guided meditation and reported he'd dreamed he finished up the weekend, went home, got a job, got married, raised a family, lived through twenty or thirty years of life—and here he was, back with us again, and all that had been a dream!

ELFRANK

And you believed him? How gullible one becomes when one loses, or even toys with, the moorings of solid faith!

PENNY

Well, he certainly acted sincere about it.

ELFRANK

The trick of acting sincere is stock in trade for every good swindler, confidence artist, or parlor jokester.

UNCLE CLIFF

Seeming to live through decades in a few minutes. There are science fiction stories based on that idea.

ELFRANK

Oh, science fiction!

UNCLE CLIFF

There was a show on one TV series where one of the regular characters lived a whole lifetime in less than an hour, and it turns out to be a record another planetary culture made of their way of life and sent out in a space probe when they knew their sun was about to go nova.

PENNY, GOTCHER, BUGSY, and OTHERS

Wow! *(with or without the exclamation point)*

ELFRANK

I repeat: science fiction. Some, indeed, question whether any television series is or can be more than "space opera" at best.

GOTCHER

Hey, man, don't knock *Space Trek!*

ELFRANK

Those who *must* have space opera in their diet, might chew on the *Space "Wars"* saga, which has at least the advantage of a solid grounding in archetypal symbology.

PENNY

A little too solid a grounding! As I understand it—I saw a PBS show about it—the *Space Wars* filmmakers went straight to Joseph Campden, modeled their plots and characters on everything he had to say based on his lifetime of studying archetypes, and then got him to endorse it. It's all *manufactured* archetypes and imitation folklore. But the real stuff has to well up from our collective unconscious—has to happen without our understanding it's happening. Like *Space "Trek,"* whose authors were only interested in telling stories—"space opera," if you will—with no pretensions about high scholarship. The trouble is, the more you learn about what's going on at the root of this kind of storytelling, the more you disqualify yourself for writing anything but scholarly analysis about it. That's why I think *"Trek"* has a much better chance than *"Wars"* of lasting another century or two.

UNCLE CLIFF

Why can't you just enjoy them both?

PENNY

Oh, I do. When I'm actually watching a *"Wars"* movie, especially in a theater full of *Space Wars* fans, I enjoy it a lot. They're great movies, and depend at least as much on movie archetypes as Homeric or fairy-tale or whatever—especially the first movie. But it's *"Trek"* I keep coming back to in the end. I doubt I'll ever read a *"Wars"* tie-in novel, but every so often I read a *"Trek"* one.

ELFRANK

Thus compounding the waste of time.

LEIF

No more a waste of time, by your own account, than reading what you write yourself, Frank.

ELFRANK

My horror potboilers, cheerfully granted. But when I am sufficiently well-read and prepared to pen my *magnum opus* in apologetic theology, I trust you will think otherwise.

ELIZA

Be careful the potboilers, as you call them, don't take over, and at the end of your day you find *they* were your great work, after all.

ELFRANK

Madam, you chill my blood.

BUGSY

"Apologetic theology"? I thought any word with an -ology in it meant the study of something. Why does anybody need any apology for studying theology?

GOTCHER

It's in the "theology," man, not the "apology." The "theo" part means "God," and God doesn't exist. So "theology" really means "the study of nothing," which is obviously a waste of time. Why shouldn't people apologize for studying nothing?

UNCLE CLIFF

Maybe because they have nothing to apologize about?

PENNY

Oh, well said!

ELFRANK (addressing Gotcher, with a glint of humor)

When the bolt from above strikes you, my benighted friend, I hope and pray it misses the rest of us. *(to Bugsy)* A more serious answer to your query, lad, is that "apologetic" in this sense does not signify what we mean by apologizing in the sense of begging forgiveness—although both senses derive from the same Latin root—but, rather, arguing the truth of a proposition.

GOTCHER

"What is truth?" Old Pilate sure spoke a mouthful there!

ELIZA

You may "apologize"—in either sense—for the truth of whatever heavy proposition you like after dessert, but please keep the dinner-table talk light. Remember the house rules we set up.

FREEDOM

I move we save the heavy talk till we're in the living room.

GOTCHER

Fine by me.... Okay, what do we buzz about in the meantime?

MARY

May we return to the apparent passage of time in dreams? There was a famous case of a long and complicated dream about the French Revolution in which, after many adventures, the dreamer was captured, sentenced by the Tribunal to death—

PENNY

And woke up right when the headboard—was it?—fell and hit his neck? Must have been a glancing blow—oh, sorry. I interrupted you.

MARY

You simply anticipated me. Yes, that's the very case. The dreamer guessed that his mind had manufactured that whole dream in the same instant it turned the sudden blow into the shock of the guillotine. Alternately, however, Jung proposes that in such cases it is only the *memory* that the dream manufactures on the spur of the moment.

PENNY

So all those years of life that fellow thought he dreamed in an hour…

MARY

Were a false memory the dream manufactured. Numerous studies indicate that actual activity takes about the same length of time to accomplish in a dream as in waking life.

UNCLE CLIFF

Which would cover my dream of going through my whole watch like I was awake, when I was actually sleeping the same number of hours.

ELFRANK

Hmpf. I should be interested in examining these "numerous studies" to which all too many experts vaguely appeal when in the throes of serious argument.

MARY

Let me have your mailing address, and I'll send you a bibliography.

GOTCHER

Yeah, man, a bibliography. That's a list of books and magazine articles and like that, most of 'em very hard to get and some of 'em maybe made up for the authoritative look of it. Ol' Pop Amisov gave his essay about the substance that dissolves before water hits it such a good bibliography of completely made-up sources, that a bunch of readers thought it was dead serious.

LEIF

And complained when the poor reference librarians failed to locate those sources. I remember something of the episode.

PENNY

So do I. Loved Amisov's article. Did you ever read it, Cliff?

UNCLE CLIFF

I'm not sure. Probably, but I don't remember much about it.

FREEDOM

Uncle Cliff can lose himself completely in a story while he's reading it, and then forget it completely in a month or two.

UNCLE CLIFF *(grinning)*

Yes, but by then I'll have read two or three more. How can I keep all the stories I've read "before" in my mind when the one I'm reading "now" pushes them out?

PENNY

Sounds like a pretty good plan. I've often wished I could swallow some kind of selective forgetfulness pill right before seeing—say—a G. and S. opera, so it'd be like seeing and hearing it all for the very first time. Of course, I'd want the effect to be temporary, so that later on I could remember all the times I'd seen or read or studied it before.

LEIF

What about the plot synopsis in the program? Wouldn't reading that rather spoil the effect?

PENNY

Oh, I never read those synopses ahead of time, any more than I ever read introductory essays to a classic novel before the novel itself, because they usually give away so much of the plot. Or assume the reader already knows it anyway. Unless they're by the original author him- or herself. Then they're usually safe to read first. Otherwise, they really ought to be printed at the back of the book, for you to read last. That's when I read 'em, anyway. Everyone has the right to be surprised on the first reading. The way the author intended. Same thing for plays and operas.

ELFRANK

I beg to disagree. Does not every author secretly cherish the dream of one day having his—or her—works achieve the status of classics, whose plots actually gain power by being well known ahead of time?

PENNY

That's how I know whether it's really any good—by how well it stands up to rereading, or to seeing over and over.

UNCLE CLIFF

But there are stories and movies that are really exciting the first time around, and lose their edge—their punch—the next time, when you already know what's going to happen.

PENNY

In one of the Oz books, Baum describes a book-tree. Its books—which have to be ripe when they're picked, or the plots are confused and the pictures poor—anyway, they last for only one reading before they dry up and crumble away.

LEIF

As all our books, even the most cherished volumes on paper of high rag content, threaten to do with the passage of centuries, unless properly treated and cared for.

UNCLE CLIFF

Doesn't that happen in *The Time Machine?*

FREEDOM

Oh, the best books will always go on being reprinted in new editions.

LEIF

Not necessarily.

MARY

Which are the "best" books? Even one's own opinion often changes from time to time. I would say that books, and films, stand up to rereading or repeated viewing in measure as they appeal to different depths in the reader or viewer. Since we ourselves are always growing and developing, in a sense it cannot accurately be said that we are still the same person when we read a book the second time; and, therefore, it is arguably not quite the same book.

ELIZA

As Heraclitus said, You can't cross the same river twice.

PENNY

That could be why authors are notoriously bad judges of their own works. That is, either they know all the thought that went into a novel—all its background—and that gives it a richness in their opinion that nobody else sees...or else they've forgotten most of that background, and seeing it the way everybody else sees it comes as a big disappointment to them, where maybe other readers, who never knew the backstory at all, find the work in question pretty good.

ELFRANK

Could that suggest that my potboilers might actually rise superior to my own estimation of them?

LEIF

Anything's possible. All I can tell you today is that they're pretty popular.

ELFRANK

So much I knew already from my royalty statements. But popularity—need I point out—is scarcely a reliable indicator of quality, unless in the negative sense.

PENNY

Dickens was very popular in his day, and his works have stood the test of time.

GOTCHER

Gilbert loved him. Thought he should have been made a duke for his literary merit.

ELFRANK

Perhaps. But Gilbert, as I recall Victorian chronology, was already in the generation following Dickens, and therefore better able to judge the lasting power of his work. It requires a certain passage of time to recognize and prove true literary merit.

PENNY

Sometimes more than a single generation. Look at Jane Austen.

LEIF

As I recall, Sir Walter Scott recognized her merit in her own lifetime.

PENNY

Few other people did. I don't think she was rediscovered until early in the twentieth century.

FREEDOM

She wrote all those romances, didn't she?

PENNY

Some people still don't appreciate her work.

LEIF

It only goes to prove that authors are as fallible as everyone else when it comes to judging one another's work.

ELMER

How about dessert?

BUGSY

Yeah, man, that's something we're all pretty good judges of!

GOTCHER

The lad speaketh a mouthful.

UNCLE CLIFF

Pun intended?

GOTCHER

Why, shore, if you like.

UNCLE CLIFF

Good.

CHAPTER 27

Dessert comprised what our British cousins call a "trifle," a designation which, in the opinion of Pearl Bonami, applied—if at all—to the fact that it could be prepared well ahead of time and dished up at the last minute: pieces of fruit, left-over white cake, and a suggestion of brandy in cherry-flavored gelatin, topped with generous dollops of real whipped cream. To a diner, the company pronounced it scrumptious.

Dessert being finished, and the evening fair and almost cool, the company repaired to the large fire pit overlooking the lake, where, during a free hour earlier that afternoon, Gotcher with some help from Bugsy had built up tinder, kindling, and logs: a campfire ready for the lighting. Here the humans arranged themselves comfortably, on the permanent rustic benches as well as half a dozen canvas lounge chairs. Pearl showed Gotcher, Elmer, and Uncle Cliff where to set down the supplies they had carried out: thermos jugs of cocoa and coffee; picnic baskets of mugs, chocolate bars, graham crackers, marshmallows, and toasting forks, after which she took her seat ready to preside over passing these things out whenever dinner should be sufficiently digested to allow of their discussion. Eliza and Freedom passed blankets around right away, and everyone settled down to await that deep blue twilight against which the lighting of the fire would show to its most aesthetic advantage.

While they waited, Penny Wright drew from her pocket a folded paper, originally one leaf from a spiral-bound notebook; unfolded it; and used the last of the fading daylight to read aloud the lines she had composed the night before, haunted about equally by the theory that God's existence might be demonstrated from the delicate conditions rendering the universe amenable to life as we know it, and by her feelings for Uncle Cliff, then newly roiled by Freedom's angry reactions to the same.

* * * *

But, don't you see?
To make "What Is" the touchstone of "What Must Be"—
To say our life depends
On a nuclear force of just the right strength,
Or a proton of just the right stability,

Or that slippery concept, a cosmological constant just barely large
enough to exist,
Or a long enough time—as *we* measure time—
And argue that all these things and others being precisely as they are
Demonstrates that God planned afar
For the Big Bang to boil forth humanity…

Is this not to make God subservient to Physics?
As if God were of Nature
Not Creator, but Creature,
And could not have blossomed life forth under any other conditions
Save some almighty Laws of Physics.

Is it not less to study the Mind and the Artistry of God as they are,
Than to cage God within a set of pre-existing principles?
As if God were that Cosmic Cow of northern myth,
Licking away upon the vast salt-ice plains of Science
Until at last she licks free the Giant of Creation.

You call it a "circular" argument
To explain the ultimate laws of nature
By the ultimate laws of nature.
Leaving aside that prejudice against circular explanations
Smacks of slavery to patterns of pure linear thought:
Your "anthropic coincidences" are equally circular, are they not?

What need, in such an argument,
For a Divine Intelligence to choose any set of physical conditions?
Is all this not to make Science our God and label it accordingly?

Or so it seems to me.

ELFRANK

Hmpf. Do you call that a poem?

PENNY

No. I call it a short essay in lines broken up oddly on the page, which
is what most modern poetry, so called, looks like to me.

ELFRANK

That is your deficiency and your loss, but I rejoice that at least you
have enough perception to recognize your own lines for the poor scrawls
they are.

UNCLE CLIFF

Well, *I* liked it.

GOTCHER

Yeah, man, I don't see your beef with it. What? You didn't like the one she read us last night because it rhymed, and now you don't like this one because it doesn't?

ELFRANK

Alas, in a few places, it does. As a poet, I regret to say, she lacks the competence even to refuse accidental rhyme in a set of verses meant not to employ it.

UNCLE CLIFF

Ordinary everyday speech just happens to rhyme sometimes. We can't avoid it.

PENNY

All right, Mr.—Frank, please define "poetry" for us.

ELFRANK

Poetry resembles God in this much: that it is by nature indefinable; but, when encountered, raises a shiver of awe in the percipient.

GOTCHER

No, man, you're wrong there: poetry exists, God doesn't.

MARY

Before we go into that, I'd like to point out that what raises a shiver in one person doesn't necessarily do so in another.

ELFRANK

That is where percipience comes into play.

PENNY

In other words, it's all a matter of taste.

ELFRANK

I trust you recognize that there is such a thing as good taste, and such a thing as bad.

LEIF

There's also such a thing as critics of equally good and educated credentials disagreeing diametrically on what's good and what's not.

ELFRANK

In all such cases—and I confess there are many—I would argue that the critics' apparent perceptual equality is merely spurious.

PENNY

Or a matter of time. It's notorious that each generation forgets works its parents found "immortal," and comes to see that works its parents hated are really excellent.

GOTCHER

Yeah, man, and maybe rediscovers things its grandparents loved and parents rejected—and decides they're really pretty good, after all.

LEIF

Some scholar has observed that in all such cases, the more favorable judgment always proves correct.

ELFRANK

That scholar was, of course, as human and therefore as liable to error as all the rest of us.

GOTCHER, BUGSY, FREEDOM, and several others

with various minor variations in phraseology
What, even you?

PENNY

Wait a minute, here! Play fair—no ganging up on him.

UNCLE CLIFF

Hasn't he been ganging up on you, all by himself?

PENNY

Well...I should have said...maybe...no ganging up on *anybody*. After all...who knows who might be next...maybe me!

MERLINA

Penny is quite right. No ganging up on anybody.

ELIZA

Or at least, since we can't always prevent some opinion or other from proving generally unpopular, let's take it one at a time to disagree, and let...whoever...answer each objection in turn.

GOTCHER

Man, we can't always control mob knee-jerk reactions, either

MARY

No, maybe not. But we can nip them in the bud whenever they happen, and stop, and take a few calming breaths. Penny did the right thing just now.

PENNY

Thank you.

> *There was a short pause, during which all contemplated the dark yet somehow translucent glow of the deepening twilight.*

LEIF

I think it's somewhere in the third *Gormenghast* volume that Peake describes the strange silence which tends to fall, unplanned, on any large gathering every twenty minutes.

BUGSY

There's the first star! Over there.

UNCLE CLIFF

Actually, planet, I think. Probably Venus, maybe Jupiter.

FREEDOM

Does the first planet count as the first star? "Planet white, planet bright, first planet I see tonight—I wish I may, I wish I might, have the wish I wish tonight…"

ELFRANK

I should wish that all poets, so called, might henceforth imitate the lucent simplicity of that simple folk verse. Scanning the more usual "star" for "planet," of course.

BUGSY

But it rhymes with the identical same word.

ELFRANK

Which technique our Medieval ancestors admired.

FREEDOM

Could be one of the reasons we use "medieval" as an insult.

PENNY

We shouldn't. We're wrong when we do. Every age—every era—has its own fashions. Who knows what clumsinesses our descendants will find in the fashions of our own era? Who knows what gross mistakes *we're* making, and can't even see 'em?

GOTCHER

Y'know, talking about not ganging up on anyone, haven't all of you kind of made a game out of ganging up on me over this God and religion thing?

ELFRANK

If you consider the problem of where you will spend Eternity in the light of a "game."

ELIZA

I hope that, at least, we have tried to keep it polite and courteous.

GOTCHER

(glancing at Frank)

Yeah, most of the time, more or less.

ELFRANK

Oh, by all means, in all situations, let us always place courtesy above truth. It matters less whether I see someone damned than whether I handle him gently while trying to snatch him from the fiery pit.

LEIF

Yes, but you won't snatch him from the pit by insulting him.

MARY

How true! Arguing by means of insult and satire tends only to harden the enemy's existing attitude and polarize positions.

PENNY

But what about Voltaire? and Jonathan Swift?—That is, I mean, what about all the writers and thinkers who fought social—and governmental—evil by means of trenchant biting satire? Didn't they help make the world a better place?

GOTCHER

Yeah, man.

ELFRANK

Did they? Look around and tell me how "good" a place you find this world we live in today.

UNCLE CLIFF

A pretty good one, all in all, I'd say. I know I wouldn't like to live any time or place in the past. Which is not to say there might not be even better times coming in the future.

PENNY

If we all work at it.

ELFRANK

I very much question your optimism, unless God takes a miraculous hand with the world, as promised in the Apocalypse.

GOTCHER

You mean the "Book of Revelation"? Man, now there's an opium trip if there ever was one!

MERLINA

How do you know that God's "miraculous hand" may not be the force inspiring us humans to work toward a better future?

UNCLE CLIFF

I like that.

FREEDOM

Yes, you two seem to think so much alike, don't you, Uncle Cliff?

ELMER

Only so many thoughts in the world to go around. Not surprising if some of 'em turn up in more than one head.

GOTCHER

Naw, man, our thoughts are like our fingerprints—no two alike!

MARY

But all made up of very similar whorls and patterns.

LEIF

So that it takes an expert to identify fingerprints with certitude.

MARY

If there were no overall similarities in our thought patterns, any scientific study of the mind would prove impossible.

ELFRANK

(Emits an odd little sound.)

MARY

Don't snort, Frank! Religion would be impossible, too!

ELFRANK

I was merely clearing my throat.

LEIF

Systematic studies of any kind would prove impossible. Actually, systems themselves would prove impossible.

MERLINA

There goes my yarn shop. Who could teach anyone else how to knit or crochet?

FREEDOM

And needlepoint?

ELMER

There goes model railroading, too.

ELIZA

I suppose that language would be impossible, as well. Since we can in fact communicate intelligibly with one another, we might as well try to get somewhere.

BUGSY

I'd like to get to the s'mores.

MUTTWUMP

Woof!

PUMPKIN

Woof! Woof! Woof!

PENNY

I'm still pretty full from that wonderful dinner.

PEARL (getting out the marshmallows and toasting forks)

Let those who want 'em, have 'em.

Soon half the company were toasting marshmallows, while Pearl readied and passed around the graham crackers and squares of chocolate, and the stars, little caring about any concerns but their estellar own, popped by twos, threes, and hundreds into view. Less impartial than the stars, those members of the Loon Lake gathering who had earlier eschewed the campfire treat, finding themselves overpowered by the scent of scorching marshmallow and the sounds of happy munching, claimed and in due course were crunching their own. Mary Arrowsmith surprised the rest by not liking chocolate and therefore eating her marshmallow—carefully browned rather than blackened—naked between its crackers; in happy compromise, the librarian was quick to beg her share of the bar and enjoy his marshmallow and crackers with a double layer of chocolate.

The dogs were not forgotten, and, seeing Gotcher slipping chocolate to Pumpkin, Bugsy slipped a small square to Muttwump as well, just so as not to let him feel left out.

LEIF

Who invented these, I wonder.

BUGSY

The same caveman or cavewoman who invented the wheel?

LEIF

Unfortunately for the popular image, the people of the Stone Age—who by and large probably did not live full-time in caves—did not invent the wheel. That came much later, at different times in different civilizations around the world. I doubt that the Stone Age had either chocolate bars or graham crackers, either.

UNCLE CLIFF

A doctor named Graham invented graham crackers in the nineteenth century, I think. That's why we call them "graham" crackers.

PENNY

Originally a health food, weren't they?

BUGSY

Poor old cave people!—wherever they lived full-time. No chocolate and no graham crackers. What about marshmallows?

LEIF

Originally made from a plant—the marsh mallow—but whether Stone Age people had yet figured out how to eat it, I don't know.

MARY (teasingly)

Can't you look it up, O Reference Librarian?

LEIF

I'm not sure *that* one can ever be definitively answered, even with the Internet. But since the Stone Age didn't have sugar, chances are they didn't enjoy confectionery.

PEARL

Had honey, didn't they? Wonderful what you can do with honey sometimes.

PENNY

I would love to try a real, old-fashioned marshmallow made out of marsh mallows.

FREEDOM

I'd love to try a really original Coke.

UNCLE CLIFF

That could be risky, Freedom

GOTCHER

Yeah, man, it was cocaine that put the "coke" in the real first-formula stuff. What a kick! And all they can use nowadays is an overload of caffeine.

PENNY

Many years ago I had a children's cookbook that told how to make these, only it called them "Pixie's Delight." I made them in a little toy oven, baking them graham cracker, chocolate, and all. It was quite a culture shock when I went to Girl Scout camp some years later and found 'em calling them "s'mores" and toasting only the marshmallow.

BUGSY

Hey, wouldn't it make a great cartoon gimmick to show Goofy or Elmer Fudd or someone stringing the whole thing on a stick—chocolate, crackers, marshmallow and all—and toasting it over the campfire whole?

ELFRANK

(after clearing his throat again)
I'm sure all this is of vital and permanent importance, but—

GOTCHER

The Great American Confection, man! As close to heaven as anybody's ever gonna get in this land. *(singing)* "This land is your land, this land is my land..."

> *All—or enough of the party to justify use of that word—joined in, taking the words where necessary from Gotcher's lead.*

PENNY

If we ever decide to change the National Anthem, that one has my vote!

FREEDOM

Hasn't "The Star-Spangled Banner" always been our National Anthem?

LEIF

Only since about 1931 or so.

ELFRANK

Another fascinating sidetrack, I am sure. At least my fellow author's not particularly poetic lines had the merit of cleaving to what was supposed to be the central topic of our weekend, as He is indeed the central topic, recognized (or not) as such of all existence: our Maker.

GOTCHER

I don't know about you, man, but it was my parents who made me, like their parents made them, and so on back to the protoplasmal primordial atomic globule. We made ourselves.

BUGSY

Yeah, but which came first, the chicken or the egg?

PENNY

The egg. Since we should probably call Pooh-Bah's ancestral protoplasmal globule an "egg."

UNCLE CLIFF

Good! We've finally got that one solved.

ELFRANK

I confess surprise that anyone calling himself or herself "Catholic" should accept at face value the heresy of Evolutionism.

PENNY

The Vatican thinks otherwise now. Where have you been?

ELFRANK

The Vatican has pronounced only that the theory of evolution might be permissible with certain cautions—

BUGSY

Gee, that's big of the Vatican!

ELIZA

Ulysses Samson, shh.

ELFRANK

—as, for example, you may believe that we are descended from the ape if you are prepared to believe that Adam and Eve were apes.

PENNY

Why not? The apes might be more alarmed than we are at the thought they might've spawned us. But I think you'd better reread the latest Vatican statements.

UNCLE CLIFF

Actually, Darwin didn't say that we descended from apes. He said that apes and humans have a common ancestor.

ELFRANK

And the Book of Genesis says that all—the first apes and the first humans—were created direct from God's own hand.

LEIF

It's an awfully small gene pool, when you think about it: one reproducing couple. Does the Book of Genesis say God made the ancestors of all species two by two, like the passengers of Noah's Ark?

PENNY

Somebody has pointed out that, since "with God one day is as a thousand years and a thousand years as one day," the "days" of the first chapter of Genesis could each have been millions of years long. Why couldn't evolution have been the means God used to shape humanity—and the rest of creation—out of the "mud" of the Big Bang?

GOTCHER

Wow! If that don't muddy the waters.

LEIF

It's true there seems to be a certain ambiguity about the opening sentences of Genesis. It seems they could mean, at least in some translations, not that God actually created everything from nothing, but, rather, that He molded an existing waste into the heavens and earth we know and love.

ELFRANK

This is why the Church long found it better to teach her children the true meaning of the Bible, rather than permit, nay, even encourage them to read it for themselves! A piece of wisdom she may have been ill-advised to abandon in our generation.

PENNY

If I hadn't heard a good Catholic like you say so, I'd never have believed our Church used to forbid lay people to read the Bible. I'd have thought it was just another Protestant slander.

UNCLE CLIFF and GOTCHER (speaking simultaneously)

Hey! We don't slander
Hey, man, a plague
    Catholics any more.
        on both your houses.

PENNY

So what you're saying is, "We Catholics don't need the Bible— we've got *Tra-di-tion!*"

> *Uncle Cliff, picking up on her pronunciation, began to whistle the Broadway tune "Tradition," in which Gotcher, Mary Arrowsmith, and several others immediately joined, humming or singing. The librarian appeared to know most of the words, but had no chance to deliver them all, for Frank Craftlove soon intervened in an overriding voice.*

ELFRANK

On the contrary, Catholics not only need the Bible, but—tradition- ally—respect it far more than any breakaway creed that throws this Pearl of Great Price to the swine of every passing popular opinion.

PEARL

Seems to me that Jesus talked directly to the common men and women, and even liked 'em a lot better than He liked the scribes and Pharisees.

MERLINA

That's right. And if He talked directly to the commoners in His time, why shouldn't we commoners read His words directly for ourselves in our time?

LEIF

All we have of his words, you mean. There's a great deal of scholarly debate as to what he actually said. At the time the Gospels were written, it was considered good biography—in so far as they thought of it as "biography"—to put into the subject's mouth not what he was known to have said, but what the "biographer" believed had been in his character to say.

MARY

Also, all of us can hear, or read, exactly the same words, and each find something variant in them: whatever he or she is psychologically prepared to find. This explains how the same sacred text can have so many different interpretations, some of them wildly opposed and mutually contradictory.

ELFRANK

Scholars and psychologists—present company excepted—are the scribes and Pharisees of our day.

MARY

"Present company excepted" is hardly a polite expression, Frank. Rather, it affirms the speaker's opinion that the generalization holds true for the "present company's" group as a whole.

ELFRANK

And does it not?

UNCLE CLIFF

I think we'd better drop the subject.

BUGSY

Aw, it's just gettin' good.

PENNY

Poor old scribes and Pharisees! They were really the educated and moral elite of their time and place. Why, Frank, back then I think *you* might've been called a scribe and/or a Pharisee—and taken it as a high compliment—right up until the time Jesus made his public appearance.

ELFRANK

I do not take it as a compliment now.

UNCLE CLIFF

More s'mores, anyone?

PENNY

Yes, I'll have one—thanks.

Most of the others following suit, soon a dozen more marshmallows were on long forks flirting with the flames. As Gotcher's flared up, he blew it out and began anecdotally,

GOTCHER

Here's one that should've made it into the printed Bible, if some editor hadn't left it on the cutting-room floor. When they bring that adulteress up to Jesus, and he says, "Let whoever is without sin cast the first stone," a fella who's just been to the bath house picks up a stone. His neighbor goes, "Hey, what's wrong with you, man? Didn't you hear him say, 'Let the one without sin cast the first stone?'" "Oh, I thought he said, 'without *scent.*'"

Uncle Cliff and several others chuckled or groaned in polite appreciation, while Gotcher went on,

So then they all start talking it over, like "What did he mean by that, man?" "Hey, I know! He's without sin, isn't he?" "Yeah, so he wants to cast the first stone!" "Here you go, Jesus old boy—here's the first stone, cast it!" So Jesus takes the adulteress and walks away with her, shaking his head and saying, "The problem isn't sin, it's stupidity."

All laughed, but Frank Craftlove quickly stifled his chuckle by turning it into a frown.

ELFRANK

The problem is dual: both stupidity *and* sin.

GOTCHER

Hey, man, watch out for Dualism.

ELFRANK

While I find at first blush nothing absolutely heretical or even particularly irreverent about your gloss, it is definitely extra-Scriptural and therefore in no way binding.

PENNY

But maybe the whole adulteress story is extra-Scriptural. Haven't I read somewhere that for generations—maybe even a century or more—it was a—what do you call it?—"free-floating logion," a sort of piece of oral tradition, folklore—

GOTCHER

"Urban legend," like we're calling the stuff now.

PENNY

—and when they finally decided to put it into the written record, they weren't quite sure where, so some ancient manuscripts insert it at a different spot in John and some even put it in Luke.

ELFRANK

That is no argument against its Scriptural status, since the entire Gospel in all its pieces existed first in the oral tradition.

MERLINA

Don't you mean that it existed first of all by actually happening?

GOTCHER

Yeah, man, but did it ever really happen? Ain't that the big question?

ELFRANK

To doubt it is heresy.

PENNY

Yes, but when one Gospel says one thing and another has an entirely different take on the same thing, which one are we supposed to believe? I mean—I'm not questioning that all Scripture is "inspired"—whatever that really means—but is every single word, every single phrase, really…golden…or is it that every book of the Bible contains some essential truth? Is it sort of like a bowl of nuts, for us to dig the kernels out of the shells—the window-dressing details?

ELFRANK

How little acquaintance you show with the devotion of *lectio divina!*

PENNY

No—I've tried that, rolling the text around word by word and syllable by syllable to get a mystical meaning out of it—to "let the text read you." Trouble is, it seems to work with *any* printed text, not just the Bible. In the right mind, you can do it with Dickens or *Moby Dick* or probably even Catharine Hartland.

GOTCHER

So, is *all* writing inspired by God?

PENNY

I'd say it is. All sincere writing, anyway. Doesn't St. Paul have a verse somewhere about "all scripture being inspired"—and then he quotes a line from a Pagan play, so he literally means "all *writing,*" not just what the Jewish people regarded as sacred texts.

ELFRANK

When the Jewish people of the Diaspora, in the generations immediately preceding the time of Christ, set out to translate their ancient holy texts into Greek, seventy of their greatest scholars first sat down to work singly, each by himself. At length coming together to compare and collate their independent translations, all seventy were found to be identical to the last jot and tittle, proving the Divine Inspiration not only of the original but also of the translation: the Septuagint.

Uncle Cliff made a short, whimsical siffle of amused negation, but immediately tried to apologize.

UNCLE CLIFF

Sorry, but…you really believe that?

PENNY

Sounds like a pious legend to me.

FREEDOM

Like little George Washington and the cherry tree.

LEIF

Or the Spartan boy who let the fox gnaw away his stomach rather than confess he had it hidden under his tunic.

BUGSY

Ych! Didn't they see the blood?

GOTCHER

The point, man, is that all these tales get made up to comfort and inspire people, forge a national identity or just bear up under the strain of everydayness.

PENNY

All I know is, it certainly didn't carry through to our own times, as witness the great number of English versions we can take our pick from.

ELFRANK

The Jewish people were united in their piety. We were divided already in ours by the time the earliest English translations were made—all of them questionable until the Douai—and now we are a veritable melting-pot of creeds as well as races.

LEIF

If you think the Jewish people were ever united in their approach to their faith, you know neither history nor humanity. No group of people has ever been or ever will be as much united as all that. In fact, a lot of the Bible itself describes and argues the pros and cons of various divergent viewpoints.

PENNY

I think religions are languages for talking about God, and no two of us anywhere speak exactly the same language, exactly the same way.

The trick is to find enough people who speak a close enough dialect to communicate and worship together.

MARY

Yet we do share a vast treasury of symbols and archetypes in our collective unconscious: a common sign language far more universal than mere words.

UNCLE CLIFF

The trick is understanding it.

PENNY

But isn't there a certain—looseness—in the symbols? Don't they mean slightly different things to different people?

ELFRANK

The Mohammedans are wise in this much, at least: that they insist their own sacred texts, so called, are valid only in the original language and therefore, as scripture, untranslatable.

GOTCHER

Naw, man, doesn't exactly work. Even if Mohammed's words all meant exactly the same thing to every last one of his own contemporaries, times change, cultures change, and language changes right along with 'em—any language, even so-called "sacred" language. You might be able to study Papa Mohammed's language till you got fluent enough to read his book in the original, but you couldn't ever get enough inside his time and place and brain to understand it exactly like he meant it.

PENNY

The Red Queen's race. "It takes all the running you can do to stay in the same place."

BUGSY

Who wants to stay in the same place all the time?

GOTCHER

Out of the mouths of babes, sucklings, and older kids, too!

LEIF

Books are like stepping-stones. Isn't it better to translate so that something can be understood, than to leave it untranslated and understand nothing?

ELFRANK

Always providing that the substance was worth comprehension in the first place.

PENNY

Maybe books are like dry stepping-stones in the original language, when it's fresh and contemporary—and become slippery, moss-covered stepping-stones in translation. The older, the more moss-covered.

LEIF

Even in the original language, moss grows over the years, with the changing fashions. A really good translator might actually manage to scrape a bit of the moss off an ancient text.

UNCLE CLIFF

Like an archeologist carefully dusting off a potsherd?

MARY

To mix metaphors.

PENNY

I've sometimes thought maybe I should have been an archeologist.

BUGSY

Yeah! Like Indy Jones.

PENNY

Not like Indy Jones! That's not archeology—crashing through the sites to grab anything made of gold and leave the total context in ruins—worse ruins than before. That's looting.

UNCLE CLIFF

It might have been considered archeology during Indy Jones's early career, when archeology was still an infant science, more or less. But in the third movie Indy's own father, also an archeologist, decries his son's approach.

GOTCHER

Also, there's lots of extenuating circumstances—bad guys mucking up the valuable sites anyway, with silly little things like world wars.

PENNY

Getting back to the subject of translations—isn't there always necessarily some question what you're actually reading, the original author's vision or the translator's? I've read two different translations of "The Little Fir Tree"—in one, the final conflagration was a glorious consummation, in the other, it was a sort of dull, existential "life is meaningless" thud. Which translation better reflected Hans Christian Andersen's own intention?

MARY

Maybe neither. Maybe Andersen was being intentionally noncommittal and leaving the effect—the moral, so to speak—entirely up to the reader.

FREEDOM

Then a good translator should be just as noncommittal, shouldn't she?

UNCLE CLIFF

Too bad none of us knows Danish.

GOTCHER

I know "uff da," man. Or is that Swedish?

UNCLE CLIFF

Norske. I'm half Norske, myself.

GOTCHER

I knew it was one of those Scandinavian lingoes, anyway.

PENNY

Yes, but which one? Even, which Norwegian? I had a college professor once—ballads and folklore—who said Norwegian has so many dialects the Norskis themselves tell a joke: "He speaks twelve languages—eleven of them are Norwegian."

UNCLE CLIFF

I think "Uff da" means pretty much the same throughout.

ELFRANK

Which is?

GOTCHER

In plain English, man, "Oy vey."

All laughed, chuckled, or at least smiled. Frank cleared his throat as if preparing to bring the conversation to heel, but before he could speak Bugsy sang out, "She'll be comin' round the uff-da, when she comes—Uff! Da!"

CHAPTER 28

This set off a minor epidemic of campfire singing, followed by a round of campfire ghost stories, beginning, by consensus, with the youngest human member of the group.

BUGSY'S TALE

There's this guy hiking up in the mountains, see, and just when night is falling and he's looking around for a place to camp, he finds this old deserted cabin. Well, the roof's half off, but he rolls out his bedroll under what's left, and builds himself a good ol' fire between it and the door, cooks his hot dogs and beans, and by now it's pretty dark, so he just crawls into his bedroll and lays there watchin' his fire while the wood pops—yeah, just like that (as the Loon Lake campfire obligingly popped)—and changes shape and all.

Then, just as he's gettin' good and drowsy, a little kitten walks in through where there usta be a door. The kitten comes right up to the fire, walks around it three times, spits its little spit into it, and sits down on its haunches between the fire and the doorway, and just sits there, looking at the guy, and he just lays there, looking back at the kitten, and thinking, kinda drowsy-like, what a cute little kitten it is, when all of a sudden a big ol' tomcat walks in through where there usta be a door, comes up to the fire, walks around it three times, spits in it, and sits down beside the kitten.

The kitten turns to the cat and goes, "Shall we do it now?"

"No," says the ol' tomcat, "we gotta wait for George."

So they just sit there looking at the guy, and he's looking back at them, and wondering is he dreaming, when all of a sudden a wildcat comes in, walks around the fire three times, spits in the fire, and then sits down beside the tomcat and the kitten.

They both of 'em turn to him and ask, "Shall we do it now?"

"No," he says, "we gotta wait for George."

So they all three sit there between the fire and the doorway, and watch the guy.

Well, he's pretty wide awake by now, but just layin' there keeping quiet, wondering what's gonna happen next, when in comes a mountain lion, pad-pad-pad on his big paws, walks around the fire three times, spits in the fire—an' he makes it sizzle some—and then sits down beside the wildcat, the tomcat, and the kitten.

The three of 'em all turn to him and go, "Shall we do it *now?*"

"No," he says, "we gotta wait for George."

So all four of 'em just sit there on the far side of the fire, which is flickering by now, and watch the guy.

He gets to thinking, should he jump up and make a break for the doorway, when here comes in a leopard, yeah, a leopard—and now the guy's too wide awake to even think is it all just a dream. The leopard walks three times around the fire, spits in the fire—makes the last flames shake—and sits down beside the mountain lion, the wildcat, the tomcat, and the kitten.

They turn to him and ask, "Shall we do it NOW?"

"No," he says, "we gotta wait for George."

So all five of 'em just sit there on the far side of what's left of the fire, five pairs a' cats' eyes in a kind of half a circle, just staring at this guy across the few little half-hearted flames and glowing embers.

By now he's so scared he can't move at all, just wishes he could, when what comes in next but a great big ol' saber-tooth tiger. Yeah!

The saber-tooth tiger walks around the fire three times, spits in it and puts it all the way out, and then sits down beside the leopard, the mountain lion, the wildcat, the tomcat, and the kitten.

So all their glowing eyes turn to him and—"Shall we do it *NOW?*"

"No," he says, disgusted like, "we gotta wait for George. And George...ain't...coming!"

So they all get up and walk out.

> *Some of Bugsy's listeners laughed heartily, some gradually, a few merely politely. Only Frank Craftlove offered criticism.*

ELFRANK

Unfortunately, suggesting a dream even to deny the possibility raises the question in the listener's mind as to whether that is not in fact the case. I should have omitted that element entirely.

BUGSY

Yeah, well, whenever you tell it, you can do what you like.

ELFRANK

I do not plagiarize the work of other authors.

PENNY

But it isn't plagiarism with retelling folk tales. Oh, yes, I've met that one before—was it in Richard Chase's collection, or one of Botkin's?—but I don't think I've ever heard it told any better, Bugsy.

UNCLE CLIFF

I'm not sure you're right, Frank, about leaving out whether or not it's a dream. If the possibility isn't denied right away, people are going to assume it *is* a dream as soon as the leopard shows up.

MARY

If not as soon as the kitten speaks intelligibly.

LEIF

But so what if it were a dream? How would you analyze it, Mary?

MARY

Without fuller acquaintance of the camper, I would not venture any analysis at all, not even during office hours.

UNCLE CLIFF

Well, you've got some acquaintance of me, so maybe I'm being brave, or even foolhardy, but I'll offer up an actual dream I had last night, just in time to be my ghost story.

UNCLE CLIFF'S TALE

There were a group of archeologists working on a dig, somewhere in South America it must have been. They discovered a cave, behind a door made out of a huge rock set in a groove so it could roll back and forth.

When they went into the cave and shone their flashlights around the walls, they found them covered with pictographs—pictures of people— each one about a hand's length tall. Most of these pictographs had faces that looked like caricatures of real people's faces, every face different... like that emperor's tomb they discovered in China with the army of statues, and every statue looks as if it's been modeled from a real individual soldier, no two statues alike. But some of the pictographs in this cave had heads that were just faceless ovals. Like eggs.

Then the archeologists hear a kind of low, grumbling sound. They look around, and there's the rock rolling back over the open doorway!

The rock's closing off the daylight fast. In a minute it'll be too late, and they'll all be shut in, trapped in the dark with nothing but their flashlights. There's a mad scramble for the opening—what's left of the opening.

They got out just in time. As the rock WHAMMED shut behind them, they heard something like a long, terrible scream. They didn't know if it was a sound the boulder made grinding shut, or what. But there the boulder was, tight and solid and still, as though the cave had never been there at all.

They look around, panting and counting heads, and to their horror, one of their number isn't there. They go up to the rock and shout his name. They can't hear anything through the rock. As far as they can tell, it's completely silent in the cave.

They're looking for whatever they can use that might be strong enough to lever the stone away from over the mouth of the cave, when slowly, with a groaning, grating sound, it rolls open again all by itself.

You can bet how carefully they venture back in, bouncing their flashlight beams up and down and around the pictographed walls, calling their friend's name... Some of them stay outside, piling stuff in the groove to keep the boulder from slamming shut again.

They find him lying face down, completely still. When they roll him over, his face...he doesn't have a face any longer, just a smooth, white oval, like an egg. They look up at the wall, and the pictograph just above him has a very definite caricature of his face.

As Uncle Cliff signified with an audibly definitive period that he had come to the end, Bugsy demanded, "Wow! Was he dead?"

UNCLE CLIFF

I guess so. At that point, I woke up.

PENELOPE

Let's hope so! How long could he have stayed alive, with his nose and mouth gone?

ELFRANK

Something might possibly be made of that nightmare, although I would not be the one to try.

GOTCHER

Okay, Madam Headshrink, how d'you analyze this one?

MARY

Who were you in the dream, Cliff?

UNCLE CLIFF

I don't know. Just watching it all, I guess. I don't very often have dreams like that.

PENELOPE

Maybe you picked up on somebody else's thoughts.

UNCLE CLIFF

Maybe, knowing we were sort of planning this campfire ghost-story session, my dream kindly provided something for me to tell.

MARY

That's good enough for me.

ELFRANK

For a psychoanalyst, you seem very easily satisfied.

MARY

Here and now, I'm just a camper like everyone else. If you want psychoanalysis, you'll have to make an office appointment.

GOTCHER

Fair enough spoken! I think, for that, you win the prize of telling the next story.

MARY

My, my! Well, let me see…

DR. MARY ARROWSMITH'S TALE

There was once a man—call him James Smith—and I want to state here at the outset that this man and his story are complete fictions, any resemblance to actual persons living or dead purely coincidental and so forth.

Very well. You've all heard of lucid dreaming?

> *Gotcher, Leif, Penny, Eliza, Freedom, and—after a blink—Uncle Cliff, all nodded. Pumpkin gave a little whine that resembled "yes" but might as easily have been a plea for Gotcher to scratch behind her ears, which he did. Muttwump, lying asleep at Bugsy's feet, twitched his legs. The others shook their heads or looked blank. Only Frank Craftlove spoke aloud into the pause.*

ELFRANK

The two terms, "lucid" and "dreaming," of course I recognize individually. May I take it that coupling them in that fashion denotes some psychoanalytic jargon which changes their common connotations beyond recognition?

MARY

Not exactly. "Lucid dreaming" simply means becoming aware while dreaming that one is in fact dreaming—that it is one's own dream and therefore the dreamer may and can change it to taste, turn it from nightmare into paradise at will—at least in theory—or vice versa if one happens to prefer nightmares, as I have occasionally found with rare individuals—met socially, outside office hours, let me hasten to add.

In any case, James Smith had the theory and technique of lucid dreaming down pat. He used looking at the back of his right hand as a signal to tell him whether he was awake or dreaming—

BUGSY

Huh?

MARY

That's one common trick. The dreamer can choose anything to serve as the symbol: the moon, a tree, a plate, even just a word or two repeated to one's self, like the question, "Am I dreaming?" The simple act of consciously looking at or mentally repeating the chosen clue triggers awareness of whether or not one is dreaming. Our James Smith had chosen the back of his right hand.

PENNY

As in "I know it like I know the back of my right hand"?—Sorry! Rule: let's not interrupt the storyteller.

MARY

The first time James Smith tried looking at the back of his right hand in a dream, ugly little worms started growing out of his knuckles. That told him he was dreaming, so he turned them into palm trees, put them on a resort island in the tropics, and settled down in a beach chair to sip a fancy drink and watch the waves roll in.

Later that week, he was walking to work through a rocky field when he found himself menaced by a growling gray wolf the size of a Shetland pony. Again he glanced at the back of his right hand, understood he was dreaming, turned the wolf into a riding horse, jumped up into the saddle on its back—even though in waking life the closest he'd ever gotten to a horse was watching the Kentucky Derby on television—and rode to the beach, where his chair and drink were waiting.

The third time it happened was at a business conference where his new boss, who looked quite a bit like Richard Nixon, was raking him over the coals for his work performance during the previous administration. Glancing down at his right hand, he saw that this was another dream—in waking life, he was CEO of a major corporation, with an annual salary touching seven figures—so he spat in Nixon's face, jumped out the conference room window, and flew to his island, with the beach chair, the cold drink, and the waves rolling in.

From then on, whenever anything got unpleasant in James Smith's life, he would glance at the back of his right hand. If nothing happened, he just put his head down and waited in silence for the storm to pass. But if it turned out to be a dream, he changed or manipulated the other characters to his liking, and soon ended up on his beach, sipping his drink and watching the waves roll in. More and more often, it turned out to be a dream, and he enjoyed his beach so much that after a while he was glancing at the back of his right hand several times a day, even when things were going well. He rarely if ever had a dream, however good in itself, but that he felt it could be improved with his beach chair and a cold drink.

Anyone who draws seven figures annually can afford to put a down payment on a beach house in the Bahamas, so James Smith did exactly that as soon as he found one to his taste, one with a shoreline that looked like the beach in his dreams. As soon as he could get away for a weekend, he chartered a plane to fly him there.

He was lounging on his private beach, sipping his cold drink and watching the waves roll in, when Richard Nixon rode up on a gray wolf the size of a pony.

James Smith looked at the back of his right hand, but it told him nothing. This time, he didn't seem to be dreaming. What should he do? Have his houseboy bring out another chair and a drink for Nixon, and maybe a couple of raw steaks for the wolf?

He looked up again, and there at the edge of the waterline was the velociraptor from a nightmare he'd had about six months ago. To the dinosaur's right, a masked terrorist. On the other side, Al Capone with his machine gun. In fact, the beach was crowded with armed enemies and monsters, all of whom James Smith recognized as characters he had snuffed out or manipulated in his lucid dreams.

He stared down again at the back of his hand, determined to find himself dreaming and wake up so he could have his beach to himself. He saw ugly little worms growing out of his knuckles.

He couldn't shake them off. He pulled at one, but it hurt like hell. At last he remembered that the first time he had turned them into palm trees, so he tried that. It worked—but this time he couldn't move them to the beach front. They stayed stuck to the back of his hand, their roots coming out through his palm, and their tops turning into scaly, reptilian heads above palm fronds like frilly green collars.

His nightmares had gotten tired of being shunted lucidly aside when they had things to tell him about himself. So they were ganging up on him while he was still awake.

BUGSY

Wow!

PENNY

Reminds me of a theory I read about, that all the troubles and temptations the ancient Desert Fathers had with demons, were their own dreams coming while they were still awake—more or less—because they believed in fasting from sleep as well as from food.

ELFRANK

(Snorts.)

LEIF

In modern times, researchers have experimented with sleep deprivation, and after about four days, sure enough, the volunteer test subjects start hallucinating like they're dreaming while awake.

MARY

That fits my little story, since lucid dreaming is best accomplished in the state so near waking that the dreamer often has difficulty remaining asleep. But Jung theorizes that we dream constantly, and usually become aware of it only when asleep.

PENNY

Really?

ELFRANK

As if Satan and his fallen angels were mere figments of our own dreaming imagination! Would that the sins they cause us to commit were likewise.

GOTCHER

Hey, man, we can sin plenty all by ourselves, without blaming everything on the poor old devil.

ELMER

Time out.

ELIZA

Yes. This campfire time is for relaxing. Frank, suppose you tell your story next?

ELFRANK

Very well. Although I generally require payment in advance for my potboilers.

How can you require editors to pay you to read your potboilers before they decide whether to buy them or not?

Unfortunately, depending on circumstances, sometimes I cannot. Therefore, let me offer our present group, in outline, one of the few tales I was unable to sell—one of my earliest efforts—and leave it to your collective judgment whether the editors were justified or foolish in rejecting it.

L. FRANK CRAFTLOVE'S TALE

On the evening of the day he turned seven years old, Danton Epworthy the Third had his first tangible experience of the Devil.

A firefly had just alighted on young Danton's arm, when there beside him, limned with a sort of sulfurous dark glow in the blue twilight, sat His Infernal Majesty.

"Dismember this insect," Satan whispered with a soft hissing in the lad's ear, snatching the firefly from Danton's silken sleeve in order to present it to him giftlike, wriggling between the talonous nails of the diabolic fingertips. "Start by slowly pulling out its wings, then its little legs, one by one. Last, its winking thorax. See how much pleasure you derive from the action—how much fun it will be."

After momentary hesitation, the boy accepted the proffered firefly and did to it exactly as Satan had suggested. As promised, he derived therefrom sufficient satisfaction that, in later months, whenever he found the voice of conscience menacing him, he stilled it by catching another insect and treating it after the same fashion.

This became so habitual that one fine day he unthinkingly dismembered a large black ant in the presence of his maternal parent, who, witnessing the act with shock and distaste, gave him a severe talking-to. "But, Mother," the boy protested, "you don't even *like* ants."

"Nor do I like seeing them, or any other creatures at all, tortured. You must always exterminate them as quickly as you can."

For a few weeks he tried to follow her advice; but neither stamping on a bug nor even popping it between thumb and forefinger provided him quite the same thrill of satisfaction as vivisecting it bit by bit. Then one day—his reflexes were both young and keenly honed—he caught a small frog.

He might have simply squeezed it to death, when once again before him he beheld the Devil, sending off a faint black smoke, in lieu of a halo, into the bright afternoon sun.

"It's well enough to kill things fast," hissed Satan, "but isn't it much, much more fun to kill them slowly?"

Agreeing that it was, Danton Epworthy the Third lingeringly stretched his latest capture limb from limb.

He was by this time nine years old and sufficiently "savvy" to hide the fragments of amphibian, but either he lacked sufficient ingenuity to hide them really well, or some not-quite-extinguished spark in his soul unconsciously yearned to be found out, because his mother happened upon the dismembered corpse whilst pruning her flowerbed. Horrified, she held consultation with his father, Danton Epworthy the Second, following which she took her offspring to a pet shop, where she directed him to choose the prettiest and most melodious bird he could find.

The idea was, of course, that by keeping a pet which he could not bear to kill, young Danton might develop some compassion toward other living things. For a number of months, the exercise seemed to augur well. From its simple yet elegant cage in the living room, the canary sent forth peals of cheery song and, when a ray of penetrating sunlight struck it at the proper angle, glowed like a blazon of heraldic gold.

Then, on the evening of Danton's tenth birthday, the Devil appeared to him again, glowing without benefit of sunlight, but glowing with an evil aura. Next morning the cage was empty, and the maid—who might otherwise have been thought to have inadvertently left the cage door open—shrieked to discover on the back doorstep a bird's broken leg with bloody stump.

Not to linger overlong upon the increasingly gory details, Danton's parents continued providing him with ever larger and more lovable pets, in the fond hope that at some point one of them would awaken his better nature. All in vain! What hope could white mouse, guinea pig, kitten, bunny rabbit, or even puppy have when thrown into the scales against the Prince of Infernal Majesty with his darkly sulfurous glow and enticing whispers? When Danton, by now seventeen, assured his parents solemnly that his new horse had escaped from its paddock to run away he knew not whither, and scarcely even blushed at his father's producing one imperfectly concealed equine forelimb and demanding to know how a creature so maimed could run—much as it might wish to—the elder Epworthies at last abandoned their futile attempts.

Never, as long as he lived under the parental roof, had they dared allow him to babysit; but at the usual age he left home for university. He had not been there five weeks when his roommate, having accidentally double-booked a calendar date, begged him to, "Help me out, Dant. Stay with the Pattersons' kid this Friday evening so I can keep my date with Shar Meyer."

Having often wondered what the experience might be like from the sitter's vantage, Danton Epworthy the Third jumped at this opportunity. Friday evening found him on the Pattersons' doorstep promptly at six-thirty. The Pattersons gave him the customary last-minute instructions—where he could find the diapers, where they themselves might be reached in emergency, and so on.

An hour after their departure, the baby started crying in its crib. As Danton rose from the TV couch, before his eyes a familiar dark, Satanic glow coalesced in the easy chair across the room.

"You saw, I think, the kitchen stand of carving knives?" inquired His Infernal Majesty.

And Danton nodded.

BUGSY

Yowp!

PENNY

That's so ugly, I'm amazed nobody bought it.

ELFRANK

I suppose that either I left the goriest details too much to the reader's imagination, or else I felt the moral too deeply in my own heart. I have never since made either mistake in another potboiler, and all have sold only too well.

GOTCHER

Moral, man? What moral?

BUGSY

Well, whenever I grow up and have kids of my own, I'm not gonna want 'em listening to stuff like that.

ELFRANK

Why, I was younger than you when first I heard this tale—in merest plot, of course—from the lips of one of the good nuns who instructed me at Saint Sebastian's. Its moral, I should have thought as obvious as it is wholesome: listening to the Devil in small matters paves the sinner's way to heeding his noxious advice in large ones.

PENELOPE

Oh! I thought the moral was about starting with a bluebottle fly and working your way up through the animal kingdom until you reached a Second Trombone.

UNCLE CLIFF

Yikes! Any flautists along the way?

GOTCHER

Gilbert and Sullivan's "Mikado," Act Two. But look, man, even in your story, the devil could as well have been in the kid's—young Danton's—imagination, as out here in actual, ever-lovin' objective reality.

ELFRANK

Even from your viewpoint, what great difference would that have made? In preaching the "Do your own thing" ideal, your generation overlooked the inconvenient fact that between unrestrained sex and unrestrained murder there is only one small, slippery step.

GOTCHER

Man, you're full of it! Sex creates, murder destroys: opposites, man, *opposites*. That's why we always said, and I'm sticking to it, "Make love, not war." Always with mutually consenting adults, of course.

PENNY

But I can still see where some people—like Danton in the story—might feel the pressure building up and up inside them to destroy something...to kill someone. Surely sometimes a little social repression can be a *good* thing!

ELIZA

Mary? As a practicing psychiatrist, can you give us any insights here?

MARY

As a practicing psychiatrist enjoying a weekend out of the office, my insight is that it's time for the next story.

LEIF

Let me take up the slack with a tale that was probably already old when it appeared in the seventeenth-century equivalent of today's tabloids.

LEIF PAGETURNER'S TALE

There was an inn, very old and shabby and rundown at the heel. A lone traveler reached it late in the day. He stood there awhile on his tired horse, studying the sign where it hung down by one hinge. "The Silent Woman." Paint faded and chipping away, but even in the dusk he could still make out the picture of a woman without a head—apologies, but that's unfortunately authentic, a little piece of very, very old-fashioned sick humor.

At last the traveler got down off his horse, tied it to the hitching post, and went in. He found two or three locals sitting around in the common room, drinking and gossiping—men gossip, too, and I don't imagine too much has changed about barroom fat-chewing over the centuries. But there was nobody to wait on them except the innkeeper and his wife, an elderly couple but still pretty hale and spry—well-weathered by life.

The traveler sat down, called for supper and a room, and asked if somebody could stable his horse. The innkeeper himself went to do that, while his wife fetched the newcomer bread and cheese, a bit of roast fowl and a tankard of fairly decent ale—rough fare, but the best they had on hand.

The locals watched him eat and, when he had finished his food and gotten his tankard refilled, they began asking him where he'd come from and what had been happening there. Newspapers in that age and area were few and hard to come by. The stranger said he was returning home from the wars. The innkeeper's wife remarked that her own son had gone off to the wars twenty-some years ago, at which the innkeeper, back from stabling the horse, eyed the stranger and observed that he looked about the same age as their boy would be now. Mayhap they had served together? The lad's name was such and such, and he had a red birthmark the shape more or less of a mermaid on his belly, right about *here*.

The stranger, scarred, sunbrowned, lean with middle age and his hair already thinning, looked shrewdly at the old couple and their few late customers before answering that yes, he had met such a fellow soldier, who had fought well and bravely when he knew him, but the tides of fortune had parted them years ago. He then spent half an hour telling stories of the battles he'd been in, growing drowsier and drowsier even while he talked, and at last yawned hugely and went up to his room.

The locals sat on talking until past their usual hour, but finally they went home, supporting one another out the door, leaving the innkeeper and his wife alone in the house with their sleeping guest.

The woman looked at her husband. "A stranger hereabout," she said. "Saddlebag fair and full," he replied.

With ten years or so of experience behind them, they fetched out their knives and stealthily mounted the stairs. Half drugged by weariness and certain herbs the inn wife had slipped into his ale, the stranger never even stirred as they plunged their knives into exactly the right places, killing him instantly.

In those days, people tended to sleep naked or almost as good as, so it wasn't long before the murderers noticed a birthmark more or less in the shape of a mermaid on their latest victim's belly, right about *here*.

He had made good in the wars and brought his booty home to surprise his old parents, but, having changed so much, had been waiting for just the right moment to reveal himself.

The mother's screams brought the locals stumbling back. All was discovered, the pair shortly hanged, and the whole story broadcast in sheet ballads.

BUGSY

Sorta like the Bates Motel.

GOTCHER

Turned inside out, but yeah, it has some of the same elements.

ELIZA

Well, it reminds me of a story I heard when I was a kid, many years ago.

ELIZA'S TALE

An English traveler came to Transylvania and stopped for the night at a quaint old inn. From the outside, it looked full of local color, but once inside, he began to think, maybe a little too much local color. The food was passable, but he noticed that all the other customers seemed careful to leave before nightfall. When they were gone, he sat there awhile listening to the sounds—wind howling and owls shrieking outside, the building itself making odd creaks and cracking noises...

At last he decided it was time to go up to his room. The innkeeper lit a half-burned candle in a tarnished old candlestick, and led the way up the creaky old staircase. Outside, the wind moaned. Inside, the candle flame dipped and guttered, sending odd shadows wavering around the dark walls and angles. The only other light came from the half-hearted fireplace in the common room, getting farther away with every step. Here and there—almost everywhere—cobwebs showed up when the candlelight happened to hit them. The stairs creaked. Something brushed the back of the traveler's neck.

At last he could stand it no longer, and asked his host, "Has... Has anything...strange...ever happened here?"

Slowly, in a low voice, the innkeeper replied, "Only once...years and years ago."

"What—What happened then?"

"A gentleman...who spent the night in the same room you shall have...next morning...came down for breakfast."

All laughed or chuckled, even Frank Craftlove. The dogs woke, looked around curiously, and nudged their noses at the nearest hands for a petting.

PEARL BONAMI

I just wanted to take a dust cloth and scrub brush to that old place.

PENNY

Maybe the dust and dirt were all that held it together.

FREEDOM

What would make a scary story for you, Pearl?

PEARL

Well, let me think... You know those "Scouring Suds"—the little guys in those TV commercials that are like soap bubbles on top and scrub brushes underneath?

BUGSY

With great big eyes and little smiles? Yeah.

PEARL

Yeah.

PEARL BONAMI'S TALE

Okay, there was one time a housewife who was just wild about those little guys. Her husband used to joke that he'd have someone to worry about if there was just one of 'em, and not so many it was more like she had a whole harem...poly...what do they call it?

ELIZA

Polyandry.

PEARL

Yeah, that. Thanks. Well, she used 'em on everything, she wanted such a clean house. Just set 'em right to work on floors, sinks, wall, ceilings...even sprinkled 'em right on her dust cloths. She'd maybe even have tried 'em in her laundry, except she took that to the laundromat and just used the detergent packets they had for sale there.

She was especially proud of how neat it kept her closet of cleaning supplies, to have just the one kind of container there: a shaker of Scouring Suds labeled "Kitchen," another one labeled "Bathroom," others labeled "Master Bedroom," "Guest Bedroom," "Living Room," "Dining Room," and so on—all lined up nice and neat, same size (giant economy), same shape, no difference except her homemade labels. It provoked her a bit when the company changed the shape of the cans and she had to decide whether to change over can by can as her old ones got used up, or throw out the partly-used ones and get a whole new set all at once.

But you can't use just one cleaning product for every last thing. There's reasons they make some of 'em abrasive and some soft, some to be used wet and some dry. What this lady noticed first was how dull her drinking glasses were getting, but she just chalked it up to the hard water and squeezed a few more Scouring Suds onto her dishrag.

Next thing, her husband complained it always looked like snow, whatever he watched on TV. Football games, he said, were one thing, but it shouldn't be snowing on a basketball court. She told him to get a new TV. She never watched the tube herself, too busy cleaning everything. He got himself a big new TV and warned her in no uncertain terms she wasn't ever to touch it—he'd keep this one cleaned off himself, like he did the birdcage. She heard just enough to give him a nod, and went back to cleaning everything else she could reach.

Next thing, he complained his food tasted soapy and gritty. She answered him that she rinsed all the dishes and pots and pans twice. He asked was that after she scrubbed 'em, or before, and took to eating his meals at restaurants and his snacks out of bags he kept apart for himself. He even bought bottled water and his own special drinking glass, that he kept hidden. She didn't care. She kept herself too busy finding new places to clean with her friendly little Scouring Suds.

Their pet canary was really her husband's, and he'd always been the one who cleaned its cage. But one day the woman looked at it, looked at her can of Scouring Suds, decided hubby must've forgotten a day or two, and cleaned it herself. Maybe she didn't get it rinsed off quite as well as she could've. Anyway, next morning the canary was gone.

When hubby found out about it, he accused her of letting it get away while she was doing the cage. She protested, she had made sure it was snug inside with the door shut—look, it was still shut—when she hung the cage up again. She had even heard it fussing during the night. He said it could have fussed from anywhere in the house, especially if it couldn't get to its food and water dishes. So they searched the house top to bottom. No bird. The man said somebody must've opened a door while it was loose, and it must've flown right out, and she'd just imagined seeing and hearing it afterwards. Well, they hung the cage up again in its old spot, this time with the cage door open, just in case. But they never saw song nor feather of that poor little canary ever again.

About a week or so later, this woman left her husband getting ready to take a shower while she went out for groceries. Right before she left, she reminded him to be sure and scrub the shower stall down when he was finished. She left the "Lower Bathroom" shaker of Scouring Suds all ready to hand on the shower ledge.

When she got back home with the groceries, there was no sign of hubby. The shower stall was spic and span, with his slippers there on the floor beside it and his bathrobe on the hook on the bathroom door, but no hide nor hair of him. She looked all through the house. She shouted out for him everywhere. Nothing. She was all alone in her nice, clean house.

She finally put the groceries away before the meat spoiled, sat herself down with a cup of coffee, and reasoned out that he must've taken it into his head to pad into the bedroom barefoot and naked, get dressed and go out for a beer without thinking to leave her a note. She spent the rest of the afternoon cleaning extra hard to work off the worry, fixed herself supper, ate it, and then sat waiting and drumming her fingers on the tabletop until nine-thirty. Hubby never showed up.

She phoned the police and was told a person had to be missing at least twenty-four hours—a grown-up, anyway—before they went into action. She paced the living room awhile, and then she went up to try and relax with a long, hot bath.

Well, she was out of bath salts, so she sprinkled some Scouring Suds in the tub. After all, she figured, they worked for everything else, why not for bubble bath, too? At least she could simplify her shopping list a little more that way. She filled the tub with hot water and got in.

The last thing she saw was the grinning little Scouring Suds coming for *her*.

Again, the listeners laughed, chuckled, or grinned. Uncle Cliff commented, "Yikes!" and Eliza remarked, "I'm not sure I'll ever see one of those commercials the same way again." Then Bugsy spoke up.

BUGSY

Hey, you know, we've had—let's see, one, two, three…seven stories so far, that's more than half of us—and not one of 'em with a real, honest-to-goodness *ghost!* So how come we call 'em "ghost" stories?

FREEDOM

Yours wasn't about ghosts, either.

BUGSY

Yeah, well, how do you know? All those cats *could've* been ghosts. Besides, I went first. How'd I know everybody else was going to go every place except real ghosts? Oh, yeah, Mom almost got there, but not quite. With the one about the creepy old inn in Transylvania.

ELMER

Well, son, let's see if I can't come up with a real ghost yarn for you.

ELMER'S TALE

Happened back in about 1898, near Homer Pass in the Rockies. Old Number Three—the Flying Zephyr—pride of the Denver Pacific, one of those old narrow-gauge lines that hadn't ever quite grown into its name—was chugging along at a nice, peaceable rate in the late evening twilight, when they heard another train behind 'em.

The engineer, John Chudden, was a new man on the line, just moved out west from Ohio. He thought he'd checked the schedule himself ahead of time, like he always did, but to make sure, he turned around to his fireman and asked, did he know any other train scheduled for this route tonight? The fireman shook his head no. The engine behind them blew its whistle in a warning kind of way.

Chudden told his fireman to pile it on. The conductor came out to the engine and asked why they were speeding up. Chudden told him about the train coming up behind them, and said, go back and do what you can to keep the passengers calm and quiet.

The train behind seemed to be gaining a little on the old Zephyr every downhill stretch, but it seemed to gain every time they went uphill, too, no matter how much fuel the fireman piled on. The fireman worked like a devil. Grinned like a devil, too, with the exertion, his face all sooty and shiny and streaky with sweat. The old Zephyr went racing up and down the Rockies like an engine half her age, with this second train gaining on her, gradual but steady. The passengers started hearing it, too, started looking out the windows, back along the curving track, and not all the conductor could do could stop 'em talking and worrying about this crazy engineer coming up behind 'em, who was he and what was going to happen.

By now it was full night, and all they could see was the lights, this other train edging up closer and closer behind, when they came down on Homer Pass.

There on the other side of the bridge, coming straight on toward the Flying Zephyr—a third train on the same track, heading toward the other two, full speed!

All John Chudden could do was hit the brakes and pray, thinking a head-on crash would probably be worse than a rear-ender. But the Zephyr was going too fast to stop right away. It was actually on the bridge before it met the oncoming train, with the one behind tickling its last car.

Well, these two other trains—to front and to rear—both of 'em just seemed to pass right through the Flying Zephyr, meet smack, head-on in about its midsection. Both these trains reared up—the Zephyr's passengers testified afterwards that they could just see the outlines, shadowy people mouthing screams—and then these two other trains toppled together, in kind of slow motion, like, into the chasm below, leaving the Flying Zephyr all alone on the bridge, safe but pretty badly shaken. That is, everybody aboard was pretty shaky. The train itself was nice and steady, all set to go on as soon as Chudden let up on the brakes.

Turned out they'd seen a real accident that happened right at that spot ten years before.

Well, son, that enough ghosts for you?

BUGSY

Yeah, okay, we didn't actually see any people-ghosts, but, yeah... How about getting that into one of your lay-outs, Pop? The old Flying Zephyr and the two ghost trains...

ELMER

Afraid that'd be pretty tough, son.

UNCLE CLIFF

Hmmm... Maybe if... Let me think about it awhile.

PENNY

Anyway, it could explain something I've never been able to figure out in one of the old "Maverick" episodes—one set on a train—Bart driving the engine, for some reason that's too long to explain—meaning I've forgotten most of the details—night, I think, and here's an oncoming train on the same tracks...and then, instead of crashing, it just seems to melt right through and disappear. Doesn't seem to have a thing to do with the rest of the plot, as well as I can remember. The sequence is just there, never brought up again. Now I finally know. It must've been one of those ghostly trains of the Old West. Maybe even the seed idea the writer started working with, and then the story developed in other directions and that little orphan sequence is all that's left of the original inspiration.

ELFRANK

And ought therefore to have been excised in the interests of internal consistency. But what can we expect of television writing, to which the worst paperback prose potboiler—even my own—is like Shakespeare?

PENELOPE

Actually, when you think about it, writing for television must be quite a discipline. They have to start with a narrative hook, build up to four or five mini-climaxes strong enough to keep people watching through the commercials, make all these segments hang together and give it a satisfying ending... It's amazing there's as much watchable TV as there is.

ELFRANK

Employing the broadest possible definition of "watchable." And for "satisfying" I should substitute "satisfactory"—barely, and, again, in the broadest possible sense of the word.

LEIF

The newspaper comic strips. They certainly helped train generations in the skill of following a storyline three panels a day.

BUGSY (speaking from hearsay)

And how about those old-time double features? When you could go in anytime, watch the end of one movie, watch the second movie all the way through, then watch the first one until, "Here's where we came in," and go, because you still remembered the ending well enough and now it made sense... Man! When you build your time machine, Uncle Cliff, I wanta go back and see a few movies that ol' double-feature way.

MERLINA

I believe those of us old enough to have done it will agree that you've described it very well, Bugsy.

ELIZA

We've told him about it.

FREEDOM

I'm not sure why, exactly, but Dad's story makes me think of one.

BUGSY

Aw, just about everything makes you think of that one, Sis!

MERLINA

How do you know which story it makes her think of?

BUGSY

It's the same one she always tells, times like this, as soon as she gets brave enough to take her turn.

MERLINA

Good. Then she'll have had lots of practice, and maybe *we* haven't heard it yet.

FREEDOM

Thank you, Merlina.

FREEDOM'S TALE

There was a young woman who had a recurrent dream. She'd had it from the time she was very young, since before she knew what the big black coach was that would come driving up. When she started having the dream, it was a coach and four, all four horses glossy black. As she got older, more and more often it was an automobile, a long black limousine that by the time she was twelve or thirteen she knew was a hearse. That was the era she lived in: just when automobiles were replacing horse-drawn carriages.

Anyway, the hearse would stop in front of her. The driver would lean down or—when it was an automobile—roll down his window and look out at her. He was a round man with a jolly face that could turn nasty and threatening all in a moment—

BUGSY

Like the coachman in the old Disney "Pinocchio."

ELIZA

Bugsy! Your sister didn't interrupt you when you were telling your story.

BUGSY

Okay, sorry, Sis.

FREEDOM

Thank...you... Bugsy. Anyway. The driver would look down—or out—at her, smile, and say, "Room for one more, Miss." His face turned menacing, he started to laugh, and at that point she always woke up. When she was very young, she used to scream for her parents. As she got older, she learned how to lie there telling herself, "It was just a dream. Only a dream. Just that old dream again," until she went back to sleep.

She graduated from high school and went away to college, and the dream came less and less often. By the time she was working on her Master's degree, she hardly thought about it at all from day to day. Then one of her college friends from undergraduate days was getting married, and invited her out to Denver for the wedding. It was a long trip, so she decided to go by train.

The nearest station was a small one, in a small town, and the train would be there to take on passengers at four in the morning. She had to get up so early, and then this went wrong and that went wrong while she was trying to get dressed, so she got to the station rushed, and hungry from skipping breakfast in her hurry, and afraid she was going to be late. But the train itself was twenty minutes late, so there she stood on the platform, relaxing until she was almost nodding off, until it finally pulled in and rolled to a stop, with the boarding door several yards away from her.

The conductor swung down the boarding steps and helped the few other waiting passengers up into the car, while the young woman hurried over to the end of the little line. When her turn came, the conductor looked up at her and grinned He was the same man she'd seen in all those childhood dreams! and what he said to her was: "Room for one more, Miss."

She stammered something about changing her mind, backed away, and then turned around and ran back to the station house. She thought she heard the conductor chuckle, and then the train pulled out of the station.

She got her older brother to drive her to Denver for her friend's wedding. He was ribbing her unmercifully about the way she had chickened out at the train station, when they turned on the car radio and heard how the train she would have been on had just had a terrible accident and everybody on board had been killed.

ELFRANK

Ah, yes! "Room for One More." Frequently if not generally involving an elevator accident. Belonging to that species of folklore currently designated, I believe, "urban legend."

LEIF

There's a reason why these things catch on and get retold. They make for darn good stories.

GOTCHER

Set that a generation or two earlier, and your heroine could just escape being killed on one of those colliding trains in your dad's story.

ELMER

What Engineer Chudden saw on the Flying Zephyr is recorded history.

ELFRANK

As all good urban legends purport to be.

PENNY

All right, I'll tell one that really is factual. I found it in Arthur Jacobs' biography of Sir Arthur Sullivan, only Jacobs doesn't make anything of it except just putting down what happened. I found a few more details in somebody else's book of readings about Gilbert and Sullivan.

PENELOPE WRIGHT'S TALE

Sullivan had been commissioned to compose an overture for one of the big music festivals—Leeds or maybe Norwich, I'm not quite sure which one. An "overture" doesn't necessarily have to be for any specific stage work—at least it didn't back then. It could be just a stand-alone concert number. The festival was getting closer, and Sullivan complained to his father, Thomas Sullivan, that he was having a lot of trouble with the new overture. His father assured him that if he just kept working on it, a new inspiration would come in time. I guess that must have been before Sullivan went to visit friends in another part of the city while he was trying to work on his overture, because a letter survives in which he complains to his father that the new overture wasn't going at all the way he wanted—he'd meant it to be bright and happy and of course Sullivan could write very bright and happy music, even when he was suffering from gallstones and other health troubles—but this particular overture was coming out all "gloomy" and "dismal," and he thought he'd probably have to back out of the contract, after all.

Later that same month—September, I think—Sullivan's brother Fred arrived in the night at the house where Sullivan was staying, to tell him their father had just died of an aneurism. Sullivan was devastated. That overture he'd wanted to be bright and happy, and that had been coming out mournful and sad, he hadn't known why, got finished after all. It became Sullivan's famous "In Memoriam," and his father's prediction about his getting an inspiration in time, came true, tragically.

UNCLE CLIFF

Yikes!

GOTCHER

I never knew that one.

MARY

Could he have been aware on some level that his father was seriously ill?

PENNY

He could've been. Isn't that the way these phenomena usually work? Nothing that can't be explained away using Occam's Razor as an absolute and not a tool, as if the probable—the "natural" or "logical" solution as they like to call it—absolutely excludes all chances of some alternative solution being the right one in any given case.

ELFRANK

For once, I agree with what I believe you to be arguing. In many cases, Occam's Razor would actually, for any truly unbiased mind, point to the supernatural as the simplest and most logical explanation. Pretending otherwise betrays the atheistic prejudice of the so-called "scientific" investigator.

PENNY

Including the Church's own Devil's Advocate?

LEIF

Is it true that Queen Victoria knighted only Sullivan because Gilbert's librettos didn't amuse her?

PENNY

Oh, I don't think so. She herself ordered a command performance of *Gondoliers*. In fact, neither Sullivan nor Gilbert—much later—was knighted for their Savoy Operas. Sullivan was the leading light of British serious music in his day, and a lot of highbrows actually thought he was wasting his time, his genius, and his dignity on these little stage works—that he himself considered "potboilers" as we call them. Besides, he was kind of a playboy, and every second or third person in the set he ran around with seems to have had some kind of title, noble or royal. Besides all that, by Victorian times musicians were a lot higher in the pecking order than mere playwrights—Gilbert preferred the word "dramatist." I think Gilbert was the first person ever knighted—much later on, in the first decade of the twentieth century, if I remember right—for his contribution to stage literature. Even today, in opera, the librettist never gets named in the same top line with the composer.

GOTCHER

What, never?

PENNY

Well, hardly ever. There's Gertrude Stein—*The Mother of Us All*—and there's W. S. Gilbert, but maybe more people say "operetta" than "opera" and class G. and S. more or less with Lerner and Lowe or Rodgers and Hammerstein. Anyway, with all those reasons, it's surprising Sullivan wasn't knighted even earlier—or Gilbert ever at all. And then maybe not only even so much for his own plays, as for making the theater itself respectable, which it hadn't been before Gilbert and Sullivan and D'Oyly Carte got at it.

UNCLE CLIFF

Actors and actresses aren't always considered quite respectable, even today.

ELIZA

We can blame a lot of that on Hollywood.

ELMER

Like always, it isn't so much what you do as who you know.

BUGSY

Well, what I know is, we've gotten off real ghost stories again, and only two more of us are left—Gotcher and Merlina.

PENNY

Oh, did Sullivan's father's death count as my story? Good.

MERLINA

You don't really expect me to tell a story, do you?

GOTCHER

Okay, kid, you want a "real ghost story," and we've gotten Gilbert and Sullivan into the conversation, so I'm just gonna dish up Gilbert and Sullivan's ghost story for you.

> *The aging hippie glanced around the circle of firelight. Penny Wright was settling down with a connoisseur kind of smile; L. Frank Craftlove was vouchsafing a nod; Leif Page-turner had his eyes shut as if mentally reviewing the G. and S. series. The rest of the company looked more or less tabula rasa. With another grin, Gotcher began.*

GOTCHER LOTSADOE'S TALE

Well, the urban legend around Rederring—a kinda flyspeck fishing village over in Cornwall, England, U.K., about the time of Napoleon (who doesn't come into this story at all, just to let you know), was that old Sir Rupert Murgatroyd, a couple of centuries earlier, had been cursed by a witch he was in the pious process of burning at the stake. That was the urban legend, anyway, good for shuddery stories around the fireside and suchlike. Well, maybe it was true. The first law of Wicca—Witchcraft—is "Do whatever you like—just so long as it doesn't hurt anyone," and the first principle of Magick is, "What goes around comes around"—pretty much like the Biblical "Cast your bread upon the waters" thing—in other words, Cast a wicked spell, and it may or may not hit its target, depending on how much the target deserves to get hit, but it definitely *will* boomerang and hit *you*, also or instead. Maybe a witch in process of getting burned alive figured she didn't have much to lose, and probably nobody deserved getting hit like old Sir Rupert M. But I've know a bunch of witches, and they're pretty decent folks—decent as Christians, any day—and me, I kind of suspect that the curse was all Sir Rupert's own idea, all along, and he started the witch story himself, or secretly hired somebody else to start it for him.

One thing's sure, and that's that keeping up the curse was all Sir Rupert's own work, and his descendants' as they joined him, one by one, and we never hear anything more about the witch involving herself with any of the dirty work at all. Because the curse was this: "Each lord of Ruddigore"—that was Sir Rupert and his heirs, "Ruddigore" being the title and "Murgatroyd" just the family name—"shall do one crime, or more, once every day, forever." Like I say, I expect Sir Rupert always was a pretty fair old sinner and criminal type himself, and putting out this tale of being cursed just gave him a good excuse to go right on with his preferred lifestyle and maybe even cadge a few tears of pity whenever he came to die naturally. And maybe however he died actually was almost as painful as he deserved, because the rest of the curse, as per the urban legend anyway, went, "This fate he can't deny, however he may try, for should he stay his hand—that day, in torture he shall die." And whether he'd added that himself and made faces on his deathbed, or whether the survivors added it after watching however he died, once the tradition got started, ol' Sir Rupert's ghost kept it up right royally.

The way the ghosts went about it, instead of messing around with, like, ectoplasmic materialization and all that, they'd get in and animate their own full-length portraits, so's they could step down out of their gilt-edged frames and interact with their living descendants. Every generation there was one more dead baronet, and always just the one who was living, so it got harder and harder for the living one to try and face all the rest of 'em down, there in the long, echoing picture gallery anyone had to go through who wanted to get from one wing of the big ol' dusty castle to the other. And those generations went down pretty quickly in the Ruddigore line, because, talk about rat races, I guess a guy just don't know what a rat race is till he has to figure out how to commit a crime every day of his life, rain or shine, sickness or health, when most of the really good crimes take weeks of planning and preparation—ask Sherlock Holmes and Professor Moriarty! I mean, like, *anything*—except maybe eating and sleeping—can get wearing for somebody who's got to do it religiously every single day without fail, so this particular lifestyle just naturally tended to wear people out in a hurry, make ghosthood look like a fairly attractive alternative, in comparison.

Only thing was, all these ghosts found their deathstyle got to be something of a rat race, too. All except ol' Sir Rupert, the first of the line, who never seemed to get tired of torturing somebody else, even his own descendants.

Well, came along baronet number twenty-two, Sir Riven, and he really, really did not want the position. I mean, like, for this guy it wasn't even so much a question of the rat race and the daily grind and like that—he just simply enjoyed being a good guy and didn't want to turn around and be a baddie. He thought it was more fun being good. (Yeah, Bugsy, I see you sitting there itching to ask, "So why didn't he just turn the job down? Why did any of them take it at all, if they didn't want to?" Well, son, it wasn't as easy as all that. It's not like it came with a draft card you could burn and hide out in a bunch of other right-minded peaceniks heading for the Canadian border. This was back in Old-World England, and when you were next in line to some hereditary title, that was definitely not a thing they let anybody just turn down and sneak away from. Believe me, Sir Riven had tried that route, but folks in his time and place liked their titled dudes, and they liked to keep 'em all in their proper place.)

I guess it could've maybe been the way Riven's uncle, Sir Roderic— sorry about all these "R's," folks, it wasn't me who named 'em—had brought him up. In his own day, Sir Roderic was a real stickler for doing things up right, even when "right" meant "wrong." In fact, Sir Roderic was the first one of the Ruddigore descendants who had the strength of will to stand up to ol' Sir Rupert. Once he was safely dead himself, anyway. And then it got to be a power struggle between Sir Roderic and Sir Rupert for who was going to end up as alpha ghost.

But let's get back to Sir Riven, who out in middle-class suburbia would maybe have been your A Number One conformist, but in the Ruddigore line he was, like, the complete and total nonconformist. Or wanted to be that, anyway, till bedtime rolled around and he had to walk down that long, dark-shadowy portrait gallery with no more'n a candlestick in his hand to light the way to his bedroom.

The first night he just tiptoed past 'em, portrait by portrait, breathing too soft to disturb even one grain of dust on the big, gilt-edged picture frames. Nothing bad happened. He made it to his bedroom okay, and went to sleep breathing a little easier. Next night, same thing. Third night, also okay, and he got to breathing easier yet. Almost a whole week went by, and he got to thinking maybe it really was just a folk legend, all of it. Maybe he didn't have to worry, after all. Maybe he could just go back to living the way he wanted to, a good, decent kind of lifestyle...

And then, boom! The seventh night, a whole chorus of hollow voices:

(Here the storyteller began to sing, in a soft, true voice.)

"Painted emblems of a race
All accursed in days of yore,
Each from his accustomed place
Steps into the world once more!"

Sir Riven fell down on his knees and held his breath. The ghostly chorus went swelling, rising and falling and rising again around the old gallery. The candle flame snuffed out and a blue-green glow took its place, coming from the portraits themselves as they stepped down to the floor and lined up behind ol' Sir Rupert for a kind of slow procession around their latest living descendant.

Sir Rupert was just opening his mouth to cut off the chorus and start the interview, when Sir Roderic finally stepped out of his frame, declaiming, "Beware! Beware! Beware!"

"Uncle Roderic!" goes Sir Riven, and he gets up, dusts off his knees, and makes to brazen it out. "How are you...uh...doing these days? I mean, how're things...uh...over there on the Other Side?"

Now that he finally has a live captive audience—just one, but obviously interested, Sir Roderic is only too ready to describe it:

> *(Again Gotcher sang, and this time Penny Wright softly supplied the occasional "Ha! ha!" syllables for him.)*

> "When the night wind howls in the chimney cowls, and the bat
>   in the moonlight flies,
> And inky clouds, like funeral shrouds, sail over the midnight
>   skies—
> When the footpads quail at the night-bird's wail, and black
>   dogs bay at the moon,
> Then is the spectres' holiday—then is the ghosts' high-noon!
> *(Penny)*   Ha! ha!
> Then is the ghosts' high-noon!
> *(Penny)*   Ha! ha!
> High no - oo - oo - oo - oon!
>   Then is the ghosts' high-noon!

> "As the sob of the breeze sweeps over the trees, and mists
>   lie low on the fen,
> From grey tomb-stones are gathered the bones that once were
>   women and men,
> And away they go, with a mop and a mow, to the revel that ends
>   too soon,
> For cockcrow limits our holiday—the dead of the night's high-
>   noon!
> *(Penny)*   Ha! ha!
> The dead of the night's high-noon!
> *(Penny)*   Ha! ha!
> High no - oo - oo - oo - oon!
>   The dead of the night's high-noon!

> "And then each ghost with his ladye-toast to their church-
>   yard beds takes flight,

With a kiss, perhaps, on her lantern chaps, and a grisly grim
  'good-night';
Till the welcome knell of the midnight bell rings forth its jolliest
  tune,
And ushers in our next high holiday—the dead of the night's
  high-noon!
(Penny)   *Ha! ha!*
The dead of the night's high-noon!
(Penny)   *Ha! ha!*
High no - oo - oo - oo - oon!
  The dead of the night's high-noon!"

* * * *

As soon as Sir Roderic finishes, Sir Rupert gets in with, "And now, young sprat, give an accounting of yourself."

"Orderly, O First-of-Our-Line, orderly," Sir Roderic tells Sir Rupert. And then *he* turns back to Sir Riven and starts out orderly with, "Monday, I think, was your first day of the onerous duty?"

"And on Monday," Sir Riven says proudly, "I committed murder!"

"Murder of whom?" demands ol' Sir Rupert.

"Of the time," Sir Riven has to confess. "I played the Minute Waltz in ninety-six seconds, in two-four."

Sir Rupert starts to shout, "You call *that* a crime—" but Sir Roderic, being more musically inclined, cuts him off with,

"*I* call it satisfactory! Tuesday?"

"On Tuesday," says Sir Riven, "I forged a Will."

This time ol' Rupert waits for Sir Roderic to ask it: "Whose Will?"

"My own," says Sir Riven.

Ol' Sir Rupert explodes with, "You can't forge your own Will!"

"A man can do what he likes with his own," Sir Riven argues. "Therefore, I can certainly forge my own Will! On Wednesday I filed a false Income Tax return."

All the ghosts hoot at this one. "That's nothing, nothing at all! Everybody does that." Sir Roderic sums it up with, "The tax forms being what they are, you could hardly file a true one if you tried. But we'll accept the implied intention, for now, and move on. Thursday?"

"On Thursday," Sir Riven says, getting a little hesitant now, "I shot a fox."

Well, this one actually pleases the ghosts, because it seems your true, sportin'-blood fox hunter never, never shoots the fox, considering it much more sporting and humane to let the dogs tear the little guy limb from limb. And Sir Riven doesn't mention that he wasn't actually out on a regular fox hunt at the time. "On Friday," he goes on, a little bit cockier again, "I forged a check."

"Whose check?" Sir Roderic wants to know.

"What does that matter?" says Sir Riven. "Shouldn't you be asking for how much?"

"Answer his question," says ol' Sir Rupert, who doesn't really understand modern banking but sees a chance to get his oar in again. "*Whose* check?"

"My faithful steward's," Sir Riven confesses.

"Your steward doesn't use a bank!" Sir Roderic objects.

"I didn't say I forged his *bank*, I said I forged his check. On Saturday I disinherited my firstborn son."

"You haven't got a son!" cries Sir Roderic.

"Not yet," Sir Riven explains. "I disinherited him in advance, to save time."

"And today?" rumbles ol' Sir Rupert.

"Today is Sunday." Sir Riven tries to stare him down. "When *any* unnecessary work counts as crime in the moral sense. I blacked my own boots."

"What it all boils down to," Sir Roderic says, just beating Sir Rupert to the punch, "is that you have managed with contrivances and arguments of dubious philosophical value to wriggle through your entire first week injuring no one seriously—except the fox—and doing nothing for which you could conceivably face legal action—except the Income Tax form, and there it would fit the general pattern if you actually falsified it to the benefit of the government. Now, unless you begin at once to take your duties more seriously…" Sir Roderic holds his right hand up menacingly, like so, and Sir Riven starts feeling some fairly serious pins and needles starting up from the soles of his feet to the crown of his head.

"Wait a minute!" he squeals, hit by a sudden panicky inspiration. "Do I understand this correctly? If I do nothing at all, it will mean my death?"

"It will," rumbles ol' Sir Rupert, holding up *his* right hand.

"But in that case," goes Sir Riven, "refusing to commit my daily crime amounts to suicide!"

Sir Roderic agrees, "Yes, so it would seem."

"But *suicide* is a crime!" Sir Riven cries.

All the ghosts stop and think about that one, looking back and forth between Sir Roderic and Sir Rupert.

Ol' Sir Rupert speaks first. "Something fails to scan here—"

Sir Roderic cuts in, "Well, *I* like it! On both the moral and the legal level, our latest living descendant is quite right. He has but to spend the remainder of his natural life committing ritual suicide on a daily basis."

The rest of the ghosts put up a cheer because, like I said before, all of them were getting pretty doggone tired of their own particular rat race and wanting to get on with a more relaxed afterlifestyle. So they outvoted Sir Rupert, followed Sir Roderic, left their portraits forever, and everybody got on with life—or death—liberty, and the pursuit of happiness ever after.

Well, Bugsy, my man, was that enough ghosts for you?

BUGSY

Yeah…well…it had ghosts, all right…but they weren't all that realistic or scary, were they? No blood and guts.

GOTCHER

Hey, man, the trick is, you gotta use your imagination sometimes. You want I should've taken a lot more time describing gory death wounds, maybe splashed some ketchup around?

BUGSY

And, hey! Doesn't "disinherit" mean cut people off from what they were going to inherit? I thought you said they got these titles, no matter what, so how could he disinherit his son?

GOTCHER

There's still the property, man. That's what he could will away to somebody else.

PENNY

Hmm? The property? Including the picture gallery? Interesting! "In this chapel are ancestors… I don't know whose they *were*, but I know whose they *are*…" And *The Pirates of Penzance* is set in Cornwall, too, a few generations later…

LEIF

Hardly seems like enough material there for a whole operetta.

PENNY (laughing)

You might say that! He's really trimmed it down to the bare bones, cutting out most of the characters and all the love interests.

BUGSY

All right!

PENNY

But I like what you've done with it, Gotcher, and I *loved* your rendition of Sir Roderic's song.

GOTCHER

Thank you kindly, ma'am. I played the part in a school production.

PENNY

I envy you.

UNCLE CLIFF

I played Colonel Pickering in "My Fair Lady." *(affecting a high-class British accent)* I say there!

PENNY

And I really, really wish I'd seen you in it!

BUGSY

Yeah, yeah, but we've still got one more story to go.

PEARL

And at least one more s'more to eat apiece, leave less to carry back to the house.

FREEDOM

Oh, I couldn't hold another crumb!

BUGSY

Don't worry, Sis, I can eat yours and mine both. How about it, Merlina? Can you tell us a story about real ghosts?

MERLINA

Oh, dear! Do you really expect me to tell a story, too?

Well, Bugsy, I'm afraid I can't remember any stories about wicked or scary ghosts, but I can try to tell one about a real ghost.

Death doesn't change people's natures, you see. If anything, it may make us…a little more ourselves, and most people try to be good most of the time. Maybe we actually find it easier on the Other Side. Being good, I mean. So it's silly being afraid of ghosts simply because they're ghosts, before we know anything about who they were on this side.

BUGSY

Like Casper the Friendly Ghost?

ELFRANK

Let us hold our peace, lad, and listen.

MERLINA

Thank you, I don't mind. I know I'm not much of a storyteller, and Gotcher is—I think they call it—"a hard act to follow."

MERLINA BATIQUE'S TALE

Well, I know a woman—she probably wouldn't like me to use her real name, so I'll call her Alice—a widow like myself, who sees…call them "wraiths"…as a regular thing in her everyday life. They're like people, or sometimes pet animals, but clear, transparent, like glass but flexible, moving around. As a rule, they tend to disappear if she tries to look straight at them. They have to be viewed from the side, "out of the corners of one's eyes," the way astronomers tell us we have to view celestial objects.

These wraiths, or apparitions, have always been quite harmless. When she first started seeing them, they seemed oblivious of her. All she could make of them was that perhaps they were people who had once lived in or visited her house or yard, and were passing through again. Eventually, some of them started seeming to take a friendly interest in her. Now she has three of them, youngsters, a little girl in a pink coat, one in a blue coat, and a little boy in a striped shirt, who often watch TV with her.

Now, a few months after this woman's husband died, she got a young dog, I'll call him Dodger, from the animal shelter. Dodger's a very well-behaved dog, doesn't chew up or disturb anything in the house; but he did explore thoroughly when she brought him home, sniffed around everywhere, especially in her bedroom. Using his nose more than his eyes. He'd stop and stare over a distance at things outdoors, but indoors he never actually *looked* at anything longer than a few seconds before turning and looking at something else.

Except for the second evening after she brought him home. That evening they were both in the living room, Alice watching TV with Dodger lying on the carpet near her feet. She glanced over and saw her new dog gazing up at something with all his might. Not at the TV—he wasn't even facing that way. She followed his line of sight and saw that it led to the framed photo of her late husband.

Dodger gazed at that photo for a full thirty seconds or more. Then he laid his head down on his front paws and dozed off into a very peaceful nap. Almost as if he were thinking, "It's all right—that man belongs here." As if the dog had been sighting the husband's ghost, and recognized his photograph in its place of honor.

But that isn't the end of it. You know the way trees occasionally fall without warning? Well, one day Alice was out walking Dodger on a path through a little woods around a lake near her home. They came to a weathered old bench overlooking the water, and she sat down to rest for a few minutes. All at once the dog sprang up from beside her—yanking the leash right out of her hand—and ran up the path, barking and wagging his tail.

He stopped about a dozen yards up the path and stayed there, pawing the air like he was expecting a treat. When Alice turned her head a little and tried looking out of the corner of her eye, she thought she could see one of her wraiths standing there, seeming to play with Dodger.

She got up and went over, and just as she reached them to get hold of Dodger's leash, she heard a cracking sound and then a crash. When she turned around—a big old dead tree had suddenly fallen and hit the bench where she was sitting half a minute before.

So we shouldn't be at all afraid of being haunted by friendly ghosts. They can be good company, and they might even be able to save your life.

FREEDOM

There! You see, Merlina, they *do* want us to go on living.

MERLINA

Or, at least, not dying in bad circumstances.

ELFRANK

Take care with that line of reasoning. There are too many who, interpreting "bad" in some such context as "uncontrolled," have sought to insure their final comfort by personally controlling their own last moments, and thus suicided their souls into Hell.

PENNY

Let's not get into that just now!

LEIF

We're too full of marshmallows and chocolate.

FREEDOM

So why not get married again, Merlina?

MERLINA

If one could find a second mate who wouldn't suffer by comparison with one's first. But then, if there were two men that good in the world, wouldn't it be selfish for one woman to have had them both?

> *Both Freedom and Penny glanced at Uncle Cliff, who was gazing at the latter. The librarian and the psychiatrist meanwhile exchanged meaningful looks with each other; and did Muttwump and Pumpkin actually nudge a bit nearer together in their doggy dozing?*
>
> *Soon after this, the party put out the remains of their campfire and repaired to their various bedrooms in Loon Lake Lodge.*

CHAPTER 29

About six o'clock the following morning, Uncle Cliff climbed out of bed, dressed, shaved, combed his hair carefully over the thinning spot, and repaired to the dining room, where he found not another living soul except…Penny Wright, whom he glimpsed through the window, sitting on a lounge chair in the screened porch, sipping something from a cup while she watched the early morning sunshine at play among the pine branches and lake ripples.

A carafe of hot water was waiting beside the row of cups and basket of tea bags, instant coffee packets, and envelopes of cocoa mix. Fixing himself a cup of hot chocolate, he went to join her on the porch.

UNCLE CLIFF

Good morning.

PENNY

Oh! Good morning.

UNCLE CLIFF

It looks like a beautiful morning.

PENNY

Yes…. "But we do want rain."

UNCLE CLIFF

I hope not. Not today, anyway.

PENNY

"Want" in the sense of "need."

UNCLE CLIFF

Well... In about another four or five days we will. If we don't get any before that. But things are still looking pretty green now.

PENNY

Very green. Dewy. It was just a quote...quotation...from that operetta Gotcher used for his story yesterday evening.

UNCLE CLIFF

Oh.... I had a dream last night.

PENNY

Oh, tell me!

UNCLE CLIFF

Well, you were in it....I was in a movie house. The movie was a new Indy Jones adventure, I think. Something about the "Lost Enterprise"? Anyway, when the movie was over and the house lights came up, there you were, sitting beside me. Only in the dream I didn't know you. You were a stranger. But you seemed to know me. You asked me if I read Sci-Fi. I said I did. You said, "So you know the theories about alternate universes?" When I answered yes, you told me that you came from an alternate universe. Somehow you had slipped into mine—my universe—in this movie theater—which must have been a sort of nub for the alternate universes—and you kept going out and coming in again, hoping to get back to your own universe, and finding yourself in a different one every time. You said, "For a minute, here, I thought I was home." When I asked why, you said...

> He hesitated so long that at last she prompted him, "Well? What did I say? Do you remember?"

UNCLE CLIFF

You said, "In the...alternate universe where I come from, you and I are married. Very happily. We're...very happy together." That's what you said. In my dream.

PENNY

....Wow.

UNCLE CLIFF

Of course, it wasn't really "you." It was really an alternate-world counterpart of you. In my dream. And it was just a dream.

PENNY

Wow, you even dream in Sci-Fi! What happened next?

UNCLE CLIFF

I woke up. But…

PENNY

But?

UNCLE CLIFF

I kept thinking about it all the time I was falling back asleep, so I don't know how much of the follow-up was dreaming, but I wanted to try to help you—the counterpart you—get back to your own universe, and you were insisting no, you didn't want me getting stuck between alternate universes, too… You wanted to get back to your own counterpart of me, and what I should do was…find your counterpart in my world. So finally we decided to see if we couldn't find somebody inside the theater who knew how it worked…the manager or someone…who might have a control panel tucked away somewhere, who could maybe dial you home… Well, that was about all.

PENNY

Maybe we could make a novel out of it.

UNCLE CLIFF

Maybe…we could make a date? "Starnet" is playing at the Lakeland in Woodward this week. It's a classic old theater. Town's about twenty minutes from Muskywater.

PENNY

I know—I came through Woodward on my way here. But do the two of us dare go into a movie theater, after your dream?

UNCLE CLIFF

As long as we stay together, it should be okay. *(His look said, though his mouth did not, "It might be kind of fun to bounce around in alternate universes with you. So long as we kept holding hands.")*

PENNY

Shall we say Wednesday?

UNCLE CLIFF

…Wednesday is my choir practice… But they have matinees in the summer. We could go to the Wednesday matinee.

PENNY

I don't like to feel rushed. How about Tuesday?

UNCLE CLIFF

Tuesday's fine. Evening?

PENNY

Let's say matinee. We'll go by daylight. Maybe a little safer than evening, if we're going to risk bouncing around in alternate universes.

UNCLE CLIFF

Together.

At this moment Mary Arrowsmith joined them, cup in hand, just in time to hear the last word.

MARY

Are you talking about carpooling to town this morning? I thought I'd go along with Leif to his U.C.C.

UNCLE CLIFF

That's my church, too.

MARY

He assures me it's very liberal.

UNCLE CLIFF

It is. We welcome everyone and never try to convert anyone. We get a lot of people, especially in vacation time, whose own religions don't have any churches in this area.

PENNY

How wonderful!... I—uh—think there's a Catholic church in Muskywater, isn't there?

ELFRANK

(having entered the porch unobserved by the others)
There is. Blessed Kateri of the Woods. I took care to ascertain the fact and procure the Mass schedule ahead of time, as is my habit whenever I spend a weekend away from home. Will you want to ride with me, or are you too liberal to place your religious obligations ahead of your own convenience?

PENNY

I wish you wouldn't use "liberal" to mean "bad." It's a sloppy use of language!

ELFRANK

Is it?

UNCLE CLIFF

Blessed Kateri's is just about a block from U.C.C. on a beeline trajectory. We can see its tower from our parking lot.

PENNY

Then I can ride with you and walk from there.

ELFRANK

Depending on the two schedules. The single Sunday Mass at Blessed Kateri takes place at ten thirty.

UNCLE CLIFF

Our U.C.C. service is at ten.

PENNY

Perfect!

LEIF

(coming in, having seen Mary already on the porch)
Yes, it's hard to sleep late on such a perfect morning. They were to ring a bell at seven-thirty, but I imagine everyone will be up by then anyway.

MARY

But not necessarily here on the dining-room porch.

ELFRANK

True. Indeed, communing in solitude with nature and nature's God might well constitute a better preparation for formal Sunday worship than mere idle chatter.

PENNY

I wouldn't call this weekend's conversations "mere idle chatter."

LEIF

If *you* do, Frank, why did you come?

ELFRANK

One may travel any distance eagerly in order to commune with another true seeker, only to find oneself, at the end of the journey, tongue-tied in the presence of the Great Mystery. Or, as sometimes happens, at the journey's end one may seek for the fellow true seeker, and seek in vain.

MARY

Maybe because what one seeks is less "Truth" than reconfirmation of one's own preconceived ideas.

PENNY

Years ago—in a writing class or maybe even when I was still in high school, a fellow student read an original short story that moved me a lot. A girl had gotten the most popular boy in the school as her date for the prom, and at first she thought she was the happiest girl in the world.

But as the evening wore on, she felt more and more disillusioned and unhappy with him. All they talked about was superficial things—small talk—and she felt he was completely shallow, all surface, no depth, a real disappointment. Then, after he brought her home, said good-night, and saw her safely inside, the story switched to his point of view, as he went back to his car, looking up at the moon and stars, singing inside with the beauty of the night, thinking how shallow his date had been, how you couldn't really talk about the deep, important things with a girl.

UNCLE CLIFF

It's hard enough to talk about them with *anybody* else, your own sex or the other.

MARY

Why do you think people pay for sessions with us psychoanalysts? So that they can sit and try to talk about what's deep inside them without the risk of being laughed at.

LEIF

Is that what we've come here for this weekend?

MERLINA (entering the porch)

I came because Freedom asked me, and because it's so nice to have someone else cook and wash the dishes for a weekend. Did you know they're about to ring the bell?

MARY

Do I hear it now?

ELFRANK

Yes, that would be the bell for seven-thirty. Actually, by my watch, it is seven thirty-three.

PENNY

Must be one of those mini time zone differences we find all over the place.

ELFRANK

Seven-thirty, if memory serves, was to be the wake-up call—superfluous, as it transpires—with breakfast to commence at seven forty-five, for those inclined to partake.

LEIF

What did you mean by that, Frank? I for one have found the meals here excellent.

PENNY

Glad to hear a man second my own opinion.

MERLINA

Don't let Eliza or Freedom hear you suggest a man's opinion could be worth more than a woman's!

PENNY

No—I only meant—in my observation—for a woman, almost anything tastes better if she hasn't had to cook it herself.

ELFRANK (clearing his throat with a hint of smugness)

Obviously, I intended no slight on the meals we have enjoyed here at Loon Lake Lodge. I, however, remain loyal to the old rules, which enjoined strict fasting from midnight until after Communion.

PENNY

You still abstain even from water?

ELFRANK

From even the tiniest sip.

PENNY

For your sake, I'm sorry they don't have an earlier Mass!

ELFRANK

For my sake, I rejoice that the breakfast about to be presented us will make my fasting a true sacrifice. For your sake, I might suggest that you would find it spiritually profitable to follow my example.

PENNY

Thank you, whatever rules are strict enough for the Pope, are strict enough for me.

ELFRANK

As Saint Luke records the words of Our Savior: "We are unprofitable servants. We have done no more than our duty."

GOTCHER (joining them, with Pumpkin trailing him)

Right on, man—just what the contract calls for, no more. And they didn't buy that for a defense even at Nuremberg, if I remember right.

PENNY

You began and ended with the same word! What do they call that? As a literary device, I mean.

ELFRANK

We can surely find weightier matters than that with which to occupy our minds, especially on a Sunday morning. For instance, we might more profitably employ our time persuading our atheist to accompany us to church.

GOTCHER

Man, I can ignore God better out in the woods than boxed inside four pious walls.

ELFRANK

From your own mouth I question your disbelief. Properly speaking, one can "ignore" only that which actually exists.

GOTCHER and PENNY (quoting simultaneously from Gotcher's G and S operetta)

"Fallacy somewhere, I fancy."

ELFRANK

One cannot, for example, "ignore" a roast that is not in fact present on the table.

GOTCHER

Too early in the a.m. for this kind of quibble, man! I spoke in short-hand. Guess I should've talked about ignoring your blabber about God.

PUMPKIN

Arf?

MUTTWUMP (just outside the porch door)

Arf! Arf!

PUMPKIN

Arf!

So hard on Muttwump's heels that their arrival might be termed "simultaneous," Bugsy appeared on the threshold of the porch. After pausing to call back, "Hey! It's okay, here they are, all of 'em!" he returned his attention to the porchful of assembled guests and inquired with some eagerness:

BUGSY

Power's out! Didn't you guys know?

FREEDOM (appearing at her kid brother's shoulder)

It's already so bright out here, I bet you didn't even have the lights on.

UNCLE CLIFF

No, we didn't.

GOTCHER

Hey, man, why didn't the generator kick in?

BUGSY and FREEDOM

Generator? What generator?

GOTCHER

The big ol' generator we used back when this was a commune. Called her Clarabelle. She was a beaut—all but state of the art, even if we did get her secondhand at a real bargain. Quite possibly the best investment we ever made. Supplied all our power needs, and didn't break down enough to need tinkering more than five or half a dozen times a year. If the rest of the commune had worked out half so well, we'd've still been here. Don't tell me you aren't still using Clarabelle Generator, man!

BUGSY (frowning in concentration)

Oh! Do you maybe mean that rusty ol' thing in the shed behind the kitchen?

GOTCHER

Rusty? Man, we painted her up with flower power all over.

FREEDOM

Yes, that's it. You can still see some of the paint. Must have been pretty "psychedelic" in its day, Mom says.

BUGSY

We thought it was an old, broken air conditioner or something.

GOTCHER

Poor old Clarabelle! How have the mighty fallen!

ELFRANK

So I see that you are not too confirmed in your atheism to quote the Bible.

GOTCHER

I think that's from Shakespeare, man.

PENNY

Pretty much the same thing.

UNCLE CLIFF (speaking quickly, so as to head off whatever Frank was about to say)

Why haven't I ever seen this generator? Assuming that's what it is.

BUGSY

Wanna see it now?

GOTCHER

Yeah, man, let's go have a looksee.

> *This point decided, the entire company, dogs crowding along, trooped to the shed behind the kitchen, where Gotcher recognized the timeworn unit as his commune's once-trusty generator, shed a few figurative tears over her dereliction, and announced his preparedness to have another go at fixing her, for old times' sake, if the power hadn't come back on by the time the others were ready to leave for church—or even if it had. Unpredictable power outages being kind of a habit around this neck of the northwoods.*

ELFRANK

With never a doubt in your complacent brain as to whether it might not be to your greater permanent benefit to join us at one or other of the churches?

GOTCHER

And pray for a miracle to cure an ailing hunk of machinery? Hey, man, even back when I believed there was a God, I also believed he mostly helped those who helped themselves.

BUGSY

Meantime, what about breakfast?

MERLINA

It must have been almost ready when the power went out?

FREEDOM

At least we have a lot of muffins and donuts and bread and dry cereal and stuff, even if the meat and eggs and pancakes didn't get cooked in time.

GOTCHER

Bugsy, my man, why don't you bring me a couple of donuts and your dad's toolbox, and I'll get started right now?

UNCLE CLIFF

Let me give you a hand. I'm good at fixing things.

FREEDOM

His father used to say, "If Clifford can't fix it, it can't be fixed."

GOTCHER

That so? Well, then, I'm glad you didn't know about Clarabelle here, or I'd've been out a handy way to repay these good people for their hospitality. Sooner than let you steal my thunder, man, I'm coming back, eat whatever we've got for breakfast, and make sure you get off on time with all the other churchophiles before I commence operations on my own hook.

CHAPTER 30

They settled around the breakfast table to partake of muffins, do-nuts, bread, and dry cereal. Of course the bread could not be toasted, but fortunately the coffee had been brewed and the water for tea and cocoa well heated before the power went out, and the large urns would retain their heat for quite some time. And, reassured by Gotcher that within an hour after eating, if the power had not come back on by then, he would surely have the generator back in service, Pearl Bonami made bold to open the fridge long enough to bring out milk for the cereal and cream for the coffee. Butter and jam for the bread and muffins were already safe on the table.

So soon as the others had helped themselves to whatever of the avail-able provisions they wished, Mr. Craftlove, surveying the assemblage from his smug perch above a plate guiltless of food and cup equally unsullied since its last trip through the dishwasher, thus remembered the Gotcher project:

ELFRANK

Very well, my friend, let us return to the basics. How, if there is no Creator, do you explain the existence of Creation?

GOTCHER (laughing)

Give us a break, man! That one was already old corn by the first time somebody asked which came first, the chicken or the egg—which I seem to remember us settling the other day, in favor of the primordial egg. Me, I think the universe jest growed.

ELIZA

Like Topsy?

GOTCHER

More like Topsy-Turvy.

ELFRANK

The great difficulty with that analogy is that Topsy did *not* "jest grow." Little as she herself, at the tender age we glimpse her, may have been aware of the fact, even Topsy had a father and a mother.

GOTCHER

And you want the universe to have just a father, man? Where's the mother?

LEIF

Sky Father, Earth Mother.

PENNY

Didn't the ancient Egyptians reverse that? Sky Mother and Earth Father...

ELFRANK

Another false analogy. My only point was that no delicate or complicated mechanism—understanding "mechanism" in the broadest sense—comes into being by itself.

BUGSY

What about a simple, uncomplicated one?

ELFRANK

Your "primordial globule" is already an organism of the most wonderful complexity. Even scientists of the least spiritual stamp tell us that.

BUGSY

What about the rocks and water and stuff that had to be around before the live globule could develop?

UNCLE CLIFF

Atoms are pretty complex, too. Even the simplest—the hydrogen atom. The deeper we go, the more amazed we are how complex.

ELFRANK

Thank you.

GOTCHER

All this sounds okay, but I expect any minute you're gonna try hitting me with adjectives like "orderly" and "well-regulated," and there's your big mistake, man. The universe just ain't orderly or well-regulated or any of that. It's a big, stupid, bloody mess.

MARY

As far as human affairs go, you're certainly justified in saying that. For the rest of creation, I'm not so sure. The universe at large seems to be reasonably well-regulated, at least until humanity interferes with it.

ELIZA

Shouldn't you say "the world"? We can make a mess of our own planet, but the universe at large? Surely that's a little like a gnat trying to deface Mount Rushmore.

GOTCHER

Actually, the gnat's a lot bigger to Rushmore than we are to the universe at large. It's religion that makes humanity out for the be-all and end-all of creation. But I wasn't blaming all the mess of the universe just on us humans. What about "Nature red in tooth and claw"? What about Black Holes at the center of every galaxy?

UNCLE CLIFF

Everything has to eat. And we're not quite sure what purpose Black Holes serve, but it could be to hold the galaxies together.

ELFRANK

Thank you. We return, you see, to the fact that the root of disorder is the peculiarly human phenomenon of sin. And the root of sin, the ground of sin, the all but unforgivable sin is disbelief.

PENNY

Now, wait a minute! Which is worse—the mass murderer, or the philanthropist who quietly doesn't believe in God?

ELFRANK (without a blink)

The latter. The former kills merely bodies. The latter, by setting a deplorable example and sheathing atheism in a false luster of respectability, murders souls.

ELMER

That's pretty strong.

ELFRANK

"It would be better for anyone who leads astray one of these simple believers to be plunged in the sea with a great millstone fastened around his neck." Saints Matthew, chapter 18, and Mark, chapter 9.

PENNY

Whereas, to feel honestly convinced in one's heart that there is no God, and go around mouthing pious sentiments anyway, just to satisfy people like you, is hypocrisy—and you know what Jesus had to say about hypocrites!

ELFRANK

You misunderstand hypocrisy, which was—and is—the masking of greed in a pretext of piety, the use of piety to oppress one's fellows. This is the hypocrisy against which Our Savior railed—not the silence that refrains from infecting other souls with one's secret disbelief.

MARY

I'll repeat what I quoted the other day about Jesus saying, "If you bring forth what is within you, it will save you; if you don't, it will destroy you." And before you object to the Gospel of Thomas, Frank, doesn't that most probably Gnostic Evangelist John himself remark that Jesus said and did many more things than he could record?

ELFRANK

That John's Gospel bears the heretical taint of Gnosticism is slander, but we will assume your repetition of it springs from simple misinformation, and pass on to your citation from the so-called Gospel of Thomas, concerning releasing what is within lest it destroy the bearer. Now, assuming this statement to possess any authenticity whatsoever, no doubt the lost context would have plainly shown the duty of evangelizing the Truth that sets believers free.

GOTCHER

Yes, our culture is very big on Freedom of Speech—just so long as everyone who practices it speaks freely whatever the culture has already decided it can either applaud, or laugh off as harmless.

PENNY

Returning to your "fact" that the root of disorder is human sin, Frank, I really don't see how human sin causes things like natural disasters and Chronic Wasting Disease.

LEIF

In his poem "Natural Theology," Kipling has a medieval man saying…let's see if I can quote it right…

> *"My sewer and well flow into each other,*
> *After the custom of Christendie.*
> *Fevers and fluxes are killing my mother—*
> *Why has the Lord afflicted me?"*

It's a longish poem pointing up how much of what we blame on God or "the gods" is really our own fault, even if it takes us a few centuries to figure it out.

GOTCHER

Right on, man! And Oriental wisdom tells us how a butterfly flapping its wings on one side of the world causes a hurricane on the other side.

UNCLE CLIFF

Possible, but not probable—as a certain science officer Frank doesn't approve would say.

PENNY

But a butterfly isn't humanity—a butterfly is part of nature, so whether hurricanes start from butterflies flapping their wings or anything else, it still isn't *human* "sin"—it's still a natural disaster.

BUGSY

Hey! Aren't we part of nature, too?

GOTCHER

Again I say, right on! Natural disasters, the job lot of us.

ELFRANK

The conversation appears to have taken a ridiculous turn.

ELIZA

Here's another problem: intentions don't always match results. The best intentions can result in harm and injury. For instance, a saint may give her grocery money to a beggar—who then goes and spends it on whisky.

ELFRANK

Let the saint choose the objects of her charity with greater care.

PENNY

I'm not sure that's exactly what Jesus taught.

UNCLE CLIFF

It's kind of like judging other people, isn't it?

ELFRANK

It is simple, prudent discernment of spirits.

MARY

I'd say that "discernment" is what one applies to one's own psyche. Trying to "discern" someone else's spirits—unasked—amounts to judging them.

PEARL

Back in the Forties, your good, healthy breakfast was bacon and eggs, and just having a bowl of cold cereal was like eating junk food. Nowadays, it's the bacon and eggs that'll kill you, and eating just the cold cereal that's the healthy breakfast.

ELFRANK

With all respect, madam, and many thanks for all your labors, what has that to say to the problem at hand?

UNCLE CLIFF

It's one more example of meaning well and doing the wrong thing. We want to do what's healthy for us, but the people who are supposed to know, keep changing the rules.

MERLINA

When I grew up, we were taught seven basic food groups. Later they changed it to four, and I even saw a TV ad made to look like an old movie showing them teaching four food groups back in my day. Then they came out with the food pyramid, then revised the pyramid, and I don't know where they are now.

FREEDOM

I've seen another commercial where a man talks about the two basic food groups as "sugars and preservatives."

Most of the party laughed.

PENNY

Wright's Kitchen Law Number One—which Wright herself often ignores: the more convenient it makes meal preparation, the worse it is for your health.

Uncle Cliff and a few others laughed. Frank cleared his throat.

ELFRANK

Granted, maintaining the health of the body is so important a responsibility that ignoring it can, under conditions of mere thoughtlessness, worldliness, or carelessness, amount to grievous sin; nevertheless, the health of the soul must always take precedence.

PENNY

So it's sinful to go anorexic for your looks but not for religious fasting, no matter if the health results are exactly the same?

ELMER

Look at the time.

Thus reminded, the breakfast party broke up and those attending services at any one of Muskywater's churches made ready to depart. Although both authors were heading ultimately for Blessed Kateri of the Woods, Penny elected to ride with Uncle Cliff, Leif and Mary taking their places in the back seat of his old Dodge, while Merlina and Freedom—who had decided to accompany her in friendly curiosity to see how the Free Bible Church embellished a Sunday morning, passengered in Frank's unpretentious Cadillac.

Pearl and Eliza got busy stacking the dishes and otherwise cleaning up after breakfast as best they could while awaiting power for the water pump, whilst Gotcher, with Bugsy and Elmer, turned to see whether faithful old Clarabelle might not be coaxed out of her long retirement of rust and neglect. The dogs tagged along, but soon grew bored by these strange machinations of men with generator, and Muttwump led Pumpkin away on a tour of the chief points of canine interest that Loon Lake Lodge had to offer. In his cage, Budgewiser began inquiring, only a trifle prematurely, whether whoever heard him had had a busy day.

After about three quarters of an hour, Gotcher succeeded with Clarabelle. The men cheered, and the women washed dishes. Perhaps ten minutes later, the power company restored its own electricity, as the men learned by toying with one of Elmer's model train layouts that had never been hooked up to the generator; but they decided to let Clarabelle continue feeling useful again awhile longer, after her long period of desuetude.

CHAPTER 31

With the help of electrical power, Pearl was able to prepare the luncheon she had planned, rather than substituting, as she otherwise must have, cold sandwiches accompanied with beverages innocent of ice cubes.

In one way, the carpooling had been less than optimally convenient. The U.C.C. service beginning a mere half hour after the Catholic, Uncle Cliff, Leif and Mary had not so very long to wait, and a Friendship Room adjoining the U.C.C. sanctuary to wait in; this same facility lay at Penny's disposal when she walked down from Blessed Kateri's after Mass, in time to enjoy the strange (to her ears) closing hymns of the Protestant service. The Free Bible Church, however, did not begin its service until 11:30. Frank Craftlove's ulterior motive in carrying his two passengers had been to persuade them to taste what the True Church had to offer; but Freedom disliked the thought of overdosing on religion, and steadfastly opted to wait comfortably with Merlina in the latter's Yarn Barn, which was only a little farther from the Free Bible Church than Blessed Kateri's was from the U.C.C., and therefore an easy enough stroll. Eschewing both the Free Bible Church as an heretical sect (though he had the grace to refrain from putting it to Merlina in exactly those words) and the Yarn Barn as of limited interest to a male of his proclivities (he added that a hunting supply store would have been, to him, almost equally uninteresting), he whiled away his after-Mass wait over toast and tea in one of the town's two small restaurants, following which he turned to the nearby general store, which stayed open on Sundays until half past one, and shook his head over the selection in its stand of paperback books, deploring most of the fiction in his own potboiling genre.

Meanwhile, after the return of Uncle Cliff's Dodge, Loon Lake Lodge settled down to await the return of Frank's Cadillac before addressing lunch.

Since Eliza gave Pearl a hand in the kitchen, and insisted on her second-born helping out in the capacity of gofer, Muttwump meanwhile continuing Pumpkin's tour of the grounds, it was only half a dozen who assembled in the lounge. Elmer as host poured appetizers for the assembly, Uncle Cliff as usual taking his cola straight. Bugsy meanwhile brought in Budgewiser, whose cage the tall Gotcher suspended from a hook set years ago into the ceiling, more probably for the use of hanging a flowerpot than a birdcage.

BUDGEWISER

Have you had a busy day?

GOTCHER (laughing)

Right on, little guy, and it's only about halfway through. Well, people, what about it? Anybody else like a go at converting the atheist while Big Poppa ain't around to breath hellfire at us?

UNCLE CLIFF

Or maybe you'd like to have your go at converting us to atheism?

GOTCHER

It wouldn't be me, man. It'd be your own native reason and intelligence.

MARY

Speaking as the non-Christian, and therefore the party Frank would no doubt have been trying to convert if you hadn't shown up to save me from that fate, I'd like to register a protest against the idea that reason and intelligence must always lead to atheism.

GOTCHER

Where else? Nope, I've gotta stand my ground. It's just plain fear—whether people understand it or not—that twists reason and intelligence into supporting religion.

PENNY

Are you sure fear can't—doesn't—cut both ways?

LEIF

True. People who fear hell find it a relief to think death ends everything, but people who look forward to heaven fear nothingness and oblivion.

MARY

We choose our fears. Reality doesn't necessarily have to pay any attention to our individual quirks and foibles.

GOTCHER

That the technical language of psychoanalysis, Doc Shrink Lady?

MARY

The language of off-duty poetry, Mr. Hippie Gentleman.

ELMER

What *do* you believe in, Gotcher?

GOTCHER

Well, man... I guess it's all give and take between us and Reality.

PENNY

We shape it, and it shapes us? Well—aren't we part of Reality, too?

UNCLE CLIFF

Believe in anything outside of and larger than yourself, and—as may have been said before—you're believing in Something that somebody, somewhere, calls "God."

GOTCHER

Semantics, man, semantics.

MARY

He could have a point there. This word "believe" is rather slippery.

LEIF

Yes. It can mean to be of the opinion that such-and-such actually exists, or it can denote pledging allegiance. In the "I think this is the actual case" meaning, we carelessly interchange it with "know"—as "k-n-o-w"—

PENNY

The way we mix up "evidence" and "proof."

LEIF

Yes. So we say in the creed, "I believe in God"—literally meaning, "I pledge allegiance to the principles I understand by the concept 'God,'" and this becomes "I 'know' the Biblical God actually exists."

MARY

Even in our own minds, the confusion grows. Language is a tricky tool.

LEIF

But it's the best one we have so far. For its own purposes, anyway.

PENNY

It's the Italians?—I think—who have a phrase meaning, "To translate is to betray." In a way, that's what happens to us all the time. We have these deep feelings, deep insights—we try to wrap words around them and—even while doing this—actually, *by* trying to do this—we misrepresent and distort what's really inside us.

MARY

Even if we were glimpsing it accurately ourselves, "from the inside," so to speak.

UNCLE CLIFF

I'm not so sure about that. Pretty often, *something* comes through.

LEIF

True. Or we wouldn't be able to communicate at all, even to complain about the inadequacy of our attempts at communication.

GOTCHER

Like, for instance, "somebody somewhere" may call "it"—whatever—"God," but that isn't to say that "it"—whatever—is what *I'd* call "God."

PENNY

Can you call *anything* "God," if you don't believe God exists at all?

LEIF

Nice point, there. Can we define things we consider nonexistent?

UNCLE CLIFF

What about mermaids, manticores, and the Loch Ness Monster?

MARY

Ah! But the people who defined those beings, thought they actually existed.

PENNY

At least, we *think* that's what they thought. But we could be doing them an injustice, there. Maybe they were perfectly well aware these were made-up creatures, and it was subsequent generations that got fooled.

LEIF

However we slice it, someone turns out to be foolish somewhere.

GOTCHER

Like with God.

UNCLE CLIFF

Or maybe mermaids and manticores actually exist in some alternate universe.

GOTCHER

Yeah, man, if you like, but that's where this argument breaks down, the one that goes, "God probably exists, so He could choose to create this particular universe—the one with the right anthropomorphic coincidences to fit us—out of all the possible universes He could have created." I mean, if all these possible universes exist, we just grew in whichever one fit us, and no divine intelligence had to choose anything.

BUDGEWISER

Have you had a busy day?

All laughed or chuckled.

MARY

As Leif said, language is still one of the best tools we've developed so far.

UNCLE CLIFF

Until we all develop our latent sense of ESP.

MARY

Maybe. Assuming ESP doesn't turn out to prove almost as tricky as physical, mouth-to-ear language.

LEIF

Like flesh-and-blood bodies. We can see language like the Greeks saw our bodies—as something that separates us—or like the Hebrews saw them—as things that make it possible for us to get together.

GOTCHER

Hey, man, I like that! With our bodies, we can make love, not war.

MARY

Although, obviously, even the Greeks sometimes got together with their bodies.

PENNY

But maybe less than willingly, if half of what I've heard about the status of women in ancient Greek society is true.

BUDGEWISER

Have you had a busy day?

GOTCHER

Hey, watch out, bird! It was just about to get really interesting.

Mary and Leif exchanged a glance, as did Penny and Uncle Cliff. Elmer grinned and poured another round of drinks. Gotcher grinned and carried them around. And so the chit-chat continued without resolving any question except the necessity of tolerance, compromise, and the art of living with unresolved questions, until Frank—a past master of living with questions that were already resolved, whether rightly or wrongly, in any case to his own satisfaction, got back with his passengers Merlina and Freedom from their respective churches, when lunch, which had awaited only their arrival, was served in the main dining room, with the doors to the screened porch wide open in order to best enjoy the day's delicious breezes.

Having heard from Uncle Cliff's musical lore the principle that concerts should end with a piece that left the audience wanting more, the Eklektiks and their cook had planned a last luncheon more nearly resembling a dinner: duck a l'orange, with ham on the side for anyone who might not want duck (in the event, everyone wanted duck, so it was as well that Pearl had prepared three, but most of the company took a slice or two of ham in addition); a medley of wild and tame rice; California vegetables; tomato aspic; a pleasant salad compounded of avocado, red onion, and pink grapefruit tossed in poppy seed dressing; and for dessert, (almost) every American's favorite, good old apple pie.

Budgewiser, whose cage Elmer had carried in and hooked to the stand in the dining room, surveyed the humans' meal while partaking of his own, consuming seed after seed and scattering their shells over his own pebbled floor paper, then attacking his cuttlebone almost as if it were an enemy. The dogs lounged lazily beneath the table, perhaps envying the bird for, although they partook of human food, they did not partake of it until after the humans had finished their own meal; this was one of the few house rules Muttwump lived by (except when Bugsy cheated), and in deference to his hosts Gotcher adopted it—at least during this meal—for Pumpkin who, with canine adaptability, suffered it patiently and nudged herself a little closer to Muttwump.

When once the ducklings had been carved, the side dishes passed around, and the feast fairly embarked upon, Frank—bolstered anew by his Sacrament—seized his final chance to broach once again the adopted project of the weekend.

ELFRANK

This being our last general gathering of the weekend, and additionally the hallowed day of Sunday, let me ask you, Gotcher my friend, atheist as you proclaim yourself to be, have you no fear of the nothingness that you believe awaits you following the dissolution of your earthly shell?

GOTCHER

Man, according to you, nothingness awaits all these other creatures *except* us humans who've managed to screw the world up so royally for them. If they don't fear it, why should we?

ELFRANK

They cannot imagine anything beyond this world. They, indeed, cannot so much as conceive of no longer being alive in the flesh.

GOTCHER

Neither can we, man, and that's why we make up these heavens and hells and summerlands and whatchamaycallems to live in after we're dead. Only some of us recognize what's going on, and we're not afraid to admit it—hey, I can't imagine myself dead, but I'm gonna be dead one of these days, just the same.

PENNY

I'm always uneasy whenever we talk about what "the animals" can and cannot imagine. I mean, how can we *know?* We can't even know for sure what other human beings think and perceive and imagine. I know what *I* see by the color orange, but I can't be sure it's exactly the same thing *you* see as orange. In fact, it probably isn't, quite, or—to switch colors—why are there so many arguments about whether something or other is "green" or "blue"?

MARY

There's a native language somewhere that has no separate words for "green" and "blue." But I believe it does have separate words for different shades of yellow.

BUDGEWISER

Have you had a busy day?

ELFRANK (after clearing his throat)

Very well, then, let us return strictly to our perceptions and imaginations. If we can imagine it, chances are that in some form it exists. Neither the griffin nor the centaur was a totally imaginary creature, but rather one made up of mismatched pieces of reality. I shall even allow, for the sake of argument, that the lower animals might be capable of imagining and therefore enjoying an afterlife. As C. S. Lewis remarks, a Heaven for mosquitoes could be very neatly combined with a Hell for humans. What we cannot conceptualize or imagine, and what therefore in all probability does *not* exist, is the absence of any awareness following corporeal dissolution.

GOTCHER

Fallacy somewhere, I fancy.

LEIF

It's a funny thing about imagining the afterlife. The better people have it in their mortal lifetimes, the worse they start fearing they'll have it after death. The record seems to show that oppressed people look forward to "that great gettin'-up morning," where the wealthy and comfortable fear the dread Day of Judgment.

ELFRANK

And rightly so, when their wealth and comfort comes through oppression of the masses.

GOTCHER

What about *your* wealth and comfort, man?

ELFRANK

I leave it up to the reasonably well-off bookbuying public whether they want to squander their excess pennies on literary tripe.

UNCLE CLIFF

People who have other people oppressing them look to God for protection and reward, which too often translates for them into Heaven and Judgment Day as "that great gettin'-up morning." People who have it very good in this life, at least in the material sense—who are on top, so to speak, and can't blame other people for oppressing them—whether it's because they're the oppressors, or not—they don't feel any need for God as avenger or rewarder, and so they start fearing Him as somebody who can take away their comforts and privileges, come the Day of Reckoning.

PENNY

Wonderful! But Frank has slid very neatly over the problem of whether animals have souls, and I think it's really much more important than that. By denying souls to animals...

ELFRANK

Show me any Biblical text to the effect that they do.

PENNY

Balaam's ass, for one. You show me anywhere in the Bible where it says they *don't*. I think it was Science that came up with that idea, to excuse its experiments on animals—as if their not having any Heaven after their death meant it was perfectly okay for us to make this life Hell for them—and in this case Religion followed Science in order to bolster its notions of humanity as something really special—probably a reaction to its own collective guilty conscience. St. Francis loved animals, and he's called the saint who was most like Jesus. Anyway. As your own story last night suggested, it might be impossible to treat our fellow human beings right, until and unless we also treat animals and all creation right.

> *Gotcher, Uncle Cliff, and several of the others applauded, which caused the speechifier to look both pleased and embarrassed, even abashed.*

ELFRANK

Indeed? Would you find it permissible, then, to rebuke Muttwump or Pumpkin as you just rebuked me?

BUGSY

We scold an' punish them for doggy misbehaving.

PENNY

I was arguing—in the debating sense—not rebuking.

ELFRANK

You have called Francis of Assisi the saint "most like Jesus." In fact, *no* mortal, however saintly, was or ever could be "like Jesus," except perhaps insofar as a fruit fly resembles an eagle. For Jesus Christ was God Incarnate.

GOTCHER

Thus spaketh the Council of Nicea three centuries or so after the fact.

ELFRANK

Clarifying what had already been recorded centuries earlier. As C. S. Lewis also observed, "Either Jesus was a raving lunatic, or else He was exactly what He claimed to be. There is no middle way."

GOTCHER

Sure there is, man. At least two middle ways, take your choice. Either the Gospel writers got it wrong, or the Council of Nicea got the Gospel writers wrong.

PENNY

Someone else points out that in the Synoptics Jesus hardly ever talks about Himself, and in John He hardly ever talks about anything else.

LEIF

So do we owe our understanding of Jesus as God Incarnate primarily to John's Gospel?

ELFRANK

I would question that, but suppose we do? Is it any the less valid for that?

PENNY

I've also found it stated somewhere—in a book with the *Imprimatur*, I'm sure—that Scripture isn't itself the revelation, but only the *record* of the revelation.

ELFRANK

So? What has that to say to the case?

PENNY

Only that language is a tricky thing. One person gets a divine revelation that he or she can't find just the right words for—probably because just the right words don't exist yet—so he or she does the best they can with whatever words are available to them. Then a lot of time goes by, and some community or other decides, "This is a Direct Revelation from God," and translates it, and translates the translation, and starts picking out and analyzing these translated words according to whatever they've come to mean by now, and never even stops to ask itself whether what they're working with is still the original revelation or something else.

ELFRANK

You come perilously close to blasphemy.

PENNY

Yes, maybe I do. Thank God, that isn't a burnable crime here and now, in this country. But the fact remains that I've only got the word of other human beings for it that the Bible is a direct, sacrosanct revelation from God. Maybe God has given some other human beings this direct guarantee about the Bible, but He—or She—has never given that assurance to me, personally.

GOTCHER

And the humans who think they've had it are just getting their own psychological quirks confused with God.

PENNY

And then, we declare our Biblical Canon closed, denying the possibility that God might have more revelations for future people in their own eras—and we never even notice that our various interpretations and glosses and commentaries and even re-translations actually result in a kind of new Scripture.

ELFRANK

The alternative to a closed Canon is chaos, nor is anyone compelled to place the same trust in any interpretation, gloss, or commentary as in the Scripture itself.

GOTCHER

Huh! Go and tell that last part of your statement to the Fundamentalists, or the Inquisition, or any other churchgoer you like, and see how far you get explaining the difference between "Scripture" and their own pet interpretation of the same.

MARY

I would have to say our hippie is in the right of it there.

ELFRANK

Of course, it is always so simple and self-righteous to hold the entire Catholic world of all ages, eras, and places to blame for the Inquisition, which was a product peculiar to its own time, clime, and structures of the secular governments, and had its strenuous opposition even among contemporary Catholics of a wiser and more far-seeing nature.

LEIF

Not to say braver.

ELIZA

To be fair, Frank, Gotcher mentioned Fundamentalism in the same breath as the Inquisition.

ELMER

And "Fundamentalism" usually means folk like the Southern Baptist Convention.

PENNY

It's always easier to laugh at another group than to take them seriously.

GOTCHER

Oh, I take the Southern Baptists very seriously. More than my life 'd be worth to go into one of their tent revivals and tell 'em exactly what I think about their particular take on religion.

ELFRANK

Indeed? Does that imply that you take my "particular take" less seriously?

GOTCHER

Man, I don't take *anybody's* religion seriously, but I *can* take people themselves seriously. Don't think I'd sit here and tell you what I think about your particular creed if we were in the time and clime of the Spanish Inquisition instead of safe in America where all we've got to fear that way is the Republicrat Right.

ELMER

I've voted Republicrat, some elections.

ELFRANK

As have I.

PENNY

We have the secret ballot as one of our rights in this country, so I'd never tell any of these exit pollsters how I'd just voted in any election. But if it seemed to me that the Republicrat was a better person than the Democritan in any given election, yes, I might vote Republicrat, too. I've even voted third party, more than once.

FREEDOM

That's throwing your vote away.

PENNY

No, it's telling the Political Powers That Be, here's someone who cares enough to vote but dislikes both of the major parties' offerings.

LEIF

Do you think any Political Power is really paying much attention, these days when fifty-two percent of the vote counts as a "landslide"?

GOTCHER

And couldn't we say that not voting at all sends the Political Powers That Be a message that here's folks who think the whole system is dirty and needs changing?

BUDGEWISER

Have you had a busy day?

ELIZA

Budgewiser has a way of being right. Let's call another time out.

ELFRANK

Rather, let us return from the temporal to the eternal verities. And are you in fact irrevocably bent, my friend Gotcher, on spending Eternity in the infernal regions?

GOTCHER

Hey, man, give me one good proof why your particular passport to the heavenly regions is valid and all the other parties who're busy waving alternate ones, each of 'em claiming to be the one, true, and exclusive way up, are wrong, and maybe I'll reconsider. Meantime, I'd just as soon take my chances with everybody else around this table, and maybe have just a few more bites of that tomato aspic, thanks!

ELFRANK

When have I suggested that *every*body else here present is doomed?

PENNY

Careful there, Frank! You're getting dangerously close to Vatican II.

UNCLE CLIFF

(noticing Pearl getting up to fetch the pie from the sideboard)
I think maybe now we should set aside the serious talk and finish up our last meal together with a dessert-round of jokes.

BUGSY

Hey, great idea!

PEARL

Who wants it a la mode and who wants it with good, Wisconsin cheddar cheese? Bugsy, please go get the ice cream.

CHAPTER 32

Elmer, Eliza, Merlina, Penny (who was among the few Americans less than wild about apple pie but who for once politely said nothing about it), and—after a moment's consideration—Uncle Cliff opted for slices of cheese, most of the others for ice cream, Gotcher for both, and Frank chose to eat his pie naked and unadorned.

ELFRANK

Since I sit accused of solemnity and over-righteousness, let me begin by asking this company to name the five things that God, even in His omniscience, does not know.

The company pondered this problem while passing their used dinner plates up to Freedom—who stacked them ready for removal to the kitchen—and accepting their desserts from Bugsy, who carried them around as Pearl cut the pie and embellished each slice to the recipient's taste. What was it that God did not know? Elmer suggested, how to balance the national budget; Gotcher, why anyone went to war—but Eliza pointed out that that way led back to serious discussion, and Frank was asking a riddle designed for laughter. Pearl proposed, where the socks went that the drier ate up. Uncle Cliff suggested, which side of a Mobius strip was "up"; Penelope, what was the difference between A sharp and B flat; Leif, where was the Muskywater Library's copy of Turgenev's Fathers and Sons *that had been missing for three years with no record of ever having been charged out; Merlina, why a raven was like a writing-desk. At length, when all the pieces of pie had been passed out, Frank answered his own riddle.*

ELFRANK

One: What a Franciscan is going to say before he steps into the pulpit. Two: What a Dominican has said after he steps out of the pulpit.

Three: What is on the mind of a Jesuit. Four: What a Benedictine does with his time. Five: What a lay priest does with his money.

> *Only Penny laughed. Leif and Mary managed a chuckle; some of the others smiled politely, but most looked more or less blank.*

UNCLE CLIFF

What's a "lay priest"? It sounds like a contradiction in terms.

ELFRANK

If you please. As it was my riddle that appears to have fallen flat, it behooves me to explain it. A "lay priest" is one not belonging to any religious order, but simply under the direction of his local bishop and receiving a living stipend which remains under his personal budgetary control. For the rest: the Franciscans were traditionally known for spontaneity; the Dominicans, for deep and sometimes abstruse studiousness; the Benedictines, for their—

GOTCHER

Liqueur! And we all know what "jesuitical" means.

PENNY

Probably unfairly; but that order had its Catholic enemies from the outset, like the Inquisition and today's Opus Dei, and weren't the Jesuits even repressed for a while by some pope or other?

MUTTWUMP

Arf.

PUMPKIN

Arf. Arf. Arf.

BUDGEWISER

Have you had a busy day?

ELMER

(clearing his throat)

Awhile back a priest and a minister introduced their pal a rabbi from the Twin Cities to fishing on our lake out there. Well, after about an hour, the priest says, "Where's the beer?"

"Oh, gosh," says the minister, "we left it back in the car."

"Never mind," says the priest, "I'll go get it." And he gets out of the boat, walks across the water to the shore, gets their little cooler out of the car, carries it back across the water, and climbs back into the boat.

Well, they open it up, and—this happened a while back, before pop-top cans got universal—no church key, like they used to call the openers for bottles and cans.

"Never mind," says the minister, "you got the beer, I'll go get the church key." So he gets out of the boat, walks across the water to the car, rummages around a minute or two, and comes back with the can opener, walking across the water.

Well, all this time the rabbi is just sitting there with his mouth open, watching his chums. Eventually he decides, if they can do it, so can I. So he says, "Y'know, I left my favorite lure back there in the car." He steps out of the boat, and plunk! straight to the bottom.

He comes up, they pull him back into the boat and find a towel, and he sits there awhile shaking water out of his ears and thinking, How can they be that much holier than I am? Doesn't make sense. If they can do it, why can't I? So finally he makes up his mind he's going to try again, tells them he's going back to the car for another towel, steps out of the boat and plunk! straight to the bottom.

This time when they haul him into the boat, the minister turns to the priest and asks, "Well, Father Mike, think we better tell him where the stepping stones are?"

After the general laughter, Bugsy protested, "That never happened anywhere on this lake, Dad!"

ELMER

Maybe it did and maybe it didn't, son. Called "local color." Like the gangsters.

PENNY

I love the priest, minister, and rabbi stories. Sometimes they all have names. I think the rabbi is "Jake" or "Ike" or "Abe."

GOTCHER

How about one about a rabbi, a Hindu, and a…let's see…a hippie? yeah, a hippie.

These three were traveling together, 'way out in the boonies, and night falls on 'em miles away from anywhere but one tiny little farm. The farmer says yes, happens he's got a little guest cabin, but it's only got two beds, singles, so one of you three guys'll have to sleep in the barn.

They get to the cabin, have a look around, and the Hindu says mortification is good for the spirit and he'll go over and sleep in the barn.

Fifteen minutes later, there's a knock at the door. The Hindu's back. "I can't sleep in the barn. There's a cow there, and cows are sacred to us."

The rabbi says, "Cows are good animals, but to us not sacred, so I will sleep in the barn."

Fifteen minutes later, there's another knock on the door, and the rabbi's back. "Oy! There is also a pig in the barn, so I cannot sleep there."

The hippie says, "Pigs don't bother me none. Cows, neither. So I'll go sleep in the barn."

Ten minutes later, there's another knock on the door.

It's the cow and the pig.

> *After the laugh, Frank observed, "That has much the sound of a priest, minister, and rabbi story, with one of the Christian clerics transmogrified into a Hindu and the other into a hippie."*

GOTCHER

Yeah, well, man, the first time I heard it, it was a rabbi, a Hindu, and a Catholic priest. Someone else in the group had heard it before with a rabbi, a Hindu, and a Southern Baptist preacher. Years later, I heard it about a rabbi, a Hindu, and an insurance salesman. It always seems to hafta have the rabbi and the Hindu, for obvious reasons, but I guess the third one can belong to any group unpopular wherever it's being told—lawyer, Norski, in the bad old days someone of some ethno-racial persuasion or other… I thought it'd be safest in this present company to pick on my own kind.

PENNY

Bless you for not using the insurance man or the lawyer. My father sold insurance, and I know first-hand how long and hard he worked to choose just the right policy to best help each of his clients. And one of my uncles was a lawyer.

ELFRANK

I notice you seem less solicitous for the good reputation of our Catholic priests.

PENNY

I take their good reputation as a given, so if a joke implies otherwise, I interpret the humor as being in the contrast between reality and implication—the topsy-turvy of it.

ELFRANK

You are overly optimistic.

PENNY

No, just careful where I tell and listen to Catholic jokes.

ELFRANK

You are still and nevertheless overly optimistic.

UNCLE CLIFF

Maybe she judges other people by herself.

PENNY

For instance—thank you, Cliff, you're very kind—let me tell my joke next.

It was a cold, wet, rainy afternoon, and a nun was standing waiting at a bus stop, shivering hard. The bus stop happened to be right in front of a corner tavern. A businessman came by and saw the nun.

"Sister, what bus are you waiting for?"

"Oh…oh…the Number Fourteen."

"Why, that one won't be along for—let's see—almost an hour. You can't stand out here in the cold rain all that time. Why don't you just step inside here and get warm?"

"Oh…oh…oh, I couldn't do that. That…that's a tavern. They sell… spirituous beverages in there. Oh, I couldn't!"

"Just inside the door, sister. Just to get warm and keep out of the rain. You can watch for the bus through the window. Just to get warm and dry."

"Oh…oh… Well, all right."

So they went in, just inside the door.

"Well now, sister, you've been standing out in that weather awhile, you must be pretty tired. Surely God wouldn't mind if you just sat down for a little rest at this table near the door."

"Oh…oh… Well, just for a few minutes…just to rest."

So they both sat down at the little table near the door.

"Well, sister, you were getting pretty cold and wet out there. You know, a little alcohol has a medicinal effect. When Saint Bernard dogs go out to rescue people in the snow, they carry little kegs of brandy on their collars. It'd be okay for you to have a little drink, just to warm you up so you don't catch cold."

"Oh…oh… Well…maybe just one. Just for…medicinal purposes."

"Fine, fine. Waitress, let us have some menus here."

So the waitress brought them two menus.

"Well, sister, what looks good to you?"

"Well…well…maybe one of these…mar-tin-EYES?"

"Fine! Waitress, we'll each have a mar-tin-EYE."

So the waitress goes back to the bar. "Hey, Joe, two mar-tin-EYES."

Joe answers, "That nun here again?"

Frank managed to look disapproval even while adding his wry chuckle to the general laugh; but before he could comment, Uncle Cliff jumped in.

UNCLE CLIFF

During the big waltz craze of the Nineteenth Century, a musician in Vienna complains to his physician, after playing for any number of all-night balls, "Doctor, I'm tired, I'm cranky, I ache, I'm short-tempered, I have no energy, I don't know what's wrong with me."

The physician replies, "You're overStraussed."

There was laughter mingled with moans, depending on what each listener regarded as the more polite response. Penny laughed most heartily, then turned her mirth into a courteous groan. Bugsy frowned a minute before responding at all.

BUGSY

Oh, yeah, I get it! "OverStraussed"—because Strauss was the "Waltz King." Good! We've gotten to Uncle Cliff's famous punning.

FREEDOM (lightly, and more in agreement with her brother than with her adoptive uncle)

And we're just going to get right away again. What's red and black and hangs from the ceiling?

BUGSY

Aw, Sis, not that one again!

ELIZA

Shh, Bugsy, it's bad manners to give away the endings of movies, books, and jokes.

> *All those present who had not yet encountered Freedom's riddle—which included everyone but her immediate family, their cook, and Uncle Cliff—hazarded their guesses, mentioning everything from a checkerboard chandelier to a white planter with red and black flowers to a side of decaying beef (Frank) to a newspaper caught on a beam (Leif). At last Gotcher guessed, "A red and black whizbang."*

FREEDOM

That's close, Gotcher, very close. Actually, it's a red and black freezgalloper, Pat. Pending. What's green and yellow and hangs from the ceiling?

PENNY

A green and yellow freezgalloper?

FREEDOM

Sorry, they only come in red and black.

LEIF (after the laugh)

And that puts me in mind of Kilroy the kush-maker.

When Kilroy joined the Navy, on his form, where it said, "occupation," he filled in, "Kush-Maker." Well, when he was assigned to a ship, his captain actually noticed what Kilroy had written, and called him in.

"I see you're a 'Kush-Maker.'"

"That's right," says Kilroy.

"All right," says the captain, "make me a kush."

Kilroy shakes his head a little and replies, "It'd take a lot of time and men and materials."

"That's okay," says the captain. "Requisition whatever you need. Just make me that kush."

So Kilroy set to work in the biggest hold of the ship. A week later the captain called him in again. "Kilroy, how is that kush coming?"

"Well, sir, we've made a pretty fair beginning, but I'm going to need more men and time and materials."

"Okay, Kilroy, whatever you need, requisition it. Just make me that kush."

Another two weeks went by, and the captain called him in again. "Well, Kilroy, how is that kush coming?"

"It's coming along fairly well, sir, but I'm still going to need more men and time and materials."

"Okay, Kilroy, whatever you need, just make me that kush."

Well, bit by bit, Kilroy had pretty well everyone on that ship except the cook and the pilots down in that hold, working with materials getting ferried over day by day. Finally, after another month, he announced to the captain that everything was ready. Next day the whole ship's company assembled on the deck in dress uniform. The band played a fanfare and everyone saluted the colors. A big crane swung over and lowered its hook into the open hold, and brought up…(*the librarians's hands moved as if expressing a roughly globular shape)*…a huge, misshapen mass of twisted beams and concrete and kitchen sinks.

Slowly, majestically, the crane swung this thing over the side, hung it suspended a moment above the ocean, then opened up to let it fall… and, just as it hit the water… K - U - S - H - H - H.

As the laugh subsided, Elmer spoke up.

ELMER

That the same Kilroy who "was here," almost everywhere?

LEIF

Most likely.

BUGSY (showing off his knowledge)

"Ha, ha, ha, I laugh for joy
'Cause I was here before Kilroy."

LEIF

World War Two era, I think, like Rosie the Riveter.

PENNY

And the Four Chaplains of the Dorchester—a Catholic priest, a rabbi, and two Protestant ministers—who gave away their own life vests when the ship was torpedoed, and went down together holding hands and singing hymns.

UNCLE CLIFF

We may owe a lot of today's good interreligious feeling to how chaplains had to mix and got to know each other, and minister at need to soldiers of other faiths, during the wars of the twentieth century.

PENNY

Showing how God can bring good even out of such an evil as war?

ELFRANK

Insofar as one may regard Truth mingling on equal terms with false or debased credal forms as a "good."

MARY

Time for my joke.

You may expect one about psychiatry from me, or maybe *(glancing at Frank)*, one of witches complaining about lax fellow practitioners who show up only at Hallowe'en, or Puritans telling the woman they're about to burn, "Oh, we don't really believe in witches anymore—we just do this for kicks." But those are more cartoon captions than anecdotes, and I'm going to dig 'way back into my old, Christian upbringing for a joke about Saint Peter and Saint Teresa.

Saint Peter called Saint Teresa into his office one Heavenly day and told her, "Saint Teresa, there are three cities down on Earth that are absolutely the worst ever. These cities are New York, Chicago, and Hollywood. The Lord wants them cleaned up of sin and corruption, and I'd like to assign the task to you. Saint Teresa, do you think you can handle it?"

"Saint Peter," said Saint Teresa, "I can only try."

"Fine, Saint Teresa, fine! You may as well start with New York."

So down she went to Earth. Two weeks later the golden telephone on Saint Peter's desk started ringing. He picked it up. *(Mary pantomimed the action.)*

"Hello, Saint Peter? This is Saint Teresa. I want to report that New York is completely cleaned up."

"Fine, Saint Teresa, fine! Now go on to Chicago."

So on she went to Chicago.

Two weeks later the gold telephone on St. Peter's desk rang again. Again he picked it up.

"Hello, Saint Peter, this is Saint Teresa. I want to report that Chicago is completely cleaned up."

"Fine, Saint Teresa, fine! Now go on to Hollywood."

So on she went to Hollywood.

Two weeks later, the golden telephone was silent.

At the end of three weeks, it still hadn't rung.

Four weeks, and nothing.

Five weeks, and the silence continued.

Finally, at the end of six full weeks, the golden telephone rang. Saint Peter picked it up...

"'Allo, Petah DAHLING? This is Tessie."

ELFRANK (after the general laugh)

I had feared worse. Indeed, your joke points out a wholesome moral: even the best among us must exercise considerable caution. As Saint Peter's compatriot Saint Paul expresses it in his First Epistle to the Corinthians, "Bad company corrupts good morals."

LEIF

Which translation?

BUGSY

An' what was the moral of *your* joke, Frank?

PENNY

I have never understood how to reconcile "Avoid bad company" with "Be as much as you can like Jesus Christ in all things," when Jesus was notorious for socializing with "sinners and tax collectors."

ELFRANK

That is where discernment enters in. Jesus had the discernment to read hearts and know which prostitutes and collaborators were capable of repentance and which were hardened and would if they could have corrupted even His morals.

PENNY

Which of course they couldn't, Jesus being God—but doesn't that still leave us with the problem: how can we imitate Jesus in all ways when we aren't God and can't possibly have the all-important discernment He had?

UNCLE CLIFF

But where was His discernment when it came to Judas?

PENNY

Every year, it seems more and more to me as if that whole episode was a kind of casting lots—drawing straws—Jesus says, "One of you will betray Me," and they don't say, "Which one?" or "What can we do about him?" or anything like that, they just say, "Not me, Lord, not me!" Then He says, "The one I pass this bread to," passes it to Judas, tells him, "What you have to do, do quickly," Judas goes out, and *they don't even guess why?* COME ON! How stupid are we supposed to think they *are?* Jesus had figured out that the Romans weren't taking the bait He'd been throwing them all week, the Scriptures suggested it was time for one of His own to betray Him, and poor old Judas drew the short straw.

ELFRANK

Next you will suggest that Jesus Himself expected, not to redeem us through His sacrifice on the Cross, but to be saved at the last minute by His Father sending celestial hosts of angels to inaugurate the millennium.

PENNY

Maybe He did. Expect that, I mean. Better than considering the Holy Trinity a collaboration of divine sado-masochists.

PEARL (authoritatively)

This old farmer lay dying. He tells his wife, "Marthy, I want to be buried nekkid. I know durn well where I'm goin', and I ain't a-goin' t' need any clothes there."

So she insists on burying him nekkid.

Two nights later his nekkid ghost comes in, stands beside her bed, and says, "Marthy, I've got t' have my overcoat, after all. Got t' be so many high-falutin' rich—what d'you call 'em's?—C.P.O.'s down there, he put in air conditioning."

ELIZA (after the round of laughter)

As long as we've gotten to the infernal regions.

A C.P.O. died and found himself in Hell. While a guide demon was taking him down to his assigned spot, they passed a place where a man the C.P.O. had known in life, a big-time confidence operator who had made his lush living by swindling people out of their life savings, was cozying up to a beautiful woman.

"Hey," said the C.P.O., "how fair is this? I know that guy from our time on Earth. Me, who always lived on my own income, you're taking to torment, while that con artist, who did nothing but destroy other people's bank accounts, sits there spending his eternity with a gorgeous babe?"

"Silence!" said the guide demon. "Who are you to question that woman's punishment?"

GOTCHER (after the laugh)

Like, things are seldom what they seem, huh?

ELFRANK

Nor do we know but that the woman's personality was such as to constitute punishment for the man as well.

MARY

It's probably best not to overanalyze that one, Frank. As with most jokes told in informal social settings.

MERLINA

Oh, my! It looks like everyone's told their jokes except Bugsy and me, and I'd rather not go last again.

A good man died and went up to Heaven. Saint Peter let him in and assigned him an angel to guide him to his own eternal home among the many mansions.

On their way, the angel pointed out one that looked like the Vatican. "There's where the Catholics live." Another that looked like—what is that place, the big center somewhere?—Cern: "That's where the scientists live." One that looked like Buckingham Palace: "The Anglicans live there." Another that looked like the Taj Mahal: "There's where the Muslims live." Then they came to a lovely big one where the angel said, "Shhh! We have to be quiet going past this one. This is where the Born-Agains live. They think they're the only ones here."

BUGSY (after the laugh)

What'd the Born-Agains think about all those other places they'd passed by on their own way in?

ELFRANK

"They have eyes, but see not…"

ELIZA

Rather a slur against blind people, there.

ELFRANK

It comes to us directly from the mouth of Jesus, as recorded in the Gospels.

PENNY

Jesus spoke for His times, and they weren't so sensitive about these things. If He had spoken today…

BUDGEWISER

Have you had a busy day?

MARY

Budgewiser seems to be telling us we'd better stop right there.

MERLINA

I'm afraid my joke works best when told about whatever group the teller belongs to himself or herself.

BUGSY

Okay, time for my joke!

There's this guy, see, who gets stranded out in the country near sunset, and stops at the only farmhouse he can find.

"All right," says the farmer, "you can sleep here tonight. But first I've got something to show you."

He takes the guy five fields over from the house, and here's this elevator, like, for a mine, going down into the ground. They take it, like, about a thousand feet down, and finally they come to a bunch of doors, all bolted. They go through ten iron doors, and then ten steel doors, and then ten reinforced concrete doors till finally they come to this great, big cage of concrete with iron bars and steel bars and alloy bars, all two inches diameter. An' there, inside the cage, a humongous big King Kong of a gorilla, just sittin' there lookin' sleepy.

"And what you must *never, never* do," the farmer tells the guy, "is touch him."

So they go back through the ten concrete doors, and the ten steel doors, and the ten iron doors, and up the thousand-foot shaft to the surface, over the five fields back to the house, and the farmer shows the guy the spare bedroom.

So they all go to bed and turn out the lights, but the guy can't get to sleep. He just lies there tossing and turning and wondering what'd happen if he touched that gorilla. Finally, 'way after midnight, he gets up, gets his flashlight, and sneaks outta the house, across the five fields to the elevator. He takes the elevator down the thousand-foot shaft, through the ten iron doors, through the ten steel doors, through the ten concrete doors, all the way to the big cage where King Kong is just sitting there dozing.

The guy reaches between the bars and stretches out his pointer finger...like so...and gives the gorilla just one itty bitty little touch on the shoulder.

Well, the gorilla wakes up and roars and beats his chest and starts smashing through the bars of his cage.

The guy runs like sixty, back through the concrete doors, heaves' 'em shut behind him an' heaves' all the solid heavy bars into place. "That'll hold him."

Nope. Here comes the King Kong, smashin' right through all these doors of solid, reinforced concrete.

So the guy gets through the ten steel doors, slams' 'em shut an' bars' 'em behind him. "That'll hold 'im."

Nope. Here comes the gorilla, smashing right through the steel doors.

So through the ten iron doors, shuttin' and barrin' 'em all good an' tight. "That'll surely hold him!"

Nope. Here comes King Kong, smashin' right through all ten iron doors.

So up the shaft in the elevator, top speed. "There—now he's gotta be stuck at the bottom."

Nope. Here comes the gorilla, climbin' right up after the elevator.

So there the poor guy is, runnin' through the fields with this big Kong on his heels, till finally he falls down, too exhausted to get up. The gorilla comes up, bends down over him…

Touches him and says, "Tag! You're 'It.'"

To this culminating joke of the round, not even Frank Craftlove offered an immediate moral application; so, after the laughter, the conversation continued, seasoned with such further anecdotes and bon mots as best suited the companionable winding-down of the weekend. By midafternoon, most of the participants had set off upon their homeward journeys, except of course those who made up the homely complement of Loon Lake Lodge: the family Eklektik, including their pets. Pearl Bonami, who had slept Friday and Saturday nights in the lodge in order to facilitate her breakfast duties, lingered until most traces of the retreat were tidied up, and the next two meals ready to fetch forth from fridge and pantry until she should return Monday mid-morning. Gotcher, in addition, who had nowhere else in particular to go, agreed to stay at least one night longer, with his good dog Pumpkin.

Uncle Cliff also lingered, on pretext of discussing a new model train layout with Elmer, but actually to discuss many things with Penny Wright, who lingered along with him, long enough to share supper before seeking their respective homes, with the promise of meeting the following Tuesday for dinner and a movie. Nor must I omit to mention that the librarian and the psychiatrist, by arrangement, broke their homeward journeys to meet for a long stroll about Muskywater, town and park, followed by dinner and drinks at the Catch of the Day Supper Club.

EPILOGUE

The weekend had seemed sufficiently successful that the Eklektiks inaugurated paying retreats on a monthly basis, to the general pleasure of themselves and their retreatants. In these projects, as well as for the day-to-day upkeep of the property, Gotcher Lotsadoe proved among the handiest of handy men. The erstwhile hippie's wandering days seemed to have reached their happy conclusion at last, for he was still on hand the following year, when the family decided to send out invitations to the veterans of their first retreat for a special and complimentary anniversary weekend. Leif and Mary attended as a married, Uncle Cliff and Penny as an engaged couple. The intervening months had been gentle with all the others as well, and even L. Frank Craftlove appeared somewhat mellowed by the passage of time. All of Elmer's trains were running comfortably around their respective layouts; both Freedom's and Bugsy's projects had prospered, if altering somewhat along the course of a youthful twelvemonth; and, fortuitously, Muttwump and Pumpkin between them had produced puppies enough to go around. So, to give the last words to perhaps the most meditative if least loquacious of the group:

MUTTWUMP

Arf!

PUMPKIN

Arf. Arf. Arf.

BUDGEWISER

Have you had a busy day?

NOTES

About the turn of the twentieth into the twenty-first century, I discovered the dialogue novels of Thomas Love Peacock. These had a great liberating effect on my spirit. I have always loved reading plays, and here were, in effect, long plays thinly disguised as prose fiction. Not that I enjoy reading pages and pages of fictional small talk; but I love conversations of philosophical, historical, cultural, artistic, and satiric content, which Peacock provides.

Loon Lake Lodge was the first new novel I began and completed after my beloved husband's death. It turned out far longer than most of the best-known of Peacock's dialogue novels, but otherwise I strove to follow his template, only adapting it to my own milieu.

Clifford Reed and Penelope Wright are my late husband and myself, but with a far different meeting than we had in our actual biographies. Everybody else is fictional and hails from my own head—any resemblance to actual persons living or dead purely coincidental. Their setting is modeled on the northwest Wisconsin area which has been my home for the last quarter century or so, but all names are fictitious and places heavily fictionalized. The actual restaurant advertising itself as Al Capone's northwoods hide-out as far as I know still exists, but it is alluded to only; and as far as I know it never had a would-be rival. I have tried to mask our contemporary authors, books, and movies under transparent fictional names, but let older authors and works stand under their own names.

There is a stronger element of autobiography here than in any of my other novels, but only in emotions, opinions, and details, not in historical plot. For instance, in youth I had a pet parakeet, Peeps, who never actually said anything, but always listened very attentively when you asked him, "Have you had a busy day? The beetle Bugsy describes in ch. 3 is one I really found on a walk near home one day, but left alive rather than collect, and was subsequently unable to find in any reference book. Some of the conversations are based on and to some extent duplicate ones in which I have partaken over the years, in different circumstances than those described. The alternate-world dream Clifford reports to Penelope is one I myself had one night in the early years of our marriage.

And so on. Our own courtship, however, ran remarkably smoothly: as smoothly as the fourteen wonderful years we spent together, before he fell victim to sCJD.

ON THE PROVENANCE OF THE CAMPFIRE STORIES

BUGSY'S.

Being unable to locate this one today in Richard Chase's *American Folk Tales and Songs*, I guess I must have read it many years ago, probably in one of Botkin's folklore collections. No doubt many details, likely including the name of whoever the felines are waiting for, got changed a bit in my mind over the decades.

UNCLE CLIFF'S.

A dream my late husband once had. It was in third person, sometimes I think called the "observing eye" by dream researchers.

MARY'S.

Original. I made it up.

ELFRANK'S.

Greatly expanded from a cautionary tale one of the teaching nuns told us during my primary-grade days at St. Mary's, Griffith, Indiana.

LEIF'S.

I found this in a seventeenth-century British folio in the Patterson Rare Book Room at the University of Louisville Library in the 1970s; and I believe I have encountered it elsewhere as well, in other versions. As Leif remarks, it is undoubtedly an old tale of the type known today as "urban legend." I added a few touches of my own.

ELIZA'S.

I think I couldn't have been older than teenage when I heard this one orally from a friend. I *think*. Or I may possibly have read it in some joke collection.

PEARL'S.

Original. I made it up. Certain names have been changed to protect the guilty.

ELMER'S.

Despite Elmer's contention that what "Engineer Chudden saw on the Flying Zephyr is recorded history," it isn't, at least not in our home timeline. I did, however, adapt it from one printed in *The Life Treasury of American Folklore* (1961; p. 188f.) as "The Phantom Train of Marshall Pass."

The "Maverick" episode to which Penelope refers is No. 63, "Easy Mark."

FREEDOM'S.

The abovementioned *Life Treasury* prints this on p. 259. I have also seen it used on a classic "Twilight Zone" episode, with an airplane at the climax.

PENNY'S.

Pieced together out of Arthur Jacobs' biography of Sullivan, Harold Orel's *Gilbert and Sullivan: Interviews and Recollections*, and other reading on the subject.

GOTCHER'S

The opera in question is, of course, *Ruddigore*. I reproduce the given name of Baronet No. 22 as Gotcher—correctly—pronounced it and therefore how all his auditors heard it, with the exception of Penelope Wright, L. Frank Craftlove, and possibly Leif Pageturner, who knew the proper spelling to be "Ruthven." Such liberties as I, through Gotcher, have taken with Gilbert's libretto grew out of a lifetime of loving study and attentive cogitation.

MERLINA'S.

Various elements have been adapted from my own experience and that of people close to me. Some details have been embellished for dramatic effect.

ON THE PROVENANCE OF THE JOKES

All these jokes came direct to me from the oral tradition with the following exceptions:

PEARL'S.

I read this one maybe half a century ago in, I believe, an illustrated Sunday supplement magazine.

ELIZA'S.

From a "jokes" daily calendar of 2009 C.E. Since the calendar boasted itself as somewhat corny, I assume its jokes were up for grabs; I have, moreover, retold it without referring back to the printed calendar text, with a few conscious and certainly some unconscious variations. A school friend of mine who had gone into gourmet cookery remarked at an early class reunion that making three changes in a recipe resulted in a new and original recipe. I rather think I must have made at least three changes, albeit small ones, in this joke.

UNCLE CLIFF'S.

My late husband made this up Feb. 19, 2003. He used to make these up almost daily, but unfortunately I did not write enough of them down. (This is not to say that any number of other people in other places may not have come up with it by process either of spontaneous inspiration or unconscious picking of one another's brainwaves.)

LEIF'S.

This one appears in the above-cited *Life Treasury of American Folk-lore* as "Murgatroyd the Klug Maker." I have, however, recounted the version told to me by a classmate ca. 1956, except that I have supplied "Kilroy" for a protagonist. I believe he was left "a guy" in my friend's telling.